The Beast of CRETACEA

The Beast of CRETACEA

TODD STRASSER

CANDLEWICK PRESS

This is a work of fiction. Names, characters, places, and incidents are either products of the author's imagination or, if real, are used fictitiously.

First edition 2015

Library of Congress Catalog Card Number 2015936912
ISBN 978-0-7636-6901-0

15 16 17 18 19 20 BVG 10 9 8 7 6 5 4 3 2 1

Printed in Berryville, VA, U.S.A.

This book was typeset in Adobe Devanagari and ITC Officina Serif.

Candlewick Press
99 Dover Street
Somerville, Massachusetts 02144

visit us at www.candlewick.com

This book is dedicated to my mother, Sheila Strasser,
whose unconditional love was the life raft I clung to.

For God's sake, be economical with your lamps and candles! Not a gallon you burn, but at least one drop of man's blood was spilled for it.

— Herman Melville, *Moby-Dick*

CAST OF CHARACTERS

Abdul • Chase-boat skipper

Ahab • Ship's captain

Archie • Ishmael's foster brother

Bartleby • Special adviser, United North America Trust

Ben • Friend of Ishmael's foster family

Mr. Bildad • High-ranking executive, United North America Trust

Blank • Pirate

Dr. Bunger • Ship's surgeon

Bunta • Lineman and brute

Charity • Ship's stasis tech

Daggoo • Yellow-haired chase-boat skipper

Diana • Islander

Fayaway • Islander; daughter of Gabriel

Fedallah • Harpooner

Flask • Third mate

Fleece • Ship's cook

Gabriel • Informal leader of the islanders; father of Fayaway and Thistle

Glock • Pirate

Grace • Trawler captain

Ms. Hussey • In charge of foundling home

Joachim • Ishmael and Archie's foster father

Kalashnikov • Pirate leader

Marion • Green-haired chase-boat lineman

Mikal • Islander

Nazik • Medic

Perth • Ship's engineer

Petra • Ishmael and Archie's foster mother

Starbuck • First mate

Stubb • Second mate

Tarnmoor • Blind old sailor

Tashtego • Harpooner

Thistle • Fayaway's younger sister

Valente • Chief compliance officer, United North America Trust

Wesson • Pirate

Winchester • Pirate

1

"Wake up."

It's dark and gelatinous. Ishmael floats in a breathable syrup. *Is this a dream?* he wonders before soft, warm tendrils reach out and draw him back into a black, foamy haze.

"Come on, everyone. Rise and shine."

Ishmael makes a fist; the gel is gone. He opens his eyes and sees hues: a woman's copper face with an unusual sheen accentuated with serpentine tattoos. Dark-brown hair, blue eyes, a gentle smile.

"Are we there?" he asks. He is lying on his back. The foamy haze has lifted, but he's still woozy and surprised by how tight his jaw feels. As if it's rusty, in need of oil. He starts to push himself up.

"Easy, honey." The woman places her fingertips on his collarbone to keep him from rising. "You're here, but you've been in deep stasis. Take it slow." She gently pushes him back into the molded foam. "I'll tell you when."

Ishmael allows himself to be eased down into the soft cushioning, but when the woman moves to the next pod, he peeks over the edge and watches while she tells the person inside it the same thing she told him. In this dimly lit chamber, there are five green oval pods, each containing a new arrival. Ishmael saw some of them the day they left Earth. Strangely, right now, that and his name are the only things he remembers.

Moments later, having awakened all of them, the woman steps into the middle of the chamber. She is wearing blue shorts and a blue shirt with the sleeves torn off, exposing arms covered with tattoos. "Listen up. My name is Charity, and I'm going to guide you through reentry. I know you're eager to get out and look around, but unless you want to do serious damage to yourselves, I recommend that you do exactly as I say. Raise your right hands."

Ishmael does as he's told. Like his jaw, his elbow and shoulder feel tight and stiff.

"That's your left hand, Billy."

A high-pitched voice flutters. "S-sorry, ma'am."

"*Now* raise your left hands."

Charity leads them through the process of moving their limbs and flexing their joints. Ishmael has never felt so stiff or feeble. Just lifting one leg leaves him momentarily breathless.

"Don't worry about feeling weak or tired," she tells them. "Just before destasis, you were infused with a biologic that'll help you regain your strength and balance. We're going to start the process of getting vertical. Most of you won't succeed on your first attempt. That's expected. When you start to feel light-headed, let yourself fall back into the pod. That's why it's got all that nice soft cushioning. What you don't want to do is fall forward and crack your skulls on the floor. Everyone got that?"

Muted affirmative replies.

"Okay, try to sit up."

Slowly propping himself up on his elbows, Ishmael feels his heart begin to pump harder. From this angle he can see into some of the other pods. He doesn't remember putting on the stiff brown uniform he and the other new arrivals are wearing. Across from him, a girl with a tangle of unkempt red hair manages to sit partway up before her eyes roll and she flops back with a soft thump.

Once his heartbeat feels steady, Ishmael lifts his torso more. Someone else tries to sit straight, loses consciousness, and falls back. Ishmael waits until his heartbeat feels normal again, then inches up.

Charity glances his way and nods approvingly.

The others adopt the gradual approach. Still in the pods, they eye one another curiously. Next to the girl with the red hair is a tall fellow with broad shoulders, and a frail-looking kid with short, curly blond hair who Ishmael suspects is the one named Billy. They are all thin and bony and have dull, ashen skin.

The next step will be to get out of the pods and stand. "Make sure you hold on to the handrail," Charity tells them. "Don't try to walk. If you straighten up gradually, you shouldn't feel dizzy, but if you do, bend your knees and lower yourself to the floor."

The pods slowly tilt forward. Grasping handrails, Ishmael and the other new arrivals place their feet unsteadily on the floor. The tall fellow is the first to stand, but then he starts to sway. As his knees begin to buckle, Charity scoots behind him, sliding her arms under his shoulders and easing him down.

"Don't anyone else faint, please. There's only one of me to catch you." She squats before the tall fellow, who is now sitting on the floor with his head between his knees. "You okay, Queequeg?"

He places his hands flat on the floor. "Yeah, I think so. Thanks."

"That was a little too fast," she says, helping him up. "Let's try it more slowly this time."

By now, Ishmael and the others are standing unsteadily, still gripping the handrails. The floor gradually tilts beneath them.

"Feels like a ship," says a boy Ishmael hadn't noticed before. He is short and chubby with neatly cut black hair and evenly trimmed fingernails. For a moment, Ishmael stares, unable to remember the last time he saw anyone with so much as an extra ounce on them.

"That's because this *is* a ship, Mr. Lopez-Makarova," Charity replies.

"You may address me as Pip," the boy says.

"W-where are we?" asks the frail-looking blond kid, his high-pitched voice quavering.

"You'll hear about that later, Billy. If I told you now, you'd just forget. Memory loss is a side-effect of deep stasis, but it will pass. Right now just concentrate on keeping your balance. Oh, and one more piece of business. Hold out your left wrists."

They do as they're told, and she scans their wrists with a tablet, starting with Billy, whose slim forearm reflects his delicate features. Ishmael focuses on the strange symbol tattooed on the inside of his own wrist. The one-inch square resembles circuitry, with clear and copper-colored filaments woven through a black matrix code. *A registry,* he remembers.

Illuminating the red-haired girl's wrist with purple light, Charity gives her a curious look.

"Got a problem?" the girl growls.

"Attitude won't help you here, Gwendolyn."

"Nobody calls me that," the girl snaps. "It's Gwen."

Charity moves to Queequeg, who holds up an unmarked wrist. "Sorry, don't have one."

That catches Ishmael by surprise. Despite his addled memory, he's certain that back in Black Range everyone had a registry — it was the law. But Charity accepts the boy's answer and moves to Ishmael. As the purple light passes over his wrist, he catches a glimpse of gold filigree he never knew was there. Charity gazes at him with an expression he can't quite decipher, then turns away.

Ishmael wonders if any of the others noticed that she didn't even try to scan the wrist of the boy named Pip.

It's not long before the new arrivals take their first steps. Feeling as shaky as a toddler, Ishmael finds it hard to separate his own unsteadiness from the mild sway of the ship. Charity is both gentle and demanding, directing them through each stage of movement. Finally she hands out goggles. "We're going up on deck. Be careful with these. They're delicate and in short supply. Once we're up top, under no circumstances are you to take them off. To do so will mean risking severe macular damage."

"Then maybe we shouldn't go up on deck." Gwen tosses her goggles back.

Charity lurches to catch them before they hit the floor. "Did you hear anything I just said? They're delicate. You can't toss them around. And you *are* going up."

When the redheaded girl crosses her arms and juts out her chin defiantly, Charity steps close, then lowers her voice. "Don't be stupid, Gwen. You're here to make money, and to do that you'll have to cooperate and take orders." She holds out the goggles. "Unless you'd rather spend the voyage in a stinking hot cell next to the reactor."

Gwen snorts but does as she's told. Charity turns to the others. "Okay, everyone, let's go meet your new world."

Eager to see what's out there, Ishmael puts on the goggles. They're different from VRgogs, which are always dark for virtual reality. These stay clear while Charity leads them out of the chamber and up several ladderways. At the end of a long passageway, she pushes open a hatch. Through it comes a blinding glare far brighter than anything Ishmael ever experienced on Earth. Hot air wafts in.

"One at a time," Charity orders.

Queequeg goes first and seems to melt into the powerful brightness outside. He's followed by Gwen, then Pip. Ishmael shuffles closer, his pulse revving with excitement. As he steps through the hatch, a blast of torrid air hits him and the top of his head begins to feel hot, as though he's standing under a heat cell. From the very edge of his peripheral vision he perceives that the source of the intense warmth and incandescence is a glowing yellow disk in the sky above. Even with the goggles darkening automatically, he has to squint in the painfully bright whiteout. Meanwhile, he's bombarded with a host of bewildering sounds, smells, and sensations.

But there is one thing he knows for certain: For the first time in his life, he is standing in a place with no Shroud.

"Wh-what is it?" asks Billy, who's shielding his forehead with his hand.

"We call it the sun," Charity answers.

Ishmael takes a deep breath, and his lungs fill with nearly stifling hot air. The goggles are meant to protect eyes made sensitive by a life spent living in perpetual gloom, so the view they provide is muted and blocked at the edges. But Charity wears only a visored cap, which gives Ishmael hope that sooner or later the new arrivals won't need the goggles either.

For now he can see that they're on the deck of a large ship that looks nothing like the vessels he saw in the VR walk-through at the Mission Office when he enlisted. Those were sleek, polished craft with streamlined superstructures. In contrast, this old tub is rust stained and battered: black paint peeling, long streaks of reddish brown everywhere. Looming overhead are the dark shapes of cranes, and amidships juts a superstructure lined with windows — some broken — and lifeboats hanging by frayed ropes at careless angles.

But Ishmael doesn't dwell on that. Not when there's an ocean surrounding them. Until now he has never seen more water in one place than could fill a small bucket. But this ship floats on a vast glittering blue-green sea that stretches away in all directions to the horizon.

And above it, for the first time in his life, he sees endless blue sky dotted by small white clouds.

So this is what an unspoiled world looks like. . . .

A sudden commotion on the deck interrupts his reverie. Several sailors rush past, and from overhead comes the high-pitched whine of a drone landing. More crewmen are hurrying toward the port side of the ship, and the new arrivals can hear excited chatter from across the deck.

"What's going on?" Queequeg asks.

Charity grabs a passing sailor and gets an excited reply: "Fedallah's stuck a terrafin!"

2

With Charity in the lead, they traverse the deck to join the sailors crowded against the ship's port bulwark. When Ishmael touches the bulwark rail, it burns, and he yanks his hand back from the sun-cooked paint. Around him others splash buckets of seawater on the rail to cool it, so he does the same. Sunlight glints off the smooth, rolling ocean, and the strange scent of salt breeze fills his nostrils.

Sailors are pointing at two specks on the blue-green horizon.

"What are they?" Queequeg asks, using his sleeve to wipe sweat from his forehead.

"Chase boats," Charity explains. "Towing the terrafin in."

"Terrafin?" Pip repeats.

"You'll see."

Gradually the specks become boats, still tiny in the distance. Ishmael estimates that they're about two hundred yards apart, each towing a heavy red line. Perhaps a quarter mile behind, the space between the lines narrows to a roiling, frothing dot.

"It's a terrafin, all right!" a sailor near him shouts. "Nothing else puts up a fight like that!"

"Ain't a big one, but it'll do!" shouts another.

"This'll help fill the pot!" cheers a third.

While everyone else watches the frenzied commotion in the distance, Ishmael leans against the rail and gazes down — then catches his breath. On a blood-soaked deck below, half a dozen sailors with long blades attached to poles stand on and around a huge greenish-gray creature lying on its side. The beast has an enormous head, a long snout filled with pointed teeth, flat, stubby flippers, and a long tail. With his elbow, Ishmael nudges Queequeg, who looks down and gasps.

"A hump," Charity says when she notices what they're looking at. "Just brought in this morning."

Ishmael and Queequeg watch in astonished silence while the sailors slice the creature apart, stacking slabs of meat the size of mattresses off to one side. Other than some insects back on Earth, this is the first nonhuman creature either of them has ever seen.

Meanwhile, the sailors around them are growing louder and more excited. The long, narrow chase boats are closer now, and the terrafin's resistance is so fierce that it looks like they are towing a small typhoon behind them. At last the boats reach the ship, and the red lines are transferred to enormous aft winches, one on either side of the slipway, which is a broad ramp that slants down into the sea at the vessel's stern.

"Here's where it gets dicey," Charity cautions. The deck shivers as the ship comes to life, slowly towing the terrafin to keep the lines from going slack and tangling. A cargo rope is thrown over the rail, and several sailors in yellow immersion suits climb down to help the chase-boat crews clamber up the side of the hull.

The appearance of the first crew is startling. They are all big, with dark glossy skin and brightly dyed hair. Their uniforms are torn away at the sleeves, displaying muscular, tattooed arms.

"That's Tashtego's crew," Charity says. "Doesn't look like they were there for the actual capture. Probably showed up later to help tow the beast in."

"How can you tell?" Pip asks.

"They're not shaken up enough."

The words have hardly left her lips when the second crew starts to appear over the rail. The first is a green-haired woman, blinking rapidly and taking unsteady steps. She's followed by a dazed-looking sailor with bushy yellow hair, a matching yellow goatee, and orange and red tattoo flames rising from yellow eyebrows. His forehead is wrapped in a red-stained bandage, and his orange personal flotation device is spattered with blood.

When the next member of the chase-boat crew is hoisted up in a basket stretcher, Charity bites her lip. "Someone's in a bad way."

A couple of sailors grab the stretcher and lower it gently to the deck. Lying in it is a big brute of a man with a shaved head. Deep-set eyes squeezed shut, he's cradling his left arm, his face contorted with pain. A short, round man with an eye patch quickly squats beside him, opens a black medical bag, and fumbles for a moment with a derma-jet infuser filled with a watery green liquid. He injects the injured sailor, who exhales with relief and goes limp.

The last of the chase-boat crewmen to climb aboard is slighter of build, with white hair balled into a knot that rests like an egg on top of his head. Long white strands escape from the topknot, and his uniform is blood-spattered and ripped at the elbow and knee. But his expression is calm, a faraway look in his dark eyes. Without a word to anyone, he crosses the deck and disappears through a hatch.

* * *

The powerful winches have drawn the furious terrafin close to the ship. Ishmael is startled by its relative slightness of size. The span of its thick, powerful wings can't be more than twelve feet, and its thin, whiplike tail is barely three yards in length. Still, it is completely unlike anything he has ever seen before, its back as black as its underside is white, with dashes of white around its large midnight eyes.

Incredibly, the nearer the terrafin is pulled to the ship, the greater its resistance grows, flinging itself about with such terrific force that it seems to spend more time above the water than in it. At the same time, the sky above the ship's stern teems with white, gray, and brown flyers circling and screeching.

The new arrivals gawk.

"Stop!" a voice suddenly shouts. Heads turn. A man stands on a short tower above the deck beside the glass-encased compartment where the winch operator works. He wears a neatly pressed black uniform, and sunlight reflects off his dark, round glasses. A carefully folded black bandanna holds back his spiky, jet-black hair.

The winches stop. Ishmael sees why: At the bottom of the slipway, the terrafin has wedged itself into the corner where the ramp meets the hull. Were the winches to continue to take in line, the harpoon would be yanked out, and the creature would escape. Indeed, as the beast's wings pound thunderously against the ship's hull, all can see that one of the harpoon's bloody barbs is slowly pulling out of the creature's back.

"They better get another stick in it before that one works itself out," Charity says.

The man in black bellows from the winch tower at the crowd of sailors below: "A thousand for the next stick!"

Ishmael catches his breath. It's a ludicrous amount of money, and he expects the sailors to fight for the chance to earn it. But the crowd goes silent, eyes hidden beneath the shading visors of their caps. The only sounds are the thrashing of the terrafin and the squawking of the flyers winging overhead.

"Two thousand!" the man shouts.

"Is that the captain?" Gwen asks.

Charity shakes her head. "Starbuck, the first mate."

"Three thousand!" Starbuck yells.

Queequeg leans toward Ishmael and whispers, "It would take *years* to earn that back on Earth."

Still, no one takes the offer.

At the mouth of the slipway, the terrafin continues to battle and flail. One of the harpoon's barbs has now pulled completely free.

"Four thousand!" Starbuck beseeches. *A small fortune!* Just to do something that won't take more than a few seconds. Ishmael knows it would go a long way toward saving up the money he came to this planet to make. But he's only been on board a few hours; would they even consider him for the task?

Before he can decide whether to act, a hand in the crowd goes up, and a wiry, dark-haired sailor steps forward.

"Abdul took the bait," Charity whispers. "Wish him luck. He's going to need it."

The sailor is given a helmet, body armor, a clear shield, and a shoulder-mounted harpoon launcher. His eyes shift nervously and his hands are trembling. Sweat runs from under the helmet and down his temples. Someone clips a heavy wire to a hook at the back of the armor.

With the shield raised and the harpoon launcher balanced on his shoulder, Abdul takes short, careful steps down the slipway. The terrafin's thrashing sends spray against the clear shield. The flyers dive and shriek more frantically, as though sensing the tension in the air.

Halfway down the slipway, Abdul stops and looks back.

"What are you waiting for?" Starbuck yells impatiently.

The other sailors concur. "Go on!" "Don't be scared!" "Think of the pot, mate!"

"He'd best go through with it now," Charity whispers. "They'll never let him live it down if he doesn't."

"The harpoon!" A sailor in the crowd points. The second barb has worked free of the wound.

"Go!" Starbuck barks at Abdul. "Before we lose it!"

Abdul takes another step. Just then, the terrafin grows still. A hush settles over the crowd. Now that the beast has been brought to the mouth of the slipway, the ship's engine has been silenced and its propellers have stopped churning. Riding the ghost of momentum, the vessel glides slowly and silently ahead.

"Go on!" Starbuck shouts.

Abdul lowers the shield and takes aim at the impassive creature half out of the ocean below. Its black hide glistens in the sunlight.

Even the flyers have momentarily quieted.

"Do it!" Starbuck commands.

But the terrafin acts first. In less than the blink of an eye, it arches its back and whips its tail forward. Abdul buckles and collapses, the harpoon launcher clattering unfired to the slipway floor.

Small waves splash against the ship's stern where an instant ago the terrafin was pinned. The creature is gone, the bloody harpoon dangling uselessly from the towline. Abdul lies on the slipway, a long, pointed white spine driven through his neck. With each beat of the sailor's heart, a stream of bright-red blood pulses from his wound.

Starbuck and the short, round man with the eye patch hustle through the crowd and down the slipway to the fallen sailor. Starbuck cradles Abdul's head in his lap while the other man once again fumbles in his black bag and pulls out a derma-jet infuser.

But his hand stops in midair.

Blood has ceased pulsing from the wound.

Starbuck's shoulders slump. "Forget it, Doc."

The man with the eye patch slips the infuser back into his bag, and the first mate gently lays Abdul's head on the slipway.

It's not the first time Ishmael has encountered death: Back in Black Range, if you rose each day at dawn to get on the Natrient line, sooner or later you would come across the corpse of someone who'd been a victim of robbery the previous night, or drunk too much benzo, or faced too much despair. But he has never seen someone perish right before his eyes and, from the looks of it, neither has any of the other new arrivals. Slack-jawed and pale, they stare while Starbuck orders sailors to carry Abdul's body up the slipway.

"Wh-what was th-that th-thing in his neck?" Billy stammers.

"We call it a skiver," Charity answers, shaking her head grimly. "Welcome to your new life, kids."

3

BLACK RANGE, EARTH:
Predeparture

They sat around the ancient baclum table, its faint bioluminescent emissions barely enough to outline the glass and jar on its surface. The rest of the small kitchen was veiled in darkness, those sitting around the table little more than silhouettes.

"How much longer?" Ishmael asked.

"Nine hours," replied his foster father, Joachim.

"It doesn't matter, Ish." Archie's voice came out of the dark. "I *want* to go. You were stupid to file that appeal. I'll be fine."

"Isn't Eliza's Law supposed to stop things like this from happening?" Ishmael asked.

From out of the shadows Old Ben leaned forward. With a trembling hand, he picked up his half-full glass of benzo. "That only applies to jobs in this solar system. Once you're out past the Oort cloud, it's more or less anarchy." The glass was empty when he returned it to the table.

"If you can go, I can go, Ish," Archie insisted. "Besides, I bet they send me someplace easy. Like that planet where all the nutraceuticals come from. What's it called?"

"Permia," said Joachim.

"I hear they just sit in labs all day, testing for impurities," Archie said. But then he added, "Though I guess that can't pay as well as working on one of those crazy planets with active volcanoes and earthquakes and people dying in mining accidents."

Old Ben leaned forward just enough for Ishmael to see his bushy eyebrows and white hair. He picked up the jar and refilled his glass with the clear, syrupy liquid. "Whatever they pay," he said, "it'll be better than what you'll get around here . . . *if* you can even find a job." As the plant manager of the Zirconia Electrolysis station — the only employer left in Black Range — Old Ben knew better than anyone the grim prospects facing Ishmael and Archie's generation.

"He's right," said Joachim.

Although Ishmael would never say so, it bothered him that his foster father seemed untroubled about Archie's going away. True, missions only lasted for one year — unless you decided to renew — but no matter what you were paid, it was worth it only if you survived.

Outside, the wind whistled and Ishmael thought he heard rough scratches of dirt and grit against the roof.

On the table, Old Ben's glass was empty again, but when his hand went in search of the jar of benzo, it was gone. Ishmael assumed that was his foster father's doing.

"Could be a storm kicking up." Joachim rose to his feet. "You'd better get home, Ben. Get the POLE, Ishmael."

"Should I take a gun?" Ishmael asked. At night it was usually advisable to carry one.

From outside came the rattle of a wind-tossed can careering down the street. Joachim hesitated, then nodded. "Hard to imagine that kind out in weather like this, but you never know."

Ishmael went to the storage closet, where he got the gun, and, after feeling around the disorganized shelves in the dark, found the Portable Organic Light Emitter. By now the wind was whistling more loudly and they could hear dry thunder in the distance. A storm was indeed approaching.

As Ishmael made his way through the gloom toward the front door, he glimpsed the barely visible silhouettes of two people, heads bent close, speaking in low voices. He stopped and listened.

"The station's down to one coal delivery a week," Old Ben was whispering. "And soon it's going to be one every *other* week."

Joachim sighed. "I'm worried about Archie. . . . Surely there'll be *some* form of Eliza's Law where they send him, won't there?"

So Joachim *was* worried, Ishmael thought.

"No way to know." Old Ben placed a reassuring hand on the taller man's shoulder. "But even if there isn't, he's a smart and resourceful boy. And you know this is the way it has to be."

"What's the way it has to be?" Ishmael asked.

Both men jerked their heads up, startled.

"It's nothing, Ish," Joachim said. "You'd better get Ben home. Take goggles and a mask. It could get nasty on the way back."

Outside, the wind stank of chemicals and soot. Except for a dim glow in a window here or there, it was pitch-black. Even on the clearest of nights, you couldn't see more than half a dozen feet before everything bled into inkiness. When Ishmael was younger, he'd sometimes pictured himself walking down the street and falling off a cliff, or perhaps off the edge of the earth itself, and plummeting forever into the empty vacuum of space. But if what he'd heard was true, at least that vacuum would benefit from the illumination of stars.

He and Old Ben followed the Portable Organic Light Emitter's beam down the cracked and broken sidewalk, the wind gusting at their backs, particles pricking their ears and necks. Sometimes months passed and the foul smoky air under the Shroud barely moved. Then a storm would blow in, followed by days of digging out.

A particularly bad stretch of broken sidewalk lay ahead, and Ishmael took the old man's arm to steady him.

"You're a good boy," Old Ben said as they passed the tall ghost poles where it was said streetlights had once hung. "Don't worry about Archie. He'll be okay."

The words did little to alleviate Ishmael's fears. Who really knew what life was like on those distant feeder planets so many light-years away? Everyone you talked to had a different story, but these were always second- or thirdhand; Black Range was a filthy blight, and the reason people signed up for missions was to earn enough money to leave and never return.

They passed a flickering outdoor holovid, one of the tallest sights in Black Range after the huge smokestacks that rose from the Zirconia Electrolysis station. A beautiful forty-foot-tall woman beckoned to them in an audio track blemished with gaps and breaks: "Want to . . . *zzzt* . . . new worlds filled with . . . *zzzt* . . . Enlistees make an excellent . . . *zzzt* . . . never been a better time to . . . *zzzzt* . . . Safe travel aboard a modern fleet . . . *zzzt* . . . Adventure and excitement . . . *zzzzt* . . . a secure financial future . . . *zzzt* . . . Volunteer today and . . . *zzzt.*"

Ishmael winced. Why had he told Archie he'd enlisted? Then again, he couldn't have just vanished without warning — that would have been unthinkable. Was there *anything* he could have done to stop Archie from hobbling down to the Mission Office and enlisting as well?

The truth was that it had never occurred to Ishmael that his foster brother would do such a thing — or even if he did, that the Mission Board would accept him. That's why Eliza's Law existed, right? To make sure children and people with disabilities couldn't be exploited. A wave of remorse swept through Ishmael. Maybe he shouldn't have enlisted in the first place. It would have meant all of them spending the rest of their lives here in dark, dismal, dilapidated Black Range, but at least Archie would be safe.

The flying grit was starting to sting by the time they got to Old Ben's place, which had once been one of the nicest homes in Black Range but was now in serious disrepair. Ishmael helped the old man through the door, wrinkling his nose at the stale, musty odor inside.

"Have a seat," Old Ben said, wheezing in the dark.

"But the storm's coming."

"Sit. We have . . . to talk, son. It's . . . important." Though the walk had not been far, it had left the old man breathless.

Knowing Old Ben wouldn't keep him in weather like this unless it was truly urgent, Ishmael felt for a chair and sat. The old man disappeared into the dark and returned with a jar and a glass. Benzo was a homemade concoction that impaired the nervous system and gave people the tremors. But Ben was old, maybe forty-five or even fifty, and surely couldn't have many years left. His thick beard and hair were pure white, save for a bit of gray at his widow's peak, and, like just about anyone still alive at his age, he had a clip on his nose feeding pure oxygen into whatever was left of his ravaged lungs. He sat down hard and inhaled deeply through the clip. Ishmael could barely make out his face in the shadows.

"There are things I have to tell you, son. . . . Things I couldn't say before . . . and now there isn't time to explain everything because of this Earth-forsaken storm." With quaking hands he poured himself a glass, some of the benzo spilling onto the tabletop. Ishmael had always been amazed by how much Old Ben could drink and still remain lucid. "Now, you know that your foster parents and I have been friends for a long time . . . but what I'm going to tell you, even they don't know. So you have to swear to me that this stays between us. You can't repeat a word of it."

Ishmael hesitated. He might not tell his foster parents everything, but he and Archie had no secrets.

"Not even Archie," the old man added knowingly. "Maybe someday, but not now. Swear?"

"Why?" Ishmael asked.

"Because . . . " The old man took a deep breath and let it out slowly. "It's a matter of life and death, son. That's why."

Ishmael felt his chest tighten. Outside, the wind buffeted the windows. A fine cloud of dust seeped in through the leaky door gasket.

Ben went on: "There's a great deal that you and your family don't know, Ishmael. Things nobody in this town knows because the Trust doesn't want them to know."

"The Trust?" Ishmael repeated.

"Just bear with me, son," Old Ben said. "Now, you're a smart boy and probably wondering how a broken-down old man like me, who's spent most of his life working in that decrepit Zirconia Electrolysis station, could know anything you don't, so I'm going to show you something." He pulled up his sleeve and placed his left arm on the table, with his wrist turned out. "Put your wrist next to mine so our registries are facing each other."

Ishmael leaned closer and did as he was told, the foul, fermented odor of the old man's benzo breath filling his nose. Old Ben slowly drew Ishmael's arm nearer his own until a sudden spark of blue light leaped between their wrists. The mild shock startled Ishmael. He yanked his arm back.

"Our registries just greeted each other," Old Ben explained.

Ishmael had never heard of such a thing. Registries were forms of identification. "What does that mean?"

The windowpanes rattled. The dirt peppering the outside walls made a hissing sound. Old Ben waved his hand dismissively. "I don't have time to explain. There's too much else I need to tell you. But remember what you just saw.

"Now, you've heard that the coal supplies are running out? That soon there won't be enough fuel left to power the systems that sustain life on this planet?"

Ishmael nodded. Those rumors had been around for as long as he could remember.

"Well, I hate to say it, son, but this time it's true. We've nearly depleted all known supplies." The old man paused to let it sink in. "Oxygen production's started to dip below acceptable levels. You've probably noticed that there are days now when it seems hard to catch your breath?"

"I thought that was the carbon monoxide," Ishmael said. When the Zirconia Electrolysis station atomized carbon dioxide, the result was oxygen and carbon monoxide — in high enough concentrations a poison itself.

"That's partly to blame. But it's mostly oxygen deficiency."

Ishmael felt goose bumps rise on his arms. If what Old Ben said was true, didn't it mean the end of life on Earth? "Are you sure? Joachim and Petra would've told me —"

The old man shook his head. "Think about it, son. More than anything, your foster parents want you and Archie to be safe. And it won't be long before the safest place will be anywhere but on Earth."

Now Ishmael understood why Joachim and Petra weren't fighting Archie's enlistment. Still, he shook his head. "If that's true, then I'm not going. They can't expect me to leave them here to . . . what? Die a slow death?"

Old Ben placed his hand on Ishmael's and squeezed. His grip was surprisingly strong. "If you stay here, son, you'll all die. The only way you can save yourself *and* your foster parents is to go."

"And abandon them?" It was inconceivable.

Old Ben let go of Ishmael's hand and sat back in the dark. He took a gulp of benzo and then contemplated his glass, gathering what he had to say next. "Listen closely, son, because what I'm about to say won't be easy to believe. What if I told you that you and I met once before — a long, long time ago? I'm not talking about here on Earth." The old man pointed a finger upward. "I mean, out there . . . out where you're going. On Cretacea, where you served aboard a ship called the *Pequod.*"

4

The new arrivals follow Charity through a hatch and into a passageway. Shaken by the death they've just witnessed, they take a moment to notice the wrinkled, bent old man trudging toward them. His skin is so pale it's nearly translucent, and his eyes are sunken and shut. One bony hand slides along the handrail while the other pulls a wheeled bucket. Liquid with a sharp chemical odor sloshes in the bucket, and the handle of a long brush pokes out.

He stops and listens for a moment, his face turned to the passageway wall. "That you, Ms. Charity? That you?"

"How are you, Tarnmoor?" Charity asks.

"How'd anyone be what'd just heared about young Abdul? Tells me, Ms. Charity, is there no folly a' beast that ain'ts infinitely outdones by the madness a' men? Now is there?"

Ishmael wonders how this old man already knows what just happened abovedecks.

"No, Tarnmoor, it certainly isn't," Charity answers.

The strange old man takes a deep sniff. "Gots some nippers with ya, eh? Eh?"

"I do."

"Ah." He addresses them. "Listen to what Ms. Charity says, ya hears? Don't want to end up like poor young Abdul. Or a blind old swabbie like me, neither, does ya? Does ya? Now tells me your names as you passes. Your names."

The new arrivals identify themselves as they file past: "Hello, I'm Pip." "B-Billy." "Ishmael." "Queequeg, sir."

"Waits a minute, waits a minute," Tarnmoor calls when they're done. "The young lady didn't say her name. Young lady?"

Gwen looks startled. "How'd you know?"

The bent old man grins, revealing gums and a few worn stubs of teeth. "How's old Tarnmoor know? How? Blinded by the light on his first day, he wassed. Aye, but he knows. . . . If it moves, if it makes a noise, he knows. If it gots a smell, he knows."

"Don't let it go to your head, Grandpa," Gwen scoffs.

"Ah, and a redheaded lass at that, she is! Ain't that right, Ms. Charity? Ain't it?"

Gwen's eyes go wide with astonishment.

"Indeed it is," Charity says.

Tarnmoor cackles, then aims a crooked finger at the new arrivals. "Keeps cares, nippers. The most dreaded creatures glides under waters, unapparent for the most parts, and treacherously hid beneath the loveliest tints a' azures."

The old man continues past, pulling his bucket. Charity leads Ishmael and the others away.

Several decks down, they stop outside a door marked MEN'S BERTH. Charity tells Gwen to wait, then motions the guys inside. Curtained bunks float at different heights between the ceiling and floor, suspended by magnetic levitation. As she leads them toward the back of the room, Ishmael notices that some of the sleepers are decorated with what appear to be large pointed teeth as well as long spines like the one that killed Abdul. Charity pushes open a door marked WASHROOM and gestures for them to look in. Lining one wall are urinals and toilets, but along another wall is a row of open stalls, each with knobs and a long pipe that arcs overhead and ends in a conical nozzle.

"Anyone know what those are?" Charity asks.

Ishmael, Billy, and Queequeg don't have a clue. But Pip—who has quick, curious eyes that never stop moving—hangs back, as if he knows something they don't.

"Try turning one of the knobs," Charity suggests with a smile.

Queequeg strides into the washroom, and Ishmael can't help noting how unlike the cautious, jittery denizens of Black Range he is. He reaches into a stall and turns a knob.

Water starts to pour from the nozzle overhead.

Queequeg jumps back in surprise, then quickly reaches in and turns it off. "Sorry! I had no idea! Really!"

"It's okay." Charity chuckles. "That's what it's there for. You can let it run all day if you want."

Is she serious? Ishmael wonders. Back on Earth you could be arrested for wantonly wasting water. He looks at the wall of stalls again and then back at Charity. "They're . . . for washing?"

"Anytime you want, guys," Charity says, training her gaze on Ishmael and Queequeg. "And based on the way some of you smelled when I opened your pods, you might want to try one right now. I'll come back when it's time for dinner." She backs out of the washroom and pulls the door closed.

Moments later, Ishmael and Queequeg are in the stalls letting water—*hot* water!—pour down on them. It's a miracle. Ishmael cannot get enough of the sensation of it splashing against his body. If only it could wash away the memory of the death he's just witnessed.

"Can you believe this?" Queequeg asks in the next stall.

"Where could it come from?" Ishmael asks.

"Charity said the ship has a nuclear reactor," Queequeg says. "My guess is the hot water's the byproduct of the cooling mechanism."

Ishmael's never heard of nuclear reactors. Though now that he thinks of it, he doesn't recall seeing smokestacks on this ship when they were abovedecks. No trails of dark soot rising into the air like back home.

"There used to be nuclear power on Earth, too," Queequeg adds. "Before the Shroud. But without lots of water, reactors can't work."

Ishmael lets the hot water splash against his face, wondering how Queequeg could know all of this.

"And the way it got him with that skiver thing in its tail," Queequeg is saying later. Their meager possessions neatly stowed, the nippers have gathered between bunks to talk about Abdul's death. "Ever see anything like that?"

"Of course not," Pip says condescendingly. "It's an ocean-dwelling creature and there are no oceans on Earth."

"Oh, yes, there are," Queequeg says. "Not much now, but there was a time when more than three-quarters of Earth was covered by water."

Pip snorts. "Rubbish."

"Oh, yeah? What if I told you I saw one once?" Queequeg asks.

Pip laughs. "That's rich!"

"May lightning strike me if it's not true." Queequeg crosses his heart. "My father took me. We walked on dirty gray salt for a week. *Crunch, crunch* all day long."

"So, wh-what made you th-think there w-was an ocean?" Billy asks.

"The wreck we found. Of a ship like this. Just a huge, rusted hull lying on its side."

No one speaks, not even Pip. When Ishmael thinks of the dry, filthy planet he left, the idea of most of it once being covered by water does sound outrageous.

"Finally we came to these cliffs," Queequeg continues. "I think my dad was afraid that the salt might give way and we'd fall in and never get out, but then we saw some coral—"

"Coral?" Billy repeats.

"Colonies as hard as rock under the ocean made by tiny creatures long since dead," Queequeg says. "There were once huge reefs of them in all sorts of strange shapes."

"Oh, for Earth's sake, what nonsense." Pip harrumphs, then says to Billy and Ishmael, "You believe that from someone who doesn't even have a registry?"

"Th-that's right," says Billy. "How's that p-possible? I th-thought everyone g-got a registry at b-birth."

Queequeg averts his eyes. "Not everyone."

"Perhaps you'd like to explain?" Pip asks.

When Queequeg doesn't answer, Pip turns to Billy and Ishmael. "Keep that in mind the next time he tells you one of his tales."

As strange as it is that Queequeg doesn't have a registry, Pip is something of a mystery as well. He enunciates his words the way the voice-overs in VR do. And there's his chubbiness, and his neatly trimmed hair and nails—all things nearly impossible to achieve in the barren and dim households of Black Range. Finally, when the nippers were settling in, Ishmael noticed that the items Pip pulled out of his travel bag were brand-new and still in their original packaging.

But before he can ask about any of that, the door of the men's quarters opens and three sailors come in. Ishmael recognizes them from earlier: The one with the bright-yellow hair, the one with the white topknot, and the brute with the shaved head, his left arm now in a sling. The sailor with the topknot climbs into a bunk decorated with many teeth and what look like terrafin skivers, but the other two saunter over to the nippers. The one with the shaved head is built broad and deep, a concrete block of a man with bulging muscles ridged with thick veins. How long must he have served on this planet to have attained such a physique?

The muscular sailor reaches into Pip's sleeper with his good hand and grabs a T-pill that Pip just removed from its box.

"What do you think you're doing?" Pip demands. "Give that back!"

The brute ignores him and displays the electronic sleep aid to his mate. "Nice, eh, Daggoo? And good timin' 'cause mine just broke."

"It's not yours," Pip snaps indignantly, and addresses Daggoo. "Tell him to return it at once!"

Daggoo chuckles and pretends to obey. "Hear that, Bunta? You'd better do as he says."

When the brute smirks and turns to leave, Pip appeals to the other nippers for help. Ishmael should have no allegiance to this well-fed, fancy-talking boy who acts so superior, and yet he feels a bond because they're both new arrivals. Besides, he knows what happens when bigger guys think they can push you around. Once these sailors bully one nipper, what's to stop them from trying to terrorize all of them?

He figures it's not in Billy's nature to fight, and Pip looks too small and soft to be much help. That leaves Queequeg. When Ishmael shoots him a quizzical look, the tall, broad-shouldered boy nods.

Ishmael steps in front of Bunta. "Give it back."

The brute stops and slowly swivels his head, pretending to look around. "Someone say somethin'?"

Ishmael cracks his knuckles. "I did. Give it back."

Bunta looks down and curls his lip, baring a row of shiny steel teeth. "You? How old are you, pinkie?"

"My name is Ishmael, and I'm seventeen."

"You ain't big enough to be seventeen."

"Maybe you've forgotten, but nutrients are scarce back on Earth."

"Then you should feel lucky you're not there and mind your own business here." Bunta winks at Daggoo as though he thinks he's said something clever.

"Maybe *you're* the one who should mind his own business," Ishmael shoots back, "and not steal from new arrivals."

The room goes silent. Bunta's face darkens. "Watch yourself, pinkie."

"I said, my name is Ishmael. Now give the T-pill back."

The brute snorts. "Make me." As he pushes past, Ishmael reaches up and taps him on the back. Bunta instantly wheels around, a huge fist swinging for Ishmael's head. Ishmael ducks and delivers a sharp jab to the brute's ribs. But it feels like he's just punched a firm slab of clay. Bunta sneers and draws his fist back. But before he can swing, Queequeg steps beside Ishmael.

"This is between me and him," Bunta warns. "You stay outta it."

Queequeg doesn't budge.

Bunta considers for a moment, then hands the T-pill to Daggoo. "All right, I'll take you both with one hand."

"No." From across the room comes the voice of the sailor with the white topknot.

Bunta looks askance. "Aw, come on, Fedallah."

His bearing impassive, Fedallah points at Daggoo. "Return what he took."

The yellow-haired sailor tosses the sleep aid to Pip.

Bunta narrows his eyes at Ishmael. "You're dead meat, pinkie."

Ishmael raises his chin. "For the last time, my name is Ishmael. See if you can manage to remember it."

Bunta's beady eyes bug out at the insult. For an instant it looks like he's going to do grievous damage, but then he glances at Fedallah and stomps away. Daggoo lingers. "You don't know what a pinkie is, do you?"

Ishmael raises his little finger.

Daggoo shakes his head. "You're in for a treat one of these days." Then the sailor's manner grows menacing. "But mark my word, *Ishmael:* the next time you get in Bunta's way, no one, not even Fedallah, will be able to stop him."

5

"Anyone kn-know which p-planet we're on?" Billy asks in the passageway while he and the other nippers follow Charity to dinner.

"Cretacea," replies Charity.

Ishmael stops. "You sure?"

Charity gives him a funny look. "Of course I'm sure. Why?"

Ishmael feels goose bumps as he recalls his last night on Earth. Is it really possible that Old Ben knew where he was going? Or was it just a lucky guess?

"Hey, friend, you just gonna stand there?" Queequeg asks. "Some of us are hungry."

Ishmael makes his feet move. As they near the mess, the passageway fills with unfamiliar smells, some oily and mechanical, others tart or smoky.

"Listen up," Charity says before they go in. "I assume most of you have never eaten solid food before. If you don't want to spend the better part of tonight puking your guts out, don't eat more than half a plate. Don't eat anything raw. Nothing that's green, red, yellow, or orange. Stick to foods that are brown or close to white. You can eat things with skin, but don't eat the skin itself. Your bodies don't have the microbiota for that stuff yet."

"Wh-what's microbiota?" Billy asks nervously.

"Bacteria," Charity answers. "In the old days, our digestive systems were full of them, but it's been so long since people on Earth ate anything except liquid nutrients that they no longer have much gut bacteria. Here on Cretacea the food's a lot more complex, and it'll take your gastrointestinal tracts a few weeks to adjust. You can't rush it without getting sick, so just bide your time."

Ishmael is still trying to wrap his brain around the idea of eating *anything* that has skin when Charity leads them into the large, noisy mess filled with sailors, their plates piled with awful-looking matter. Some of the sailors are trim, while others have clearly been so well fed since their arrival on Cretacea that their uniforms are stretched tight over their bellies.

Charity directs the nippers to the far end of the mess, where they get trays and eating utensils, which she calls silverware. Next stop is the galley, a hot, cramped room filled with pungent aromas that make Ishmael's stomach rumble hungrily. Behind steamy glass cases, sailors wearing stained white aprons serve portions of grossly unappealing fare. Despite his growling stomach, Ishmael is repulsed by the dark-brown lumps, the crusty, light-brown sticks, and things with tails, glassy eyes, and mouths filled with tiny teeth, lying in shallow pools of oily yellowish liquid. They're supposed to *eat* this stuff?

"Believe me, it tastes a lot better than it looks," Charity assures them. "It just takes getting used to. Sample a few things and see what you like. Then you can come back for a few bites more."

Moments later, carrying trays, the nippers follow her back into the mess, where she instructs them on the use of the silverware. They watch in fascination as she spears a morsel with a fork, then chews and swallows. “Delicious!” she pronounces.

Queequeg is the first to follow her example, stabbing a small brown lump and placing it in his mouth. His eyes go wide and he quickly begins to tear at another piece with his spoon and fork.

“Use the knife to cut, and don’t forget to chew,” Charity advises. “Otherwise you can choke.”

Ishmael’s head is spinning. Food with eyes and tails? Food that was once alive? Food that can *kill* you? Back home, all they had was Natrient, a sweet, gooey “natural nutrient” squeezed out of hermetically sealed pouches. Why would anyone choose to eat these weird-smelling, awful-looking lumpy things instead?

But Queequeg’s blissful expression and eagerness to eat more motivate Ishmael to pick up his fork and sample something. The food feels strange in his mouth, and he has to remind himself to chew, but it does indeed taste far better than it looks, and like nothing he’s ever had before.

“Slow down,” Charity cautions. “Chew for as long as you can before you swallow. It helps with digestion.”

They try, but it’s difficult to pace themselves. Ishmael and Queequeg hunch over their plates with knife and fork tightly in hand, their mouths working busily. Billy uses the spoon to try small bits of the blandest-looking lumps. Once Gwen discovers how delicious the food is, she sets her arms on either side of her plate protectively. Pip, however, eats slowly and delicately, resting his knife and fork on his plate while he chews. But then, given that he’s the only plump one among them, perhaps he isn’t as hungry.

“What is this stuff?” Gwen asks with bulging cheeks.

“Mostly what we catch,” Charity answers. “Hump, long-neck, basher.”

"Wh-what about that?" With his knife Billy pokes one of the things that have eyes, a mouth, and a tail.

"Scurry. Someone must've caught it, or maybe we traded for it. The *Pequod* doesn't trawl for game like that."

Ishmael stops chewing. "The *Pequod*?"

"It's the name of this ship."

Ishmael puts down his silverware as Old Ben's words come back to him: *"On Cretacea, where you served aboard a ship called the* Pequod*."* There's no longer any doubt in his mind that the old man knew where he was going. *But how?*

"Lost your appetite, honey?" Charity asks.

Ishmael blinks. "Sorry?"

She gestures at the uneaten food on his plate. He forces himself out of his daze and continues to eat, but his thoughts are far off. *How could Old Ben have possibly known?*

It's not long before everyone except Pip and Billy has cleared his plate. Pip is still eating in his slow, deliberate way. Billy has tried a few morsels and left the rest untouched.

"Can we have some more?" asks Queequeg.

Charity nods. "But not too much, or, believe me, you'll be sorry."

Queequeg, Ishmael, and Gwen head back into the galley. Heeding Charity's advice, Ishmael and Gwen don't ask for much, but Queequeg tells a server to fill his plate.

"Hold up, friends." He pulls out a spoon he's hidden in his pocket and quickly shovels food into his mouth.

Moments later, when they leave the galley, it appears that Queequeg's taken no more of a second helping than Ishmael and Gwen.

By the time they finish their meals, a heavy, languorous sensation has settled upon them. Charity goes into the galley and returns pushing a cart with two meals on trays. "I have to take these up to the bridge. You guys head back to your quarters. Get a good night's sleep. First thing tomorrow, you're going to work."

Later that night, in the pitch-black, Ishmael wakes to the sounds of whimpering and sniffling. For a second he wonders if it's Pip. Earlier, when they returned to the men's berth, Pip found that his electronic sleep aid had been ripped apart, foam and fiber circuitry hanging out like the guts of a small, disemboweled creature. But it's not Pip who's sobbing; it's Billy.

From around the room come rustling and grousing as Billy's moans begin to wake the others.

"Aw, for Earth's sake, shut it," someone gripes in the dark.

"I w-wanna g-go h-home," Billy whimpers.

"Wait a year and you'll get your wish, bud," another voice croaks.

"I want to g-go now!" Billy blubbers.

"Put a sock in it," someone — sounding like Bunta — growls.

"Leave him alone," Ishmael warns.

"Mind your own business, pinkie. No one wants to listen to that snivelin' crybaby all night."

"The more you threaten him, the more frightened he'll feel," Ishmael says. "If you really want to get back to sleep, just drop it."

Some mumbling follows, but the room soon goes quiet except for Billy's sniffling.

"Billy," Ishmael whispers.

"Y-yes?"

"You're not alone. We're all kind of scared. And these jackasses aren't making it any easier. But Queequeg and I have your back. Right, Queequeg?"

"Right, friend" comes a yawning murmur from the sleeper below his.

"Try to get some rest," Ishmael tells Billy. "Things'll be better in the morning."

"N-no, they w-won't." Billy sniffs.

Knowing not to argue, Ishmael says, "Okay, maybe not. But after a good night's sleep, at least you'll feel better."

Silence. Then Billy whispers, "Th-thanks, Ishmael."

Ishmael lets his head sink into his pillow and soon falls asleep — but not for long. A short while later he's awakened again, this time by a warm breath close to his ear. He can just make out the silhouette of Bunta's large, shaved head.

"You're a dead man, pinkie," the brute whispers in the dark. "When you least expect it . . . when it's the farthest thing from your mind . . . you're going down."

Bunta moves away without a sound. Ishmael closes his eyes and waits for his heartbeat to steady. In the quiet he hears someone retching in the washroom. He peers down at Queequeg's sleeper. It's empty.

· 6 ·

BLACK RANGE, EARTH:
Predeparture (Pt. 2)

In Old Ben's place, Ishmael listened to the wind whistle. He should have started home already. It was not uncommon for people to get lost in storms, often suffering lung damage from breathing in too much soot and grit. Sometimes they even died. But despite the looming danger, he stayed. What Old Ben had just said about them meeting on another planet was impossible — nonsense, really — but Ishmael had never known him to lie. "They haven't told me where I'm going yet. And wherever it is, we can't have met there before. I've never been off Earth."

In the shadows, the old man drummed his fingers, as though struggling to find a way to explain. "For now, just humor an old man and *pretend* you and I met on Cretacea thirty-five years ago. Would you do that for me?"

Old Ben might have used the word *pretend,* but Ishmael knew this wasn't a game. If the old man was telling him this, it was because he believed it to be true. But Ishmael hadn't even been *alive* thirty-five years ago. . . .

"Back then, I was just a kid myself," Old Ben went on. "Maybe twelve years old at the most. All I knew were Grace and the ocean."

"Grace?"

The old man's voice turned wistful. "The captain of our pinkboat. I was her crew."

Pinkboat? Apprehension began to slither through Ishmael. This was starting to sound more and more like a fantasy, the imaginings of an old, lonely man. Or could it be the benzo talking? "We met when you were twelve?" Ishmael repeated, trying to show the old man how ludicrous the whole thing sounded.

But Old Ben took it differently. "You're thinking they don't allow kids as young as twelve on missions?" He leaned across the table, his craggy face faintly visible in the dark. "I wasn't on a mission, son. Cretacea's where I grew up."

Ishmael sat back, unsure what to do. The wind rattled the house's roof. By now, Joachim probably assumed that he'd stay the night at Old Ben's. But Ishmael was determined to get home and spend his last night on Earth with his foster brother.

A loud *plink!* made them both start. A gust of wind must've picked up a small pebble and hurled it against a window. Old Ben poured himself another glass of benzo, liquid overflowing the rim. "Mark my words, son: The next time you see me, it'll be on a scurry trawler in the middle of an ocean the size of which you can't imagine."

He raised the glass and drained it. But instead of relaxing, he suddenly hunched forward, his demeanor intense. "Here's what you need to remember: Do *not* rendezvous with the *Pequod*. When Grace tells you that's what she's going to do, you *have* to stop her. Understand? Lives are at stake, son. Don't let her do it. If she insists, you go down below and disable the RTG. Do whatever you have to. Just don't let her near that ship."

Outside, the wind no longer whistled; now it screamed. *Scurry trawler? RTG? The* Pequod *again?* Ishmael didn't know what to make of any of this.

"Promise me," Old Ben said.

The roof rattled so loudly that Ishmael wondered if it would blow right off. It was definitely time to go. He started to rise.

"Son?" said the old man.

"How can I promise? Nothing you've said makes sense."

Old Ben mulled it over. "All right, if it's all nonsense, then what harm is there in promising?" He offered his hand. "I've been waiting most of my life for this moment. Shake on it, son."

Ishmael hesitated, then reluctantly grasped the old man's quivering hand and shook. But instead of letting go, Old Ben tightened his grip and pulled Ishmael close. "There's one more thing. As soon as you've got a decent chunk of money, you transfer it to me."

Ishmael scrunched his face. The old man's benzo breath was foul.

Old Ben squeezed his hand, refusing to let go. "Promise?"

"Why do you need money?"

"To save your foster parents. They've aged out of the mission parameters, but there are still ways to get them off this planet. Only it's going to take a lot of cash." The old man let go of Ishmael's hand and slumped back in his chair, breathing heavily. "I know . . . I'm putting a huge burden on your young shoulders . . . but there's no other way. You just . . . you've got to take a leap of faith, son. I'll need at least six thousand. Maybe seven or eight. Ten thousand would definitely do it."

That cinched it: Old Ben had lost his mind. Ψ10,000 was an absolute fortune, more than most people earned in an entire lifetime.

"I know it sounds like a lot," the old man said, "but it's not impossible where you're going. You've heard the stories. You can make that and more if you're smart. Just remember, son: As soon as you've got that money, transfer it to me. And don't let Grace rendezvous with the *Pequod*."

Outside, the wind continued to howl and sand and dirt pelted the windowpanes. "You better get going," Old Ben said, reaching again for the benzo jar. "And son?"

Ishmael hesitated. "Yes?"

"May good luck and fortune go with you."

7

A loud, insistent bleating comes through speakers in the ceiling of the men's berth — speakers that Ishmael hadn't even realized were there. With no windows in the sleeping quarters, it's impossible to know whether it's dark out or light, but to Ishmael it feels much too early to rise. He and the other nippers nestle groggily in their sleepers while the older sailors wash and dress.

The door opens and in hurries a short, portly, balding man wearing a neatly pressed black uniform much like Starbuck's, as well as wire-rimmed glasses. He's carrying a tablet and wearing a headset, and his skin is pallid. The nippers watch him from under their blankets while the other sailors brush past without a word. "Well, what are you waiting for?" the man asks in a high, squeaky voice. "Come on, it's time to get up. This is your first full day. Lots to do. Come on. Up, up, up!"

Billy, Queequeg, and Ishmael drag themselves out of their sleepers. Queequeg looks especially bleary, his eyes puffy from spending half the night in the washroom giving back his dinner. Only Pip rolls over and covers his head with a pillow.

The portly man passes his tablet over Pip's bare wrist. "Oh, uh, it's you, Mr. Lopez-Makarova." The man's tone becomes deferential. "You really should get up. You don't want to be left behind, do you?"

"Bugger off," Pip murmurs from under the bedding.

Ishmael and Queequeg wait to see how the man will react, but he simply forges ahead politely: "Now, now, Mr. Lopez-Makarova, is this really the way to begin your sojourn with us here on the *Pequod*? As I'm sure you've been informed, no one gets to sleep in, except for an extra hour on Sundays, and today is not Sunday."

A wiry man with tattoos of coiled vipers on both cheeks enters the room. He, too, wears a black uniform, but it's wrinkled, and several days' worth of stubble darkens his jaw. When he hears the portly man meekly admonishing Pip, he stomps over to the bunk. "Aw, fer Earth's sake, Stubb, step aside." He reaches into Pip's sleeper and grabs the boy by the hair. "Get up, ya lazy slug!"

Pip lets out a cry, and the man named Stubb gasps. "Stop, Mr. Flask! You don't know what you're doing!"

Ignoring him, Flask yanks Pip's pale, round face close to his own. "Listen, mate, when ya get an order, ya snap to it. Otherwise you'll spend yer time here cleaning toilets with yer tongue."

Stubb scoots close and whispers something in Flask's ear that makes him instantly let go of Pip's hair. "Oh, er, is that so? Still, shouldn't mean a basher's snout who he is," he splutters and backs out of the quarters.

"I'm terribly sorry about that, Mr. Lopez-Makarova," Stubb apologizes while Pip sits up and rubs his eyes. "But it is breakfast time, and Ms. Charity asked me to make sure you were all up. She said she'll meet you in the mess. So do hurry. You don't want to be late on your first day, as that would —"

"Oh, for Earth's sake." Pip swings his legs over the side of the sleeper. "You won't cease blathering unless I'm up, will you?" He hops down and stalks off toward the washroom.

A few minutes later, on their way to the mess, Ishmael gets a better look at the *Pequod.* Like its exterior, the interior of the ship is in a state of disrepair, with reddish-brown rust creeping along the corners where walls and floors meet, lights broken or missing, hatches that either won't stay shut or must be forced open, portholes with cracked glass . . .

"So just who are you, Mr. Lopez-Makarova?" Queequeg asks, imitating Stubb.

"My father's acquainted with some people, that's all," Pip replies vaguely.

"My father used to know some people, too," Queequeg says. "But that never got me special treatment."

Pip's lips remain pressed tight. Meanwhile, Ishmael notices that Billy has fallen behind them. He slows down, letting Pip and Queequeg go ahead.

"You okay?" he asks in a low voice.

The thin blond boy shrugs. "I d-don't know. But th-thanks for doing what you did last night."

"No problem. It's too bad some of them have to be idiots."

Billy lowers his voice. "I heard what Bunta said. Aren't you scared?"

Now it's Ishmael's turn to shrug. "Worrying about guys like him is a waste of energy."

Billy absorbs this, then nods at Pip and whispers, "Y-you believe that stuff about his f-father knowing some people?"

"Right now I'm finding *a lot* of this hard to believe," Ishmael replies, only half kidding.

When they arrive at the mess, Charity and Gwen are already eating. "Anyone lose their dinner last night?" Charity asks.

Queequeg sheepishly raises his hand.

"Right. So this morning take it easy, okay, honey?"

Once again the meal looks unappetizing but tastes delicious. They're almost finished eating when the mess door swings open and in marches Starbuck, followed by the pale, bespectacled second mate, Stubb. Starbuck stops beside a row of tall chrome canisters near the nippers' table to fill a mug with a steaming brown liquid.

"I must tell you that I have spoken to Mr. Bildad himself, and he is not at all pleased with the production of this ship, Mr. Starbuck," Stubb says, clutching his tablet to his chest like a newborn baby. "At this point in the voyage, he says there should be twice as much weight in the hold."

"Is that so?" Starbuck replies, bringing the mug to his lips.

"Yes, sir. And I'm sure you know that the crew isn't happy either. With our catch being so meager, their common fund is far lower than on previous voyages. Far, far lower. And pardon me for saying this, sir, but we both know that when the crew isn't happy—"

"They work even harder to make up for the shortfall." His round black glasses steamed by the hot drink, Starbuck turns on the fussy man. "Is that what you were going to say, Stubb?"

"Why, n-no, sir," stammers Stubb. "That wasn't what I was going to—"

"How many voyages have we been on together?" Starbuck cuts him short.

"Uh, five, sir? Well, officially five and a half if you take into account that we're halfway through this one and—"

"And have we ever ended a voyage with less than full weight?"

"Well, uh, no, sir, not really."

Starbuck adjusts his glasses. "Then I don't see a problem, do you?"

Stubb swallows. "Well, to be honest, sir, yes, I do." He offers his tablet. "You see, sir, at this point in the voyage—"

"At this point in the voyage doesn't mean a blasted thing," Starbuck snaps. "The only thing that matters is what the weight and common fund look like at the *end* of the voyage. So talk to me about it then."

"But Mr. Bildad says—"

"Mr. Bildad can shove a terrafin's skiver up his—" Starbuck's eyes find the table of nippers watching and listening. The first mate's forehead furrows. "Why aren't you at work? Get your sorry carcasses into the galley, now!"

The startled nippers jump to their feet. Starbuck points at Pip. "Not you, Lopez-Makarova."

· 8 ·

BLACK RANGE, EARTH:

Predeparture (Pt. 3)

In the storm outside, Ishmael adjusted his goggles and tightened the thin dust mask covering his nose and mouth, but he could still taste grit. He felt for the rope that led out to the street. This length would lead to another that he could follow home while gusts whipped around, soot getting into his hair and working its way beneath his clothes through every possible crevice. The important thing was to count the number of steps. When he got to three hundred, he'd begin feeling for the rope that ran along the path to his home.

Later, he stood inside the front door, shaking the grime and filth out of his clothes and hair and wiping what he could off his skin. Washing wasn't an option. Water was too scarce for anything except drinking. After returning the gun to the storage closet, he went into the tiny bedroom he shared with his foster brother. It wasn't large enough even for two small beds, so Joachim had rigged a bunk. In the shadowy dimness, Archie was barely visible sitting on the side of the lower bunk, undoing the Syncro straps on the metal braces that ran the length of both legs. Ishmael had been listening to the tearing sound of Syncro for almost as long as he could remember.

Recalling the electric shock he'd felt earlier at Old Ben's place, Ishmael had an idea. "Show me your registry?" he asked.

Without asking why, Archie held out his left arm. Ishmael pressed his own registry close to his foster brother's.

There was no shock.

"What was that for?" Archie asked.

"Nothing," Ishmael said. "Any word from the Mission Board?"

Archie shook his head.

On impulse Ishmael said, "Maybe we should run away."

"In the middle of a storm? And go where?" Archie chuckled as he braided his long black hair so that it wouldn't get tangled in his dreams. He was right. There was nowhere to go. For many hundreds of miles outside Black Range, the territory was said to be barren, parched, and uninhabitable. Even if they packed supplies, how far could they possibly get with Archie on crutches?

And if Old Ben was telling the truth about the looming end of oxygen production, what would it matter?

"Stop agonizing, Ish. Wherever they send me has got to be better than this place," Archie said. "And we both know they're not going to make me do anything I can't do. You'll see. I'll probably get an auditing job while you're slaving away in a mine. And with both of us out there, we'll have twice the money when we get back. Imagine having our own rooms, Ish. Or are you still afraid of sleeping alone in the dark?"

That's how Archie was. Even at a time like this, he could tease. Ishmael watched his foster brother lift his useless legs into the lower bunk and cover them with the blanket. "And seriously? If something *does* happen to me — if I die, I mean — it won't be bad, it'll just be what happens. Saying death is bad is like saying night is bad. Night isn't bad, it's just not day. You can't expect me to stay here in Black Range. This isn't living, Ish. It's . . . it's hardly even existing."

Ishmael didn't argue; the appeal deadline had passed, so there was no point. But it was agonizing to think that after tomorrow, the next place Archie would undo his braces would be in some distant solar system. An auditing job? If such a thing hardly existed on Earth, why should it exist on some wild, uncivilized feeder planet?

9

"Welcome to purgatory, urchins. Prepare to toil the longest hours for the least amount of pay and the most abuse."

In the galley, Gwen, Billy, Queequeg, and Ishmael, all wearing aprons, stand at attention. The speaker is Fleece, the ship's cook and a great bearded blob of a man sitting on a stool and wearing a bedsheet-size apron covered with red and brown stains. His vast stomach stretches the apron tight, and his brown beard fans out from his face like a bib. Ishmael is certain that three or four average-size men could fit into the cook's trousers. He is without doubt the roundest human Ishmael has ever seen.

"Behold the sacred shrine at which you shall daily worship." Fleece waves a fat hand at an ancient, boxy machine with a spiky black conveyor belt running through it. Stacked on one side are a dozen gray tubs filled with greasy, food-encrusted eating utensils, plates, glasses, and cooking implements the cook calls pots and pans.

Fleece assigns them stations. Gwen's job will be to place the dirty items on the conveyor belt. Ishmael will stand at the other side of the machine and transfer the clean plates and utensils to racks, which Queequeg will carry to the serving areas. Billy is given a bucket of rags and a mop and ordered to wipe down the dining tables and swab the mess floor.

"Get to work!" Fleece orders.

"Ow! Mother of Earth!" A little while later, a knife clatters to the floor and Gwen yanks off her glove. She hurries to a porthole on the other side of the galley and inspects her finger in the sunlight.

Ishmael grabs a medical kit from the wall and goes toward her. "Let me help with that."

"Blast off!" Gwen snaps and turns her back.

Over her shoulder Ishmael can see blood running down her hand. "You need a bandage."

Silence.

"Seriously."

"Get lost."

Ishmael stares at her, then says softly, "Look, we don't have many friends on this ship. It's going to be a really miserable year if we don't stick together."

Gwen keeps her back turned, her face hidden by her unruly mop of red hair. Drops of blood have begun to splatter on the floor.

"Must be pretty deep," Ishmael says. "Come on, let me help."

She licks her lips, about to say something, then stops. Without looking at him, she slowly holds out the bleeding finger. As he suspected, the cut is serious, but her hand is trembling so hard that Ishmael can't aim the closure strip properly. He glances at Queequeg and signals for him to join them.

"Yeesh, that looks nasty," Queequeg says. But when he tries to close his hand around Gwen's, she jerks hers away.

"Don't!" she snarls.

"Whoa. Easy does it, friend." Queequeg retreats. "Just trying to help."

Gwen glares over her shoulder, wary eyes flicking back and forth between Ishmael and Queequeg. Meanwhile, blood continues to drip onto the floor.

"Would you feel better if we got Charity?" Ishmael offers.

Gwen considers, lets out a sigh, and once again holds out her wounded finger. This time when Queequeg takes her hand, she stiffens but doesn't pull back. Ishmael wipes away the blood, then carefully applies the closure strip and wraps the finger in gauze. When he's finished, Gwen's pale-green eyes are glittery. She turns away and stays by the porthole, squinting out for a long time.

It's late when the nippers finally drag themselves out of the galley. They've been on their feet all day; as soon as they finished cleaning up after one meal, it was time to set the tables for the next. Back in the men's berth, they find Pip in his sleeper, his face hidden behind a top-of-the-line head-mounted display.

"Where'd you go today?" Queequeg asks.

"Drone control," Pip answers without taking off the HMD.

A rare frown crosses Queequeg's face. Back on Earth, being a drone operator is a posh job. They sit in comfortable chairs all day, looking at screens while controlling joysticks. Not that it isn't demanding work; drones are expensive, and if you crash one, you'll get in a lot more trouble than you will dropping a plate on the mess floor. But it sure beats toiling long hours in the ship's galley. "How come you get to go to drone control while we're stuck washing dishes?"

"I suppose Starbuck took one look at me and decided I wasn't suitable for that."

It's a lie, and they all know it.

· 10 ·

BLACK RANGE, EARTH:
Predeparture (Pt. 4)

"Guess neither of us is gonna get much sleep tonight." In their cramped, dark bedroom, Archie switched on an old tablet he and Ishmael had found years before in an abandoned shack. The boys had toiled for weeks to get the thick, heavy device to function, but when they'd finally succeeded, the result had been disappointing. It contained screen after screen of annoyingly tiny, indecipherable symbols. But Archie had become fond of the few strange images interspersed here and there and could spend hours scrolling through them.

Now, his face illuminated in blue light, he studied one of his favorite designs: a circular shape with a thick column in the center and intricately interwoven lines branching out from each end.

Ishmael sat down on the edge of the bunk bed and pressed his forehead against Archie's. It was something they'd done often when they were younger, but not recently. Archie's skin was cool; he wasn't at all worried.

"Nervous?" Archie asked.

"Hard not to be," Ishmael replied, still wondering about Old Ben's crazy story, and regretting that he'd promised not to tell his foster brother about it.

"Don't know why I'm not." Archie grinned. "Guess I just keep imagining how incredible it's going to be. Getting off this dry, filthy rock and seeing what's out there."

Archie's irrepressible optimism nearly brought tears to Ishmael's eyes. Though Archie was two years older, Ishmael's knuckles were scarred from years of protecting his foster brother from being bullied about his small size, gentle nature, and disability. But now what would happen? Once Archie went away, he'd be defenseless.

"It's gonna be hard on Petra and Joachim," Ishmael said, forcing himself to change the subject.

"Only for a year," Archie reminded him. "And then it's going to be so much better. Imagine moving to a place where dirt doesn't blow in through the cracks every time there's a storm. And having a baclum table so bright it lights a whole room, and a holodeck where all the colors work. And Petra and Joachim not having to work sixty-five-hour weeks. And me having my own room without you around doing your stupid workouts and stinking up the place with BO."

Ishmael turned his head toward the dark and blinked hard. He couldn't help imagining something else: never seeing his foster brother again.

11

"Hey, mop boy!" comes a shout from the mess.

In the galley, Billy's eyes dart apprehensively.

"Get out there and attend to your responsibilities!" Fleece orders from his stool.

Taking a mop and bucket, Billy inches out the door. At every meal chatter, laughter, and arguments filter in from the mess, so when a roar of amusement explodes among the dining sailors, no one in the galley gives it much thought.

But when another voice calls, "Hey, mop boy, over here!" and more hilarity follows, Ishmael goes to the galley door and peeks out. Sailors have interrupted their dinners to watch Billy frantically mop up a spill, while at another table Daggoo whispers to Bunta, whose arm is still in a sling. The brute surreptitiously nudges a bowl off the edge of their table.

Crash! The bowl shatters on the floor, spilling its contents.

"Hey, mop boy, over here!" Daggoo calls mirthfully.

Having seen enough, Ishmael pushes through the galley door. He stops beside Billy and takes the mop from him, feeling the vibrations of Billy's jitters through the handle. "It's okay," he whispers. "Go run the dishwashing machine."

"B-but F-Fleece s-said . . ."

"Don't worry," Ishmael reassures him. "I'll take care of it."

The sailors in the mess go silent while Ishmael pulls the mop bucket toward the splatter on the floor where Bunta dropped the bowl. He locks eyes with the brute and holds out the mop. "You made it, you mop it."

Murmurs begin to ripple from table to table. Bunta grits his steel teeth. "Don't think I heard you right, pinkie."

"You heard me just fine."

Bunta looks to Daggoo. "You believe this squirt?"

Daggoo crosses his arms and glowers. Bunta turns to Ishmael and juts out his chin. "Make me, pinkie."

"I would . . ." Ishmael nods at Bunta's injured arm. "But unlike you, I don't take advantage of defenseless people."

The sailors around them snigger, and Bunta's face goes red. Ishmael leans the mop handle against the table. "I know you've got only one working arm, so take your time cleaning up. Just make sure you do a good job."

Hoots and hollers follow. Ishmael starts back to the galley, but stops when he hears chair legs scrape behind him. He spins around just in time to see Bunta take the mop bucket with his good hand and fling it, losing his balance and falling forward. Ishmael tries to duck, but the bucket clips him on the shoulder and he crashes into a table, sending plates and mugs flying as cursing sailors jump out of the way.

Bunta grabs him, but Ishmael is now slick with soapy mop water and manages to wriggle out of the brute's one-handed grasp. With sailors circling around, cheering and shouting, Ishmael scrambles onto Bunta's back and hooks an arm around his thick, muscular neck. Bunta bends and twists, trying to wrench the clinging nipper off his back while Ishmael delivers punch after punch to the brute's remarkably hard skull. Finally Bunta gets a handful of Ishmael's hair and starts to pull.

"That's enough!" a voice yells. A hand closes on Ishmael's collar and yanks him off the brute. Breathing hard, Ishmael finds himself looking at his reflection in Starbuck's dark, round glasses.

"Let me have him!" Bunta lunges for Ishmael, but the first mate shoves him back.

"That's enough, Bunta. I'll deal with this nipper and be back for you later."

With Starbuck firmly grasping his collar, Ishmael is strong-armed out of the mess, down passageways, and up ladderways until they enter a spacious, well-appointed cabin that seems to belong on an entirely different sort of ship. Starbuck slams the door and plunks Ishmael into a high-backed chair before a large, neat desk.

The first mate straightens his uniform and leans against the desk, scrutinizing Ishmael, whose bloodied knuckles have begun to throb from repeated contact with Bunta's concrete cranium. "What in Mother Earth is wrong with you, boy?"

Breathing hard, heart drumming, Ishmael looks around at the couch, table, and vast holodeck over which floats the three-dimensional image of a planet that is mostly covered with water. Beyond that, through a partly open door, is a bedroom with a large hovering sleeper, upon which lie two T-pills.

"Well?" Starbuck is waiting for an answer.

"He was bullying Billy, sir."

He feels the first mate's eyes bore into him from behind the dark glasses. "Haven't you ever heard the saying 'Never pick a fight you can't win'?"

"Yes, sir."

"So?"

"I don't believe everything I hear, sir."

A muscle twitches just below the rim of the dark glasses. Starbuck leans toward him. "Listen closely, boy. There's only one reason why any of us are on this ship, and it isn't to prove how tough we think we are. It's to grab the biggest share of the pot we can. And getting into fights for the sake of some weakling isn't going to help you do that, understand?"

Ishmael's eyes have gone to a shelf and a small static holograph of an attractive blond woman and three small blond children.

The first mate knits his brow. "I said, 'Do you understand?'"

Ishmael nods slowly. He understands; he just doesn't agree.

Starbuck leans back and presses the tips of several misshapen fingers against his forehead, rubbing in a circular motion. "Listen, I've got enough headaches with this crew already; I don't need some green nipper like you looking for trouble. Daggoo and Bunta may be loose cannons, but they are also part of the top-producing crew on this ship. *They're* the ones making coin for us, not you. So know this, boy: Next time you get into a scrape with either of them, I don't care what it's about or who started it—*you're* the one who's going to stew in the brig until you're so pale you're practically see-through. Do I make myself clear?"

"Yes, sir," Ishmael answers. But he's distracted by something he's noticed about the first mate's appearance. Starbuck's crooked fingers and worn-down nubs of teeth don't fit with his youthful skin. And there's something artificial about the blackness of his spiked hair. The first mate places his hands flat on the desk, and Ishmael looks at them closely. He's never seen so many scars.

12

"Pay attention!" shouts Flask, the wiry third mate with the tattoos of vipers on his cheeks. He's sitting on a wave racer, bobbing in the ocean. A dozen yards away, clad in personal flotation devices, or PFDs, and wearing caps with visors, Gwen, Billy, Queequeg, and Ishmael stand in a chase boat, also called a stick boat, just as a harpoon is sometimes called a stick. Flask has just finished assigning them positions. Since Billy admits to some experience with hovercraft back on Earth, he'll be the skipper. Queequeg, undoubtedly the strongest among them, will be the harpooner, and Gwen and Ishmael will be linemen who handle the ropes. The chase boat's hull is lined with inflatable pontoons for stability. Mounted in the stern is a light machine gun, while in the bow is the harpoon gun, which looks like a small cannon armed with a pointed steel arrow with slanting fins and a shaft as thick as a man's thumb.

It's the nippers' day off, but not a day of leisure. Starbuck has ordered them to begin training as a chase-boat crew. A quarter mile behind them, the *Pequod* floats amid the gentle ocean swells. By now, the nippers have been aboard the ship for a month, long enough to figure out that the chase-boat crews make the most money because they take the biggest risks. So the fact that Starbuck has decided to have them train as a crew so early into their mission gives them the best start imaginable.

Apparently Flask disagrees: "I've heard a' desperate times calling fer desperate measures, but this is a new low, training nippers fer a stick boat. The four a' ya combined ain't got the strength a' one Daggoo."

"Maybe not, but each of us has at least twice his brains," Gwen cracks.

Flask raises an eyebrow. "What have we here? A jester, huh? Well, good fer you, Red, but a quick wit won't go far when yer face-to-face with a beast what weighs a hundred tons. Still, Starbuck wants ya trained in the art a' the stick, so trained you'll be."

The third mate points at the harpoon gun. "Obviously, Queequeg's not gonna fire no stick at me. What I'm gonna do is hook the towline to the tail a' this racer and then take off like a large sea creature would. Yer job is to try to apprehend me. Any questions?"

The nippers don't answer; they're watching an approaching chase boat, its RTG whining, bow lifting and crashing over the swells, arcs of white spraying out from both sides. It's Fedallah's boat — Daggoo at the wheel and Bunta beside him — and it's bearing directly down on them.

"Don't mind that other —" The rest of Flask's sentence is lost. At high speed, Daggoo is just seconds from ramming the nippers' chase boat. With panicked shouts, Queequeg, Gwen, and Billy leap overboard. Only Ishmael stands his ground.

At the last conceivable instant, Daggoo veers sharply away, missing the nippers' craft by inches, creating a wake so violent that

Ishmael is almost thrown into the water with the rest of his crew. Daggoo slows his boat and circles around. Beside him, Bunta displays a sadist's grin. "Sorry, we didn't see you."

"Yeah, right," Ishmael replies while the others, buoyed by their PFDs, splash back toward the chase boat.

"We're looking for Fedallah," Daggoo announces. "Heard he was out here, swimming." Shading his face with his hand, he scans the waters around them, then points. "There he is."

Surprisingly, not far from them, someone is undulating through the water like a sea creature. It's the first time that Ishmael has ever seen a human swim.

While Daggoo steers toward Fedallah, Ishmael reaches over the side to help his crew climb back into their chase boat. They're drenched and quaking.

Flask motors the wave racer close to them. "Don't get yerselves in a snit over those two. Ya want revenge? Hang around fer a second year. Become a good stick-boat team and stick more beasts than that yellow-haired scurry-sucker and his pea-brained mate. That'll show 'em good."

It takes hardly any time for their uniforms to dry under the broiling sun. When the nippers have collected themselves, Flask speeds away with the bright-red towline tied behind his wave racer. In the chase boat, Gwen and Ishmael let the line stream through their gloved hands from a large yellow tub on the floor. As skipper, Billy is supposed to keep a steady pace behind the pretend beast, but he bumbles at the chase boat's controls. Gwen has trouble keeping the line from catching on oarlocks and cleats. And more then once Ishmael gets tangled up trying to deploy the big orange float.

After several hours of bungled maneuvers, the chase-boat crew is tired and dejected. Flask sits on the wave racer nearby with a sour look on his face. "Yer gonna have to do an awful lot better than that."

"We just need more practice," Ishmael suggests.

"Or maybe yer just a bunch a' green nippers wastin' everyone's time." Flask gazes back at the *Pequod,* seemingly trying to decide what to do next. It's nearly lunchtime, and while they have meals stowed in the chase boat, they could just as easily return to the ship and eat in the mess.

Ishmael feels disappointment spread over him like the Shroud over Earth. To make the kind of money Old Ben said he'd need to save Joachim and Petra, it's crucial that he be part of a successful chase-boat crew. "Why don't we take a break, eat lunch, then practice some more this afternoon?"

Flask gives him a skeptical look. "I can only bang my head against a wall fer so long, mate."

"Just a few more hours," Ishmael implores.

"Yeah, come on, friend," Queequeg joins in. Even Gwen and Billy start pleading for more practice.

Flask presses his lips tightly together, then speaks: "Waste a' time, but . . . oh, all right."

They're in the middle of lunch, floating under the sweltering midday sun, when there's a splash behind them. Twenty yards away, a huge shadow moves slowly below the surface. It must be eighty or a hundred feet long, by far the largest living creature the nippers have seen yet.

"Well, I'll be." Flask chuckles. "It's a big ol' hump. 'Scuse me while I see if any stick boat's close enough to put a stick in it." He starts to lift a two-way to his ear.

"What about us?" Gwen asks.

Flask snorts. "Get real, Red. That's serious weight down there. And a good chunk a' coin fer a pot what dearly needs it."

"But wouldn't it be the perfect way for us to practice?" Gwen persists.

The third mate ignores her. Meanwhile, the huge creature drifts lazily past as though the chase boat weren't even there. The nippers can hear only the third mate's side of the conversation over the two-way: "Well, how long till he can get here? . . . Naw, it'll be gone by then. Humps don't stay this close to the surface fer long. Come on, there's gotta be someone. Where's Fedallah? . . . A hundred clicks? Blast it. . . . Oh, sure, great, thanks."

Flask lowers the two-way, his sun-chapped lips pressed together in frustration.

"Come on, let us take a shot," Gwen cajoles. "Otherwise, all that money's just going to get away."

"Grow some brains, Red," Flask snaps. "If yer crew can't manage with me on a wave racer, what makes ya think ya could ever handle a great big wild creature like that?"

By now the hump is forty yards away.

"Oh, come on!" Gwen begs. "There's nothing to lose from letting us try!"

Flask casts his eyes up at the clouds dotting the blue sky. A moment passes, and then he shakes his head and spits into the ocean. "Aw, what's it matter? You'll never come close. Go on, knock yerselves out."

Gwen wheels around. "Start her up, Billy!"

While Billy gets the chase boat running, Queequeg pulls the tarp off the harpoon gun, and Ishmael checks the spools of red towline to make sure they're clear. Gwen hooks the big orange float to the line's end.

"Ready?" Billy asks, trying to sound brave.

By now the hump is fifty yards off and several fathoms deep. Gradually steering the chase boat nearer, Billy positions them about twenty-five yards away, at which point he starts to run parallel with the hump.

Flask motors beside them on the wave racer, coaching. "Suppose it surfaces, Queequeg. Gonna aim the harpoon gun straight at it?"

"No, sir," Queequeg answers. "If I do that, the stick'll fall short."

"So what's yer plan?"

"Got to fire on an arc, sir."

All the while, the dark shadow of the hump continues along languidly.

"Can't we get closer?" Gwen asks.

"We might spook it," says Billy.

"But Queek's never practiced from this far."

Queequeg kneels in the bow, his hands on the harpoon gun, making minute adjustments to the angle at which he hopes to fire. The sea around them sparkles, rising and falling in gentle swells. Sometimes in the trough of a wave, they lose sight of the hump. But when they rise back up on the next swell, the creature is there, swimming slowly, oblivious to the threat so close by. Still, sooner or later Ishmael expects to come to the top of a swell and discover that it's gone.

"The other boats ever try to stick a hump from this far away?" Queequeg asks Flask.

"Not if they can help it," the third mate answers. "I was a harpooner fer years, and I can tell ya from experience, it's too easy to miss at this distance. There's ways to approach on the sly, distract and trick 'em. Only ya ain't had time to learn that stuff yet."

"So tell us," Gwen says.

"Easy does it, Red. I told ya, ya ain't ready."

The chase boat dips down into a trough and starts to climb out. At the top of the swell, Gwen lets out a gasp.

The hump has changed course.

It's crossing their bow a mere fifteen feet ahead!

Not only that, but it's coming up for air!

"Well, mother of terrafins, will you look at that!" Flask mutters.

As it reaches the surface and lumbers past the chase boat's bow, Ishmael feels like he's watching a slow-moving coal transport. The hump is so close it will be impossible to miss with the harpoon gun.

But Queequeg, as startled as the rest of them, looks back quizzically, uncertain if he should really fire. Gwen hisses urgently: "Go on! Before it gets away!"

Queequeg takes aim.

"Wait!" Flask cries. "Ya ain't—!"

Ker-bang! Too late. With a big puff of white smoke, the harpoon rockets from the gun and into the hump's flank.

In a flash, the creature sounds. Length after length of red towline whips away at blurring speed. Now that they've scored a hit, Billy is supposed to accelerate and follow the hump, but he flounders at the controls, and when he guns the engine, the boat lurches *backward*!

The crew tumble forward. Billy reacts too quickly, shifting out of reverse and into forward so abruptly that the RTG stalls. The chase boat dies in the water.

"Clear the line!" Flask shouts while the crew stagger to their feet and Billy tries to restart. The harpoon line is still whipping out, and there's hardly any left in the tubs. Suddenly Ishmael realizes what's going to happen and cries out to Queequeg, who has just enough time to duck before the last of the coil disappears and the big orange float shoots toward the bow.

Whack! The boat takes off with such dispatch that they're all thrown back into the stern. Ishmael hears a cry and a splash and knows someone's gone overboard, but in the tangle of bodies, arms, and legs, it's impossible to see who. In no time the chase boat is bumping and slapping across the ocean swells, being pulled by the hump while in the bow the big orange float is jammed tightly against the harpoon gun.

Groping for a handhold, Ishmael pulls himself into a kneeling position on the stern thwart and catches a glimpse of Flask far behind them, hauling Billy out of the water and onto the back of the wave racer. By now Queequeg and Gwen have also managed to get handholds and kneel.

"Cut the line!" Ishmael shouts. Each of them carries a knife for just such emergencies and Queequeg starts to inch forward, always with a tight grip on a thwart or gunwale to keep from being thrown out of the boat. He's almost reached the bow when the chase boat suddenly stops.

Ishmael, Gwen, and Queequeg share mystified glances. Have they caught a lucky break? Queequeg is reaching for his knife to cut the line, when the bow is suddenly yanked down with such force that the stern flies up —

And Ishmael and Gwen are catapulted into the air.

Ishmael smashes face-first into the ocean, then bobs to the surface in his PFD, dazed and coughing up salt water. The seawater is nearly as hot as the *Pequod*'s showers, and with a jolt he realizes that he's in the middle of an ocean and has no idea how to swim. His body goes stiff with panic. Will the PFD keep him afloat?

A wet head of dark-red hair pops up a few feet away. It's Gwen, coughing and spitting.

But where's Queequeg?

· 13 ·

The Foundling Home

One day, when Ishmael was around seven, he was playing on the floor with some children. On the other side of the room, a door opened and Ms. Hussey, the sour-faced woman who was always yelling at the children, came in with a boy on crutches, his legs strapped into long metal braces. Ishmael and the others stopped what they were doing and stared.

The two boys grew close, often playing games with a handful of parts they'd scavenged from the insides of broken tablets, navigating the pieces over a landscape of old circuit boards and touch-screen assemblies spread out on the floor.

Sometimes Ms. Hussey accompanied grown-ups into the playroom. And now and then, the grown-ups left with a child. While no one had ever wanted to adopt Archie, the boy with the leg braces, couples had often expressed interest in Ishmael, and on three occasions he'd been placed with families. Each time, he'd run away and found his way back to the home.

One day while he and Archie played, they became aware of two men, a woman, and Ms. Hussey standing a dozen feet away, observing. They'd seen one of the men before, watching them through the window from the street. He was stocky, with a broad forehead, thick black hair, and a beard.

The other man and the woman were new. They appeared to be a couple, the man tall but stooped, with a lined, wizened face and the thick hands of a laborer. The woman was petite, with bright, watchful eyes.

"We've tried to separate them," Ms. Hussey was saying, "but no matter where we place the younger one, he always finds his way back here. He's got an uncanny sense of direction, I'll say that for him."

"Does he say why he keeps coming back?" asked the man.

"He doesn't say anything," said Ms. Hussey. "Both boys could speak when they came here, but now they refuse. We don't know why."

The couple whispered to the man with the broad forehead, and then the woman turned to Ms. Hussey. "What about the other boy?"

"Archie?" Ms. Hussey shook her head. "You don't want him." She gestured to the leg braces propped against the wall.

In the past that had been enough to end the conversation, but when the three visitors began to whisper again, Ishmael and Archie eyed each other uneasily. Then the tall, stooped man said, "What if we took them both?"

Archie's eyes instantly widened with hope. No one had ever suggested that before. But Ms. Hussey looked down at her tablet and shook her head. "As much as I'd love to get them both off my hands, it appears that you were fortunate to be approved for even one foster child given how small your home is. But why don't you follow me? There are some excellent candidates in the room next door."

She started away, but the couple and the stocky bearded man lingered for several moments more, speaking in low voices. When they'd gone, Ishmael and Archie shared a disheartened look. Being taken together would have been a miracle, but they were old enough to know that there was no such thing.

14

Fifty feet away, the chase boat bounces wildly as the hump tries again and again to dive. Somehow Queequeg has managed to remain aboard and is being tossed around inside the boat like a doll. Ishmael can't imagine how he's able to hold on and keep from being flung off. Why doesn't he just let go and jump overboard?

Then Ishmael sees why: Queequeg's not holding on — he's being *held.* The back of his PFD is caught on something, and in the mayhem he can't reach around to free himself.

Flask rushes up on the wave racer with Billy riding on the back. "What in the universe is he doin'?"

"He's caught!" Ishmael yells from the water.

Crack! A plank of the chase boat's flooring breaks off, sails into the air, and smacks down into the water near them. The hump is pulling the boat to pieces. Sooner or later it's going to jerk down hard enough to yank the hull right off the pontoons, and when that happens, what's left of the chase boat is going straight to the bottom — and Queequeg with it.

A loud ripping sound fills the air as one of the pontoons tears free of the hull. The chase boat cants to one side, and Queequeg is slammed silly.

"Can't we do something?" Ishmael shouts at Flask.

"Like what?" the third mate yells back.

Ishmael doesn't have an answer, but he's not going to bob around and watch his friend perish. His fear of drowning momentarily forgotten, he begins mimicking the movements of Fedallah swimming. He lacks the grace of the older sailor, and the PFD slows his progress, but even so, he's able to propel himself forward.

"Stop!" Flask shouts. "You'll get yerself killed!"

Ishmael ignores him.

"Come back! That's an order!"

As Ishmael splashes closer to the chase boat, a burnt-chemical smell hits his nose and the water's surface becomes oily. The chase boat is being pummeled so violently that it's spilling lubricants.

Strangely, when he's about ten feet away, everything goes still. The remains of the chase boat float peacefully, and Ishmael can see that this would be the perfect moment for Queequeg to free himself. But his friend hangs limp and stunned, thanks to the beating he's taken.

Ishmael splashes closer. Five feet away . . . three feet . . . He can almost reach out and touch Queequeg.

"Get back!" Flask bellows behind him. "It's breaching!"

Ishmael doesn't know what "breaching" means, but there's no retreating now. He's reached Queequeg. A loop of fabric on the back of his friend's PFD is caught on the float hook.

"Ishmael, it's going to surface!" shouts Gwen.

Deep below them, a dark spot is rapidly growing larger.

"W-watch out!" Billy shouts from the back of the wave racer.

The water around the chase boat begins to roil. Ishmael gropes for his knife.

"Leave him!" Flask shouts.

Ishmael reaches up and slices through the fabric loop — just as something slams into them from below.

· 15 ·

The Foundling Home (Pt. 2)

In the morning, the couple and the man with the beard were back with Ms. Hussey. Ishmael and Archie were in the exercise room, swinging on overhead bars. As soon as Ishmael spotted the grown-ups, he felt anxious. Usually when people came back for a second look, they ended up taking him with them, at least temporarily.

Sensing that a child might be chosen, the youngsters in the room stopped playing. Ishmael and Archie crept toward the playhouse near the wall, Archie walking with his hands, his legs dragging behind. They slipped inside, hoping the visitors would forget about them and leave.

Footsteps echoed in the silent room, and then Ms. Hussey's sour face appeared through the playhouse window. "I'd cooperate if I were you," she warned Ishmael under her breath. "The people who come here looking for children want the ones who are young, cute, and cooperative. The longer you play these games, the more likely it is that you'll never be chosen."

But that, of course, was exactly what Ishmael and Archie were hoping for. The boys stayed inside and huddled close to each other. Exasperated, Ms. Hussey said, "It's no use. You'll never separate them. If you insist on trying, all you'll do is create a great deal of trouble for all of us."

The tall man eased himself to his knees and gently pushed open the playhouse door. "You two must be pretty good friends, huh?"

Ishmael and Archie remained silent.

"My wife, Petra, and I would like a foster child," the man said. "But we're only allowed to take one of you."

The boys backed farther into the playhouse. Now the petite woman with the bright eyes kneeled down beside her husband. "We would so love to have you both in our family. We tried to get them to change their minds, but they just won't."

Archie squeezed his eyes shut. Ishmael watched the grown-ups warily. No one had ever spoken to them like this before, and he didn't know what to make of it.

Ms. Hussey harrumphed loudly. "I really don't see the point in going through all this. You're just wasting everyone's time."

The tall man looked over his shoulder at her. "Just a few more moments." He turned back to the boys. "What if we let the two of you decide who comes with us? Would that make it easier?"

"Oh, for Earth's sake!" Ms. Hussey blurted out in exasperation.

Ishmael held the man's gaze. Had he understood him correctly? Slowly, he began to creep forward. Archie stared at him uncertainly but didn't resist.

"Well, well, isn't this interesting," Ms. Hussey clucked. "The younger one must really like you two. Either that, or he's gotten tired of having that little cripple around all the time."

Leaving the playhouse, Ishmael crossed the room and collected Archie's leg braces and crutches . . . which he brought back and offered to the couple.

The woman drew a loud breath. Her husband took her hand in his. Ishmael crawled back into the playhouse and pressed his forehead against Archie's.

"Pay them no mind," Ms. Hussey told the couple. "I'm sure it's just a trick meant to make you feel even guiltier about separating them."

"Have they ever done it before?" asked the man.

"Well, no," Ms. Hussey admitted. "But there's always a first time."

The two boys stayed inside the playhouse for more than a minute with their foreheads pressed together. Then Archie began to drag himself out. Ishmael remained where he was, tears running down his cheeks as the bright-eyed woman drew the whimpering Archie into her arms. Archie's eyes stayed fixed on Ishmael.

The tall man slowly rose to his full height and gave Ms. Hussey a meaningful look. "Now tell me that you honestly think these boys should be separated."

For once, Ms. Hussey appeared uncertain. She swallowed. "But you don't have the space."

It was then that the stocky bearded man with the broad forehead and widow's peak took the director aside and began to speak to her in hushed, forceful tones. Ishmael could see that Ms. Hussey responded differently to him than she did to most grown-ups, listening instead of arguing.

When the man had finished, Ms. Hussey turned to the couple. "All right. I'll see what I can do."

16

Ishmael rouses to the sensation of dozens of liquid fingers tickling his skin. There's a tightness around his chest and a loud hum in his ears. His jumbled thoughts slosh in a murky mist.

Water flows around his body as the ocean slides past.

Overhead the sky is deep blue. . . .

This could be a dream, but it's not. He's being pulled slowly through the hot sea. The hum is from the wave racer running just a fraction over idle. The tightness around his chest is Gwen's arms holding him. When Ishmael tries to move, pain shoots through his shoulder. Still, he swivels just enough to see that behind Gwen is Queequeg, his arms around her waist. Billy, still sitting on the back of the wave racer, has a grip on Queequeg's PFD.

Ishmael's eyes meet Queequeg's. His face and arms are bruised and scraped, but otherwise he appears unharmed. "You saved my life, friend."

As he tows them back to the *Pequod,* Flask can't stop grumbling. "Never seen anythin' like it. Neither a' ya has any right to be alive." He looks back at Ishmael. "Especially you, sonny. That hump came up right beneath ya. Woulda thought you were a goner fer sure."

"Did we get it?" Ishmael asks, despite the throbbing pain in his shoulder.

"Ha!" Flask laughs harshly. "*That's* all ya want to know? We ain't got him yet, but we will. He's still got Queequeg's stick in him and he's draggin' the float so's we can track him. This time tomorrow they'll be slicin' and dicin' him on the deck."

"So we did good?" Gwen asks hopefully.

Flask frowns. "No! Ya did terrible—ignorin' a direct order not to fire, gettin' the float caught, and not cuttin' yer line, practically destroyin' yer stick boat! Mark my word, Red, when we get back to the *Pequod,* there's gonna be bloody bilge to pay."

Twenty minutes later, they're lined up on the deck, their uniforms and PFDs dripping, while Starbuck demands, "What happened out there?"

"They stuck a hump, sir," Flask answers weakly.

Starbuck stares incredulously at the four soggy nippers, then turns to the third mate. "You *let* them do that?"

Flask lowers his head. "Didn't happen like that, sir."

"Just how *did* it happen?"

"I told 'em not to fire, sir."

"Forget the stick, Flask," Starbuck snaps. "How'd you let them get close enough to do *anything*?"

"We wasn't that close, sir. We was running thirty, maybe forty yards parallel. You know, just fer a thrill before the beast dove. But then the hump, he . . . changed direction."

Just then, Stubb arrives breathless, adjusting his glasses and clutching his tablet. "I heard there was some kind of incident, Mr. Starbuck?"

Subtle shifts in Starbuck's expression make it plain that he's not happy to see the fussy second mate. Flask, on the other hand, perks up. "This new young team here stuck its first hump. A big 'un. Got to figure the crew'll appreciate it, considerin' how little's in the pot."

Behind them, cogs creak as a crane swings the dripping wreck of their chase boat overhead and lowers it to the deck.

Stubb inhales sharply. "Oh, my!"

The chase boat's harpoon gun hangs loosely from its broken mount. One of the pontoons is gone, and seawater flows from the RTG compartment. While two sailors open the engine's cover and douse it with fresh water, the crane angles back overboard and hauls up the missing pontoon. Stubb circles the wreckage, carefully recording the damage on his tablet before engaging in a hushed but heated discussion with Starbuck.

Finally, the second mate addresses Flask. "The estimated damages will be approximately one thousand, Mr. Flask."

The third mate goes pale. "But, sir, with all due respect, the damages was incurred in the course a' apprehendin' a beast—"

"Reckless endangerment and irresponsible judgment, Mr. Flask," Stubb states officiously.

Flask looks stricken. "I got kids back home, and I promised my wife this would be my last voyage."

"Be that as it may—" Stubb begins, but is interrupted when Ishmael clears his throat.

"Excuse me, sir, but I don't think it was Mr. Flask's fault."

"Stay out of this," Starbuck warns.

"Seriously, sir," Ishmael perseveres. "It really was an accident. We just happened to be in the right place at the right time. When the hump surfaced, it was so close that Queequeg could've reached out and touched it. Anyone would have fired a harpoon in that situation."

"Just because anyone would have done it doesn't mean it was the correct thing to do," Stubb replies primly. "Company policy states that damage caused by reckless imprudence must be paid for by the guilty party." Once again he turns to Flask. "As I was saying —"

"Then suppose I pay for it?" Ishmael asks.

Everyone goes quiet. Starbuck scowls. Flask looks at Ishmael in astonishment while Stubb quickly enters something on his tablet. "At your current pay rate, it will cost your entire year's salary, young man. Even more if the pot doesn't fill up soon." The portly second mate fixes his eyes on Ishmael's. "You're aware that you won't be permitted to return home till your debts to the company have been satisfied?"

"Yes," Ishmael answers, wondering if there'll still be a "home" to return to.

"You're being crazy, friend," Queequeg argues.

"It wasn't your fault," Gwen adds.

"Don't d-do it," says Billy.

Even Flask protests. "I appreciate it, sonny, but there's no way I can let you take the blame."

Unswayed, Ishmael says to Starbuck, "I've heard that a productive stick-boat crew can easily make that up."

"Indeed, boy, a *productive* stick-boat crew can." Starbuck looks at the third mate. "Well, Flask, how did the nippers perform this morning? Would you say they showed promise?"

Flask starts to answer, then catches himself. He scrutinizes Ishmael for a long beat, then coughs into his fist. "I'd, ahem, say they was a mite rough around the edges, sir. But given more time to learn the ropes . . . they just might . . . make a good crew."

17

By dinner, word of what happened has spread through the crew. Tables of sailors stop talking and marvel when Ishmael and the other nippers pass. Waiting at their table, Pip gives Ishmael a confounded look. "You gave up your *entire* year's pay to save Flask's neck?"

"To save *all* our necks is more like it," Queequeg says.

"How?" Pip asks with a frown.

Queequeg drops his voice. "We totally bombed in practice, but genius over here"—he winks at Ishmael—"figured that if he took the cost of the chase boat off Flask's shoulders, the third mate might feel obligated to give us another chance."

Pip grins. "So much for the martyr act."

"More l-like self-preservation," says Billy.

Queequeg pokes Ishmael playfully. "I wonder if Starbuck was on to you."

"I doubt much gets past him," Ishmael says. He turns back to Pip. "Hopefully the thousand won't matter once we start hunting for real — even if we make only half of what Fedallah's crew makes."

At that moment, Daggoo and Bunta come out of the galley, carrying trays heaped with food. When they see the nippers, they change direction and head toward them. "Enjoy your swim today, kiddies?" Daggoo asks archly.

Ishmael's face hardens. He'd almost forgotten that Daggoo had nearly rammed them that morning.

The yellow-haired skipper leans in closer. "Congratulations on *accidentally* sticking your first hump, *nippers*. But don't let it go to your heads. You've got a long way to go, and if you ever do make it to full stick-boat crew, which I strongly doubt, just remember this: Once you're out of sight of this ship, the rules don't apply. It's every crew for itself."

"At least we stuck a beast today," Gwen shoots back. "What'd *you* add to the pot?"

Daggoo's jaw muscles tighten. "Pure luck. And believe me, we would've gotten it without wrecking our boat."

After dinner the guys return to the men's berth to check the message lights on their VRgogs for word from home. Fretful about how — and where — Archie is, Ishmael has been anxiously waiting to hear from Joachim and Petra, but the entire month has passed in silence. Rumor has it that solar flares have been interfering with communications.

Tonight, the blue message lights are finally blinking. Pulling his VRgogs on, Ishmael feels the buds find their way to his ears while the dark lenses adjust to projection mode. For an instant he is in his gloomy kitchen at home, but the room keeps degrading into clouds of pixels, and the audio is broken up by buzzing distortion. Ishmael shuts off the optics, which improves the audio, but only slightly. It's Joachim's voice:

"Hello, Ishm . . . We . . . happy and re . . . hear you've made it . . . Cret . . . a ship. You're . . . enjoying the experience . . . far. We wish . . . rchie, but . . . no news . . . solar interfere . . . very worried . . . Things here continue . . . difficult to breathe . . . sometimes isn't . . . empty stores . . . but . . . hope that you . . . Love . . ."

Repeat plays don't make the VR more intelligible. One thing is undeniable, though: There's been no word from Archie.

When Ishmael slides off the VRgogs, Queequeg asks, "What did you hear?"

"Mostly buzz." Ishmael is about to ask Queequeg the same when he notices that the broad-shouldered boy's VRgogs are still hanging in his sleeper, untouched. Close by, Billy removes his VRgogs and shakes his head glumly. Only Pip is still wearing his HMD. And if the smile on his lips is any indication, he's getting much better VR than anyone else.

On the other side of the room, Fedallah sits cross-legged on his sleeper, examining something that looks like the skeleton of a small flyer. Ishmael signals Queequeg, and they slip off their bunks to take a closer look. Fedallah is shirtless and as thin as any malnourished denizen of Black Range, but he has an unusually broad chest and rib cage, as if he possesses an inhumanly large pair of lungs.

Closer now, Ishmael can see that the skeleton has a thin tail. It's not a flyer, after all, but the bony carcass of a miniature terrafin. With long, slim fingers, Fedallah gestures behind and above the terrafin's head. "The eyes are far apart. Blind spots here, and here."

"Is that its weakness?" Ishmael asks.

"Yes and no. It cannot see in those places, but it can feel: A propeller's cavitation. Or if a man splashes when he swims. But here"—Fedallah touches a place on the skeleton just behind the head—"is the real weakness. A harpoon stuck like this"—he angles his finger in—"and the battle is over."

"If you can get close enough," Queequeg observes.

The great harpooner's eyes are pools of fathomless black. "Yes, exactly."

Ishmael touches one of the many long barbed spines that decorate Fedallah's sleeper. "All from terrafins?"

"Yes."

"Ones you caught?"

"No man captures a terrafin alone." The harpooner looks up at them. "You show promise. You will be a good team."

Ishmael hopes he's right.

Something makes Fedallah glance up at the ceiling. Across the room, Billy sits up attentively, listening. At first Ishmael doesn't hear anything, but then his ears perceive faint, distant drumming.

Fedallah points a finger upward. "Go see."

18

Billy, Queequeg, Pip, and Ishmael make the three-stairways climb to the main deck. The drumming from above is growing louder. Soon it begins to sound like thousands of pebbles falling on a vast sheet of metal. They stop inside a hatch. From the other side comes a steady roar.

"Go on, take a look," Queequeg urges eagerly.

When Ishmael opens the hatch just enough to look out, a warm mist blows in. Outside in the dark, liquid is pouring down, but not from some hose aimed upward. It appears to be water . . . *pouring out of the sky*!

Suddenly the hatch swings wide and Charity's standing there, water running down her face, her uniform shirt a dark shade of green and hanging heavily off her frame.

"Not afraid of a little rain, are you?" She laughs and grabs Ishmael's hand, pulling him out into this thing he's never heard of.

The rain is warm. Being on deck feels like taking a shower with clothes on. Charity lets go of Ishmael and twirls around, the ends of her hair spitting trails of water that cut horizontally through the air. By now Billy and Queequeg have stepped out and are barely more than shadows in the sheets of falling drops and mist. Queequeg tilts his face upward and opens his mouth wide. Billy's curly blond hair hangs in limp wet spirals on his forehead, and for the first time since they arrived on the *Pequod,* he's actually laughing.

Only Pip declines to come out. When Ishmael looks back toward the hatch, he's gone.

The rain ends and the clouds start to break up, allowing the glitter of stars — actual stars! — to peek through. The hatch swings open again and a figure steps out, wearing a long black slicker. It takes Ishmael a second to recognize Starbuck without his dark glasses. The first mate's forehead wrinkles with consternation when he sees the nippers and Charity in their drenched uniforms.

"Better make sure Stubb doesn't catch you," he jests. "He might dock you a day's pay for the cost of drying your clothes."

"Money, money, money!" Charity shouts as she dances and splashes in the puddles around the first mate. "That's all you ever think about!"

Starbuck watches while she circles him. "What else is there?"

"There's life! Rain! Color! Look!" She points through a break in the sky at a faint crescent of blue, yellow, orange, and red against the dark.

"What is it?" Billy asks.

"A rainbow," Queequeg answers.

"Can't be," Starbuck says. "You need the sun. I've only seen them during the day."

"I think it's from that." Queequeg points at an opening between the clouds where they catch a glimpse of a huge, pockmarked orb in the sky a thousand times larger than any star.

"I'm never going back!" Charity starts to dance again. She is in a strange and wild mood.

"Really?" Starbuck counters. "You don't think you'll get homesick?"

Charity stops. "Homesick? For that ruined piece of dirt?"

"It's still your native planet."

Charity bows her wet head; the spell has been broken. "Killjoy," she grumbles, brushing past Starbuck and climbing back through the hatch.

The night sky continues to clear. Rainwater trickles from the crane towers and rails. As the clouds overhead thin, the great orb becomes more prominent, glowing full and bright. On the rain-slick deck, Starbuck nods at Billy and Queequeg. "You two go below. I want to talk to your friend."

Billy and Queequeg shoot Ishmael uneasy glances but do as they're told. Alone with Starbuck on the deck, Ishmael feels a chill caused only partly by his soaked uniform. Even though the first mate isn't wearing his glasses, Ishmael can't see his eyes in the dark.

Starbuck gazes out at the ocean, where a thick ribbon of rippling orblight tapers as it grows distant. The *Pequod* motors steadily through the night, still on the trail of the big hump Queequeg harpooned earlier in the day.

The first mate lowers his voice confidentially. "No matter what anyone says, that was a good stick today, boy. We get another dozen humps like that and the mood on this ship will be vastly improved."

An orange-billed flyer swoops out of the dark and disappears again.

"I asked Perth, the ship's engineer, to take a look at the stick boat's RTG," Starbuck continues. "If it didn't take in too much salt water, it might not have to be rebuilt. Could save you some serious coin."

Starbuck is full of surprises tonight. Ishmael thanks him and, looking at the star-stippled night sky, now almost clear of clouds, wonders if one of the stars up there supports the solar system where Archie's been sent. Or maybe one is the star around which orbits that "ruined piece of dirt" where his foster parents are stranded, quietly hoping for a way off.

"One more thing," Starbuck says. "From now on, you're the skipper. Billy'll train to be a lineman."

"Does Billy know that, sir?"

"You're the skipper now. You tell him."

19

"That rain last night," Ishmael says the following afternoon. "What makes it happen?"

"When sunlight heats the ocean, water evaporates into the air," Queequeg explains. "That's what clouds are. Then, when the atmospheric conditions are right, fresh, drinkable water pours freely out of the sky. It used to happen on Earth, too."

Pip sniggers. "What a fertile imagination."

"Shut up and let him talk," Gwen snaps.

The big hump Queequeg harpooned has been hauled in. Down on the flensing deck, sailors cut the creature into pieces that will be reduced to micronutrients for cryogenic transport back to Earth. During a short break between lunch and dinner, the nippers have gathered on the main deck to relax and get some sun. Pip has joined them. Ishmael suspects that he's lonely; while he spends most of his time in drone control, he never seems to hang out with the drone operators outside the control room.

Queequeg continues: "For millions of years there was rain on Earth, until pollutants from industry and transportation caused the Shroud."

"Scientists debunked that theory centuries ago," Pip states.

"Scientists whose r-research was p-paid for by the same industries that were being b-blamed for the Shroud," Billy adds incisively.

"Balderdash," Pip insists. "The Shroud is a natural astrophysical phenomenon. Maybe you've forgotten that the majority of planets in this galaxy are permanently covered by clouds. Even in Earth's solar system, the only ones that aren't are Mercury and Mars."

The conversation goes no further. Ishmael glances at Gwen. "Some Z-packs came through last night."

Gwen makes a face. Like Queequeg, she's torn the sleeves off her uniform shirt, and in addition the legs off her slacks, turning them into shorts. Her skin has become tawny, and her tangled red hair has sun-bleached streaks of orange. "I heard. No one's going to contact me."

"Could you make out your message, Billy?" Ishmael asks.

"N-not very well. There wasn't much. My p-parents are always busy."

"Doing what?" asks Queequeg.

"They have a business."

"Their *own* business?" Pip says, skeptically.

Except for a few shopkeepers around Black Range, whose shelves were empty most of the time, Ishmael has never known anyone who owned a business.

"What do they do?" Gwen asks.

Billy remains tight-lipped; apparently he'd rather not say. Last night, when Ishmael took him aside and told him what Starbuck had said about Ishmael becoming the skipper of their chase boat, Billy hadn't seemed surprised, muttering that it would just be another disappointment for his father.

"If your parents are so busy, wouldn't they want you around to help?" Queequeg wonders out loud.

Billy hangs his head. "N-not really. I-I'm only here because m-my father sent me. He th-thought it would be good for me."

An awkward silence falls. Then Queequeg says, "How about you, Pip? Looked like you were in VR for a long time last night. What's the word from home?"

Pip looks surprised; it's obvious that he didn't expect anyone to ask. "Uh, nothing."

Gwen lifts her eyes upward in aggravation. While they've all grown used to his evasiveness, he rarely lies this clumsily. "How about for once you tell us the truth?"

Pip's round face reddens.

"Don't you think you should get back to drone control?" Ishmael cuts in. "They're probably wondering where you are."

Pip throws him a grateful look and heads off.

"Why didn't you let him answer?" Gwen demands.

"He didn't want to talk about it," Ishmael replies. "We're only going to alienate him if we keep pressing him for answers."

"So?" Gwen says. "I don't need him to be my friend. I'd just like to know why everyone lets him do whatever he wants."

"Y-you really d-don't know?" Billy asks.

The others gaze at him curiously.

"H-he's . . . of the Gilded."

Gwen makes a face. "The what?"

Before Billy can explain, he tenses, staring past the others with a look of alarm on his face. Bunta, the human block of concrete, is coming toward them, running his thumb along the blade of a long knife.

Jumping to their feet, Ishmael and Queequeg look for something to defend themselves with.

Bunta stops and snickers. "Not in broad daylight, pinkie." With the tip of his knife, he points off the starboard side of the *Pequod.* In the distance a boat has appeared. It has two broad, winglike booms from which nets hang.

"That's a pinkboat," Bunta says. "Now you'll see what you're nicknamed for."

Pinkboat? The word jars Ishmael, even though he knows at this point it shouldn't. Like the name of the *Pequod,* like the name of this planet, Old Ben knew. *But how?*

"The boat's not pink," Billy says.

"Just wait," says Bunta. "May not be much in the pot, but at least we'll eat well tonight."

The pinkboat — which is blue and white — has tied up alongside the *Pequod,* and the captain, a stocky woman with short gray hair, exchanges sarcastic greetings with Starbuck, who leans against the *Pequod*'s bulwark.

"I see you haven't aged a bit," the woman calls from the deck of the pinkboat, speaking around a stem with a small bowl at the end that's clamped between her teeth.

"Jealous, sweetheart?" Starbuck yells back.

"You won't catch me putting that poison in my eyes."

"So what'll it be today, my love?" Starbuck asks.

"Got sixty pounds of hump meat?"

"Yes, ma'am, nice and fresh. What else?"

"A gallon of marine grease, five pounds of red berry, a couple of quarts of alcohol. And you wouldn't happen to have any VR appropriate for a twelve-year-old boy, would you?"

"I'm sure we can scare up something," Starbuck replies. "Twelve's about the average maturity of the men on this ship. So for all that, I'd assume we're talking fifty pounds of pinkies?"

"Funny, sounds to me more like thirty," replies the captain.

"Settle on forty?" Starbuck proposes.

"That's a deal."

The nippers watch sailors hoist up baskets of small translucent gray sea creatures with black eyes and long pink antennae. In return go the hump meat and other supplies. Finally, a sailor from the pinkboat climbs a rope ladder and boards the *Pequod,* then stands on the deck, looking around. He has a pack slung over his shoulder and looks to be about nineteen or twenty. "Say, mates, where's yer stasis tech?"

"I'll take you," Ishmael volunteers. They start across the deck. "Been on that boat long?"

"Couple a weeks," the sailor replies, in an accent Ishmael has never heard before. "Hopscotching me way to a tub with a workin' stasis lab. After three years, this salty dog's ready to git home and feel some dirt 'tween his toes."

Ishmael leads him belowdecks. "Three years, huh? On what kind of ship?"

"Factory vessel," the sailor answers. "Big old can of rust like this one. Called the *Town-Ho.*"

"Hunting humps and terrafins? Things like that?"

"Humps, for sure," the sailor answers. "But terrafins? No way, mate. Ain't worth the trouble."

Ishmael makes a mental note of that. "Whereabouts did you sail?"

"Darned if I know. All open ocean to me. Seen land a few times, but we stayed clear. They say it's dangerous."

"Catch a lot of beasts?"

"You kidding? The ocean's full of 'em, mate — though I probably don't have to tell you that. The weight we put in, I got enough in the bank so's I'll never have to work another day in me life."

Ishmael brings him to the stasis lab and knocks. Charity answers, looking distracted. "Help you?"

"Here to get transported, miss," the sailor says, then adds with a leer, "but now that I seen you, I might decide to stick around."

"And I might send you back to Earth missing a few parts," Charity replies sharply.

The sailor goes pale. "Sorry, miss. Just been a while since I seen a pretty lady. Promise you'll send me back whole and I'll be a perfect gentleman."

Charity smiles. "That's more like it."

That night festive sailors gorge themselves on boiled pinkies, which are more delicious than anything Ishmael has yet eaten. The mess is jammed. There's an entire table of mud-skinned belowdecks "bilge rats"—mechanics, nuclear techs, engineers—their dirty olive uniforms stained with grease and oil. At another table sit the drone operators, who are as dull-skinned as the bilge rats but whose uniforms are pressed and clean. They sit apart from everyone else and confer quietly while they eat. At other tables are the flensing crew, the deck hands, and "slimers," who prepare the catch for cryogenation and transport back to Earth.

The nippers are on their feet nonstop and barely have time to feed themselves. There follows a long cleanup, and they're exhausted by the time they drag themselves back to their quarters.

Ishmael climbs into his sleeper and closes the curtain. But sleep doesn't come easily. Earlier that day, the sailor from the pinkboat reinforced something he's been wondering about. Compared with humps and the other large sea creatures they're supposed to be hunting, terrafins are smaller, more difficult to capture, and much more dangerous. According to the sailor, the ocean is full of beasts, and yet the *Pequod*'s caught only a few of them since the nippers came aboard. Why are they spending so much time and energy pursuing terrafins?

20

"Battle stations! All hands! Battle stations!"

The next day the nippers are in the middle of cleaning up lunch when Starbuck's strident voice blares over the speakers, followed by a steady, pulsing alarm.

"Cadwallader's cuticles! Not again!" Fleece gripes as he and the other kitchen staff strip off their aprons and hurry out of the galley, leaving the bewildered nippers behind.

"Battle stations?" Queequeg repeats.

A sudden *rat-a-tat-tat!* of gunfire rings out, and those in the galley flinch and duck. Their ears fill with the sharp *ping*s and *plang*s of what must be bullets ricocheting off the ship's hull. It's clear that they're under attack, but from whom? The nippers dash to the portholes and peer out. At first there's only endless blue ocean, but then a fast-moving black skiff speeds into view. Half a dozen men crouch in the seats.

Bam-bam-bam-bam! From the deck above them, the drum of heavy machine-gun fire rips through the air, and the sea around the skiff begins to dance and splash. The skiff cuts hard to starboard and peels out of range, leaving an ever-spreading white wake. Now there's the loud trampling of feet, and gunfire erupts from the other side of the *Pequod*. Is the crew firing at another vessel?

"Who are they?" Gwen gasps.

Ka-blam! An explosion on the port side makes the entire vessel shudder. Plates and pots crash to the floor, and everyone grabs the nearest handhold.

"T-torpedo?" Billy asks, shaking.

"Or some kind of cannon." Queequeg squints out the porthole. "Nothing on this side. Must be a gunboat on the port side."

Rat-a-tat-tat! The heavy machine-gun fire resumes. Whoever these raiders are, they've smartly picked the middle of the day, when the chase boats are far away hunting and the *Pequod* is running with a skeleton crew.

Blam! Another shell slams into the port side. More plates crash.

"Look!" Gwen points. Through a porthole they see a crudely made rope ladder. It's being pulled taut, the strands slowly twisting under the weight of someone climbing up.

"They're tr-trying to b-board!" Billy cries.

Suddenly Ishmael realizes what's happening. The firefight on the port side of the ship is meant to distract everyone while raiders sneak up on the starboard side. He sticks his head out the porthole. Five feet below, a grizzled face covered with crude black tattoos glares up at him from the rope ladder. Ishmael is momentarily transfixed by the man's eyes, the whites of which are bloodred, making him look like some kind of demon. The man sneers. The few teeth he has are discolored stumps.

Other raiders are climbing up rope ladders to the left and right. Ishmael ducks back inside and grabs a plate from the floor to fling at the raider, but when he sticks his head out the porthole, he finds himself staring down into the black barrel of a gun.

BLAM! Ishmael jerks back, the bullet whistling past just inches from his face. Next to him, Queequeg has opened another porthole and is throwing everything he can find down on the raiders, who respond by firing pistols. *Bang! Bang!*

PIT-CHOING! A bullet ricochets off the rim of the porthole. Queequeg staggers backward, and for an instant Ishmael fears that he's been hit, but his friend steadies himself and waves that he's okay.

A hand grabs the lower edge of the porthole. Ishmael smacks it with a pan. The hand slides off but returns an instant later with a gun, waving it around blindly. Ishmael grabs the man's wrist and forces his arm upward.

BANG! PIT-CHOING! The gun fires and a bullet ricochets off the galley ceiling. Ishmael's ears ring painfully from the sharp, impossibly loud report.

Gwen rushes over and helps him force the man's arm back.

BANG! PIT-CHOING! The gun fires again, the bullet ricocheting dangerously close. The blast is a hundred times louder than the loudest thunderclap. Gwen clamps her hands overs her ears, and the raider yanks his arm free.

"O-over here!" Billy yells. A meaty, tattooed arm has reached through a porthole and closed around Queequeg's throat. Queequeg's hands are clamped on the raider's wrist, and he's gagging while the man tries to choke him.

Gwen and Ishmael dash over and try to pry the thick, mangled-looking fingers from their friend's neck.

"A knife!" Ishmael shouts to Billy, who stands openmouthed, staring. Ishmael starts to bend one of the raider's fingers back until he hears a sharp *crack!* But the man's grip on Queequeg's throat remains tight.

"Here!" Billy holds out a dinner knife.

Ishmael does a double take, but there's no time to argue. He grabs the knife and tries to stab the attacker, but manages only a glancing blow. The man's grip still doesn't loosen.

Queequeg's eyes are bulging and his face has turned bright red. Ishmael rears back with the knife and strikes again, this time burying the dull blade in the man's forearm.

The raider lets go. Queequeg collapses to the floor, gagging and coughing. While Ishmael kneels to make sure his friend is okay, he sees that the wounded raider has climbed up the rope ladder past them, the dinner knife still embedded in his arm.

From the deck above comes the scuffling of hand-to-hand combat. Closer by, a door slams in the mess, followed by rapid footsteps. Billy peeks out the galley door. "It's Pip!" he cries. "Someone's after him!"

Ishmael and Gwen sprint into the mess. Pip's on one side of a table, a tall, rail-thin raider on the other. The man's long hair is jet-black and greasy, his black clothes tattered, and his eyes are that eerie bloodred. He chases Pip around the table once, twice, and then they stop and face each other, breathing hard.

"Well, now, what a plump little marsupial you are." The raider cackles. "Surrender, Pudgy. You'll make a suitiful hostage."

Pip responds by hurling a handful of salt in the man's face. When the raider squeezes his eyes shut, Ishmael sees a crossbones tattoo on each of his eyelids. The man grabs the edge of the table and heaves it over. Plates, mugs, and silverware crash to the floor, and the chase begins anew.

"Hey!" Ishmael shouts.

The raider pivots and draws his gun. Ishmael and Gwen spring out of the way.

BANG! PIT-CHOING! A shot rings out and ricochets off the wall.

"Decrease, Pudgy. You're worth a fortunate ransom!" The raider chortles as he chases Pip.

Crouched under a table, Ishmael catches Gwen's eye and signals to a pair of chairs. A moment later, after Pip rushes past them, they both jump to their feet, grab the chairs, and swing as hard as they can.

Smack! Wham! Gwen gets the man square in the face, while Ishmael's chair smashes into his chest. The raider goes down on his back with a thud and lies there stunned, the gun still in his hand.

But a moment later he's up again, blood rushing from his nose. Spitting a disgusting glob of blood and short, blackened teeth onto the floor, he aims his gun at Gwen, who dives away.

BANG! PIT-CHING-CHING! A bullet ricochets off the leg of a table inches from Gwen's face. Having missed her, the man points the gun at Ishmael, who also dives.

BANG!

The bullet whizzes by as he hits the floor.

"Wheresh Pudgy?" the raider slurs, now almost completely toothless. A door slams on the other side of the room. Ishmael hopes it's Pip escaping. The man starts to follow but suddenly grunts and falls face-first; Gwen's grabbed his ankle and tripped him.

On the floor, the attacker rolls over and aims his gun at her.

Only a few feet away, Gwen's eyes widen with terror. She starts to crab backward on heels and hands, but this time the man with the gun is too close to miss.

21

Sweeeeee!!!! A shrill whistle pierces the air. In the mess, the raider with the gun looks up. There's a second whistle, and he jumps to his feet and dashes away, squeezing through a porthole and dropping out of sight.

Rat-a-tat-tat . . . A fusillade of machine-gun fire strikes the *Pequod*'s hull again, and the whine of drones is in the air. Ishmael helps a trembling Gwen to her feet, and they hurry into the galley, where Billy's kneeling beside Queequeg on the floor. Queequeg gingerly traces the red choke marks on his throat with his fingertips. Through a porthole, Ishmael watches as black-clad raiders fire from the skiff to provide cover while their comrades jump off the ship and swim back.

"Hold your fire! Don't shoot!" Starbuck's voice roars out of loudspeakers all over the *Pequod.* Through the porthole Ishmael sees why: In the raiders' skiff, a big man yanks a drenched Charity to her feet and presses a gun against her head. The skiff starts to speed away.

The *Pequod's* all-hands bell rings. Ishmael turns away from the porthole. Gwen and Billy are helping Queequeg to his feet.

"You all right?" Ishmael asks.

Queequeg nods, and winces when he tries to swallow. "May not be saying much for a while," he rasps.

"Is that a promise?" Gwen asks archly.

The door swings open, and Fleece waddles in, mopping his broad, sweaty brow with a dish towel and breathing hard. "From up on deck, it appeared as though someone down here was engaged in hand-to-hand combat with those carnal criminals."

"Th-those three." Billy points at Ishmael, Gwen, and Queequeg.

Fleece raises his eyebrows. "Well, I'll be Melville's mother!"

The door opens again, and Starbuck sticks his head in. "Everyone okay?"

"Aye-aye, sir." Fleece points at Ishmael and the others. "These're the brave young souls who slowed those slimy savages down."

Starbuck gives them a surprised look, then hurries off.

"Wh-who were they?" Billy asks the cook.

"Pirates." Fleece positions himself on his stool. "Good-for-nothing scum of the oceans."

"Where'd they come from?" Queequeg croaks painfully.

"Mostly ship deserters who'd rather maim and plunder than toil for an honest wage," the cook says. "I must say, I'm glad this is my final voyage. I'm too far along in years and belt loops for this nonsense."

"What about Charity?" asks Ishmael.

"I imagine that's what Starbuck's attending to right about now," Fleece replies grimly, then aims a plump finger toward the mess. "Better start straightening up. They're always extra ravenous after a good melee."

Out in the mess, the nippers straighten tables and chairs and sweep up the broken plates.

"Anyone notice that those pirates didn't seem to feel pain?" Ishmael asks. "I'm sure I broke that one guy's finger, and he still kept choking

Queequeg. I stabbed him in the arm, and he just kept climbing."

Billy points at Gwen. "Sh-she practically broke a chair on the f-face of the one chasing Pip. And it barely stunned him."

"Back on Earth, I used to hear stories about planets that were so overrun with deserters and renegades that we stopped sending missions to them," Queequeg adds, a fraction above a whisper.

"Y-you think *this* planet's overrun with them?" Billy asks nervously.

Before anyone can respond, the galley doors swing open and Fleece pushes a cart with two trays toward Ishmael. "One tray goes up to the first mate's quarters. Take the officers' lift. Knock first. If he's not there, go in and leave his meal on his desk. The other tray goes to the A level. You'll find a black door up there. Knock and say, 'Your meal is here, sir.' Then leave the cart. No dawdling. Proceed back here pronto."

"Yes, sir."

Fleece focuses on the other nippers. "Who said you could loll around yakking, you malingering mollusks? Back to your drudgery!"

Ishmael takes the cart and heads abovedecks. The ship's superstructure has four levels — C, B, A, and topmost, the bridge. On the B level he knocks on Starbuck's door. When there is no answer, he lets himself in and places the tray on the desk.

A low humming from beneath the desk draws his attention. Ishmael ducks down and finds a square lockbox about the size of a low stool. The light on the optical thumbprint scanner is glowing red. He wonders what's in it; what sorts of things a man like Starbuck holds dear.

Before leaving, he pauses by the shelf to look more closely at the woman and children in the static holograph. They are smiling, and the woman wears a wedding ring. If ever there was a portrait of a happy wife and children, this is it. But didn't he hear Starbuck say this was his sixth voyage with Stubb? *Why would the first mate stay away from his family for so long?*

When Ishmael pushes the cart back out into the passageway, old Tarnmoor is there with his mop and bucket. The bent blind man presses himself against the wall. "The meal cart, aye, but who's pushin' it? Who? Not Charity, not hers. Poor lass's at them pirates' mercy. Who, then? Who?"

"Guess."

The old man's face lights up. "Ah, a fine, brave lad, I heared. Fought off them pirates, he did." The light fades from Tarnmoor's face. "And here's how they rewards him? Pushin' the dinner cart about? I'll tells ya, lad, there's queer times in this strange mixed affair we calls life. Times when a man takes this whole universe for a vast practical joke, is there nots?"

"What'll they do about Charity?"

"Aye, that's a hard one. Hard, indeed. Sometimes alls you can do is appeals to a higher authority."

"Like who?" Ishmael asks.

"There be layers, lad. Stratums. Mysterious forces and behinds-the-scenes doings. One never knows around heres. Never."

There are more questions Ishmael would like to ask, but he has another tray to deliver, up on the A level. "I guess I'd better get going."

But before he can go, the old blind man reaches out and grabs his hand. "One lasts thing, lad. Ask yerself where lies the final harbor, whence we unmoors no more? Where's the foundling's father hidden? Our souls is like those a' orphans. The secrets a' our paternity lies in their grave."

Ishmael stares at him for a long moment, then bids him good night and takes the cart up to the next floor. When he comes to the black door, he catches the sounds of a conversation within.

An unfamiliar voice rasps: "There's a fair price for everything."

The angry reply sounds like Starbuck: "Not for her, there isn't."

The rasping voice: "Ya gettin' soft on me, mate?"

"You know what they'll do to her if you don't give them what they want!"

"In case ya haven't noticed, mate, we're dangerously low on toxin at the moment. Can't go givin' away the last of our supply."

Starbuck: "We can put Fedallah on it. He always comes through. In the meantime, I want Charity back. You know who to talk to."

There's silence, then the rasping voice: "I'll see what I can do, but I warn ya, it's gettin' harder and harder. You've seen the reports. Things back in the Anthropocene are comin' unglued fast."

Starbuck growls: "Just. Get. Her. Back."

From inside the room, footsteps approach the door. Ishmael quietly backs the cart down the passageway, then pushes it forward again, pretending that he's just arrived when the black door opens and Starbuck storms out. The first mate stops. "Leave it," he snarls, then calls over his shoulder, "The cart's here."

Through the doorway, Ishmael catches a glimpse of a dark room. A long white tapered object leans in one corner, stretching from the floor to the ceiling. It looks like one of the terrafin skivers on Fedallah's sleeper, only a hundred times larger.

"Let's go." Starbuck motions for Ishmael to join him heading back down the passageway. They walk in silence, and Ishmael suspects that Starbuck is ruminating over what just happened in the room with the black door. But then the first mate says, "You and your crew put up a good fight this afternoon. Saved your friend Pip's hide."

"Just doing what anyone would've done, sir."

Starbuck gives him a dubious look. "In my experience, most nippers would've run and hid. Truth is, a lot of seasoned sailors *still* run and hide."

At the end of the passageway, they start down the ladderway to the B level.

"Can I ask a question, sir?" Ishmael asks. "Those pirates . . . it seemed like they couldn't feel pain. How's that possible?"

"I wouldn't know, boy," Starbuck replies. "Certainly does sound peculiar."

22

"So I take this pirate over me head like this —"

In the mess, Bunta is entertaining the dinner crowd with the story of how he threw a pirate overboard. The mood is jovial as the sailors celebrate their victory and swap tales about their individual exploits against the attackers. But when Ishmael passes Tashtego on his way back to the galley, the barrel-chested harpooner from Chase Boat Two interrupts Bunta's story and grabs Ishmael's wrist. "How about this squirt, eh? Only a nipper and already fightin' pirates with his bare hands!"

The sailors cheer, though not Bunta or Daggoo.

"So what do ya have to say for yourself, squirt?" Tashtego asks.

"Uh, thanks," Ishmael says, "but if I don't get back to work in the galley, Fleece'll have a fit."

The crowd roars with laughter. Ishmael tries to pull his wrist out of Tashtego's grasp, but the harpooner holds it tight. "How about that, huh? Ain't afraid to fight pirates but scared of that big tub of blubber!"

The crowd guffaws merrily.

"Okay, squirt." Tashtego lets go of Ishmael's wrist and pats him on the head. "Get along now. Wouldn't want to make that big bad cook angry, would we?"

Ishmael is half tempted to throw a punch into Tashtego's broad gut, to let him know that he's no "squirt." But he resists and heads for the galley, the laughter of the sailors ringing in his ears.

Fleece has gone off after dinner, leaving the nippers to clean up. Still, Ishmael lowers his voice when he tells his friends what he heard up on the A level. "Sounded like Starbuck was practically threatening someone to get Charity back."

"Any idea who?" Queequeg asks while placing clean dishes on a shelf. His voice sounds better.

"Couldn't tell. The captain, maybe?" There's been no sight of the ship's captain so far on this voyage, and more than once Ishmael has wondered if this is unusual.

"Or m-maybe it was Stubb," Billy says. "Seems like he's got c-connections. Always g-going on about th-this Mr. Bildad."

"Didn't sound like Stubb," Ishmael says.

"Anyway, aren't his connections back on Earth?" Gwen asks while she loads dirty plates into the dishwashing machine. "What good could they do here on Cretacea?"

Billy starts to say something, when the galley door opens and Pip comes in. Glancing at the piles of dirty dishes and the steaming dishwashing machine, he looks surprised. Clearly he had no idea what kitchen work entailed.

Ishmael and the others pause, their hot red faces slick with sweat.

"I . . . I just want to express my appreciation," Pip announces awkwardly. "For saving my life today."

"No problem." Ishmael wipes the perspiration from his forehead with his stained apron.

Pip scuffs his foot against the floor. "Well, that's all I wanted to say." He turns and departs.

For a moment, the only sounds in the galley are the clanks and hisses of the dishwashing machine. Then as Gwen starts to scrape a dirty plate, she says, "Is it my imagination, or did that sound like the first time in his life he ever thanked anyone for anything?"

Back in the men's quarters, the lights are out and sailors wheeze and snore in their sleepers. Ishmael and the others tiptoe into the washroom. Queequeg is quick about it, and before long only Billy and Ishmael are left at the washbasins. Ever since the pirate attack earlier that day, Billy has been more morose and contemplative than usual.

"You okay?" Ishmael whispers when his eyes catch Billy's in the mirror.

Billy averts his gaze. "I was a c-coward today."

"Not everyone's born to fight."

"You're just s-saying that."

"My foster brother, Archie, isn't a fighter, but he's the strongest person I know. It's something inside him. Strength of spirit, I guess."

Billy dries his face with a handheld evaporator. "I d-don't seem to have much of th-that, either."

"Maybe you just haven't found it yet."

Billy smiles wanly and turns to go.

"Wait," Ishmael says. "The other day, when you said Pip was of the Gilded, what did you mean?"

Billy shifts his eyes. "I sh-shouldn't have s-said it."

"But you did. What is it? How come the rest of us have never heard of it?"

What Billy tells him next comes as a shock. Although the more Ishmael learns, the less surprised he realizes he should be.

BOOM!

Ishmael bolts upright in the dark, certain the *Pequod*'s reactor has exploded.

An instant later the ship tips so far to the starboard side that even his magnetically levitating sleeper can't adjust, and he has to hang on to keep from tumbling out. Things bang and crash, and there's a loud thud followed by a groan when a sailor falls to the floor.

BOOM!

"Mother of Earth!" Billy cries.

Now the ship lists heavily to the port side. Boots and shoes slide across the floor and bang into the wall. A holoset lies on its side, still projecting the stereoscopic image of a woman dancing, only now she's horizontal.

CRACK! A huge burst makes their ears ring painfully.

Billy wails. "P-please make it st-stop!"

"Quit your bellyaching!" Daggoo grouses from his sleeper. "It's only a bloody storm."

The ship rocks again, followed by another loud thump. A second sailor has fallen from his sleeper. Now when the ship rolls, bodies slide across the floor along with the shoes and other loose things. Men curse as they try to find handholds. Billy whimpers.

"It's okay," Ishmael tries to comfort him. "Just hold on. The ship's built to take this. It won't last long."

But it goes on for hours. And though he continues to reassure Billy that they're going to be okay, even Ishmael starts to wonder how much punishment the *Pequod* can take.

23

An endless procession of unfamiliar faces, beds, and smells. Groups of children crying and fighting. Pressed together at long tables that stink of old food and disinfectant. Adults shouting threats. Meager helpings of bland-tasting paste — and sometimes, no helpings at all. Children curled up on filthy floors, whimpering. Others backed into corners, eyes vacant, retreating deep into themselves.

The terrible fear that he will soon become like that himself.

Until he meets the strange boy with the useless legs.

Ishmael opens his eyes, surprised that he's gotten any sleep at all. An inner clock tells him it's morning even though the wake-up call hasn't sounded. Perhaps Starbuck canceled it, knowing that no one got much rest during the storm last night. Ishmael eases out of his sleeper and checks on Billy, who's suitably sacked out. Then his eyes meet Queequeg's, who looks like he's been up for a while. They dress and quietly pad out.

It feels like the *Pequod* is running at close to flank speed—unusual for early in the morning unless they're chasing beasts. In the passageway the only sound is the hum of the ship's reactor. The air smells of chemicals, and when they reach the bottom of the stairwell, they see why: Tarnmoor's bucket has tipped over, his mop and brushes scattered on the wet floor.

"Where is he?" Queequeg whispers.

They find the old blind man asleep at the top of the stairs, head dangling, one arm wrapped around the newel to anchor himself. Without a word, Ishmael and Queequeg gently lift him. Tarnmoor moans groggily and, still half asleep, allows himself to be helped down the stairs and into the men's berth, where they put him in Queequeg's sleeper.

"Thank ya, lads." He rolls over, presses his face into Queequeg's pillow, and goes to sleep.

Back out in the passageway, the boys collect the swabbie's pail and brushes and leave them by the door to the men's berth. Then they head abovedecks.

The sun is out, the sky is blue, and there's a rare cool breeze as the ship cuts across the sea. The deck is nearly empty, and there's little sign of damage despite the ferocity of last night's gale. The few crewmen who are up have gathered on the port side. Ishmael and Queequeg join Fleece, whose great belly is pressed against the bulwark.

"Feast your eyes, urchins," the cook says. "I'd say we were swept a considerable ways off course last night."

"Is that . . . *land*?" Ishmael asks, staring at the strip of green in the distance.

"Indeed so," Fleece says.

"Why's it green?"

"Not a clue. In all my years on the briny deep, this is about the closest I've ever been to terra firma."

Ishmael continues to stare in wonder, wishing the strip of green weren't so far away. Were they back on Earth, he doubts he'd even be able to see through the polluted haze. But that's another thing that's different about this planet. The air is so clear.

Fleece wanders off. In a low voice, Queequeg says, "It's green because that's plant life, Ish. Like there used to be on Earth, before the Shroud. An entire kingdom of organisms that ceased to exist after the Shroud formed. It's why they don't need Zirconia Electrolysis stations here. Those plants use photosynthesis to produce oxygen."

It's hard for Ishmael to imagine how a simple living thing could produce the same life-supporting gas that takes so much coal, heat, and industry to produce back home. And yet, he senses that—despite Pip's insinuations—Queequeg isn't making it up. "How do you know about things like that?" Ishmael whispers. Queequeg looks away, and Ishmael surmises that whatever the reason is, his friend is not yet willing to reveal it. He looks at the greenery again. Is it really possible that Earth once looked like that? Suddenly he feels a yearning to stand on solid ground without the incessant need to balance and adjust, and to see close up what looks so exotically beautiful from here. He can't know for certain what the other sailors pressed against the bulwark are feeling, but he suspects it's something similar.

Starbuck joins them, the bright sunlight glinting off his dark glasses. "Looks tempting, doesn't it? But get it out of your heads, boys. There's more ways to die over there than you can count on both hands. Beasts that'll run you down and tear you to pieces. Poisonous creatures that slither and crawl. All manner of disease-carrying insects. You'd be better off locked in a cage with an angry terrafin than to be left over there."

A white flyer with a black cap floats on the breeze alongside the ship, appearing to hang motionless in the air.

"Feels like we're full ahead this morning," Ishmael observes.

"The drones are on a couple of good-size humps," the first mate says.

Just then, Queequeg points toward the starboard bow. "What's that?"

A quarter mile ahead, debris is scattered over the ocean's smooth surface. It looks like the remains of a vessel: broken pieces of hull, torn netting, an overturned life raft, empty PFDs. As the *Pequod* nears the scene, word spreads through the ship, and sailors come up to the main deck to see.

"Think the storm did it?" asks someone standing near Ishmael.

"Doubt it," another sailor says. "The wreckage would be more scattered. This was somethin' else."

"Pirates?" asks another.

Flask has joined them. "Pirates woulda taken what they wanted and gone. No reason to waste their energy doin' this."

"Look!" A crewman points from the bow. Out in the middle of the debris, a lone survivor is clinging to an otter board.

Starbuck hurries toward the bridge, shouting, "Quick turn starboard! Back her down, then dead slow ahead! Put a ladder over. Rescue!"

It takes a few minutes for the *Pequod* to slow and come about. Two rescue swimmers in immersion suits have already gone over the side and are kicking toward the survivor with a bright-orange buoyancy torp.

A short time later, the grizzled, waterlogged survivor is lifted on board in a rescue basket. The man's skin is gray, his lips blue, and he is moaning in pain. Dr. Bunger, the ship's white-bearded surgeon who wears an eye patch, fumbles through the crowd of sailors and kneels beside him, scanning his body with a tablet no doubt loaded with biodetection software. Even before the results are back, the ship's surgeon attaches a saline injector to the man's forearm. He hands Ishmael a clear plastic bag of solution. "Hold this."

Ishmael takes the bag and watches while Bunger cuts away the sailor's sea-soaked clothes. Standing this close to the ship's surgeon,

Ishmael catches a familiar whiff of fermentation; Dr. Bunger smells like he's saturated in benzo.

The injured man's torso is covered with dark-purple bruises. When his eyes start to roll back into his head, Starbuck kneels and gently pats his cheek. "Stay with us now, you hear?"

Bunger cuts through the legs of the man's pants, and gasps rise from those who've crowded close to watch. A ragged red gash runs the length of the man's right thigh, so deep that Ishmael can see the white of bone. Despite the severity of the wound, hardly any fresh blood seeps out. Is it possible the man has no more to give? Bunger and Starbuck share somber looks that speak volumes.

The crowd stirs and begins to part. Ishmael hears an odd alternating step, *clank*, step, *clank*, and through the silent throng limps a man he has never seen before, wearing a long black coat with the collar turned up. His pale, bearded face is lined but free of tattoos, and his dark eyes are fierce and determined. The clanking comes from the metal shaft of a harpoon where his lower left leg should be.

Bunger hunts around in his disorganized medical bag and finds a derma-jet infuser filled with green-tinted liquid. He flicks it with his finger.

"Not yet," the man in black rasps, and slowly lowers himself beside the sailor. Ishmael recognizes the voice. It's the man Starbuck argued with about Charity.

"He should have it, sir," Starbuck says.

"I'll decide what he'll have and when," the man in black snaps in a way that no one else speaks to the first mate. *This must be the captain,* Ishmael realizes.

The injured sailor's eyes have begun to roll back into his head again. The captain shakes his shoulder roughly. "What species of creature did this?"

The wounded man's eyes close, but not for long. *Slap!* The captain strikes him across the face with his open hand. Some in the crowd gasp, but, Ishmael notices, they quickly school their expressions. The survivor of the wreck starts and blinks.

"I said, 'What species of creature did this?'" the captain demands.

The sailor's cracked, bluish lips part. "A . . . a terrafin, sir. A giant. . . . The size of . . . I don't know, sir. Never . . . seen nothing like it."

The effort to say even this much seems to exhaust him. The captain leans closer. "Its color, man. What was its color?"

The man's eyes start to roll.

Slap! "Its color!" The captain orders.

"All I saw . . . was white."

The captain looks up at Starbuck. Something deep and meaningful passes between them, and then the captain looks at the sailor again. "When?"

But the sailor's eyes have closed.

Slap!

The sailor's eyes open, unfocused. "The pain, sir. . . . If I could just have something . . ."

"When did this happen?"

"At dawn, sir. Just . . . after we put out the nets. . . . It got caught . . ." He grimaces. "The pain, sir."

"You'll get what you need soon. Caught it in the net, you say?"

"Snagged it, sir. But as soon as we saw . . . we cut the nets free."

"And?" The captain presses, but the sailor's eyes have begun to roll again.

Slap!

"And?"

The sailor cringes, and a tear rolls from the corner of his eye. "For the love of Earth, sir . . . something for the pain . . . *I beg you!*"

"First tell me: You cut the nets free, and then?"

"The . . . strangest thing." The sailor's voice sounds far away. "We swung the trawler around and ran . . . but the white terrafin . . . it . . . came . . . after us."

Murmurs ripple through the crowd. This time when the sailor's eyes close, there's no slap. The captain looks up at Starbuck. "If she was here at dawn, she can't have gotten far. Put every drone you have on it. Tell the operators to sweep a twenty-five-mile radius."

"Two of the drones are on humps, sir," the first mate answers. "Big ones we've been trailing all night. Easy prey."

"I said call them in, now!" The captain rises and goes face-to-face with the first mate, his eyes steely. "She could be close — maybe only five, ten miles away!"

Starbuck stands his ground. "I'm thinking of the crew, sir. The pot's awful low."

"The pot?!" the captain shouts, spittle flying from his mouth. "You heard the man — she's out there! Within our grasp!" He steps toward the first mate, their faces mere inches apart. "You want to see that wench of yours again? You'll call those drones in *now*!"

Starbuck's face hardens; he doesn't reply.

"Captain Ahab, sir?" Bunger calls.

The captain — Ahab — sees the derma-jet infuser of greenish liquid that the doctor is holding up. "Don't waste it."

"But the man's in —" Bunger begins.

"Is he a goner?" Ahab asks.

"Yes, sir, almost certainly, sir," Bunger replies. Just then, the sailor lets out a deep, anguished groan. His eyes have closed, but his face is pinched and contorted.

The captain starts away. Step, *clank,* step, *clank* . . . Once again, the crowd parts to let him pass.

Still holding the infuser, Bunger gazes quizzically up at the first mate. "Sir?"

Starbuck turns his furious glare from Ahab's back and whispers harshly, "Give it to him." Bunger infuses the green-tinged liquid into the sailor's arm. The man shudders with relief and then goes limp.

24

Ishmael sticks his hand out of one of the galley portholes into a world nearly as white as bone. His hand comes back wet. Around the ship, they say the rainy season has begun. While there are still periods of bright sunlight on many days, there are always clouds in the distance, trailing long gray tails of rain. Dense fogs like this are not uncommon. Peering into the heavy mist, he can't help wondering how much longer Captain Ahab will insist that they keep to this mad pursuit, ignoring an abundance of catchable beasts while searching for a huge white terrafin.

Queequeg joins him at the porthole. He's gained weight and filled out, his skin is sun-kissed glossy copper, and his brown hair has grown long enough to fan out from his head. Ishmael, whose light-brown hair now nearly covers his ears, is certain they've both grown taller as well.

Queequeg looks over at Fleece on his stool, shoveling fried scurry into his mouth straight from a large pan. "How long do you think this gloom will last?" he asks.

Cheeks bulging, the cook shrugs. "Might as well be forever, considering the mood aboard this rust bucket."

Because of the fog, the drones haven't launched, and no chase boats have been sent out to hunt. In the mess, sailors sit in knots at tables, sipping red berry, the savory brew that, after a few sips, usually leaves one feeling as if everything is in brighter, sharper detail. But today, even this exotic concoction can't lift the crew's spirits. Their grumblings seep into the galley.

"Nothin' in the pot an' he still wants to go chase that monster. A damn waste of time."

"We ain't on this ship to appease that madman's nightmares."

"If we don't start making some coin soon, he's gonna have serious trouble on his hands."

Ishmael only half-listens. He has frustrations of his own: It's been weeks since he last heard from Joachim and Petra, and he can't shake the feeling that the delays between messages mean things are getting worse back home.

Fleece wipes his mouth on his sleeve. "Anyone seen the redhead?"

Gwen hasn't shown up for work.

"Maybe she got called upstairs," Queequeg says. "Know what's going on?"

All morning, sailors have been called, one at a time, to Starbuck's quarters on the B level.

Before the cook can reply, Gwen comes through the galley door, carrying a mug of red berry and looking bleary, with bags under her eyes.

"W-where've you been?" Billy asks.

"With Charity," she answers.

The guys gape wondrously. Even Fleece looks up. It's been almost a month since the pirate attack.

"She came back late last night," Gwen says. "Really agitated. Wouldn't let anyone near her. Not even Starbuck. Finally said she wanted a female, and they asked me." Despite her weariness, Ishmael detects a sliver of pride behind her words. "I was up most of the night with her, in the sick bay."

"She gonna be okay?" Queequeg asks.

"Don't know." Gwen angrily works her jaw. "But believe me, if I ever get my hands on a pirate . . ."

"She's fortunate to be alive." Fleece heaves his great girth off his stool and carries the empty pan to the sink.

The galley speaker crackles on. "Ishmael, report to B level."

Queequeg pats him on the shoulder. "Good luck, friend."

A few minutes later, Ishmael stands in the passageway outside Starbuck's cabin. Someone is with the first mate in his quarters — Stubb, from the sound of it — and Ishmael can't help overhearing.

Stubb: "Mr. Bildad insists that you give up this ridiculous pursuit immediately."

Starbuck: "Take it up with Ahab."

Stubb: "The captain ignores me. Perhaps if you spoke to him . . ."

Starbuck: "Perhaps if *you* had kept your mouth shut, Mr. Bildad would be none the wiser."

Stubb: "As the official representative of the Trust on board this ship, I have a responsibility to keep my superiors apprised of everything that happens."

Starbuck: "And have you informed your superiors of what they stand to gain if we succeed?"

Stubb: "The Trust does not indulge in hypotheticals, Mr. Starbuck. At the rate you're going, this voyage will actually lose money. Are you prepared to tell your crew that they've worked all this time for nothing more than their paltry base pay? Some who've been sailing with you for *years*?"

The Trust? Ishmael remembers Old Ben mentioning it the night before Ishmael left Earth. But what is it?

Starbuck lowers his voice, and Ishmael can't make out his answer. A few moments later, the door opens and Stubb emerges, his face flushed. When he sees Ishmael, he stops and scrolls down his tablet. "Let's see. Ah, yes, here you are. Ishmael . . . Still nearly a thousand in debt for that damaged chase boat. What a pity." The punctilious second mate shakes his head disapprovingly and starts down the passageway.

Ishmael knocks and Starbuck beckons him inside. The first mate sits behind his broad desk, but today there is no chair for visitors; apparently he intends to keep these meetings brief. Starbuck appears weary, his black hair falling limply and his uniform open at the neck. The cabin is quiet except for the faint humming sound coming from the lockbox Ishmael knows is secreted under the desk.

The first mate sits back in his chair, presses his fingers together, and scrutinizes Ishmael, but he doesn't speak. Several moments pass. Finally, as if he's made a decision, he rocks forward.

"Congratulations, boy. Starting immediately, you and your crew will be full-time on Chase Boat Four. We need to put serious weight in the hold, and it's going to take every stick-boat crew we can muster. A new group of nippers will arrive this afternoon and take over in the galley. Your pay levels will be adjusted accordingly."

Ishmael fights a smile. "Thank you, sir."

"You'll be hunting smaller creatures for now," the first mate continues. "Bashers and whatnot. We'll see how you do with those, and then maybe you'll be allowed to go after the larger beasts."

Ishmael feels his heart beat faster. They're a full-time chase-boat team!

"That's all. You may go," Starbuck says dismissively.

Ishmael hesitates. "One question, sir?"

Starbuck sighs. "What a surprise."

"Charity's back, sir. Did we make a deal with the pirates?"

Starbuck's eyes may be hidden, but the dark round lenses don't cover the wrinkles around them, which deepen. "Don't stick your nose where it doesn't belong, boy." He points. "There's the door. Use it."

At dinner that night, Ishmael and his crew quietly celebrate in the mess, wearing new blue uniforms, while the latest batch of scrawny, gray-skinned nippers in brown uniforms hurry around on mess detail.

"We never looked that bad, did we?" Queequeg jokes.

"Time to make some *real* money," Gwen says with a rare gleam in her eye.

Tashtego, the harpooner, stops at their table. "Congratulations, and welcome to the best job on this ship."

"The drone ops would disagree," Pip says.

Tashtego waves the comment away. "All you bobbit worms do is play with joysticks. We're the ones who bring home the goods."

"When you're not chasing phantom terrafins," Pip says.

"Where you been?" Tashtego hooks his thumbs through his belt loops. "We're done with the white terrafin. As of tomorrow, assuming this blasted fog lifts, we'll be putting weight in the hold like nobody's business." He salutes the crew of Chase Boat Four. "See you out there."

He goes off.

"That was n-nice," Billy says.

"He seems like a good guy," agrees Queequeg.

"Especially compared to who's next." Gwen gestures toward a familiar head of bright-yellow hair coming their way.

Daggoo stops by their table. He's using a knife to carve a large beast's tooth into something that resembles the grip of a gun. They've heard that he's been promoted from skipper of Fedallah's boat to harpooner on Chase Boat Three.

"Congratulations." Queequeg tries to be friendly.

"Took me nearly three years to be promoted to stickman," Daggoo replies sourly, launching small white bits of whittled tooth onto their table. "Then you come along and do it in a few months."

Ishmael's in too good a mood to argue. "With all the catching up they need to get the pot where it should be, guess they're willing to send out just about anyone. Truth is, we got lucky."

"Sure, luck." Daggoo nods contemptuously at Pip. "Or maybe it's who you know." He gouges a larger piece of tooth and launches it into the air. It lands with a splash in Pip's bowl.

25

"Yee-ha!" Queequeg cries early the next morning while Chase Boat Four races away from the *Pequod,* skimming over gently rolling ocean swells. The fog has finally lifted, and they've received word that a drone has detected subsurface activity several miles away.

As the chase boat whisks along, Gwen and Billy let out gleeful whoops of their own, the wind whipping their hair, their new blue uniforms flapping. Ishmael feels hopeful as he steers toward their quarry. If they work hard and are a tad lucky, it's possible that by the time his year is up he'll have made enough to pay what he owes for the chase boat's repairs *and* to send Old Ben the money to help his foster parents leave Earth. And after that, whatever he earns he can keep for himself.

In the bow, Queequeg points excitedly. Ahead, several dark shadows glide beneath the waves. From their slender, pointed snouts and long, sleek bodies, Ishmael thinks they're bashers — not particularly large beasts, but valuable nonetheless. And given that no other crew has caught anything yet this week, a fortunate find.

Heart thudding with excitement, Ishmael positions the boat parallel to the pod while Queequeg aims the harpoon gun. A shadow begins to darken as one of the bashers rises toward the surface, and Ishmael angles the chase boat closer to give Queequeg a better shot. Gwen and Billy have slipped on their line-handling gloves and crouch at the ready.

The basher's pointed dorsal fin breaks the surface thirty feet away.

Bang! Queequeg fires. With a white cloud of smoke, the harpoon rockets toward the beast.

It's a hit!

With a frantic splash of its tail, the basher starts to flee. Red line begins to whip out of the tub. Now the linemen take over. Ishmael keeps an eye on Billy, who handles himself well and makes sure the big orange float goes over the side without a hitch. The red line goes tight and the basher begins to drag the float behind. Ishmael follows with the chase boat.

It's not long before the creature tires. Gwen and Billy start hauling in line, slowly bringing the exhausted basher closer.

"How about that?" Queequeg beams. "Our first day and our first beast!"

"If you don't count that big hump that nearly destroyed this boat," Gwen reminds him.

The basher is only fifty yards away when they hear the whine of another chase boat. As it gets closer, Ishmael sees that it's Chase Boat Three, with Daggoo in the bow on his first day as a harpooner. Ishmael signals that they don't need any assistance and points to the west, the direction in which the rest of the bashers are headed. Hopefully Chase Boat Three will find the pod and stick another beast.

But instead of veering away, Daggoo's boat shoots past Chase Boat Four, headed toward the basher that Queequeg just harpooned.

“What’re they doing?” Gwen asks.

The answer comes quickly. Chase Boat Three pulls close to the beast and Daggoo aims his harpoon gun. *Bang!*

Ishmael doesn’t get it. What Daggoo’s done makes no sense. There was no reason to fire another harpoon. It’s not a terrafin or even a big hump that might require two chase boats to tow it in.

But no sooner has Daggoo put a stick in the creature than his skipper guns Chase Boat Three around to the other side of the beast. A knife blade flashes in the sunlight and Chase Boat Four’s line goes slack.

“They c-cut our line!” Billy yells.

“They’re stealing our basher!” Queequeg cries as Chase Boat Three begins to tow the exhausted beast away.

“No Earthly way,” Ishmael growls through gritted teeth, angrier than he’s felt in years. But before he can take action, Gwen and Billy must haul in fifty yards of slack line. While the linemen pull as fast as they can, Queequeg joins Ishmael behind the controls.

“What’re you planning?” he asks quietly.

“Not to let them get away with it,” Ishmael replies tightly.

“Careful,” Queequeg cautions. “Daggoo’s not stupid. He’s got to know what you’re thinking.”

As soon as the slack line is in, Ishmael guns the engine, but Chase Boat Four’s RTG suddenly quits, leaving them adrift under the bright sun. Ishmael tries to restart the RTG, and again it quits. For a moment Ishmael wonders if Daggoo has somehow disabled his boat. He tries once more. This time, the engine starts and they take off.

Moments later they catch up to Daggoo, who’s been slowed by the task of towing the basher. But when Chase Boat Four nears, Daggoo calmly steps behind the machine gun in the stern of his boat and trains it on Ishmael and his crew. Ishmael can’t believe it. This whole incident has become bizarre. Twenty-five yards from Chase Boat Three he shifts into neutral and idles.

"That's our basher!" he yells.

"Not anymore!" Daggoo replies, still behind the machine gun.

"What are you gonna do?" Gwen shouts. "Shoot us if we try to take it back?"

"I might."

"And exactly how would you explain that to Starbuck?" Queequeg yells.

"Pirates."

Ishmael and his crew watch in disbelief while Chase Boat Three continues to tow the basher. Billy looks upward, probably hoping there's a drone around to record what happened, but the sky is an empty azure. Ishmael guns Chase Boat Four back toward the *Pequod*.

Forty-five minutes later, his crew and chase boat back on the *Pequod*'s deck, Ishmael climbs the ladderways to the B level and raps on the first mate's door.

"Who is it?" Starbuck calls from inside.

"Ishmael, sir."

"Go away."

"It's important, sir."

"Are you deaf? I said go."

"Sorry, sir, but I really have to speak to you."

"I don't think I heard you correctly, boy."

"You did, sir. I'm not going away."

From inside the cabin comes shuffling sounds, mumbling, and a woman's voice saying something Ishmael can't decipher. Thudding footsteps grow loud, and then the door swings open. Buttoning his uniform, his glasses askew, Starbuck glowers at him. "This better be good."

Ishmael is in the middle of explaining how Daggoo stole the basher when Charity, wearing a sheer pink robe, shambles out of the bedroom and stands beside the first mate. This is the first time

Ishmael has seen her since her return from the pirates. She looks thin and has faded bruises on her jaw and arms. The sparkle is gone from her eyes, and her lips are a flat straight line. The first mate glances at her with displeasure, though Ishmael can't tell if that's because she's revealed herself in his quarters or because he doesn't want her interfering in this matter.

When Ishmael has finished telling the story, Starbuck folds his arms. "Sorry, boy. It's Daggoo's word against yours. Nothing I can do."

"Are you serious, sir?" Ishmael asks. "You really think I'd make that up?"

Charity shoots the first mate a lethal look. "You know it's true. It's exactly the kind of thing that idiot Daggoo would do, and Ishmael's not the type to lie."

Starbuck knits his brow. "That's not the way it works, woman, and I'll beg you to stay out of it." He turns back to Ishmael. "Let it be a lesson, boy. Next time don't let him steal your catch."

The door closes, leaving Ishmael standing stunned and furious in the passageway. A few minutes later, back on the main deck, he tells his crew what happened.

"No way is Daggoo getting away with that!" Gwen starts for the hatch that leads up to the B level. "Wait till I give Starbuck a piece of my mind!"

Ishmael grabs her arm. "Don't."

"You're going to let him cheat us?" Gwen challenges him.

"I didn't say that."

On the deck behind them, sailors cheer when Chase Boat Three appears in the distance, towing in the first captured beast of the week. Ishmael feels his hands ball into fists.

"Easy," Queequeg cautions. "You don't want to do something you'll regret."

The basher is hauled up the slipway, and the flensing crew begins to cleave it for processing. The cargo net has gone down the side of the ship so that the crew of Chase Boat Three can climb up. Ishmael casually strolls along the deck, getting to the gunwale just when Daggoo's head appears over the rail.

As soon as they lock eyes, Ishmael hauls back and punches him in the face as hard as he can.

It's something he knows he'll never regret.

26

The brig is scalding — no surprise, given that it's deep in the ship's bowels beside the nuclear reactor. Ishmael lies bare-chested on the slab of metal that serves as a bed, his face and body glossy with sweat. The hum of the reactor is loud, but oddly soporific. As he drifts off, he savors the memory of his fist smashing into Daggoo's smug face, knocking him off the cargo rope ladder and back down into the sea.

The boy with the leg braces is hunched over a broken tablet. He sees Ishmael watching and motions for him to help. The boy has squeezed his fingertips into a seam along the side of the tablet and is trying to open it. Together they press their fingers into the seam and pull.

Sensing that something interesting is happening, other children collect to watch. The boys are on opposite sides of the tablet now, faces contorted with effort, using all their strength, and then —

* * *

Clang!

A hatch bangs. Ishmael's eyes burst open. Footsteps are coming down the passageway. Starbuck appears on the other side of the cell's bars and studies Ishmael through his dark glasses. "Do you have any idea how stupid that was? When Daggoo fell, his head missed the stern of his stick boat by inches. *Inches,* boy."

Ishmael props himself up on his elbow. "I wasn't trying to kill him, sir, just teach him a lesson."

"A lesson?" Starbuck repeats, incredulous. "You've been on this ship for, what, four months? Daggoo's been here almost three years. He's a foot taller than you and probably weighs a good sixty pounds more."

"I couldn't let him take advantage of my crew like that, sir. We're in it for the money just as much as everyone else."

Starbuck sucks his lips pensively and wraps his gnarled fingers around the cell's bars. "Listen, boy, you keep trying to teach thugs like Daggoo lessons, you're liable to spend the rest of your life dead, understand?"

Ishmael gazes at the tangle of pipes in the ceiling, knowing he'd do it again if he had to.

"I mean it, boy. I've seen men die for a lot less." When Starbuck starts to back away from the bars, Ishmael realizes the first mate intends to leave him locked up a while longer.

He sits up. "With all due respect, sir, as long as you keep me down here, my crew can't do the ship's pot any good."

Starbuck gives him an appraising look. "You think I'm keeping you here as punishment? Think again, boy. You're here for your own protection until Daggoo calms down. If I were you, I'd spend less time worrying about the pot and more time thinking about how to avoid getting your throat slit."

* * *

Another day passes and another night falls. At the back of the cell is a porthole no larger than a man's head, and through it Ishmael can see the bright stars that fill the black night sky. He lies on the metal slab and does what Starbuck told him to do — sort of. He doesn't think about the pot, but nor does he think about Daggoo. Instead his mind wanders: What kind of deal was made to get Charity back from the pirates, and who could have made it? How could Old Ben possibly have known that he would be sent to Cretacea? If the person named Grace isn't aboard the *Pequod,* then where is she, and how is he supposed to stop her from rendezvousing with them? Why hasn't he heard from his foster parents recently? And where in the universe is Archie?

Archie presses a thin green wire against the exposed copper circuitry of the holoset, and the ghostly image of a spacecraft appears in the air. The image is so diaphanous that Ishmael can see his best friend's dark eyes through it. Nonetheless, it is a triumph: the first time they have ever gotten something broken to work.

A hand reaches in and grabs the holoset. It's Ronith, the biggest boy in the foundling home. Ishmael leaps to his feet and grabs the boy's arm. Ronith hits him hard in the face with his free fist. Blood flows from Ishmael's nose, but he holds tight, punching and fighting to get the holoset back.

Grown-up hands try to pull him off the bigger boy, but Ishmael refuses to let go. Someone shouts his name.

"Ishmael?" The whisper of his name rouses him. Three figures stand outside the cell in the dark. He sits up and rubs his eyes. "How'd you guys get in here?"

Queequeg grins in the dimness. "Gwen made friends with the jail keeper."

"He should wake up again in an hour or so." Gwen twirls a key ring on her finger.

"Just w-wanted to see how they're tr-treating you," Billy says.

"They're treating me to solitary confinement." Ishmael stretches. "And if they find you down here, you'll be in serious trouble."

"With who? Starbuck?" Queequeg scoffs. "He's got far bigger problems. No one's caught anything in the past three days."

"You sh-should see Daggoo," Billy adds in a whisper. "N-nose broken, and both eyes black and blue and n-nearly swollen shut."

"He hasn't been giving you guys any trouble, has he?" Ishmael asks.

"Naw," Queequeg answers. "He and Bunta talk big, but they both keep their distance."

"Good."

"That engineer, Perth, took another look at our RTG," Queequeg says. "He thinks the seawater might've done more damage than anyone thought, but it's working okay now."

Ishmael nods. "Any word from home?"

"N-nothing's come through," Billy answers. "They say the s-solar flares are worse than ever."

Not for the first time, Ishmael wonders if solar disturbances are truly to blame, or if the worsening situation back home is causing Earth's communications systems to fail. "I'm sure that's it," he lies. "We've all probably got half a dozen Z-packs waiting to come through."

"How long's Starbuck planning to keep you down here?" Gwen asks.

"Until Daggoo calms down," Ishmael says. "Who knows what that means?"

They chat a little longer, and then Queequeg and Billy head back up. Gwen lingers, waiting until the guys have disappeared down the passageway. Then she leans close to the bars. "Every day you're down here is a day Chase Boat Four hangs on its davits and we don't make money. I didn't sign up for this voyage to see justice served on this ship. I signed up to get rich and never worry about money again. So the next time you're tempted to punch someone, for once try acting smarter than you look and think of our crew instead, okay? Because you're not doing us any favors."

Ishmael knows she's right. That's why he signed up for this mission, too. It's just hard to remember it when he stares into that yellow-haired joker's face.

27

In the morning the sounds of trudging footsteps, creaking wheels, and sloshing water come down the passageway. Old Tarnmoor parks his bucket outside the cell and takes a deep sniff. "That be Ishmael? Aye? Aye?"

"You're good, Tarnmoor," Ishmael says with a yawn.

"Ears and nose for eyes I gots. Heared you was down here for puttin' Big Bad Daggoo in his place. You gots spunk, lad. But kindness, too, puttin' me in that nice soft sleeper afters that stormy night. All my years no one's dones that."

Ishmael likes this strange old man. "How many years has it been?"

"Many, many."

"How many voyages?"

"One perilous and long voyage ends, only begins a second; and a second ends, only begins a third, and so ons."

"What about Starbuck? How long's he been on the *Pequod*?"

Tarnmoor gives a little shiver. The empty sockets that once held eyes twitch. "Don't knows, don't knows."

"I thought I heard him say this is his sixth voyage," Ishmael prompts.

"Sixth? Aye, aboards the *Pequod*. That sounds about rights."

"'Aboard the *Pequod*?'" Ishmael repeats. "You saying you know him from somewhere else? Some other ship?"

The old man goes quiet.

"What about the captain? Known him long?"

Silence.

"Why're Ahab and Starbuck so eager to catch the white terrafin?"

Tarnmoor leans against his mop's handle. "What makes you think I knows anything 'bout that?"

"I think you hear things. People are so used to you being around that they don't take notice. I bet you probably know more about the goings-on aboard this ship than just about anyone."

The bent old blind man grins, flashing pink gums. "Yer a smart lad, alls right. Knowed it the first times I smelled you." He tilts his head to one side, perhaps listening to make sure they're alone. "Only one other ship Ahab ever commanded. Called the *Essex*. A vessel likes this, it were. He was a young'un backs then. Full a' bluster and dreams a' riches. A handsome rake, too, but a hellion likes all you young'uns is. Wells, one day a new batch a' nippers arrives, amongs them a creature a' beauty the likes a' which never setted foots on Cretacea afore. The mens was beside theyselves. Some a' the womens, too. The cap'n, he kept a eye on her, makin' sures nothin' untowards happened on his watch. A' course, somes whispered it were because he had designs on her hisself, but I knowed that weren't true."

"How?" Ishmael asks.

"Because Ahab wassed a hard, greedy one, that's how. Only thing that mades his heart race were the sound a' coins in the till. But there's the irony a' it, lad. Slowly, withouts even realizin' it, he falled for her.

A year later she comed to the end a' her mission and were makin' to return to Earth, and the only way he could prevent that were by askin' her to wed. Just stay with him for ones more voyage, he promised, and they'd returns to Earth together. Well, she'd falled for him, too, so that were that.

"Off they sailed for one more voyage ons the *Essex* and lets me tell you, lad, you never seened a fella so changed as Ahab was. 'Specially after his son was borned. From night to day, I tell you. But love'll do thats to a man. He doted over those two like a —"

"Tarnmoor," Ishmael interrupts gently. "You're supposed to be telling me why he wants the white terrafin so badly."

The old man screws up his face. "Ain't I? Ain't I? Now pays attention, lad. So Ahab knowed it were his last voyage, and his last chance to makes some real coin for him and his new young family afore they wents back to that Earth-forsaken coal bin a' a planet. He heared abouts the monster from other sailors and knewed it were the greatest prize on all a' Cretacea. And as much as he loved his beautiful wife and son, he wanted that beast, he did. But his wife, she were dead set against it. Said they had coin enough — more'n enough. But Ahab, he couldn't resist. That old money love were strong and he couldn't let go."

"What happened?" Ishmael asks. "Did he ever find the white terrafin?"

Tarnmoor parts his cracked lips as if to continue the story, then freezes. He cocks his head, then reaches for his bucket. "Times to sail, lad. Times to sail." He starts to pull the bucket away.

"Wait!" Ishmael whispers urgently, pressing his face to the cell's bars. "If you lost your sight looking at the sun when you first came here, how'd you know she was that beautiful? And that Ahab was handsome?"

But Tarnmoor has vanished, the splashing of his bucket echoing behind him.

* * *

That night, shortly after lights-out, Starbuck appears and unlocks the cell. "Don't make me regret this."

"Yes, sir." Ishmael steps out. "Thank you, sir." He starts down the passageway.

"Just one thing, boy," the first mate calls behind him.

Ishmael turns. "Sir?"

"Watch your back."

Ishmael climbs the ladderways to the men's berth. The room is dark and the others are asleep. He stops beside his sleeper and is about to strip out of the clothes he's been wearing for days when he notices that the blue light on his VRgogs is blinking. He slips them on and finds two Z-packs, both storms of random pixels until he switches to audio only:

"Ishm . . . conditions worsening . . . best if you send . . . money soon . . . your . . . parents safely . . . before . . . too late. . . . Ben"

"Dear . . . ael, . . . derful news! Arch . . . he's . . . ship . . . *Jeroboam* . . . also on Cret . . . well, thank . . . safe. . . . But here on Ear . . . conditions . . . etting worse. . . . riots and looting in other part . . . Ben . . . rumors . . . oxygen production . . . slowing . . . very frightening . . . not safe . . . look for Archie! Love, Petra and Joa . . ."

Awash with emotions, Ishmael slides off the VRgogs. It sounds like things are getting worse on Earth; Joachim and Petra aren't the sort of people who'd want to worry him if they could avoid it.

But if he's understood correctly, there's also fantastic news: Archie's on Cretacea, aboard a ship called the *Jeroboam*!

The ocean is a ghostly, glowing white. Ishmael stands at the ship's rail in the dark. Tonight the sea reminds him of the surface of an old baclum table back home. *Home* . . . He closes his hands around the warm metal rail, wishing he could have deciphered more of the Z-packs so that he knew the specifics, but one thing seems certain: Ben needs that money for Petra and Joachim as soon as possible.

"Don't tell me you broke out." It's Gwen, traversing the deck.

"Starbuck let me go."

She joins him at the rail, catching her breath when she sees the glowing white ocean. "What in the stars?"

"Not sure. I think maybe it's like what illuminates the baclum back home."

They take it in. An entire ocean, the color of scurry flesh, white and luminescent.

"Trouble sleeping?" Ishmael asks.

"Always. I heard some messages came through tonight?"

Ishmael nods. "Sounds like things are bad back on Earth."

"So what else is new?"

"No, I mean worse than before. Maybe worse than ever. The end could be near."

Gwen regards him uncertainly. "Seriously?"

"Someone I know—and trust—warned me about it before I left. I wasn't sure whether to believe him at the time, but . . ." Ishmael pauses for a moment. "He says he can help my foster parents, but it's going to take a huge amount of money. Thousands."

"You believe him?"

"I've known him my whole life. . . ."

Gwen looks out at the phosphorescence. "You realize what you're saying? That—at least according to this person you know—by the time our missions are over, there might not be an Earth to return to?"

Ishmael nods solemnly. "I know it sounds extreme, but something in my gut tells me he might be right."

The cloudy white sea sloshes against the ship's hull. From somewhere in the distance comes the splash of an unseen creature. "You really don't have people back there?" Ishmael asks.

Gwen glances away. When she looks back at him, her eyes are glittery with tears. "It's always been just me."

The harsh memories of life in the foundling home before he met Archie are always with Ishmael. He'd only had a few years of it. It's hard to imagine how Gwen could have survived a whole lifetime of it. No wonder she's so wary and suspicious of everyone.

Gwen wipes her eyes. "You never saw this."

"Don't even know what you're talking about."

She gazes out at the luminescence again. "It's strange. I hated it back there, but still it's sad to think of it becoming uninhabitable. Even at its worst, it's still home. Know what I mean?"

Ishmael knows exactly what she means.

28

"Hold your fire!" Starbuck orders.

Wearing rain gear and pressed against the port bulwark, the *Pequod*'s crew brace themselves against the whipping wind and stormy seas. Not far away, Chase Boats Two and Three bob in a confusion of red lines. Now and then, the black tips of a terrafin's wings poke through the surface, and the sea erupts when the creature tries to fight free of the tangle.

"Sir! I've got a clear shot!" Tashtego shouts from the *Pequod*'s bow where he's aiming down with the big harpoon cannon.

"I said, hold your fire!" Starbuck yells back through the wind and driving rain. The hood of his black slicker dips low on his head, and rainwater speckles his black glasses.

"But sir, I can do it!" Tashtego pleads. Blood from a gash under his left eye dribbles down into his thick mustache. In the mess, he may be easygoing and jovial, but when it comes to putting a harpoon in a beast, he's as intense as any other stickman.

"No!" Starbuck shouts back.

An hour ago Daggoo harpooned his first terrafin. Tashtego's boat joined his and the two chase boats began to tow the creature in. It was a contest to see if they could make it back to the *Pequod* before the intensifying storm made the task impossible. But as the squall grew stronger, something went wrong; the towlines crossed and snagged, and both crews were forced to abandon the task. In the chaos, Daggoo went missing — and Starbuck is unwilling to let Tashtego fire until they locate him.

The terrafin and a morass of lines drift only a few dozen yards off the *Pequod*'s bow. This terrafin looks twice the size of the one that killed Abdul. Despite the winds gusting under fast-moving dark-gray clouds, and cracks of lightning followed by sharp booms of thunder, the crew are riveted.

"There!" A sailor points. Barely visible in the wind-whipped swells, Daggoo is caught in the snarl of lines and gear. It's impossible to tell if the harpooner is merely stunned, or injured — or worse.

Step, *clank,* step, *clank* . . . Through the crowd limps Ahab. Strands of rain-soaked black hair whip his face, and his long black coat is sodden. "Well, Mr. Starbuck, where's my terrafin?"

"It's Daggoo, sir." Starbuck points at the jumble of lines below. "He's in Tashtego's line of fire."

The captain squints down and is quiet for several moments. "Let's not let *this* one escape, shall we?" he grumbles and limps away. Step, *clank,* step, *clank . . .*

Through those dark, round glasses Starbuck stares at Ahab's back, then turns to the crowd of sailors on the rocking deck. "I need one more stick in that terrafin before we winch it in. But someone's going to have to get close enough that he doesn't accidentally stick Daggoo."

The crew goes silent. Wind whistles through the cranes overhead. No one's forgotten what happened the last time Starbuck asked for a volunteer to harpoon a terrafin.

"That beast could be ten feet below the surface," mutters one sailor near Ishmael. "You'd have to get right on top of him to get a stick in."

"Close enough that it could thrash ya to death," adds another.

"In these waves ya might even have to stick it by hand," says a third. "Now, there's a suicide mission."

"I'm not asking for comments," Starbuck snaps in the rain and wind. "Just a volunteer. Who'll go for four thousand?"

Ishmael's heart jumps. That's enough to pay for the damage to the chase boat and still have Ψ3,000 to help Petra and Joachim. But it's not enough to save them.

"Five thousand?"

Sailors glance at one another. It's a tantalizing number but still less than he needs. Ishmael's muscles tense. If someone else volunteers before he does, he'll lose the opportunity.

"Six thousand?"

A fortune, and maybe enough. The temptation is too great. Ishmael starts to raise his hand, but Queequeg grabs his arm and whispers harshly, "Are you crazy?"

Ishmael's eyes meet Starbuck's. The first mate turns away. "Seven thousand? Anyone?"

Ishmael can't wrest his arm from Queequeg's grasp, but he can speak out: "I'll do it, sir!"

In the whipping gale, Starbuck locks eyes with him. "I'm looking for someone to put a stick in the terrafin, not in Daggoo."

"I'll put the stick where I'm paid to put it," Ishmael replies.

The others regard him with mixed expressions, some in awe, others rolling their eyes, certain he just sealed his fate. Gwen hisses, "Ishmael, don't."

"It's suicide, friend," Queequeg agrees. "You don't stand a chance."

But Ishmael can't help thinking about Joachim and Petra and how they may not have a chance either, unless he can send Old Ben enough money, and soon. One stick in that terrafin could do it.

"Eight thousand?" Starbuck offers, ignoring Ishmael.

Ishmael tears himself away from Queequeg. "Me, sir! I'm serious!"

"Get it out of your head, boy," Starbuck growls. "You know what your chances are?"

Instantly murmurs start filtering through the crowd.

"What's this?"

"Never heard the first mate turn down anyone willin' to take the bait before."

"Playin' favorites, is he?"

The spidery wrinkles around Starbuck's hidden eyes deepen. With frustrated resignation, he orders, "Put Chase Boat Four down on the starboard side!"

The *Pequod* continues to pitch in the heaving seas. Bracing himself against a crane mast, rain slashing into his eyes, Ishmael buckles on a PFD. On the wet, seesawing deck, the crowds of sailors stand wide-legged for balance, watching silently. Someone comes toward him, but the wind and rain are so fierce it's hard to see who until she's close.

"Don't do it." Gwen grasps a turnbuckle to keep from falling. "Don't you realize that deal to get your foster parents off Earth could be a scam? There'll be other chances to make money. This is stupid."

Ishmael shakes his head. "If it's not a scam and my friend back on Earth is right, there may not be time for other chances."

Gwen contemplates him with pursed lips, then wearily shakes her head and picks up a PFD.

"What are you doing?" Ishmael asks.

She gives him an exasperated look. "How are you going to do it alone? Position the boat over the terrafin *and* harpoon it?" She closes her eyes and draws in a deep breath. "You're an idiot. . . . But I could use the money, too."

"Who said I'll share it?" asks Ishmael.

Gwen shouts to Starbuck. "You said ten thousand, right?"

"No, I said—" the first mate begins.

"Ten thousand, nothing less," Gwen cuts him short. "You couldn't get anyone to do it alone for seven thousand. Think you'll find any other two sailors who'll do it for ten?"

Starbuck thinks it over. "All right. Ten thousand for the both of you."

Gwen faces Ishmael. "Five and alive beats eight dead, eh?"

Ishmael could argue. Ψ5,000 might not be enough to save his foster parents. But Gwen's right that he can't do it alone.

Now Queequeg approaches, windmilling his arms for balance until he grabs a windlass to steady himself. "Don't do this, friends. It's insane."

"Too late," Gwen says.

Queequeg looks from Gwen to Ishmael, then reaches for a PFD. "Then I'm coming, too."

Ishmael wipes rain from his eyes. It's bad enough that he's gotten Gwen mixed up in this mess; he can't stand the thought of endangering *two* of his friends. "No. It won't be worth it if we have to divide the bait between the three of us."

"You think I care about the money?" Queequeg says. "I just don't want to go to sleep tonight without seeing your ugly face."

But before he can slip on the PFD, Starbuck yanks it away. "Absolutely not. I can't afford to lose any more harpooners today. You're not going, Queequeg. That's an order, understand?"

Queequeg lowers his head and backs away. Meanwhile, Bunta looks at Gwen strapping on her PFD and snorts derisively. "You really think you'll make a difference out there, princess?"

"More of a difference than you've ever made," Gwen shoots back.

The sailors around Bunta chuckle, and the big sailor grits his steel teeth. By now, Chase Boat Four has been lowered on the lee side of the ship, where the hull protects it from the crashing waves and driving rain. But the cargo rope they must climb down slams against the hull each time the ship heaves.

The others start to drift back to the port side. Ishmael is about to climb over the starboard rail when out of the wind and rain comes Fedallah, carrying a long, thin harpoon with a barbed point and a padded grip. His white hair is whipping wildly, and with no rain gear to protect him, his uniform is soaked and clinging to his wiry frame.

"Use this," he says, his wet face close to Ishmael's. But before he hands the stick over, he tests the tip with his thumb and, appearing displeased, pulls a whetstone from his pocket and starts to hone the point. "Remember the soft spot behind the head. Drive the stick in as deep as possible."

But just when he finishes sharpening and holds the harpoon out to Ishmael, a hand reaches through the rain and grabs the handle. It's Queequeg, wearing a PFD.

"You're disobeying Starbuck's orders," Ishmael warns.

"That'll only be a problem if I'm still alive after this." Grasping the harpoon, Queequeg starts to climb over the rail. "I swear, Ish, Gwen's right: This is the worst idea you've ever had."

Ishmael turns back to Fedallah to thank him, but the harpooner has disappeared.

Gwen, Queequeg, and Ishmael climb down the swinging cargo rope and into the rocking chase boat. Ishmael starts the RTG, but it instantly stalls. "Thought Perth fixed it!" he shouts to Queequeg.

"I thought so, too!" Queequeg shouts back.

This is bad. The task ahead will be dangerous enough without having an engine that might or might not work. Ishmael tries again, and this time the RTG catches. They start around the *Pequod*'s stern and slam into the fierce waves, wind, and rain. Crouched beside Ishmael at the console, Gwen grips the grab rail while the chase boat rises and dives over the cresting waves.

"What's your plan?" she shouts.

"Circle upwind, cut the engine, and drift down!" Ishmael yells back. "In these heavy seas and with all that line floating above it, hopefully the terrafin won't notice us."

It's not long before Ishmael has positioned the pitching chase boat upwind of the terrafin. As soon as he cuts the engine, the chase boat turns sideways in the waves and begins to rock violently, the crew holding tight to keep from being tossed out. From this angle it's impossible to spot Daggoo in the raucous seas. Is he still there, or has he vanished beneath the waves?

The fierce winds propel the chase boat closer. It's obvious now why Fedallah gave them the thin harpoon: In these conditions it would be impossible to maneuver the boat to the right spot over the terrafin to fire the harpoon gun. Ishmael indicates that Gwen should take the wheel. "As soon as we drift into the tangle," he shouts, "Queek and I'll try to get Daggoo. If anything goes wrong, you start the engine and get out of here!"

"They're not paying us to save Daggoo!" Gwen yells over the howling wind.

"You'd leave him to drown?" Ishmael shouts back.

Gwen shakes her head in frustration but takes over behind the wheel.

They reach the tangle of lines. Below the surface the dark shadow of the terrafin looks even bigger than it did from the *Pequod*'s deck. Trying not to think about how violent and dangerous the beast that killed Abdul was, Ishmael spots Daggoo bobbing half a dozen feet away. He's being kept afloat by a PFD, and it's impossible to tell if he's conscious, or even alive.

Bracing themselves, Queequeg and Ishmael pull at the mess of confused ropes and manage to haul Daggoo close enough for Ishmael to place his hand on the harpooner's neck.

"I feel a pulse!" Ishmael shouts. Together, he and Queequeg start to pull the listless sailor into the chase boat. Below, the terrafin looms like a bomb waiting to explode.

They've just gotten Daggoo into the boat when Queequeg suddenly trips and falls against the gunwale with a thud.

Instantly, the ocean below them erupts in a frenzy of spume and froth, and the terrafin forces its head up out of the water. For one instant in the seething surge, Ishmael and Queequeg find themselves staring into the black eye of the beast. A moment later, the terrafin arches its back and its long, black tail slashes up from below.

Ishmael and Queequeg dive out of the way an instant before the tail whips out of the water, its deadly skiver burying itself in the side of the tub that holds the harpoon line. *Crack!* The terrafin's tail snaps back, taking the tub with it.

The beast begins to writhe furiously, trying to dislodge the tub from its tail. Waves and water explode around them, and the chase boat pitches crazily.

Girding himself in the bow, Ishmael watches Queequeg reach for the long, slender harpoon. "Aim for the back of the head!" he reminds him.

But before Queequeg can do anything, they hear a distant voice yell, "Fire!"

Ishmael and Queequeg look up at the *Pequod*'s bow, where Starbuck is now beside Tashtego at the harpoon cannon.

Instead of pulling the trigger, the mustached harpooner says something that's lost in the storm. Ishmael imagines he's arguing that by all rights it should be Chase Boat Four's terrafin.

"I said, fire!" the first mate screams.

BOOM! The percussive smack of the blast nearly knocks Ishmael and Queequeg over. It's a direct hit, and the huge steel harpoon is buried deep in the terrafin's back.

Ishmael spins and shouts to Gwen at the controls, "Get us out of here!"

29

The storm has strengthened, and the *Pequod* tosses and yaws. Down in the mess, Gwen and Ishmael huddle under blankets, adding white powder and brownish granules to mugs of steaming-hot red berry. The aroma rises tantalizingly to their noses and the resulting brew tastes piquant and exotic. The tablecloths have been wetted down to keep their mugs from sliding off when the ship rocks.

Queequeg is hunched over, hands clasped, a woeful look on his face. Ishmael puts his arm around his friend's shoulder. "Maybe Starbuck'll forget."

"He doesn't seem like the type who forgets anything," Queequeg replies forlornly.

The mess door swings open, and Billy and Pip come in.

"I j-just saw Dr. B-Bunger," Billy says. "Daggoo's going to b-be in the sick bay for a few d-days, but after that he should be okay."

Pip gives Ishmael and Queequeg a curious look. "Whatever compelled you to save him?"

"Of c-course he had to save him," Billy says proudly. "Besides, n-now his biggest enemy on this ship owes him his life." He pats Ishmael's wet forearm. "What you d-did wasn't only brave. It was nothing sh-short of genius." He turns to Gwen. "Even *you'd* have to agree, right?"

Gwen shrugs.

Ishmael forces a weak smile, knowing that he's not even close to being a genius. But Billy is right about one thing: No matter how low a sea slug Daggoo might be, there is no way he could have left him to perish beneath the waves.

The mess door opens again and Tashtego enters, rainwater dripping off his foul-weather hat, and a bandage under his left eye. "They just dragged it up the slipway! First terrafin of the voyage." He rubs Ishmael's damp head. "This crew owes you big time, squirt."

"Not just me." Ishmael nods at Queequeg and Gwen. "It took all three of us."

"True, true." The barrel-chested harpooner leans close and continues in a hushed voice: "If I was you, I'd find Starbuck quick. There's mutterin' that you don't deserve the bait because you didn't actually stick the beast."

Billy rocks back. "That's c-crazy! If they hadn't risked their lives to s-save Daggoo, you never could have fired that harpoon!"

"Hey, if it was up to me, you'd have that bait and more," Tashtego tells the chase-boat crew, and then focuses on Ishmael. "I'm just sayin', you better speak to the first mate before the naysayers get too much of his ear."

Ishmael starts to rise. Gwen does, too. "I'm going with you. No one's cheating me out of that money."

But Ishmael slides his hand over hers. "Let me go first and see what I can do. If that doesn't work, we'll try it your way."

* * *

The first mate isn't in his cabin. Ishmael hesitates at the bottom of the ladderway that leads up to the captain's chambers on the A level. If Starbuck is up there with Ahab, should he interrupt them? Doing so might work against him. Then again, Tashtego made it sound like time was of the essence. Ishmael starts up the steps.

"Ain't up there, lad," a voice croaks behind him. It's Tarnmoor, one knurly hand clinging to the rail, the other to his bucket. "Outs on the flensing deck, he is."

"How'd you—?" Ishmael doesn't bother finishing the sentence. He should be used to old Tarnmoor's mysterious abilities by now. "On deck? In this storm?"

"Just a spot a' heavy weather, lad. Nothin' he ain't seened a hundred times before."

Ishmael throws on rain gear and pushes through a hatch out into the storm. The wind is blowing even harder than before, the warm rain stinging his eyes, but he can make out the terrafin spread flat on the flensing deck, the yellow tub still impaled by its tail. The beast is crisscrossed by heavy ropes lashed tight to keep it from sliding loose while the ship tosses and rolls.

In the middle of the terrafin's back is a great gaping red wound left by the cannon's harpoon. The wound is big enough that a man could practically crawl through it. Surely the harpoon cannon is overkill for a creature even this size. It's like using an ax to chop scurry. Ishmael is wondering how massive a creature such a large harpoon could be for when the ship pitches sharply and he has to grab onto a hoist cable to keep from sliding clear across the deck. Tarnmoor must have been wrong; it's crazy to think that anyone would be up here in a storm like this.

But out of the corner of his eye he spots a figure in dark rain gear near the tail of the terrafin. It's Starbuck. Ishmael begins to move closer, but stops when the first mate surreptitiously glances around.

Ducking behind a crane tower, Ishmael watches Starbuck carefully cut into the base of the terrafin's tail. From the dark folds of skin and red flesh he extracts a small sac that glows bright chartreuse, and places it in a container. Then, walking with a wide gait to steady himself on the rocking deck, the first mate starts making his way toward a hatch.

Ishmael waits before following. What did the first mate remove from the tail of the terrafin? What could glow so brightly and yet come from inside a living creature? Whatever it is, Ishmael knows enough not to let on that he's seen the first mate take it.

A minute later, he pretends to run into Starbuck in the passageway. The first mate frowns when he sees Ishmael in rain-soaked gear. "You up top just now?"

"Making sure Chase Boat Four was secure, sir. It's pretty rough out there."

"Good thinking." Starbuck starts around him.

"But sir? I'm glad I bumped into you. Wonder if we could talk about the terrafin?"

Starbuck stiffens.

"About the bait," Ishmael adds.

"Oh, that." The first mate relaxes. "Not now, boy. I've got something I need to do."

"Maybe in half an hour?" Ishmael asks.

"All right. Half an hour." Starbuck brushes past and hurries off.

Thirty minutes later, Ishmael knocks on the first mate's door. Starbuck answers, wearing a red silk robe, his black hair disheveled. Ishmael notices a tuft of white chest hair poking out at the point where the robe closes.

"What is it, boy?"

"About the terrafin, sir."

"What about it?"

"With all the excitement, I wanted to make sure you remembered the bait, sir. We agreed on ten thousand."

The first mate mulls this over. "Well, I don't know about that anymore. You didn't stick the beast."

"Sir, with all due respect," Ishmael begins to argue, "if we hadn't risked our lives to save Daggoo, Tashtego could never have —"

Starbuck glances back into his quarters, then cuts him short. "Now's not the time, boy."

"But, sir —" Ishmael can't allow this to be swept aside. Not after he risked his life and the lives of his crew. And not when the lives of his foster parents are in the balance.

The first mate's jaw sets, and his face begins to harden. He's about to say something when Charity comes into view. She's tottering unsteadily, tugging her fingers through her brown hair. Still, she looks much recovered from her ordeal with the pirates. The bruises on her face are gone, and her skin is practically glowing again. Ishmael is so distracted by the changes to her features that it takes a moment to realize that her eyes have a strange pinkness. To Starbuck she says, "There's only one reason you got that terrafin, and it's because of Ishmael's crew."

Starbuck gives her a frosty look. "Did I ask for your opinion, woman?"

"If it weren't for the three of them, you'd almost surely have lost the terrafin *and* Daggoo," Charity goes on. "Looking at it that way, I'd say you got quite a bargain for a mere ten thousand."

Starbuck's countenance goes flat for a moment while he gazes off. "The *three* of them? I ordered Queequeg not to go, did I not?"

"For Earth's sake, Starbuck, leave it alone." Charity takes his arm and turns him toward her. "You got what you needed, didn't you? Let it be." Something deep and wordless passes between the two, then Charity nods to Ishmael. "Don't worry, honey. You'll get the bait."

"I'll think about it," Starbuck snorts.

"Yes," Charity says firmly, "you certainly will."

She closes the door.

The storm continues into the night, the ship lurching and tossing so severely that once again the crew's magnetically levitated sleepers can't compensate. Even when sailors can keep from falling out, their possessions topple to the floor and go sliding this way and that.

Ishmael and Pip are exiting the washroom, hands tight on grab rails, when the ship lists violently, slamming them both into the wall. A palm-size tablet tumbles out of Queequeg's curtained sleeper, clatters to the floor, and skids toward Ishmael's feet.

The small tablet lies faceup, the screen white and covered with lines of black symbols grouped in twos, threes, fours, and sometimes more. They are the same undecipherable sequences of characters that Ishmael saw on the tablet he and Archie found years ago in the abandoned shack in Black Range.

Now several things happen at once:

Queequeg jerks his sleeper curtain open, a look of alarm on his face.

Ishmael and Pip both reach down for the tablet.

Their wrists graze.

Ishmael is jarred by the electrical shock he feels.

Pip straightens up and stares at him with astonishment.

Queequeg hops out of his sleeper and snatches up his tablet just as the ship again rocks violently, causing them all to grab for handholds to keep from falling.

His face only inches from Ishmael's, Pip asks, "Who are you?"

But without waiting for an answer, Pip turns to Queequeg. "And *you*!" He points to the tablet. "You're . . . a Lector?"

Queequeg averts his eyes.

"Of course! I should have known," Pip goes on. "All that business about oceans and coral reefs and rain on Earth." He gestures at the tablet. "This is where you got that nonsense."

The tablet once again in his possession, Queequeg scuttles back to his sleeper, closing the curtain behind him.

The ship pitches again, and Pip and Ishmael struggle to secure their footing.

"Were you sent here?" Pip whispers.

"To Cretacea?" Ishmael shakes his head. "I volunteered."

Pip gives him a deeply perplexed look. Then the lights go out, and in the crazed reeling of the ship, he and Pip climb back into their sleepers in the dark.

· 30 ·

BLACK RANGE, EARTH

"Here's where you'll sleep," Petra said. The room wasn't much larger than the playhouse at the foundling home — the bunk bed Joachim had built for them hardly wider than their shoulders — but for the first time in memory, Archie and Ishmael had their own places to sleep.

Despite almost immediately feeling comfortable with these new adults, at first the boys were reluctant to speak to them. After being so insular for so long, they found that words were slow to come. But Petra and Joachim were patient. Every day and night, one or the other would go away to a place called "work." When one was gone, the other would sleep for a few hours and then spend time with the boys — taking them outside to play, telling them the names of unfamiliar things, or teaching them how to add and subtract in their heads, but never allowing them to run free with the packs of children who roamed the grimy streets and abandoned lots.

It was only after the boys had begun to communicate with their foster parents that Ben started taking them for walks and on adventures.

"That's the Zirconia Electrolysis plant, where your parents and I work," he said one afternoon, pointing at the huge, soot-covered, nearly windowless complex over which loomed four tall smokestacks spewing black exhaust into the Shroud-blanketed sky.

"What happens there?" asked Archie, propped on his crutches.

"The conversion of carbon dioxide into oxygen and carbon monoxide. We need the oxygen to breathe."

"What's that?" Ishmael pointed at several black hills behind the building.

"Coal. They burn it to produce the energy for Zirconia Electrolysis."

"Will we work there someday?" Archie asked.

Ben looked out over the blackened rooftops of the hovels and shanties that made up most of Black Range. He coughed and then spit on the ground. "Not if I can help it."

31

Rat-a-tat-tat-tat!

Machine-gun fire whistles overhead. In Chase Boat Four, Ishmael and his crew duck. A quarter mile astern, raised up on hydrofoils, a black ship races toward them. They see a bright muzzle flash, and an instant later another volley of rounds whizzes past.

"Pirates!" Queequeg shouts.

"Hold on!" Ishmael jams the accelerator forward, praying the RTG won't stall. It doesn't, and the chase boat lurches ahead.

Only moments before, they'd paused from hunting to behold a wondrous sight in the distance: a turquoise lagoon edged by a thin ribbon of white sand, with lush, jade-colored hills rising up behind. Flyers soared over the summits, and a thin white waterfall cascaded from a distant peak. The sight was so stunning that they'd almost forgotten they were following a pack of long-necks.

Now they're running for their lives. "C-call the ship?" Billy yells, bracing himself while the chase boat bangs over the waves.

"We're out of range!" Ishmael yells back. The two-way is usually good up to fifteen miles, and he estimates that they're at least thirty from the *Pequod.*

"Can we outrun them?" Gwen shouts.

Ishmael has pushed the chase boat to top speed, but up on those hydrofoils, the pirate ship has no problem closing in.

Clinging to his seat, Queequeg catches Ishmael's eye and nods at the machine gun in the stern. Ishmael shakes his head. So far he suspects that the pirates have been firing warning shots over their heads. Should Chase Boat Four begin shooting back, it could become a real firefight.

The pirates are being smart, angling their vessel to force the chase boat nearer to shore. As Chase Boat Four's lead over the pirate ship shortens, Ishmael is aware that they're getting dangerously close to the rock outcroppings and shallow reefs that separate the placid lagoon from the rest of the ocean. The crew glances worriedly at him, clearly wondering about his plan for escape.

Except Ishmael doesn't have one.

The green coast is close now — too close. Ishmael can make out the brown shafts of the tall plants lining the shore. Ahead off the starboard side, waves rise up and crash into white foam on the long, barely submerged reef.

Rather than avoid the reef, Ishmael steers toward it. Billy grips the gunwale, his knuckles turning white when he realizes what Ishmael wants to do. "Y-you're going to try to g-go over that?" he yells.

"If we catch a wave, maybe we can surf over!" Ishmael yells back.

"Or capsize and sink!" Gwen shouts.

Rat-a-tat-tat! Above the whine of the RTG and the howl of the wind comes the smack of machine-gun fire much closer than before. A bullet whizzes past Ishmael's ear. Others splash into the water around them, kicking up bursts of spray. The pirates are no longer aiming high with warning shots. Now they're trying to draw blood.

"Everyone down!" Ishmael jerks his head at the machine gun in the stern. "Queek!"

Queequeg scrambles behind the machine gun and returns fire. Bullets whiz back and forth, pinging off the pirate ship's metal hull and peppering the water on either side of the chase boat's pontoons. By now the heavy surf crashing on the reef is only a dozen yards away.

Rat-a-tat-tat, rat-a-tat!

The pirate ship is angling in at high speed, its machine gun blazing. Crouching low, Ishmael steers Chase Boat Four up along the backs of swells, searching for a gap in the reef or a large enough wave to carry them —

Rat-a-tat-tat, rat-a-tat!

"Ah!" Billy clutches his thigh. Blood begins to spread around his fingers.

"Hold on!" Ishmael cuts the chase boat's wheel sharply. They speed up the back of a large swell . . . and take flight.

In the swamped chase boat, Queequeg kneels beside Billy, who's still clutching his thigh and grimacing while his blood turns the seawater pink. A moment ago, a torrent of hot water crashed over them when the nose of the boat plunged into the lagoon. Only the pontoons kept them afloat. The RTG quit, and now they wallow in the calm, sunlit waters, the thunder of crashing waves — and machine-gun fire — behind them.

Rope and loose rain gear float around Ishmael's knees while he watches the very top of the pirate boat's cabin cruise past outside the reef, the breaking waves blocking its approach. Gwen starts bailing, and he tries to restart the RTG.

Nothing happens.

"Bet the water's shorting out the battery," Queequeg says while tightening a tourniquet around Billy's leg to slow the bleeding. Billy groans in pain as Queequeg helps him to a seat.

Suddenly Gwen looks up and points.

Two hundred yards down the reef is something Ishmael hadn't seen earlier — a gap where the waves aren't breaking. That means the water there must be deep enough for a boat to broach.

Maybe even a pirate boat.

Ishmael's stomach knots. Without a functioning RTG, Chase Boat Four is easy prey. They watch helplessly while the pirate boat starts to nudge its way into the gap. In the bow a pirate with a long pole is testing the depth to be certain their vessel can make it.

Once the pirate ship clears the gap in the reef, there'll be nothing to stop them from seizing the chase boat and its crew.

32

Sploosh!

A thick white column of water bursts up into the air near the pirate boat. The man in the bow drops the long pole and staggers backward. Ishmael searches for the large humplike beast whose spout he assumes caused it.

But almost immediately there's another huge splash, and then another. They're not beasts spouting, but massive stones falling out of the sky! The crew of Chase Boat Four watch, stupefied.

Crash! An enormous stone smashes onto the deck of the pirate boat, causing the entire vessel to shudder. Pirates scream and dash this way and that. As more stones fall, the engine roars and the boat begins to reverse back through the gap in the reef.

The chase-boat crew cast their eyes upward, searching for the source of the barrage, but there is only the empty blue of sky. Ishmael glances curiously at Queequeg, who seems to know so much about so many things.

"Don't look at me," Queequeg says. "I know it rains water, but I've never heard of it raining rocks."

Another groan from Billy brings them back. Queequeg tightens the tourniquet and presses a rag against the wound to stanch the bleeding.

"How bad is it?" Ishmael asks.

"I don't think it hit an artery, or there'd be a lot more blood, but I'm worried the bone may be broken," Queequeg answers.

"It h-hurts." Billy moans through clenched teeth.

By now the pirate boat has fled and the big stones have ceased falling, but Chase Boat Four is still adrift in the lagoon, and there's only so much Queequeg can do for Billy. Getting him the care he needs means bailing out the chase boat, coaxing the RTG to start, and hustling back to the *Pequod*. But it also means leaving the protection of the lagoon and going back into the ocean, where the pirate boat may be lying in wait.

The blistering sunlight has started to dry the shoulders of their soaked uniforms. Gwen, who's been bailing water nonstop, suddenly pauses and stares. Ishmael follows her eyes. A narrow craft with a white sail and outrigger is coming toward them from the green shore.

"Keep bailing." Ishmael steps behind the machine gun, swinging the barrel toward the approaching outrigger. There are six figures in it: four rowing, one steering in the stern, and one crouched in the bow.

"See any weapons?" Ishmael asks.

"Not yet," Gwen replies, as the outrigger draws closer. When it's about fifty feet away, the strangers stop paddling. They are muscular, simply dressed men and women, their skin the same rich bronze as the sailors who've been aboard the *Pequod* the longest. The rowers place their paddles in the bottom of their outrigger. All at once they raise long, thin tubes to their lips.

Gwen slaps her upper arm like someone who's been stung by an insect. A second later she collapses with a splash into the water that remains in the bottom of the chase boat. Before Ishmael can react, he feels a sting in his thigh. Instantly he is light-headed and dizzy. The bottom of the boat comes flying up toward him.

33

He feels like he is floating on air, looking up through a kaleidoscope of bright greens and yellows. He would try to move, but can't feel his arms or legs. It's like they aren't there. If he is sure of anything—though he isn't—it might be that his chest is rising and falling with each delicious breath of air.

And it feels wonderful.

A dark shadow moves over him, blocking the colors and light. It's a blurred face. In fact, it resembles Petra's face, only with darker skin. His foster mother's here! He is thrilled to see her and would like to reach out and hug her.

A faraway voice says softly, "Be . . . pay . . . chant."

Petra's face shrinks back, and the bright greens and yellows return. Ishmael doesn't mind. Now that Petra is here, he will be, he will pay, he will chant.

* * *

The patchwork of greens and yellows is made of thousands and thousands of flat, thin things that remind him of scurry scales. Some are nearly oval. Some come to a point. Some spread out like a hand with stubby fingers. They are attached to ever-thinning limbs that spread from a single thick brown shaft rising out of the ground. Up close, he sees the shafts are covered by a coarse, wrinkled skin. A soft breeze makes the green and yellow scales flutter, revealing bits of blue here and there. By now Ishmael knows that he is lying in some sort of hammock. He can feel his arms and legs but still can't move them. A woman's face appears over him, her long black hair tickling his cheeks and forehead. She is not Petra, but she has a kind, soft smile.

"How art ye?" she asks.

Ishmael tries to speak, but only jumbled sounds come out. The woman softly smooths his hair. "'Tis all right. Be pay chant."

The sun glimmers through the green and yellow scales, heating Ishmael's skin, leaving him damp with sweat. He hears voices and rustling, tweeting and chirping, and, strangely, a distant melody. Lifting his head, he sees a hut with a thatched roof. A girl comes out of it. She is about his own age, with dark eyes, long black hair, and bronze skin. A reddish birthmark surrounds her left eye like a pink patch. She is the most beautiful girl he has ever seen. When he stares too long at her, her face clouds and she departs.

Ishmael turns his head in the other direction and is startled to find Gwen lying in a hammock beside him. She tilts her sweat-freckled face toward his and smiles broadly, aglow with happiness.

It is dark, and through the patchwork overhead Ishmael glimpses glittering stars. Unseen creatures hoot and call, and from the distance comes a soft, rhythmic crash that sounds vaguely familiar. The breeze raises goose bumps on his arms.

The dark air bears unfamiliar, fragrant scents. Ishmael can move his arms and legs a little, though not enough to climb out of the hammock. A distant part of his brain warns that he should feel apprehensive about being so openly vulnerable in this strange place. And yet he has never felt so completely serene and at ease.

Daylight.

The warm, moist air makes Ishmael suspect it is morning. He looks at Gwen. Her eyes are closed and she sleeps with an angelic expression. Ishmael slowly lifts his arms, but still can't feel or move his fingers. The dark-haired woman's face appears over him again. "Do not worry. It works from the core out. 'Twill be able t'feel ye fingers and toes soon."

Once again Ishmael tries to speak, but the sounds that come out bear no resemblance to words. The dark-haired woman places her fingers gently on his forehead. "Be patient."

Ishmael sits up in the hammock. He can curl his toes and cup his hands into loose fists. He can make his fingers open and close like scissors. The strange, euphoric feeling has subsided, and he wonders where he is. The air has turned hot and is filled with chirps and other new sounds that he assumes are animal calls. He swivels and finds that Gwen is also sitting up, and now he can see Queequeg beside her in a third hammock. All three hammocks are tied by rough rope to the brown shafts of plants. There is something naggingly familiar about these particular plants, but Ishmael doesn't know why.

Around them are huts of varying sizes, all with thatched roofs, built on stilts but also suspended from limbs overhead. Walkways connect them—also on stilts, with ropes stretching down from branches for extra support. The result is an elevated village more than a dozen feet above the ground.

A woman with two children goes by. Two long-haired men pass

in the other direction, carrying bundles of sticks on their shoulders. With friendly nods, they acknowledge the chase-boat crew.

Another man approaches. His long, straight black hair is pulled back, and his ears are pierced with very small white spines. Scurry bones, perhaps? Ishmael wonders if he's the one who was in the bow of the outrigger that came out to greet them. . . . And then shot them with darts.

The man helps them out of their hammocks one by one. Once on his feet, Ishmael feels as unsteady as he did that first day on the *Pequod* months ago, but the man leads him to a woven mat and motions him to sit. He does the same for Queequeg and Gwen, then squats before them. "What ship art ye from?"

"The *Pequod,*" Ishmael answers.

"Where are we?" Gwen asks, wiping her forehead with her arm.

"Here," the man says.

Gwen makes a face. "Where's here?"

"'Tis just here," he says. "We don't have a name for it."

A dozen questions could follow, but one rises above the rest. Ishmael asks, "Where's our friend Billy?"

"We're caring for him," the man says. "He needs rest."

"What about our boat?" Queequeg asks.

"'Tis here."

"Can we have it back?" Gwen asks.

"Be patient."

Gwen's eyebrows dip. "Who are you? Do you have a name, or *art* you just 'here,' too?"

Her sarcasm doesn't seem to bother the man. "Ah, sorry. We don't often have visitors. Gabriel is my name. And ye?"

Ishmael, Gwen, and Queequeg introduce themselves, but before they can ask Gabriel anything more, a tall woman wearing knee-high boots made of hide approaches with a bow strung across her shoulder. She eyes the new arrivals suspiciously, then kneels and whispers something into Gabriel's ear. He rises, telling the chase-boat crew that he'll return soon.

They sit on the shaded mats and wait. Smoke has begun to drift from cooking fires. Simple music floats down from a platform where a boy plays a long, slender instrument. People of all ages continue to pass.

"There was something in those darts," Gwen says.

"You're telling me," Queequeg says. "I thought I had wings. Kept dreaming that I was flying, and every time I woke, I thought I was in some kind of nest. But it felt great. I mean, I almost wish I were *still* dreaming."

"How do you know you're not?" Gwen asks.

Queequeg takes a deep breath of the fragrant air. Near them, a small winged creature — bright-green, red, and blue — alights on a limb and begins to sing. Queequeg grins. "If this is a dream, it's okay with me. I just wish it weren't so hot."

It does feel steamier here than on the ship. Ishmael suspects it's the humidity, trapped by all the greenery around them. And speaking of greenery. "I thought land was supposed to be dangerous," he says.

"Maybe it is," replies Queequeg. "Could be why this village is elevated."

Gwen looks around. Whatever euphoria she appeared to feel earlier has by now ebbed. "I don't like this. They shot us with darts. They have our boat and won't tell us where Billy is. All we know is we're on land, and they keep saying be patient."

"I understand why you're concerned," Ishmael says. "But let's give it some more time."

Gwen frowns. "Until what?"

34

The sun has begun to drop, casting long shadows. Gabriel hasn't returned. The tall huntress passes again, this time dragging a lifeless, fur-covered creature with an arrow protruding from its side. Ishmael and the others are riveted by the sight. It is the first land creature any of them has ever seen.

"Dinner?" Gwen guesses.

Still sitting on the mat, Queequeg runs his finger along the railing that lines the walkway. "See this?" He touches a joint where two lengths of rail meet. The ends of both are intricately interlocked, and the joint is smooth and firm. Queequeg raps his knuckles against it. "This material? I think it's wood. The huts and walkways look like they're made of it, too." He points at the shaft of one of the tall plants with branches. "I think it comes from these. There's a name for them, but I can't remember what it is."

"Something you know about from your tablet?" Ishmael guesses.

Queequeg's mouth falls open, and he looks as though he's about to deny it, but then catches himself.

"What is a Lector, anyway?" Ishmael asks.

"A what?" Gwen says.

Queequeg bites the corner of his lip. "Those lines of symbols you saw on my tablet? They're an ancient form of communication. Each character represents a sound. You see the symbols, sound them out in your head, and re-create the word they represent."

Gwen makes a face. "It seems so complicated. Why would anyone bother?"

"It's just a really old, pre-electronic way of storing and disseminating information," Queequeg explains. "From a time before tablets and virtual reality. Although I think they were still using it even in the early days of electronics. . . ."

"Pip made it sound like being a Lector was really bad," says Ishmael.

"*Worse* than bad." Queequeg chuckles bitterly. "We're outlaws. Back on Earth, if they caught you, you'd never be seen or heard from again."

"Is that why you didn't want to tell us?" Ishmael guesses.

Queequeg nods.

"My foster brother and I once found an old tablet that could access those symbols," Ishmael says. "It was the only one I ever saw that could do that."

"Those tablets didn't have to *access* anything," Queequeg says. "The information was in their electronic memories. Now, imagine every single person having one. From the point of view of those who want to control us, it was chaos. There was no way to monitor or govern what information people could exchange, what ideas they could share. The powers in charge wanted one central memory that only *they* controlled. My father once told me they called it the 'cloud' because they wanted to cloud people's access to information. Make it impossible to see things clearly, the way they really were. And to make sure everyone was in this cloud, they outlawed private ownership of electronic memory, and eventually they outlawed the use of those symbols, too."

Gwen makes a face. "But who are those people you say want to control us?"

"The Gilded?" Ishmael guesses.

Queequeg raises an eyebrow. "What have you heard?"

"That on Earth they have much better lives than the rest of us," Ishmael says, repeating what Billy told him. "And the reason towns like Black Range are so poor is that the Gilded try to keep as much money as they can for themselves. But there's something that doesn't make sense to me, Queek: Even if it's true that the Gilded outlawed ownership of electronic memory, people still had their own memories. No one could stop them from sharing what they knew."

"True, but people die, and with them go those memories." Queequeg gestures at all the greenery surrounding them. "Remember how you'd never heard of plant life? Eventually everyone who remembered Earth from before the Shroud died, and their memories turned to stories and then to rumor, and myth, and eventually faded away entirely."

Gwen swivels her head, taking in the vegetation encircling them. "Wait a minute. You're saying there was a time when all *this* existed on Earth?"

Queequeg nods vigorously. "Absolutely."

Gwen is quiet for a moment, probably trying to imagine how the arid, sooty planet she left could have ever looked like this. "I don't know, Queek. That sounds really far-fetched. And how come during all the time I lived on Earth I never heard about these Gilded whoevers?"

"Because they don't *want* you to hear about them," Queequeg says. “They don’t want you to know anything about them. And since they control all the information, they control what you know . . . or, more likely, what you don’t know.”

Gwen ponders this, then sweeps some unruly red hair from her face and places her hands on the walkway floor. “Sure, Queek, whatever you say. Anyway, I’m tired of waiting for that Gabriel guy. Let’s see if we can find Billy ourselves.” She starts to get to her feet, then wobbles and has to put a hand on Ishmael’s head to steady herself. “I think there’s still some of that dart stuff in my system.”

Queequeg tries to stand and grabs the wooden railing to keep from toppling over. “Whoa! I’ll say.”

“Come on.” Gwen offers her hand to Ishmael. His legs feel rubbery, but he manages to get up.

“Gabriel told us to wait . . .” he says.

Gwen waves at the people of the village, who are going about their lives, hardly paying the three of them any attention. “Does it look like they care?”

35

It's hard to know which direction to go. The huts that line the elevated walkway have no windows or doors, just openings barely large enough for a person to slip in and out. Billy could be in any one of them, and Ishmael doesn't feel comfortable wandering into one unannounced. But Gwen has no such qualms; she ducks into the closest hut and comes out with a girl of seven or eight, who signals for them to follow her. The girl wears a bracelet of flimsy red, purple, and yellow scales. As she leads them along the walkway, she looks often at Gwen's bright-red hair, seemingly fascinated by it.

She brings them to a large hut. Unlike the others, it has some windowlike openings to allow light in. Inside, several people, including Billy, lie on woven mats. Billy's eyes are closed, and his face is serene. A bandage of some rough type of material covers the wound in his thigh.

There's a foul, rotten odor in the air when they kneel close to him.

Queequeg wrinkles his nose. "What's that smell?"

Gwen places her palm on Billy's forehead. "No fever."

Just then, a small white larva crawls out from under the bandage.

Gwen yanks her hand away. "What in the universe!?"

"'Twill help," the young girl says.

Ishmael reaches down and carefully lifts a corner of the bandage. The edge of the wound is raw and pink, and more white larvae mill about, some burrowing under the skin.

"They're maggots, for Earth's sake!" Gwen gasps, disgusted. "How's *that* supposed to make him better?"

"'Twill," a deep voice says behind them. It's Gabriel. "His wound is infected. 'Tis what makes the odor. 'Twill help him heal."

Gwen crosses her arms over her stomach. "Try telling Billy that when he wakes up and finds them crawling around under his skin."

"He shan't wake up till we want him to," Gabriel says. "By then the maggots 'twill be gone."

Ishmael looks around the hut. In one corner is a low table with mortars and pestles, clumps of dried vegetation, and several vials that contain various shades of green liquid—from a watery light green to a chartreuse so dense it glows. The color reminds him of the glowing green sac Starbuck removed from the terrafin's tail.

"You're keeping them asleep?" Ishmael says of the other patients lying peacefully on mats.

"Yes."

"How?"

"Be patient," he says.

"Who's taking care of them?" Gwen asks.

"We all do. 'Tis not hard." Gabriel beckons for Ishmael and the others to rise and join him. "'Tis time to eat. Ye must be hungry."

As they follow him out of the hut, Gwen mutters under her breath, "I'm starting to get really *impatient* with all this 'be patient' crap."

Gabriel leads them along a walkway through the tall plants with brown shafts. Long, ropy green plant life drapes and loops through some of the limbs, and here and there small, colorful winged creatures hop and sing. Other, more delicate creatures with nearly translucent wings flutter by.

They continue to a widened area of the walkway where long tables are lit by flames flickering in bowls filled with an oily amber liquid. The creature that the tall huntress killed earlier is being turned on a spit over a fire.

Gabriel gestures for them to join the two girls they encountered earlier — the young one who led them to the hut where Billy lay, and the beautiful one with the pink patch of skin around her eye. "They art my daughters, Fayaway and Thistle," he says. "'Twill answer ye questions." He leaves to join a group of older men and women at another table. One of them is the tall huntress.

The crew sit with Gabriel's daughters. Thistle, the younger one, is still trying, but mostly failing, to mask her fascination with Gwen's red hair, while Fayaway tries — and mostly succeeds — not to meet their eyes.

Finally, Gwen collects a lock of hair in her hand and offers it across the table. "Would you like to touch it?"

When her sister eagerly accepts the offer, Fayaway rolls her eyes disdainfully. And when Thistle seems to fondle Gwen's hair for a moment too long, her older sister fires a look of disapproval. "'Tis enough already."

"But 'tis so beautiful," Thistle gushes.

"It's all right," Gwen says. "I don't mind."

"See?" Thistle sticks her tongue out at her older sister.

Fayaway looks away, right into Ishmael's eyes. Until that moment, he wasn't aware that he'd been staring at her. Fayaway gives him a baffled look, then gazes off. Ishmael feels his face grow hot.

Dishes of yellow and green plant foods are passed to them, along with a bowl of fibrous brown meat, which Ishmael suspects is the cooked flesh of the fur-covered creature the huntress slew. At first he and the others have difficulty picking up their food with the long, pointed spines the islanders use as utensils.

"Takes practice," Thistle says sympathetically. "Be —"

Gwen holds up a hand. "Don't say it. Believe me, we know."

Near them, at the table where Gabriel and some of the others sit, a discussion grows heated. The huntress appears to be doing most of the talking, while others cast furtive glances at Ishmael and his crew.

"Is that tall woman your mother?" Gwen asks the girls.

"'Tis Diana," Fayaway replies. "Our mother's ceased."

The corners of Gwen's eyes soften. "I'm sorry."

"'Tis no need t'be sorry." Thistle waves her arm. "She is still here, in the animals and plants and trees of the jungle."

"Trees!" Queequeg motions toward the tall, sturdy plants with the brown shafts that help keep the village elevated. "That's what they're called!" He picks up a few of the yellow and green scales that have fallen. "And these are leaves, right?"

Thistle nods, bemused.

"What's jungle?" Gwen asks.

Thistle sweeps her arm toward all the dense greenery surrounding them. "All of this."

After several minutes of silence during which the crew concentrates on the strange new foods they've been served, Ishmael has a question for Fayaway: "Why did your people shoot us with darts?"

"Didn't know were ye friend or foe," Fayaway answers simply.

"How do you know now?" Gwen asks.

Fayaway glances at the table where her father and the others sit. Could that be what the argument is about? Ishmael wonders. Is that why the huntress Diana keeps casting wary looks in their direction? Fayaway turns back. "Ye have no weapons. Shan't matter."

"There was something in the darts that temporarily paralyzed us," Gwen says.

"Nectar," Thistle answers.

"Hush!" Fayaway snaps at her.

"Why?" Thistle asks.

Fayaway's eyes peek at Ishmael and the others. "'Tis not a thing t'discuss with outsiders," she says harshly.

Sensing that it would be impolite to press the issue, Ishmael continues eating. In the dark, beyond the reach of the flickering lights, creatures make strange, eerie sounds. Ishmael feels edgy, but their hosts don't appear bothered.

Gabriel leaves the other table and joins them. "We art curious," he says. "Have ye news of Earth?"

They tell him what they've been able to piece together from the few Z-packs they received while aboard the *Pequod:* Conditions back home are deteriorating.

Gabriel accepts the news with a wistful sigh.

"How long have you been here?" Ishmael asks.

"'Twas born here," Gabriel answers.

Queequeg raises his eyebrows. "We were told it's really dangerous on land."

"On the mainland, perhaps, but on this island 'tis not too bad. No more than at sea. Maybe less so."

"If you were born here, how did your parents come to be here?" Ishmael asks.

"'Twere born here, too. And their parents. Goes way, way back to the ship that ran aground on the reef."

"And you've never tried to leave?" Gwen asks.

Gabriel smiles softly. "'Tis no reason to."

Later that night the chase-boat crew lie in hammocks, listening to the distant crash of waves and the calls of animals.

"Think they're looking for us?" Queequeg asks hopefully.

"Not likely," Gwen says. "The *Pequod*'s on the move, trying to make up weight. And the longer we stay here, the farther away she'll go."

"What do you think we should do?" Queequeg asks.

"Leave," Gwen says. "As soon as Billy's well enough."

36

In the morning, Ishmael and the others watch a scrawny man inch his way up a tall, limbless tree. At the top is a burst of long, skinny green leaves and several clusters of what look like large round green and yellow plant foods. When he's climbed high enough, he pulls a stick from his waist and swats at the clusters until they break loose and thump to the ground below.

"Hungry?" Thistle asks the chase-boat crew. The scrawny man climbs back down and hacks at one of the round things with a hatchet. Close up, he's older than he looked. His short, curly hair is gray, his wrinkled skin sags from his bony frame, and he doesn't have many teeth left.

"Mikal, these art my friends," Thistle says. "'Twill try a treestone."

The old man cuts a hole into one end, then offers it to Gwen, who hesitates. "What am I supposed to do?"

"Drink," Thistle says.

When Gwen declines, Mikal offers the treestone to Ishmael, who presses the hole to his lips. The liquid inside is fresh and sweet, but the taste is foreign, and he's not sure he likes it. He hands the treestone to Queequeg, who sips, makes a face, and hands it back. The old man shrugs, presses the treestone to his lips, and drinks what remains.

But he's not finished. With the hatchet he splits the treestone in two. Inside is a hard brown nut the size of a large man's fist, and inside that is an almost pure-white substance. Mikal scoops some out and offers it around. Ishmael tries a small bite and is surprised to find it delicious and chewy. When he quickly takes a larger bite, Gwen and Queequeg decide to sample theirs. Cheeks bulging, both nod approvingly.

With a toothless smile, Mikal starts to hack open more.

From that day forward, the crew begin with a breakfast of treestone meat, then visit Billy. He's still asleep, the maggots still infesting the wound, but the foul odor is less and less evident. Afterward the chase-boat crew are free to do whatever they choose — which usually means exploring the island. With Thistle as their guide, they trade their shoes for animal-hide boots and climb the hill behind the village, where she shows them the row of enormous catapults that launched the stones that drove the pirate boat away. Another time, she leads them to a place where clear, cool water actually burbles out of the ground and is collected for drinking and cooking. From there she points out the cave where the first inhabitants of the island — the survivors of the shipwreck — took shelter centuries before.

One afternoon she takes them to a beach where, for the first time in their lives, they feel sand between their toes. A pack of children passes, several of them guiding a sightless boy, his eyelids closed over sunken sockets. While he sits at the water's edge, the others bring him shells and pieces of oddly shaped white stone to feel.

Queequeg picks up several pieces of the white stone. One is shaped like a leafless plant with many offshoots. Another is round and furrowed, and a third is covered with a dozen thick, stubby appendages.

"Coral." He offers them around.

The coral is rough and porous. "Like what you and your father stood on?" Ishmael asks.

"Uh-huh."

So his story was true, Ishmael thinks. *Coral exists. And if Queek has seen it on Earth, doesn't that mean there really were oceans at one time?* Why did this become a secret? Why was such information banned, along with the knowledge of how to decipher those long lines of symbols from which Queequeg has learned so much?

Suddenly, a large shadow passes over the beach. Ishmael looks skyward. A huge gray flyer with broad wings and a long, pointed beak circles overhead. Thistle jerks her head up and shouts, "To the trees!"

The children splash out of the water and scamper up the beach. The biggest among them scoops up the blind boy and carries him. The flyer glides lower, tilting its head as it searches for prey. Cowering under a shady canopy of leaves, a few of the younger children whimper while the older ones press them protectively close to the thick, hard trunks.

The flyer flaps its wings and rises higher in the air, then banks and disappears from view. "Wait," Thistle whispers, then steps cautiously out into the sunlight and scans the sky. Finally she turns and waves to those still huddled under the trees. "'Tis gone."

The children creep from their hiding places, but there's a palpable sense that playtime is over. Glancing warily at the sky, they lead the sightless boy back toward the village.

Watching them, Ishmael feels an ache. The way the islanders care for one another reminds him of how he and Archie always looked after each other.

· 37 ·

BLACK RANGE, EARTH

Petra woke them in the dark. "Get dressed, boys."

"Why?" Archie yawned and rubbed his eyes.

"Ben's run out of Natrient, and he's not feeling well. We have to get him some."

Ishmael and Archie dressed, hunting around in the murk for their clothes and shoes, then joined their foster mother.

"Stay together." Petra unlocked the front door. "No going ahead, Ishmael."

At that moment, going anywhere was the last thing on his groggy mind. He mostly wanted to crawl back into bed. "Why do we have to go so early?" He yawned.

"The dispensary's been running out. If we wait until later, there may not be any Natrient left."

"What happens to people who don't get any?" Archie asked as he hobbled out into the dark on his crutches.

"They don't eat." Petra locked the door behind them.

"Don't they get hungry?"

"I'm sure they do. So they're probably the first in line the next day."

In the inky predawn blackness, they found the rope that led out to the street.

"What's a hundred and fifty-seven divided by twelve?" Petra asked.

"Thirteen, remainder one," Archie answered almost instantly.

"Good. Two hundred thirty-three divided by four?"

"Fifty-eight remainder one," said Archie.

"Right again. Let's let Ishmael answer. One hundred ninety-one divided by six."

"Uh . . ."

"I know," said Archie.

"We know you know, sweetheart."

"Thirty-one, remainder five," said Ishmael.

"Very good. Another word for *scared.*"

"Frightened," said Archie.

"And?"

"Terrified."

"Give Ishmael a chance."

"But he used all the good ones," Ishmael complained.

"Afraid, fearful, horrified." Archie rattled off three more.

Ishmael didn't really mind that Archie was smarter, or at least a quicker thinker than he was. Joachim always said that Archie would need to be extra quick-witted to get along with his disabled legs: "The world is full of people who'll try to take advantage of you. Your best defense is to be shrewder than the lot of them."

They found the street rope and started to follow it, Ishmael's ears attuned to any sound that might mean danger.

"Is Old Ben related to us?" he asked.

"No," Petra answered. "He's just a good family friend."

"Then why are we getting him Natrient?"

"That's what friends do, they help each other. For instance, Ben helped us find you. He's the one who spotted you in the window of the foundling home."

"How come you needed help finding us?" Archie asked.

"We didn't *need* it, but when he saw the two of you, he knew you were the right children for us. And he helped persuade Ms. Hussey to bend the rules so that we could take you both. We have a great deal to thank him for."

Even though it would be another three hours before the Natrient dispensary opened, a line of people already stretched down the block in the first faint light of day.

"Can Ish and I go look around?" asked Archie.

Petra shook her head. "It's still a little too dark."

"Come on, we're not kids anymore." Archie was eleven and Ishmael was nine.

"All right. But don't go far — and stay together."

Archie began hobbling away down the sidewalk, Ishmael a step behind. When they were out of earshot, he dropped his voice: "Where are we going?"

Archie grinned. "You'll see."

38

As the days pass while they wait for Billy's wound to heal, the crew of Chase Boat Four find different ways to occupy their time. Queequeg joins those who go in outriggers to net scurry. Gwen has befriended some of the hunters and often joins them in search of game. Ishmael finds himself interested in how the villagers cultivate plants.

Fayaway is among the islanders who tend the fields where vegetation is grown. Ishmael often sees her in the mornings, before the midday sun becomes so scaldingly hot that everyone heads down to the sparkling blue water of the lagoon to cool off. Ishmael sometimes joins them, though he never wades in deeper than midthigh.

One day, as he reaches down with cupped hands to splash water on his sunburned shoulders, Fayaway suddenly rises out of the lagoon before him. Her drenched black hair is stuck close to her skull, and water runs down her face. "Do ye never go deeper?"

"I don't know how to swim."

From the vexation on her face, Ishmael knows she finds that difficult to imagine. The island children learn to walk and swim at practically the same time. He's seen three- and four-year-olds glide through the water like scurry.

"'Twill teach ye." She reaches for his hand. At her touch, Ishmael feels a strange fluttering in his chest. She tugs, trying to lead him deeper, but he resists, recalling the sensation of nearly drowning when he tried to save Queequeg the day they harpooned the big hump. She gives him a puzzled look, then lets go.

"Watch." She lies back and floats with her arms spread, only her chest and face above the surface. When Ishmael peers into the water beneath her to see what's holding her up, she laughs and stands. "'Tis not trickery. Come on, try."

With Fayaway standing beside him, Ishmael lies back stiffly. Even with her hands under him, he can't relax.

"Let yeself float," she coaxes softly. "Ye won't sink."

Ishmael's heart is beating with such agitation that he expects to see small waves rippling away from his chest. But at least the water here is shallow and he can get to his feet if he has to.

"Fear not," Fayaway gently assures.

He closes his eyes and feels the midday sun's heat on his face. His heart is still thrumming and his breath is quick.

"'Tis good." Fayaway removes one hand from under his back.

Ishmael tenses, certain he will go under as soon as her other hand is no longer supporting him.

"Easy now." Fayaway is holding him up with only fingers. He takes a deep breath, preparing to plant his feet on the bottom when he feels himself start to sink. But miraculously, when Fayaway withdraws her fingers, he bobs with just enough of his face above the surface to breathe. He opens his eyes and sees her smiling down at him. Can he actually be floating? It's a confounding sensation, but he still doesn't trust it. After a moment, he tucks forward and stands, breathing hard, water streaming off him.

Fayaway claps proudly. "'Tis enough for today."

Back onshore, she bends over and wrings out her hair. Ishmael is about to look away—he doesn't want to be caught staring again—when he spots a circular design tattooed on the nape of her neck.

Fayaway straightens up, whipping her hair behind her shoulders. When she sees Ishmael's face, her brow creases. "What?"

"That tattoo on the back of your neck . . . Where'd it come from?"

"'Tis something we art given at birth. Everyone has one. Why?"

"I've . . . I've seen something like it before," Ishmael says.

Fayaway glances toward the fields where the other islanders have gone back to work. She doesn't seem particularly curious about Ishmael's discovery. But Ishmael is certain that the tattoo on the back of her neck is the same as Archie's favorite design from the old tablet they found in that shack in Black Range. What's it doing here?

· 39 ·

BLACK RANGE, EARTH

There was no point in reminding Archie that Petra had told them not to go far; he wouldn't listen anyway. Besides, she was back in the Natrient line and would never know. And Archie wasn't foolish — he stayed away from alleys and crossed the street whenever someone questionable approached.

"Where're we going?" Ishmael asked again.

"There." His foster brother gestured toward a building barely visible in the deep grayness. Beside it rose a smokestack like the ones at the Zirconia Electrolysis plant. But while those stacks spewed black smoke twenty-four hours a day, this one appeared dormant.

When they got closer, Ishmael saw that the building was abandoned and crumbling, the windows shattered, and rubble was strewn about.

"Careful." Archie gestured at the jagged rusted ends of pipes jutting out of the ground here and there. Ishmael knew better than to ask what they were looking for; Archie would always say they were looking for whatever they found.

Archie stopped at the base of the old smokestack and gazed up. It was still dark enough that the top of the stack was indistinguishable from the void above it. A row of metal rungs ran up the side, the lower ones sawed off by scrap poachers.

Ishmael immediately understood what Archie wanted to do. "But there's nothing up there."

Archie smiled. "Let's see." He propped his crutches against the stack's base, then held his hands out. Ishmael gave him a boost, and Archie was able to grab the lowest intact rung, then started to hoist himself up. While his legs weren't much good, Archie's upper body was strong, and when he needed to rest, the stiffness of the leg braces provided support. Ishmael jumped up and grabbed the first rung, then began to follow.

It wasn't long before he understood why his foster brother wanted to climb the smokestack. It was an opportunity to see Black Range from a new perspective. While it was still too dark to pick out much detail, they could see that the town was clustered around the huge Zirconia Electrolysis station. Beyond that were the chopped and gouged undulations left from hundreds of years of strip mining. Black Range had once been renowned for its anthracite — pure and with a high carbon content — but the supply had been exhausted centuries ago. Now the station depended on imported, low-quality lignite, which burned so dirty that some mornings you could sweep the previous night's soot with a broom.

About two-thirds of the way up the stack, Archie stopped. Ishmael glanced back down and felt queasy. He was no great fan of heights, and this was undoubtedly the highest he'd ever climbed. He looked up at his foster brother, who had let go with one hand and was pointing into the distance.

Far, far away in the blackness was a small, faint bluish-green dot. It might have been convex in shape, but it was too distant to know for sure.

"What is it?" Ishmael asked.

Above him, Archie shook his head and scanned the horizon, perhaps to see if there were any other places like it. Ishmael also peered out, but he couldn't see any.

"Maybe we should go higher," he suggested, his curiosity overcoming his discomfort about heights.

"Can't." Archie reached up to the next rung and shook it. It wasn't securely anchored.

Suddenly voices rose up from below. Ishmael looked down and saw three figures searching among the rubble. One of them had Archie's crutches. The other two had taken hold of one of the rusty pipes and were working it back and forth, trying to free it from the ground.

"Scrap poachers," Archie whispered.

Joachim and Petra had often warned their foster sons that scrap poachers, like other wrongdoers, were also capable of kidnapping children and holding them for ransom — or worse.

There was nothing the boys could do but wait, clinging to the metal rungs and hoping they wouldn't be seen.

40

"Do ye know many girls on Earth?" Fayaway asks.

She and Ishmael sit together on the sand, catching their breath after a long swim.

Fayaway no longer frowns when she sees him; in fact, she smiles. In the broiling afternoons they swim and tease each other and laugh. Ishmael is distressingly aware that he is finding himself growing more comfortable, not only in the water and with Fayaway, but with the islanders' way of life as well.

"A few," Ishmael answers.

"Art they pretty?"

"Not as pretty as you."

Fayaway looks hurt. "Don't make fun."

Ishmael's surprised. "I wasn't."

The small waves turn the sand near the water's edge dark. Fayaway touches the patch of pink skin around her left eye. "Can't be pretty with this."

"There's nothing wrong with it."

"No one else has it."

"Then it makes you unique. I think it looks nice," he blurts out before he has time to think. His face quickly feels hot, and it's not due to the sun.

Fayaway turns her head, but Ishmael senses that she's pleased. Suddenly she swivels around, punches him mischievously on the arm, and jumps up and runs toward the woods, laughing. Ishmael gets to his feet and sprints after her.

Moments later he catches her beside the trunk of a large tree. He grabs her arm and spins her around. They look into each other's eyes. Fayaway's go wide with uncertain excitement.

Thwack! A knife whistles past inches from their faces and buries itself deep in the bark. Fayaway jumps back, and Ishmael feels the breath rush from his lungs like air from a burst balloon.

Wearing tall hide boots, Gwen steps out of the brush and works the blade out of the tree. "Sorry to ruin your fun, but I thought you should know that Billy's awake."

Sliding the knife back into its sheath, she heads up the trail toward the village. "Go," Fayaway tells Ishmael. "'Tis time t'get back t'work."

When he gets to the healing hut, Gwen is helping Billy sit up. Strangely, the whites of his eyes are a deep pink. As Gabriel promised, the maggots are gone and there's shiny, healthy-looking new skin on Billy's thigh.

They get him to his feet and walk him outside, where he squints dumbfounded at the elevated village perched in the trees. "W-we're . . . on l-land?"

"An island," Gwen says.

"Wh-what's that m-music?"

A soft melody floats through the air. Just as he's become accustomed to the heat, Ishmael realizes that he's been here long enough to become so used to the music that he isn't always aware of it.

Queequeg joins them, and they sit in the shade and answer Billy's questions. He seems gleefully fascinated by this place. When Queequeg offers him a sweet and sour plant food, he first takes a tentative nibble, then quickly devours the rest and asks for a second.

Gabriel arrives, and Billy is quick to thank him when he learns that the islanders were instrumental in his recovery.

"Just don't ask *how* they did it," Gwen quips, then says to Gabriel, "Looks like it's time for us to say good-bye."

But Gabriel shakes his head. "Not yet. 'Tis still weak and needs t'get his strength back. The *Pequod* shall pass again. Be patient."

41

A week later, in a distant corner of the lagoon, two outriggers drift together under the midday sun. Fayaway and Ishmael have tied their outrigger to Gabriel's, and they share a lunch of treestone meat and dried scurry.

"'Tis Gwen still eager t'leave?" Gabriel asks.

"We . . . haven't talked about it lately."

"'Tis busy hunting," Fayaway adds. Each day, Gwen joins the hunters, and she is becoming skilled in their techniques.

"'Tis good for Billy t'have the time," says Gabriel. To help Billy regain strength in his leg, Mikal has been teaching him to climb the tall, limbless trees and harvest treestones.

Ishmael chews on some dried scurry, feeling the distant tug of the *Pequod.* What if there's been news about Archie and his foster parents? "It does seem like his leg is better."

“The leg, yes, but ’tis his spirit that still needs t’heal.” Gabriel takes a drink from a treestone and glances up at the sun. “’Tis time t’get back. And ye?”

Fayaway lifts a long, pointed stick. “’Twill dive for dinner.”

Gabriel unties his outrigger and sails away, and Fayaway and Ishmael slip into the water with spears. Now that he is comfortable swimming, Fayaway has been teaching him to hunt large scurry.

Soon, Ishmael finds a fat brown spot swimming lazily among the pink, green, and yellow corals. But each time he gets close, the plump scurry scoots just out of range. The large ones are skittish, but Ishmael has learned that with time even the biggest will tire of constantly swimming away, and that’s when they become vulnerable. He swims behind the scurry for what feels like a considerable distance, and gradually the creature ceases to flee quite so far when he comes near.

Finally, taking a deep breath, Ishmael dives and kicks down. But the brown spot, sensing that this approach is more aggressive, shoots behind a big coral formation. Ishmael follows — and comes face-to-face with a terrafin!

Air bursts from his lungs and he bolts toward the surface, fearing that at any moment he’ll feel the poisonous skiver that will spell instant death. But he makes it to the surface unscathed. Gasping for breath, he looks down and watches the terrafin glide away, apparently unbothered by the confrontation. He looks in the direction the creature is headed and sees something he can barely comprehend: poles and netting jutting up from the water and, inside the nets, dozens — maybe even *hundreds* — of baby terrafins!

An outrigger floats inside the netted area, and the woman in it gently pats the water with her hand. Moments later, the black-and-white wings of small terrafins splash on the surface, and the woman begins to toss out handfuls of what appears to be ground-up scurry. Other men and women stand waist-deep in the shallows while dozens of juvenile terrafins swim around them. Ishmael watches, mystified, while the men and women work in teams, one lifting a small, docile terrafin out of the water while the other gently massages the base of its tail over a vial. Even from a distance, Ishmael can see the iridescent green liquid slowly drip into the vial.

Hearing splashing, Ishmael turns to see Fayaway paddling their outrigger toward him, an alarmed grimace on her face. He climbs aboard and she gives him a grave look. "Ye shan't have seen that. If anyone finds out . . ." She shakes her head unhappily.

Though eager to ask her about what he's just seen, Ishmael merely assures her, "If it's a secret, I can keep it."

They paddle back to shore in silence.

· 42 ·

BLACK RANGE, EARTH

Clinging to the smokestack rungs, the boys watched the three scrap poachers slowly toil to free one of the old pipes from the ground. It was taking a while, and the poachers frequently paused to rest and sip from flasks. Ishmael knew that it wouldn't be long before Petra began to wonder where he and Archie were. In the meantime, it was getting harder to stay motionless on the rungs. Ishmael's hands grew numb, his shoulders ached, and his back felt stiff.

Ishmael feared his foster brother would accidentally bang a rung with one of his leg braces while shifting position, but that didn't happen. Instead, they were discovered by dumb luck: One of the poachers happened to look up.

"Hey, look!" He pointed, and the others saw them. The sky had grown lighter by now, and Ishmael could see that the poachers had scruffy beards and long, unkempt hair and wore tattered clothes.

"What're ya doin' up there?" one of them called in a jocular tone.

Neither boy answered.

Below, the three men huddled, speaking quietly. Then one called up, "You can come down. We won't hurt ya."

Ishmael and Archie remained silent.

While the men huddled again, Ishmael hoped that as the day grew lighter and visibility improved, he and his foster brother might be spotted by someone heading to work at the plant.

The three men must've been thinking the same thing.

Because they began throwing rocks.

43

When Fayaway and Ishmael return to the village, the mood is somber, and there's no music in the air. At first Ishmael wonders if word has gotten back that he's seen the terrafins, but then he and Fayaway encounter a teary-eyed Billy, who tells them that Mikal has suffered a bad fall.

"W-we were up in trees near each other." Billy sniffs and wipes his eyes. "Then something hit the ground with a th-thump that was too loud for a t-treestone. I looked down, and th-there he was." He points at a knot of men and women moving toward the healing hut. Ishmael catches a glimpse of the old man in their arms.

"Is he . . . ?" Ishmael begins.

"S-still alive, but j-just barely."

As word of the accident spreads, the islanders abandon their chores to sit in circles and tell stories about Mikal that are more often accompanied by laughter than sobs. The time they found him hanging upside down in a tree, his britches caught on a limb, unable to free himself. The time he went out to spear scurry in a small dugout and was so successful that there was no room in the dugout for him when it was time to paddle back to the village. The crab races he would conduct for the entertainment of the children.

Later, there is more music than usual in the air. Islanders wearing necklaces and garlands of sweet-smelling, flimsy petals — which Thistle calls "flowers" — play wooden flutes and stringed instruments. Gabriel and a few others sit with Mikal's family and speak quietly.

At a table nearby, Queequeg leans toward Fayaway and whispers, "What are they talking about?"

"'Tis time t'decide," she whispers back.

"Decide what?" Gwen asks.

"Shall Mikal cease."

The table goes quiet. Ishmael isn't sure which is more shocking — the idea that they are deciding the old man's fate, or the casual way in which Fayaway speaks of it.

"Shouldn't Mikal have a say?"

"'Tis not for him t'decide."

"But it's *his* life," Gwen says.

"'Twill happen t'all of us someday. 'Tis the path. The old make way for the young."

"Can't decide where 'tis best t'go," Thistle muses. "Perhaps t'be like Grandpa and spread in the sea."

"But then ye shan't be here among us," Fayaway says.

"Be the whole sea. Here and everywhere."

Gwen gently pats Thistle's hand. "Hopefully you won't have to worry about that for a long time."

Ishmael, Queequeg, and Billy trade a look. This is a side of Gwen they've not seen before.

Meanwhile, Thistle says, "Orson ceased last year and 'twas only a year older than me. 'Twas playing under a tree and a big branch fell."

"Well, hopefully you'll be luckier than him," Gwen says.

Fayaway gives Gwen a curious look. "Luckier?"

"You know, that something bad like that won't happen to you," Gwen explains.

Thistle and Fayaway both display uncomprehending expressions.

"What happened t'Orson was sad," Fayaway says, "but not bad. T'cease 'tis not bad; 'tis not good. 'Tis just what happens. "

"Just another way of looking at it, I guess," Queequeg concludes.

Ishmael feels the itch of memory. The night before they left for their missions, didn't Archie say nearly the same thing?

· 44 ·

BLACK RANGE, EARTH

Ishmael and Archie were stuck, unable to climb out of rock-throwing range because of the loose rung above them. Fortunately, the poachers had poor aim, and the few rocks that hit the boys were slowed by gravity. The worst were the stones that flew too high, striking the smokestack above, then falling and clunking them on their heads.

Then the rocks stopped. Ishmael looked down and saw why: One of the poachers had started to climb.

Suddenly, the only thing racing faster than Ishmael's thoughts was his heart. He and Archie were completely defenseless. What would happen when the poacher reached them?

Riiipp! From above came the unmistakable sound of Syncro tearing. Archie had hooked his arm through a rung and was undoing one of his braces.

He handed it down to his foster brother.

Ishmael grabbed it and lowered himself a few rungs, then waited. When the climber got close enough, he'd club him.

"Stop!"

On the ground below, Petra, Joachim, and several others were running toward the smokestack. Joachim and another man were carrying guns. The two poachers on the ground instantly ran off with Archie's crutches, leaving their comrade on the smokestack to fend for himself.

Ishmael, Archie, and the last poacher began to climb down. "I didn't mean no harm," the poacher yelled to the small crowd below. "I was only tryin' to help them down."

"Is that why you and your friends threw rocks at us?" Archie asked from above.

The poacher dropped from the lowest rung and faced the group. "They're just kids. Don't believe them."

"They're *my* kids and I *do* believe them," Petra growled back furiously. "And your friends stole his crutches."

"Get going." Joachim waved his gun. "If we ever catch you around here again, you won't get off with just a warning."

Without another word, the poacher took off, soon disappearing in the gray haze.

Joachim and Petra thanked their friends and then took Ishmael and Archie home.

It would be a month before the boys were allowed outside again. And much longer before Petra or Joachim would let them out of their sight. But the boys had learned a lesson: not to put themselves in a dangerous situation without an escape route. Ishmael, though, would never pass a tall smokestack again without a yearning to climb up and see if the faint bluish-green dot in the distance was still there.

45

"Anyone else noticed that there are no chairs here?" Queequeg asks. "Only benches. And they never say 'I.' It's always 'we.' As though the whole idea is to always be part of the group."

Fayaway and Thistle have gone off somewhere. The crew of Chase Boat Four sit on mats in the shade. Despite the somber occasion, Ishmael feels a sense of peace and well-being like nothing he has ever felt on Earth or on the *Pequod.*

"They tr-truly care about one another instead of j-just th-thinking about enriching themselves," Billy says. "It's about as f-far from Earth as you can get."

Gwen makes a face. "Sorry, Billy, but I still intend to enrich myself. And if you're well enough to climb trees, why aren't we headed back to the *Pequod*?"

"It could be hundreds of miles away," Ishmael says.

"Gabriel said the *Pequod* passes by here fairly often," Queequeg adds.

"Who knows what 'often' means to them," argues Gwen. "Could be every ten years, for all we know. You really want to sit around here and wait?" She smirks at Ishmael. "Well, *you* probably do."

"What're you talking about?" Queequeg asks.

"You don't think Ish would rather stay here with his girlfriend than get back to the ship?" Gwen asks.

"She's not my girlfriend," Ishmael protests.

Gwen lifts her eyebrows in disbelief. "You're practically joined at the hip."

"Why? Because she taught me to swim and hunt scurry?" he asks. "She'd teach you, too, if you asked."

"I don't need to learn that," Gwen counters. "I need to return to the *Pequod* and do what I came here to do: make money."

She's right. As pleasant as it is living on this island, they need to get back to their ship. Ishmael doesn't even know if Charity was able to persuade Starbuck to grant Gwen and him the bait money for helping to capture the terrafin the day they rescued Daggoo.

"So what do you suggest?" Queequeg asks Gwen. "That we stock up on food and water, set out in the chase boat, and just hope we run into the *Pequod*?"

"If our supplies get low, we can always come back here and get more," Gwen says.

It's a long shot, but Ishmael agrees. "Maybe we'll get lucky."

"Right," Gwen concludes. "So tomorrow we leave."

When Ishmael glances at Billy, he looks away.

The decision has been made: Mikal will cease. Later that evening, when it's dark, a pyre of branches, sticks, and dried leaves burns at the lagoon's edge, orange and yellow flames leaping while red sparks fly overhead to mix with the stars and then fade. Fayaway sits beside Ishmael, her face flushed with the apricot light, and her long dark hair glowing. Night-blooming flowers release their perfumed scents, and again music plays. Ishmael knows without asking that the islanders will stay as long as the fire burns, watching over Mikal while he rejoins the elements from which they all sprang, to become part of something new in the great cycle of life, death, and renewal that pervades every corner of the universe.

The next day, Ishmael and Queequeg are crouched over a net on the beach, picking out scurry. A shadow falls over them. It's Fayaway.

"What art ye doing?" she asks.

When Ishmael tells her that they are preparing provisions for their search for the *Pequod,* her face falls, and she hurries away.

"I get the feeling she's not real happy about that," Queequeg says.

Ishmael watches Fayaway go, wondering if he should follow. But what could he say or do?

A few minutes later, Diana and Gabriel approach across the sand, both looking agitated. Ishmael and Queequeg rise to greet them.

"'Tis true ye've seen our terrafins?" Diana's bearing is severe.

"Your terrafins?" Queequeg repeats with a scowl.

"I came upon them by accident," Ishmael says. "Fayaway told me to keep them a secret, so I did."

Diana turns to Gabriel. "'Tis a lie. 'Tis why they art in such a hurry t'get back t'their ship."

"No, it's because Billy's better," Ishmael says.

Diana snorts derisively. "'Twill tell them of the terrafins and 'twill come here and take it all."

"Take all of what?" Queequeg asks, bewildered. "What are you talking about?"

"They can't be allowed t'go, *ever*!" Diana vehemently tells Gabriel.

Gabriel gives Ishmael a grave look, but before he can speak, a voice down the beach suddenly screams, "Thistle!" Ishmael is almost certain it was Fayaway who cried out.

Islanders are pointing at the sky, where a huge winged beast is flapping away, the tiny figure of a struggling girl clenched in its talons.

46

Gabriel and Diana dash toward the outriggers. Gwen comes running up. "Did you see it? It took Thistle!"

"The chase boat!" Ishmael yells to his crew. By now some of the islanders are in outriggers, paddling madly, but the winged beast is already growing smaller in the sky. The chase boat is the only vessel that stands a chance of keeping up with the giant flyer.

Billy joins them as they shove the boat into the water and climb aboard. Ishmael tries the engine. The RTG starts, then quits.

"Not this again!" Gwen groans.

Ishmael restarts the engine, and this time it keeps going and they accelerate past the outriggers and out of the lagoon. As they splash across the ocean, they watch the creature swing west, Thistle a tiny dark spot in its claws.

"For Earth's sake, don't drop her!" Gwen cries into the wind.

Thankfully, the beast is flying at an unhurried pace, certainly unaware that it's being followed. Ishmael trails at a safe distance.

Behind them, the island grows smaller and more distant. Queequeg shoots Ishmael a concerned glance. Ishmael suspects that his friend is wondering how far they'll go in this chase, and what they'll do when — or if — it eventually ends. Gwen and Billy, however, never look back; their eyes stay fixed on the giant flyer and its prey.

A strip of green appears on the horizon and slowly grows, rising and broadening into a jagged coastline of cliffs with tall emerald mountains in the background. The beast flies toward the shore. If this is another island, it's much bigger than the one they just left.

"What now?" Queequeg asks.

Ishmael doesn't know. Unless the chase boat grows wings, they won't be able to follow the creature inland.

"There!" Gwen points at a broad, murky river emptying into the ocean from between the cliffs.

"Think we can go up it?" Billy asks.

"We'll find out." Ishmael steers toward the mouth of the river, where the sea goes from sparkling blue to muddy brown. The riverbanks are jammed with thick green trees dotted with long-necked white flyers that burst into the sky when the chase boat nears. The air begins to feel warm and moist.

Queequeg points off the starboard side, where large river creatures with bumpy green snouts, bulging eyes, and long, pointed teeth watch them for a moment before slowly receding into the turbid depths. Billy and Gwen take their eyes off the flying creature long enough to glance worriedly at the beasts, and then look up again.

As they travel up the river, the banks begin to narrow, the tree canopy sometimes blocking their view of the huge flyer and Thistle. Soon the roar of rushing white water is in their ears. The river squeezes into a torrent. Ishmael has to gun the RTG to keep the boat headed upstream while he steers around the massive rocks that jut up from the riverbed. The crew hold tight as the chase boat struggles against the surging current.

Finally, the river grows too narrow and rocky, and the deluge too strong. Ishmael has no choice but to nose into the tree-lined bank, where the crew jump out and pull the boat partway out of the water.

They stand on the rocky shore, trees and thick green undergrowth on one side, the turbulent river on the other. Clouds of tiny insects swarm overhead, and feathery flyers dart from branch to branch. Pointing at a tall, limbless tree, Ishmael shouts to Billy over the river's roar, "Can you climb that? Maybe you can see where it went."

Like a born islander, Billy scampers up the tree. Near the top he points at a nearby peak. "I th-think it landed up there!" He scrambles back down. "We'll need some l-line from the boat."

Moments later, with coils of red rope over their shoulders, the crew start through the jungle. Billy has taken the lead, hacking with his knife through the thick underbrush. There are broad silken webs and nasty-looking eight-legged vermin to avoid, while flyers screech in the trees and delicate metallic-blue creatures flutter and dance in the air around them.

Their path begins to slant uphill, and they have to find handholds among the tree branches and vines to pull themselves along. From the undergrowth come the scratching and slithering of unseen creatures fleeing through the thick brush. Now and then the limbs of trees rustle and clatter when some larger beast is startled into a quick departure. Recalling the stories about the dangers of the mainland, Ishmael, Gwen, and Queequeg cast jittery glances at one another, but Billy forges ahead with single-minded determination.

The slope becomes steeper and the ground rockier. The air grows cooler and drier. There's less foliage up here, and between the last remaining trees they can see the rocky crown of the peak.

Billy stops to catch his breath, then presses a finger to his lips. "Listen."

Sounds of whimpering are coming from somewhere above.

"Thistle?" he calls.

The whimpering stops. Several dozen feet above them, Thistle's face pokes out from a rocky ledge. Her cheeks are smudged with dirt and tears. Her eyes widen when she sees the chase-boat crew.

"Is the flyer up there?" Billy calls.

"'Twent away."

"Can you climb down?"

"Art scared."

"It's okay. We'll come get you." Billy turns to the others, who hold on to roots and rocky edges to keep from slipping down the steep grade. "Who's coming with me?" he asks while tying one end of the red rope around his waist. He plays out a couple of dozen yards and then secures the other end around the base of a tree. Ishmael volunteers and ties a line around his own waist.

"You guys sure about this?" Gwen asks uncertainly. From where they stand to the crown of the peak is about forty feet of steep bare rock. A fall could spell death.

Billy nods determinedly. Ishmael wishes he shared his crewmate's confidence.

"We'll keep a lookout for the flyer," Gwen says.

"Good luck, friends," Queequeg adds somberly.

Billy and Ishmael begin to climb. It's slow, painstaking toil, and they're not even halfway to the peak when there's a sudden loud flapping of wings. Gwen shouts a warning and Thistle screams from above. Billy and Ishmael look up just in time to see huge, outstretched claws diving toward them.

Crash! The creature slams into the rocks where, at the very last instant, Billy and Ishmael have squeezed into tight crevices. The flyer gives a shrill cry and flaps back into the air, kicking up dust as it prepares for another strike.

Heart thudding in his ears, Ishmael crams himself deeper into the shadows and braces himself.

But the second strike doesn't come. Instead, the creature flaps higher. Thistle screams again.

Everything goes still. In his shadowy crevice, Ishmael presses a cheek against cool rock and waits for his heart to slow down.

"You guys okay?" Queequeg calls from below.

"Yeah," Billy calls back, hidden in a cranny. "Thistle? You okay?"

Silence. There's no way to know. Ishmael leans out from between the rocks to try to see.

Snap! A beak filled with rows of needle-sharp teeth spears down, missing him by inches. Ishmael jerks back into the rocks, his pulse galloping. Had he been a second slower, the creature would have had his head.

"Billy?" he whispers. "Any ideas?"

"Not yet" comes the reply.

Across the river valley, the cliffs are beginning to glow a golden hue; the sun will be setting soon. Once it's dark, it will be almost impossible to climb back down from this rocky peak. And what are the chances that Thistle will still be there in the morning? They don't even know if she's okay now.

A loud rustle of leaves comes from the canopy below when some unseen creature leaps from one branch to another. On the sun-bathed peak across the river, Ishmael catches a quick movement of shadow when the huge flyer above them turns in the direction of the sound.

He has an idea, and calls down to Queequeg and Gwen: "Climb up a tree, but stay out of sight."

A few minutes later, when Queequeg and Gwen are in position, Ishmael tells them to rattle some branches. They do so, and once again, the shadow on the sun-bathed peak turns in the direction of the sound.

"See that?" Ishmael whispers to Billy.

"Yeah."

"Get ready to climb fast."

"Gotcha."

Ishmael whistles, and Queequeg and Gwen shake the branches again.

While the flyer is distracted, Billy and Ishmael slip out of their hiding places and scramble up to higher crevices. A minute later, they do it again. Soon, they've reached a spot just below the ledge.

Ishmael lets out a long, low whistle, the signal for Gwen and Queequeg to start thrashing branches like crazy.

"Now!" Ishmael whispers to Billy, and they both pull themselves onto the ledge.

Before them is a large, rocky nest. Ishmael's spirits are buoyed when he sees Thistle on her hands and knees beside one of the creature's huge clawed feet. Thistle's mouth falls open, and Ishmael quickly presses a finger to his lips. Now he sees a new problem: The enormous flyer is standing on her long black hair to keep her from escaping.

Gwen and Queequeg are still rattling branches, but it's hard to know how long they can keep the flyer distracted. Ishmael inches deeper into the nest, careful not to make a sound. Soon he's close enough to feel the warmth of the creature's body over him. At last, he's on his hands and knees beside Thistle, sliding his knife from its sheath and gesturing to her hair. But Ishmael quickly discovers that it is not easy to cut hair with a knife. Locks slide and pull away. He must regather them again and again, and it is impossible to cut without pulling painfully against Thistle's scalp.

As soon as he's able to free her, Thistle immediately skitters away, determined to crawl over the ledge and clamber down by herself. When Ishmael tries to grab and stop her, the knife clatters out of his hand.

Above them, the flyer starts, swinging its long neck around until its eye — the size of a large treestone — is staring unblinking at the two humans crouched at its feet. Ishmael can feel its breath on his face.

Snap! The huge bill darts down, but Ishmael nimbly rolls out of reach.

Thistle cries out when the flyer closes one claw around her and starts to flap its wings. Quickly Ishmael unties the rope from his waist and loops it around the creature's free leg.

A cloud of dirt and dust rises as the flyer begins to take flight.

But an instant later, the line from its leg to the tree below goes taut.

The flyer lets out a bellowing caw and crashes back into the nest.

The last thing Ishmael hears is Thistle scream.

Then everything goes black.

47

Hands are dragging him across rough, jagged rocks. Close by, the flyer shrieks and convulses as it snaps at the rope around its leg. Ishmael is pulled over the ledge, then bumped down through the rocks to the loose stones and gravel, where he slides into the underbrush and thuds into the trunk of a tree.

Dazed, the edges of his vision going dark, he lies on the ground, barely aware of the commotion on the ledge above. Then Queequeg's blurred face comes into view, blood running from a deep gash on his chin. "Come on, beautiful." Ishmael feels hands dragging him farther down the hill. "We're not out of the woods yet."

Is he making a joke? Ishmael wonders groggily as they struggle through the underbrush. "What about . . . uh . . . ?" He can't retrieve her name.

"Thistle? Billy's got her."

"And Gwen?"

"She's okay."

As Queequeg half drags and half carries him through the thickening brush and trees, Ishmael's thoughts slowly begin to clear, despite the painful throbbing in his skull. "I think I can walk."

Queequeg helps him to his feet. The gash on his friend's chin isn't bleeding anymore, but damp blood sticks to the wound.

Ishmael tries to take a step — and starts to list like a sinking ship.

"Whoa!" Queequeg catches him and hoists him onto his shoulders. "Nice try, Twinkle Toes."

With Queequeg carrying him, the way down to the riverbank is treacherous. Queequeg teeters under branches and around tree trunks. Several times he almost loses his footing. Ishmael can hear branches snapping and rocks crunching as the others struggle to descend as well.

Soon there's another sound: the rushing of water. The air becomes warm and moist. When they reach the shore, Queequeg has Ishmael sit on a rock. The taste of iron is in Ishmael's mouth — blood.

Billy comes through the trees, carrying Thistle, her face dirty and a patch of her black hair chopped short. When Gwen arrives, Billy orders everyone into the boat. Even in his wobbly state, Ishmael finds it hard to believe that this is the same boy who cried himself to sleep in the men's berth not so long ago.

Gwen helps Ishmael into the boat, then smirks at him. "Next time you want to break rocks, try using a hammer, not your skull."

Ishmael's head continues to throb painfully. He must have really been hit hard before he blacked out. "I think I'm lucky I still *have* a skull," he mumbles.

It's nearly sunset now, and the river is deep in the shadows. Instead of starting the engine — and possibly alerting other dangerous creatures to their presence — Billy uses a long branch to pole the boat from shore, then takes the wheel and steers with the current, which catches the chase boat and takes it on a rapid, bumpy ride downstream. They dip and splash around boulders, tepid white water soaking them. Ishmael feels Gwen's hands on his shoulders, pressing him down to the floor, where he'll be less likely to tumble out.

Gradually the current slows and the ride becomes smoother. Despite the pain in his head, Ishmael slowly props himself up on his elbows, wondering why Billy hasn't powered up the RTG. It takes his eyes a moment to adjust to the deep twilight shadows, but when they do, what he sees is enough to make his heart stop: Along the riverbanks, scores of creatures have come to drink — in groups, in pairs, and sometimes alone. They vary in size from smaller than a man to much, *much* larger.

"Amazing!" whispers Gwen. "Thistle, have you ever seen these creatures before?"

Thistle shakes her head. "There art only flyers and smaller creatures where we —" She stops short and draws a sharp breath.

Up ahead, an enormous greenish-brown beast lumbers along the shore, the very ground seeming to shake with each step. The creature's head alone is the size of a boulder and it has thick legs and powerful-looking thighs, but its arms are surprisingly slight. It bends forward and tips its huge head into the river, its jaws working as it laps up water. Ishmael is astounded that anything so large walks on land.

They're all staring in silent fascination when suddenly Thistle looks skyward and screams. Out of the deep-blue evening, the huge flyer is swooping down on them with claws extended.

"Jump!" Queequeg shouts.

Billy scoops up Thistle and plunges overboard, followed by Gwen. Queequeg grabs Ishmael, and together they topple over the side a split second before the creature's claws clack shut where their heads just were. Ishmael strokes to the surface and spits out a mouthful of murky liquid. The boat floats a dozen feet away. Billy clings to the gunwale, helping a soaked and trembling Thistle to climb back in. For the moment, the flyer has banked high. Treading water, Ishmael is relieved to see Queequeg bobbing near him, then remembers that Gwen had stubbornly refused to learn to swim while they were on the island. He looks anxiously around, but before he can find her, something strange happens. Back in the boat, Billy lunges for the machine gun. Ishmael assumes he's going to fire at the flyer, but instead he swings the weapon around until Ishmael can see the dark mouth of the barrel aimed at *him and Queequeg!*

Orange and yellow flames burst from the machine gun, and the *RAT-A-TAT-TAT* is impossibly, painfully loud in Ishmael's ears. He ducks underwater. Why is Billy shooting at them?

A moment later the shooting stops. Ishmael lifts his head. Smoke drifts from the machine gun's barrel, and his soggy ears still ring with the harsh report.

"Swim! Hurry!" Billy waves frantically. But a second later he starts to aim the machine gun again.

RAT-A-TAT-TAT! The blasting weapon is deafening. At any moment Ishmael expects to feel the savage jab of a bullet. But somehow — even at such close range — Billy misses him.

What about Queequeg? Ishmael swivels around and sees his friend stroking away toward Gwen, who is splashing and gurgling in the water, struggling to keep from drowning. Just a few feet from her are several of the huge aquatic beasts they saw earlier, their bumpy nostrils and eyes drawing nearer and nearer.

Now Ishmael understands: Billy hasn't been shooting at *them,* but at something very close behind them.

RAT-A-TAT-TAT!

One of the beasts erupts in spasms, kicking up sprays of reddish foam. But the others keep coming. By now, Queequeg has reached Gwen, who's latched on so tightly to him that they're both struggling not to drown. Ishmael splashes toward them.

RAT-A-TAT-TAT!

Close by, another river beast starts to writhe.

At last Ishmael gets to his friends, and together he and Queequeg pull Gwen toward the boat.

RAT-A-TAT-TAT! Billy fires one more volley and then reaches over the side to help them climb aboard.

Moments later, they lie drenched and panting in the bottom of the chase boat. Billy, taking the controls again, presses the throttle forward and powers out toward the ocean.

The night sky is a star-speckled dome. When the chase boat passes through the gap in the reef, several outriggers with torches are waiting to guide them to shore. Gabriel is in one, and when he sees his daughter, he joyfully holds his arms out. Billy steers the chase boat close enough for Thistle to climb into her father's arms. In the light of the torches, tracks of thankful tears glisten on his cheeks.

Despite the late hour, a great celebration ensues, during which Gabriel embraces and thanks each member of the chase-boat crew for saving his daughter's life. Seeing the lump on Ishmael's skull and hearing that his head still throbs painfully, Gabriel takes him to the healing hut and has him lie on a mat. In the fluttering light, Ishmael leans on an elbow and watches the islander sort through the vials filled with various shades of green liquid.

"What's the difference?" Ishmael asks.

"'Tis much diluted." Gabriel holds up the vial with the palest solution. "For minor injuries and mild pain."

"So that's not what you put on the darts you shot us with when we first arrived?" Ishmael guesses.

Gabriel shakes his head. "'Twas stronger. Mixed with herbs t'cause sleep."

"What about that?" Ishmael points at the vial with the densest-green fluid.

“’Tis nearly pure nectar waiting t’be diluted. T’use in that form ’tis forbidden.”

“Why?”

“’Tis too strong.” Gabriel comes toward him with a vial of the weakest solution. “Can change a man in unnatural ways. Lie back.”

Gabriel kneels over him, dipping a slim stick into the vial and drawing out a drop of the pale-green liquid. With his free hand, he gently holds Ishmael’s eyelids open and taps the drop in. Ishmael blinks reflexively, and the pain in his head immediately vanishes.

He sighs wondrously.

“Come.” Gabriel offers his hand. “Let us celebrate.”

Ishmael allows himself to be helped up. The pain is gone, as well as the hazy, addled sensations that accompanied it. His thoughts are not only clearer but feel deep and astute. His senses seem sharper, and he is embraced by an aura of profound well-being.

As he and Gabriel leave the hut, he asks, “If such a small amount is so powerful, why do you farm so many terrafins?”

“Nectar spoils quickly, and we can only harvest it from very young terrafins with little nectar t’give.” Gabriel holds his hands about eighteen inches apart. “When they art this size, wild instincts take over and they go t’the ocean.”

They continue on in silence, the sounds of revelry growing louder. But Gabriel stops in the shadows a few yards before the celebration.

“If ye art still determined t’leave, we shan’t stop ye.” Gabriel searches the crowd, and his gaze comes to rest on Diana. “After what ye’ve done for us, we’ll pray we can trust ye t’keep our secret. But never forget, ye art going with our fate in ye hands.”

Fayaway’s father extends a large, work-roughened hand. Ishmael grasps it firmly. “You have my word.”

They join the jubilant crowd. The islanders have draped the

chase-boat crew with flower-and-shell necklaces. They are gathered around the fire while Billy tells them of the rescue: "Ishmael knew we had to distract the flyer. Gwen and Queequeg shook the tree branches to get its attention, and then Ishmael and I started climbing . . ."

As Ishmael listens, he realizes that Billy isn't stuttering. He glances at Gwen, who silently mouths, *"I know,"* to show that she, too, has noticed. Ishmael would like to wait until Billy finishes the story and then take him aside and ask if he's aware of what's happened, but he's suddenly so tired he can barely keep his eyes open. Is it the residue of the day's excitement? A side effect of the nectar? He crawls into a hammock and is instantly asleep.

48

"Ishmael?"

He opens his eyes. Fayaway is leaning over him, her eyebrows dipping in concern, her dark hair hanging down like a curtain. "Who art Grace?"

Ishmael feels his drumming heartbeat begin to slow. He's been dreaming that he's in the bow of the *Pequod* while it pursues a trawler. Beside him Tashtego is aiming the big harpoon cannon at the trawler, preparing to fire.

"Ye yelled her name."

"She's someone I'm supposed to know but don't," Ishmael tries to explain.

Fayaway gives him an uncertain look but lets it pass. "Come." She takes his hands and helps him sit up in the hammock. Stippled sunlight slants through the leaves overhead, and the air is heavy with morning dew. The village is still except for a few feathered flyers that chirp in the trees.

"Can't I sleep a little longer?" Ishmael yawns groggily.

"'Tis something that shan't wait." Fayaway slowly pulls him to his feet. When they start down the walkway, Ishmael becomes aware of a raw stinging sensation in his earlobes. Reaching up, he feels tiny barbed spines.

"When did this happen?" he asks.

"Last night," Fayaway says sheepishly. "Spines so small art rare and an honor. T'show our thanks."

At the end of the walkway, they pull on high boots and start along one of the brush-lined paths going uphill behind the village. The jungle is filled with floral scents and every conceivable shade of green. Under the tree canopy, delicate yellow-and-black creatures flutter, and flyers sing melodies from the branches. Stepping out of the trees and into the bright morning sunlight, Ishmael must shut his eyes for a moment. The insides of his eyelids are bands of soft colors — no doubt another side effect of the nectar — and he pauses to ponder their beauty until Fayaway again tugs at his hand.

"'Twas wrong to tell Diana that ye knew of our terrafins." Fayaway's eyes are downcast with shame.

He squeezes her hand. "It's okay."

They reach a clearing, where Fayaway points out at the vast blue ocean. Far on the horizon a ship moves slowly. Ishmael feels his breath catch; while it is too far away to see clearly, there is no mistaking the thick brown stripes of rust. It's the *Pequod.*

Fayaway tightens her grip on his hand. "Ye art all welcome t'stay here."

If a heart could wince, Ishmael's would. He knows it cannot be easy for Fayaway to show him the ship. And he is tempted by her offer to stay. The ways of the islanders remind him of the life he once had with Archie and his foster parents — filled with love and caring.

"I can't," he says.

Fayaway's face falls. This island is all she's ever known. It must seem like madness to her that he'd want to go back to that floating hunk of rust.

"I have people I have to help. And a foster brother somewhere on this planet who I need to find." A thought occurs to him. "Your father said ships sometimes pass near here. Have you ever heard of one called the *Jeroboam*?"

Fayaway pauses to think, then shakes her head. She looks up into his eyes, and once again her grip on his hand tightens. "Once ye've found him, ye could bring him here."

Ishmael can't imagine how that would work. How could Archie navigate the ladders and walkways of the village? How could Ishmael ever hope to keep him safe in a place where giant flyers snatch people from the beach?

Fayaway must see the doubt in his eyes. Her grip loosens, and her fingers slip out of his. She turns back down the path.

"Wait," Ishmael says.

She stops, her face at once filled with hope.

"Thank you for showing me the ship," he says. "I know you didn't have to."

Her gaze slants away and she blinks hard. Her shoulders stoop and she hurries off.

Later, while the crew prepares to depart, Billy keeps gazing at the islanders who've gathered on the beach to say good-bye. Queequeg, Gwen — her long red hair braided by Thistle — and Ishmael trade looks until a silent consensus is reached. Ishmael puts a hand on Billy's lean shoulder. "Stay."

Billy looks shocked by the suggestion. "But —"

"What do you have waiting for you back on the *Pequod*? Back on Earth?"

Billy hesitates. "What will you tell Starbuck?"

"We'll make up something . . . something that will make your father proud."

Billy gazes across the lagoon, past the waves breaking on the reef, and out at the ocean. "You know, he sent me here hoping I'd become the son he always wanted me to be. Instead, I became the person *I* always wanted me to be. If that's not enough to make him proud . . ."

Ishmael squeezes his shoulder. "After how you helped save Thistle? Believe me, he'd be proud. And we're proud of you."

Billy smiles wanly. "I'm going to miss you, Ish."

Near them, Gwen and Queequeg have begun saying their good-byes to the islanders. Thistle, with a lock of Gwen's bright-red hair woven into the spot where Ishmael chopped hers off, hugs Gwen tearfully while Queequeg clasps the hands of the men and women with whom he netted scurry. They wade out to the chase boat.

Ishmael lingers on the beach with Fayaway, feeling a mixture of emotion and awkwardness, uncertain what to say, until Gabriel approaches and draws both of them into his arms. For a moment they press their foreheads together the way Ishmael used to do with Archie. "Wherever ye go, goodness 'twill go with ye, Ishmael. And should that lead ye back to us, ye shall always be welcomed."

Ishmael thanks him, embraces Fayaway one last time, then plods through the shallows out to the chase boat. Moments later, he pushes the start button. The RTG sputters and fails. He tries again with the same result.

"How embarrassing is this," Queequeg whispers, glancing back at the crowd of islanders on the beach. "They agree to let us go and we can't?"

Ishmael tries again. This time the engine starts. As they motor away from the island toward the gap in the reef, they wave their final farewells. Fayaway and Billy wade out into the water. Theirs are the last faces Ishmael sees.

* * *

Out beyond the reef, Ishmael turns Chase Boat Four to the west, so that they run parallel to the *Pequod* rather than toward it. Queequeg gives him a quizzical look. "Not going straight back to the ship?"

"Not right away."

"So they won't know where we're coming from?" Queequeg guesses.

"Exactly."

"And what are we supposed to do until you decide it's time?" Gwen asks.

"Get our story straight," Ishmael replies.

Just after sunset, Ishmael gets on the two-way.

"Who is this?" the *Pequod*'s radio operator asks. When Ishmael answers, he hears excited chatter on the other end of the connection. The operator comes back. "No kidding! We thought you were down in Davy Jones's locker. Hold on."

Ishmael waits. The next voice he hears is Starbuck's. "Ishmael?"

"Yes, sir."

"What's the story?"

"We've been on land, sir."

Silence. Then: "Is anyone injured? Showing any signs of illness?"

"No, sir. We're all fine. Uh, except for Billy, that is. He's . . . he's not with us. We'll be alongside in about fifteen minutes."

"Negative," Starbuck orders. "You are not to approach the ship until told to. Come no closer than two hundred yards and then wait. We'll send a boat."

"But, sir, there's no —"

"That's an order," Starbuck snaps. "You haven't forgotten what orders are, have you?"

"No, sir."

Ishmael keeps the chase boat on a course parallel to the *Pequod*.

"Looks different." Queequeg points at the ship's broad hull.

"Rustier," says Gwen. Even in the fading evening light it's apparent that the streaks of reddish brown on the hull have spread and multiplied.

A drone buzzes overhead and circles, no doubt inspecting the crew with infrared biodetection. Next, a tender is lowered from the *Pequod* and starts toward them. The crew of Chase Boat Four soon find themselves staring at sailors wearing orange biohazard suits, complete with gloves, helmets, and breathing masks.

Queequeg rolls his eyes skyward. "They can't be serious."

49

The crew must strip down and don white jumpsuits, gloves, and breathing masks before they're allowed on the tender, while a sailor in biohazard gear clambers onto the chase boat and sprays it with disinfectant from a tank on his back. The chase-boat crew exchange stumped glances. Is there some horrible disease on land that they haven't been told about? If there is, why do the islanders seem so healthy?

Once aboard the *Pequod*, the crew are quarantined in the sick bay overnight. In the morning, Dr. Bunger and Starbuck enter. Thankfully, neither wears a biohazard suit.

The ship's surgeon hovers over them, the ripe smell of benzo enveloping him like a cloud. With unsteady hands, he places sensors on Gwen's and Ishmael's registries to check vital signs, and asks questions about insect bites and bowel movements.

Starbuck is curious about Gwen's long braids and the way her sleeveless shirt is knotted across her stomach. He notes the thin beard that runs along Queequeg's jawline and the half dozen colorful beads that have been woven into his hair. Ishmael himself has the beginnings of a mustache, and the scant stubble on his chin is the longest it's ever been.

The first mate also scrutinizes the tiny terrafin skivers in their ears. "What's the story with these?" he asks.

"Found them on the beach, sir. Not much to do for the past month."

"And Billy?"

Ishmael releases a sigh. "We're not sure, sir." He begins a rehearsed story of how they took turns standing guard at night, and one morning woke to find the bloody evidence of a struggle but no sign of their crewmate. "We tried to search for him, but . . . You know how dangerous the mainland is, sir. We didn't dare venture too far from our camp on the beach."

"And precisely how *did* the rest of you avoid being eaten?" Starbuck asks.

"Don't really know, sir. We were lucky, I guess. We lit fires at night to keep the creatures away and hid in caves during the day when we had to. Still, I couldn't tell you why we survived when Billy didn't. But it looks like he put up a valiant fight."

Something about Starbuck's silence asserts his doubts, but Ishmael holds his gaze.

"What about food and fresh water?" the first mate asks.

"Ate a lot of scurry, sir. And luckily we came across a spring of clean water we could drink from."

By now Dr. Bunger has finished examining them. "Considering what they've been through, they appear to be in good health."

Starbuck shakes his head slowly. "A tad *too* good if you ask me."

* * *

Ishmael is eager to find out if there have been any new Z-packs from Earth, and whether Charity succeeded in getting Gwen and him their bait money, but the three crewmates are ordered to remain in the sick bay. The next time they see Starbuck, the first mate herds them up several ladderways to the A level. Every sailor they pass stares — but not with surprise that they're still alive after all this time. Instead, their looks convey wariness, and in some cases even disgust.

"What's going on?" Queequeg asks in a low voice. "Why's everyone looking at us like we're pariahs?"

They've reached the black door. Without answering Queequeg's question, Starbuck knocks.

"Who is it?" the captain rasps from inside.

"Starbuck, sir. With that stick-boat crew."

"Bring 'em in."

The captain's cabin is semicircular and lined with windows that look out over the *Pequod*'s bow to the ocean beyond. But Ishmael barely notices the view. The room is a shrine to terrafins. Everywhere he looks are holographs, screens, ancient paintings, and models of the creatures. His eyes halt on the long, tapering white shaft that he'd glimpsed once before. It must be a sculpture or maybe a carving of a massive terrafin skiver, a hundred times larger than the biggest in Fedallah's collection.

With hands clasped behind his back, Ahab stands in profile by a port window, staring out at the blue-green sea. His long, scraggly black hair hangs over the collar of his black coat, and the skin not covered by his scruffy beard is deathly pale.

Without turning to look at the crew, the captain asks, "How do you know when you're being lied to?"

Ishmael feels his stomach sink.

"Well?" the captain demands.

"When it sounds too good to be true, sir?" Ishmael ventures.

Ahab harrumphs. "Correct, sailor. So you'd like us to believe you spent more than a month on land in the midst of wild beasts, pestilence, and all manner of danger, and, except for the one you say died valiantly, you've all returned looking healthy, well fed, and unscathed?"

Ishmael can't resist risking a glance at his boatmates. Both look uneasy, but neither seems on the verge of confessing. Heartened by their courage, he stands straighter.

Ahab whirls around, his deep-set, pink-tinged eyes piercing. "Who's going to give me an *honest* answer?"

The chase-boat crew is silent. The captain steps close to Queequeg and reaches out a disfigured, scarred hand to touch the tiny skivers in his earlobes.

"Tell me how you got these, sailor," he growls.

"We found them on the beach, sir." Queequeg repeats the answer Ishmael gave to Starbuck earlier.

Ahab snorts. "Lying there in the sand, I suppose?" He turns to Ishmael. "And I suppose you also want me to believe that malarkey about how you caught enough scurry to sustain you for all those weeks? And found a miraculous supply of fresh water to drink?"

Ishmael swallows. Their rehearsed story suddenly seems ridiculous. "I know it sounds unlikely, sir —"

"Unlikely?" The captain cuts him off. "Try *impossible,* sailor."

Ishmael feels a trickle of sweat run down his back. "It's true, sir —"

"Like a hump with wings, it is!" The captain's lip curls in disgust. He limps so close that Ishmael can practically feel the heat radiating from the old man's body. "I've heard tales of such atrocities, but never — *never* — did I expect it of my own men!"

Ishmael is about to ask the captain what he means when the realization strikes. No wonder every sailor they've seen has looked at them like they were bilge scum! He almost starts to argue, but at the last moment manages to keep his mouth shut. Ahab limps back to the windows and once again surveys the blue horizon. Gwen and Queequeg shoot Ishmael puzzled looks, but he shakes his head.

"Before your recent disappearance, I'd been hearing good things about this crew," the captain says. "That Queequeg has a natural talent with the harpoon, and Gwendolyn possesses the kind of quick thinking and daring that are key to a successful stick boat. As for you, young Ishmael, rarely have I heard my first mate speak so highly of a seasoned sailor — let alone a green-gilled nipper."

Ishmael braces for the blow that he's sure is coming.

"But your departed friend — Billy, was it?" Ahab goes on. "What I'd heard about him wasn't so encouraging. . . . So as much as I'd love to keel-haul the lot of you for this atrocity, I'd be a fool to do away with such a promising crew. Especially when we're so near the goal."

"Atrocity?" Gwen repeats.

Ahab levels his steely gaze at her. "Don't pretend you don't know, missy. I'm talking about cannibalism."

50

Gwen gasps.

"C-cannibalism?" Queequeg stammers, nearly struck dumb. "We . . . Is that . . . ? Sir, are you serious? Never! Not in a million —"

"It's okay." Ishmael places a firm hand on his friend's arm and gives Gwen a cautionary look. "They were bound to find out sooner or later." He turns to the captain. "Sir, if I could ask one favor? Billy was mortally injured in a fall. He knew he wasn't going to make it. The only thing that brought him comfort at the end was our promise that we'd tell everyone he'd died a hero, to make his father proud. I mean, what's the harm, sir?"

Ahab taps a knuckle against the window frame. "Few men in this world get to make their fathers proud," he mutters. Outside, two dark-headed flyers with black wings and white breasts appear to float beside the ship while they glide on the breeze. Finally, the captain says to Queequeg, "Tell me, sailor, how much money did you imagine you'd have at the end of your year?"

Queequeg bows his head. "Don't really know, sir."

"Let's take a guess. Ten thousand? Fifteen?" Ahab turns to Ishmael. "And you. Starbuck tells me you've already made ten thousand—nine once you factor in the repairs to your stick boat."

Ψ10,000!? Ishmael shoots Starbuck a questioning look.

Starbuck juts an elbow toward Gwen. "It's her you should be thanking."

Ishmael gawps at Gwen. "You . . . gave me your half?"

"It's a *loan,*" Gwen says with emphasis.

"I . . . are you *sure*?" Ishmael stammers. "I mean, it's incredible . . . that you'd do that. I don't know how to thank you." And he'll have to make sure he thanks Charity, too, for persuading Starbuck to give them any money at all.

"All right, enough of this maudlin drivel," the captain snaps. "Normally in a case like this, you'd be stripped of your share of the pot and confined to the brig for the rest of the voyage. But instead, picture going back with forty or even *fifty* thousand! Enough not only for you to live a life of luxury but for your children and their children to enjoy comfortable lives, too."

The chase-boat crew stand in bewildered silence. What he's talking about sounds impossible.

"Well?" Ahab awaits the answer.

"It . . . it sounds amazing, sir," Ishmael acknowledges. "But even if such a thing were possible, sir . . . I hear things on Earth aren't so good."

Ahab waves the suggestion away with a gnarled hand. "Baseless fear-mongering! Man's an exceptionally adaptable species, sailor. He's been on Earth for more than two hundred thousand years and he's not finished now."

Ishmael knows the captain is lying. A few months ago, he stood outside these chambers and heard Ahab tell Starbuck that things back on Earth were quickly becoming unglued. But he can hardly say as much now.

"So answer my question," Ahab continues. "Imagine going back with more coin than you ever dreamed of. Wealth beyond anything you thought possible. Never having to worry about money again for as long as you live. You'd all like that, wouldn't you?"

"By capturing the white terrafin, sir?" Gwen guesses.

A wry twinkle appears in Ahab's eyes. "Precisely, sailor. I'll let this recent atrocity pass . . . in return for your pledge of undying commitment to our pursuit of the beast until its bloody carcass is on the cleaving deck. Unfortunately, some of the spineless cowards aboard this ship lack the foresight necessary for such an endeavor. They'd rather spend their time naysaying and fostering discontent. That's why I want your word, each of you, to stay the course. Do I have it?"

One by one the crew of Chase Boat Four agree.

"Very good." The captain waves his hand. "You may go."

As they leave, Ishmael notices a lockbox with a red optical thumbprint scanner — similar to the one he saw in the first mate's cabin — partially hidden on a low shelf. Starbuck stays behind in the cabin to speak to Ahab.

When the door closes, Gwen whispers, "Was that strange? *Buying* our cooperation with a pardon for our supposed crime and promises of obscene wealth? Since when does *the captain* have to do that?"

"Maybe when the rest of the crew is fit to be tied over chasing the white terrafin," Ishmael says as they start to take the ladderways back down to the main deck. "But Gwen, what Starbuck said back there about the money — "

"Don't get all mushy on me," Gwen warns. "I *said* it was a loan."

"Still, I can't thank — "

"Don't make me tell Starbuck I've changed my mind."

Ishmael makes a show of zipping his lips shut. Farther down, in the C level passageway, the squeak of bucket wheels and the smell of chemicals announce Tarnmoor's presence. The bent old man presses his ear to the wall. "I hears the footsteps a' three that ain'ts been aboard lately. That's you, Ishmael? And Queequeg and Gwendolyn?"

"Right you are, Tarnmoor."

"Aye, right I ams. But nots the fourth one. The one whats always smelled a' fear and timidity. Heared we won't be seeing much a' him no mores." Tarnmoor drops his voice to a whisper. "Word around the ship's he been et."

"Don't believe that, do you?" Ishmael says.

"Aye, I knows whats to believe and what ain't." The old man takes a deep sniff, and the furrows in his wrinkled forehead deepen. "What's that strange scent? Not the flesh a' man nor beast thats. Scurry, for sure, but somethin' strange as well."

"Treestones?" Queequeg guesses.

The old man tilts his wrinkled face up. "What's that? Treestones? Never heared a' them. What is it, then, heh? Heh?"

Queequeg describes the sweet white flesh of treestone nuts.

"I knewed it! Knewed it!" Tarnmoor exults gleefully. "Not cannibals, not this bunch. No. Treestones and scurry is what you been livin' on! Treestones and scurry!"

"You don't miss a thing, do you, Tarnmoor?" Ishmael says.

"Not much, no." The old man's manner grows somber, and the lines between his unseeing eyes deepen. "But I fears you'll regret leavin' such sweetness. Comin' back to a ship whats cursed."

"Cursed?" Gwen echoes.

"Aye. Cursed and damned so longs that monster roams free. It be the prospect a' sudden disasters, perils a' life and limb; these and death itself. I been on ships long enough to knows their moods, and this one's gone dark. Dismal and frightened she's growed since you was last aboard. Fear walks these decks with a heavy foot, it do."

"Fear?" Queequeg repeats.

"Aye, a' what looms ahead, lad. A' what looms ahead."

Stares greet the crew in the mess at dinner, and Ishmael knows it isn't just Gwen's braids and the facial hair he and Queequeg have decided to let grow. Pip approaches their table, carrying a tray, but stops a few feet away. "Sure you've got enough to eat?"

"Very funny," Gwen grumbles.

He sits. In the month since they've last seen him, he's grown slimmer, though he's still the same dull color they all were when they first arrived. He leans in and whispers. "So what really happened out there? Because I know you didn't eat Billy."

Ishmael, Gwen, and Queequeg share a cautious look and don't answer.

"You don't trust me?" Pip sounds hurt.

Ishmael drops his voice. "Billy's fine. Probably better than he's been in his whole life."

"What do you mean? Where is he?"

"On land."

"Land? By himself?"

Ishmael looks down at his plate. "That's all I can say. Sorry."

Pip scans the others and sees that he's not going to get anything more from them. During the meal, he tells them what's happened aboard the *Pequod* while they were gone. "We had a few good weeks of hunting, but then one of the drone ops spotted the white terrafin. Now it's back to the chase. The captain keeps harping on how rich everyone will be, but you can tell that the crew's skeptical. Lots of griping and groaning. Though, personally, I can't wait to get a look at the beast, you know?"

"Even after you saw what it did to that trawler?" Gwen asks.

"This ship's ten times bigger and stronger." Pip makes light of it.

"Anyway, now that you're back, there'll be four chase boats again. It's hard to envision a creature that four crews couldn't tow in if we all work together."

"Excuse me," Gwen interjects, "but did you just say 'we'?"

Pip looks surprised. "Starbuck didn't tell you?"

Ishmael and the others swap befuddled looks. Queequeg asks, "Tell us what?"

"I'm your new lineman."

51

"No Earthly way is he joining our crew," Gwen states up on deck, where she, Queequeg, and Ishmael have gone to talk before a scheduled briefing of the chase-boat crews. "I say we go to Starbuck right now and tell him."

"I'm not sure he wants to hear it," Ishmael says.

"So?" Gwen asks. "*He's* not the one whose life is at risk with a lineman who doesn't know what he's doing. If we were still chasing bashers and humps, then maybe Pip could learn on the job. But do you really want him aboard when we're going after this so-called monster?"

Queequeg, who's been gazing up at the large, luminous orb in the dark sky, nods in agreement. "Might not be a lot of room for error out there."

"I'm not saying you're wrong," Ishmael admits. "I just don't think anything we say is going to change Starbuck's mind. He knows there are more qualified sailors aboard. So I'm guessing we're stuck with Pip."

"You think it's got something to do with him being of the Gilded?" Queequeg asks.

"What?" Gwen stares at him like he's gone loony. "Give me a break."

"Easy, Gwen," Ishmael says. "I think he might be right."

"You mean, like it was *Pip* who gave the order? Or it came from those Gilded whoevers?" Gwen asks. "What about the captain? You really think Ahab would have to answer to them out here, a gazillion miles away from Earth?"

"Who knows how it works?" Queequeg says. "But if you're asking how Pip gets to be our lineman, that's the only reason I can think of."

Gwen chews on a fingernail. "Well, I don't believe it. And even if it were true, it's not the Gilded who'll get hurt by this. It's us. Seriously, Ishmael, you could at least *try* to talk to Starbuck. After all, since he speaks *so highly* of you, he might actually listen."

Ishmael agrees reluctantly. "I'll try, but don't hold your breath."

It's time to go belowdecks. They find the first mate in the passageway outside the briefing room, marking a tablet with a stylus. Queequeg and Gwen nod encouragingly at Ishmael, and then file inside.

Starbuck gives Ishmael a curious look.

"I wanted to thank you for giving me and Gwen the bait money from the terrafin," Ishmael begins.

"Thank the two women, not me."

"Yes, sir. I already spoke to Gwen, and when I see Charity—"

"Is that all, sailor?" the first mate interrupts, looking back down at his tablet.

"Well, actually there is something else. I need to have the money transferred back to Earth as soon as possible."

Starbuck raises his head and stares at him with a seriously irked expression.

"It's a matter of life and death, sir. Truly. I wouldn't ask otherwise."

The first mate sighs. "Give me the information."

Ishmael gratefully provides all the necessary details.

"All right. I'll make sure it's done. Now, I suggest you —" Starbuck heaves a deep breath. "Don't tell me there's something else."

"Well, yes, sir. I was wondering why you selected Pip to be our new lineman. That is, if you don't mind my asking, sir."

Behind the dark glasses, Starbuck's eyes are unreadable. "I do indeed mind, boy."

"Is it because he's of the Gilded?"

"What do you know of that?"

"All I know is that it was a choice you'd never have made yourself, sir," Ishmael says. "But why would the Gilded suggest it? Doesn't it hurt them, too, sir, if we don't produce as much as possible?"

Starbuck doesn't answer. He's done with Ishmael's questions. Without a word, the first mate folds his tablet and heads into the briefing room.

Ishmael follows him inside, where Queequeg, Gwen, and Pip are sitting in a row at the back. Ishmael takes the seat between his boatmates.

"Well?" Gwen whispers.

Ishmael shakes his head.

Gwen balls her fists.

Tashtego's crew file into the briefing room, followed by Fedallah's and Daggoo's. This is the first time Ishmael has seen Daggoo since the incident with the terrafin. The sailor stops, locks eyes with him, then nods slowly as if he hasn't forgotten.

But Bunta sniggers. "Is it hard goin' back to eatin' scurry and hump?"

"Shut up," Tashtego says. "They look like cannibals to you?"

"Don't know, never met any — till now." Bunta displays his steel teeth.

"Anyone know what this briefing is about?" Daggoo asks, his voice low so that Starbuck won't hear.

"I imagine he's gonna tell us again why we should be wasting our time chasing the Great Terrafin instead of putting meat in the cooler and money in the pot," Tashtego gripes.

"Waste of our blasted time," grouses Marion, one of the linemen on Fedallah's chase boat. "No one's ever got close to it."

"Ahab has," says Tashtego.

"And look what it done to him." Marion runs a hand over her short green hair. "All the money in the world ain't worth *that,* is it?"

At the front of the room Starbuck raps his knuckles against a desk to get the sailors' attention. "All right, let's get it out in the open. Who wants to go first?"

Tashtego raises his hand. "Who cares if the Great Terrafin is worth a fortune if we never capture it?"

"If we go back to hunting long-necks and humps, at least we'll end the voyage with some coin," adds Daggoo.

A chorus of agreement rises until the first mate holds a hand aloft to quiet them. "Okay, pipe down! I know you all feel that chasing the beast is a fool's errand. But the captain is prepared to make it worth your while. Here's the deal: The first crew that puts a stick in the beast gets forty thousand. Ten thousand per man — or woman."

For a moment there's stunned silence. Then the murmurs begin. Daggoo's the first to speak up: "A stick that leads to the terrafin's capture? Because that's pie in the sky."

"No, forty thousand for the first stick, period," Starbuck states. "The captain isn't stupid. He knows what you're up against."

More chatter breaks out around the room. "Ten thousand a man, for *one* stick?" Bunta says, as though waiting for Starbuck to correct him.

"Given how little's in the pot, it could be our only chance to make some decent coin on this voyage," says Marion.

Ishmael's eyes settle on Tashtego, curious to see how he is taking to the news. He's both respected enough and sensible enough that the others will listen to whatever he says. But Tashtego hooks his thumbs into his belt loops and remains silent.

"Any other questions?" Starbuck asks.

The roomful of sailors is quiet.

"All right," says the first mate. "Be prepared to launch first thing in the morning."

The chase-boat crews tread out. Ishmael's is the last, and they're passing Starbuck when Charity appears in the doorway. The pink is gone from her eyes, but she looks distressed as she addresses Starbuck: "How can you live with yourself when you know you're sending these sailors to almost certain death?"

Starbuck frowns. "I know nothing of the sort. And no one's making them do anything they don't want to do."

"No, you're just offering them the one thing they can't resist," she spits back.

The first mate gives her a stony look, then strides away. "Don't fall for this," Charity warns Ishmael and his crew, now the only ones in the briefing room. "There'll be other voyages."

But other voyages mean more years away from loved ones, something Ishmael can't imagine. On the other hand, he *can* imagine making an extra Ψ10,000 fast, paying back Gwen, and still having plenty of coin left over. Charity's right. It's the one thing none of them can resist.

52

"So what's everyone going to do now?" Pip asks out in the passageway.

"Take a long, hot shower," Queequeg replies. "That's the only thing I missed on that island."

"And I need to talk to Ishmael," Gwen says. "In private."

Pip makes a face, clearly not happy at being left out now that he's one of the crew.

"We won't be long," Ishmael promises.

Abovedecks, a warm wispy fog wafts out of the dark, making the deck beneath their feet slippery. The great orb is barely visible. Gwen stops beside a crane mast. "What did Starbuck say about Pip?"

"He didn't argue when I suggested that the Gilded were behind it. He seemed pretty upset that I even knew about them in the first place."

"You *really* think they exist?"

"I'm starting to. Between the things Queequeg and Billy said and the way the first and second mates treat Pip, how else can you explain it?"

"But why would anyone go to such lengths to make sure Pip becomes part of our crew?" Gwen asks. "You think Pip learned ahead of time about the new bait Starbuck's offering?"

Ishmael shrugs. "Don't know. I get the feeling these Gilded folks like money, but not enough to risk dying for it."

The thickening fog drifts across the *Pequod*'s dark deck. The ship creaks, and waves splash against its hull. Ishmael's uniform is growing damp in the mist. "Guess I'll head below."

"Wait. There's something else." Gwen looks around, then lowers her voice. "A way we can all get rich without risking our lives."

Ishmael stares at her uncertainly. "How?"

"Tell Ahab and Starbuck about the islanders raising terrafins."

Ishmael feels a chill that has nothing to do with his damp uniform. "You . . . know about that?"

"Queek told me," Gwen says. "Don't be mad at him. I asked him why Diana didn't want to let us leave the island. I guess he felt I had a right to know."

Ishmael can't really argue with that. "But why would telling Starbuck and Ahab about the islanders change their minds about hunting the Great Terrafin?"

"The night I stayed up with Charity, after she came back from being held by the pirates? She said some things about her and Starbuck. And about this green neurotoxin that terrafins have. I think it's what was in those darts the islanders shot us with."

Ishmael nods. It's just as Gabriel said.

Gwen continues: "The way Charity talked about the neurotoxin, you'd think it has magical powers. She said that the amount the Great Terrafin has would be worth an unimaginable fortune."

To have that much neurotoxin, it would have to be incredibly huge . . . Ishmael goes cold, recalling the enormous skiver leaning in the corner of Ahab's quarters. It *couldn't* be from an *actual* terrafin. But what if it was? They've seen enormous humps, and huge beasts on land. Why couldn't there be an even larger creature? The sailor who'd been hopscotching across the sea to a working stasis lab had said terrafins weren't worth the bother. But what if he didn't know about the neurotoxin? Now it makes sense why Ahab and Starbuck want the Great Terrafin so badly.

All this raises another question: "Worth a fortune to who?"

"That's what I was wondering, too," Gwen says. "And I'm thinking maybe it's these Gilded people. Charity never identified them. She just said there're people who are desperate for the stuff. They'll pay anything."

Ishmael hasn't forgotten how euphoric he felt while waking up after being shot with a dart, and how a mere drop of the most-diluted form of the nectar instantly healed his head after he'd been hurt while saving Thistle. Nectar, serum, neurotoxin — it was all the same.

But there's something else he remembers as well: Gabriel saying, *"Can change a man in unnatural ways."*

"All we have to do is tell Starbuck and Ahab about the islanders' terrafins," Gwen continues. "Then they'll have all the neurotoxin they want *without* risking anyone's life. . . . That means *our* lives, Ishmael, now that we're stuck with an incompetent lineman."

The logic of Gwen's suggestion is undeniable. They've seen the battle that "normal" terrafins put up when harpooned. He can't even begin to picture what trying to capture a truly *giant* terrafin would be like, but certainly many lives would be at risk. He gave his word to Gabriel, though — and even if he hadn't, he'd never be able to live with himself if he betrayed the islanders' trust. "We can't. We'd be destroying their lives."

"You don't know that for sure. Maybe the islanders would welcome trade with the *Pequod.*"

"If they wanted to trade their nectar, they would have done it by now," Ishmael argues. "You didn't see how crazed Diana got when she heard I knew about their terrafins. They want to keep them a secret. And I swore I wouldn't tell anyone."

"*You* swore, not me."

Ishmael eyes her warily. "Don't do it, Gwen. Even if you don't care about the islanders — about Thistle and Billy — you're better off keeping your mouth shut. Remember the money Ahab's offering. You think you'll get anything close to that if all you do is tell Starbuck and Ahab about the islanders' terrafins?"

Gwen bites the corner of her lip and mulls it over. "You could be right. But how are we *ever* going to stick a terrafin that big with Pip as a —"

They're interrupted by a *thump* and moan that come from the other side of the crane mast. When Ishmael and Gwen go around to see what it is, they find Pip getting to his feet like someone who'd just slipped on the wet deck.

"You okay?" Ishmael asks.

"Uh, yes." Pip brushes himself off. "I . . . uh . . . came up here for some fresh air. Or, I guess, fresh fog. Finished your *private* conversation?"

Gwen's eyes narrow. "It's none of your business. Just because you've been made a lineman doesn't mean —"

"Hold on." Ishmael cuts her short and turns to Pip. "Gwen's not the only one around here who has certain things she'd like to keep private. So unless you'd like to tell us why you've gotten special treatment since the day we got here, maybe you ought to respect that."

Pip's eyes tighten on Ishmael. "Point well taken," he says, then heads belowdecks, leaving them alone again.

The ever-thickening fog drifts past. Gwen's hair hangs dark and wet. "I don't trust him."

"We have to give him a chance."

"If you say so, skipper," Gwen replies sourly, then pulls her damp uniform away from her skin. "It's too wet up here. I'm going down."

"Wait." Ishmael gently takes her arm to stop her. "Not a word about the islanders and their terrafins, right?"

Gwen sighs. "For now."

53

Lying in his sleeper that night, Ishmael once again tries to imagine a terrafin large enough to possess a skiver the size of the one in Ahab's cabin. The chase boats would be mere toys in comparison with such a beast. Now he understands why that huge harpoon cannon sits on the bow of the *Pequod:* When it comes to the Great Terrafin, the *Pequod* itself will be the chase boat.

From out in the passageway comes the squeak of creaky wheels. Ishmael slips out of his bunk and leaves the men's berth. In the dim light, he finds Tarnmoor sitting on the bottom step of a ladderway. The old swabbie takes a deep sniff, then yawns and pats the step next to him. "Ah, Ishmael. Can't sleeps, lad? Troubled, are ya?"

Ishmael sits beside the old man. "Where did Ahab get that huge terrafin skiver in his quarters?"

"Aye, a souvenir that. And a reminder that the monster tooked his ship, the *Essex.* Tooked his men. Tooked his beautiful young wife and son. Tooked his leg."

Ishmael digests the tragic end to the tale that the old swabbie had begun telling him that night two months ago while he sat in the steamy brig, his knuckles sore after breaking Daggoo's nose. "Why didn't it take Ahab?"

Maybe it's his imagination, but Ishmael could swear that the old man's blind eyes open just enough for him to get a glimpse of two shrunken pink orbs before they shut again. "Why? Because she *knowed,* lad. She knowed that for Ahab, there were a fates even worse than death. And that were to go on living with the memory a' what he'd lost, what he'd still have if'n he hadn't been so blinded by greed. Losin' a fortune he never had to begins with don't necessarily change a man. But lose a wife and child, and he'll never be the same. Steals the humanity right out a' a man. Leaves an empty, vengeful husk."

Sitting on the step in the middle of the night, Ishmael can hear the faint hum of the *Pequod*'s heart — its reactor. But now he knows that its captain's heart has been broken beyond repair.

"So it's revenge he wants?"

"Aye, revenge — always revenge," Tarnmoor says and stretches his arms. "He'll say it's coin he craves, but it ain't. He lives only to destroy the thing what destroyed him."

Ishmael sits back. "Tell me something, Tarnmoor. Why do you make it sound like you were there? Like you actually saw that beautiful wife and child?"

The old blind man is silent. The *Pequod* forges through the waves and from here and there come the creaks and groans of an aged, rusting ship plowing through the sea. Finally, Tarnmoor moves closer and lowers his voice, even though there's no one around to hear. "Smarts you are, lad. Smart, smart. I'll tells ya, but only so longs as ya swears never to tell another soul. Although if ya dids, I reckon it wouldn't matter sinced they'd never believes ya, no never."

Ishmael promises to keep the secret.

"I were Ahab's first mate, lad, on the *Essex.* Had the rank Starbuck gots on this ship, and sailed under our captain when he were young."

"You said you were blinded by the sun when you first got here."

Tarnmoor chuckles. "Only a fool would look at the sun, lad. Ya takes me for a fool?"

"No, but—"

"Serves a good purpose, don't it? Charity always makin' sure new nippers runs into me on their firsts day. 'Here's the old fool swabbie whats looked at the sun and now he's blinded, so don'ts go makin' the same mistake, kiddies.' Scares the Earth's dry dirt out a' them."

Ishmael can't help but feel amused. "You do it every time a new batch of nippers shows up?"

"Aye, lad, every time. Saved more'n a few a' them their eyesight, I reckons."

"So how *did* you lose your eyesight?"

Tarnmoor presses a bony finger across the bridge of his nose, covering his useless eyes. "The Great Terrafin, how else? Whipped acrost the eyes, I were. Left floatin' on a piece a' decking whiles all around me mens screamed and cried as the big-tooths moved in and mades a feast a' them."

"Big-tooths?" Ishmael repeats.

"Good-for-nothin' scavengers that'll eat anything what's hurt or strugglin'. Terrafins is their favorites, but they're too cowardly to attacks ones whats healthy. So they waits and follows a terrafin whats hurt or injured until its defenses is low and then attacks it. We been out a' their waters these last few months. But nows we're going back in, as it seems that's wheres the Great Terrafin be headed."

Ishmael sits quietly for a moment more. "You think we'll find it, Tarnmoor?"

The old man is slow answering. With a yawn, he says, "Ahab knows this may be his last chance. The Trust won't pay for another voyage if he don't come back with a full pot. This time there'll be no turning back. It's the Great Terrafin or it's him."

The Trust again, Ishmael thinks, remembering what Old Ben said about it not wanting the people of Black Range to know certain things. And how Stubb claimed he was its official representative on the *Pequod.* And now Tarnmoor saying it pays for these voyages. He turns to ask the old swabbie what, exactly, the Trust is. But Tarnmoor's head hangs forward, and he begins to snore.

54

“My third day as a lineman, and we’re on the trail of the Great Terrafin!” Pip exclaims excitedly. Under the blazing midday sun, Chase Boat Four floats peacefully on a vast glittery aquamarine bay. Overhead, drones buzz and zip like giant insects. An hour ago the beast was briefly spotted here, and now the chase boats drift silently, waiting to see if it will reappear.

“Just remember what you’re supposed to do,” Gwen grumbles. A warm breeze pushes the chase boat slowly along, and the crew sweat in their PFDs. This jungle-lined bay is so broad that the other chase boats are mere dots. Far away, waiting outside the mouth of the bay, the *Pequod* looks miniature. Schools of silvery scurry burst from the water now and then, fleeing some larger predator. Queequeg stands in the bow behind the harpoon gun, his visored cap pulled low.

“Look.” Pip points into the water, where the rusted hulk of a large ship lies on its side, caked with lumpy orange and red growths. Long green and brown blades of underwater plants gently wave in the current, and scurry of all sizes and colors dart in and out of the wreck's many holes and crevices.

"What's all that orange and red stuff?" Gwen asks.

"Coral," Queequeg answers, grinning triumphantly at Pip. "Those are its colors when it's alive. That ship must have been down there for hundreds of years. It takes a long time for that much coral to grow."

This time, Pip doesn't challenge Queequeg as they all stare, fascinated, at the wreck below. Rusted and bent crane booms jut from its main deck, and in the stern, there appear to be a slipway and the remains of two large winches, though not nearly as large as the ones on the *Pequod.*

Suddenly, Queequeg points. Fifty yards away, something enormous and white glides slowly beneath the surface.

"Mother of Earth!" Pip blurts.

Ishmael catches his breath. Alarm barrels through him like an electric charge. The creature is gigantic! More the size of a submerged island than a living thing. Firing a harpoon at it will be like jabbing a splinter into the ankle of a giant.

Gwen and Queequeg glance anxiously at him, awaiting instructions. Right now the Great Terrafin is too far away for Queequeg to get off a shot with the harpoon gun. Ishmael suspects that if he were to start the RTG, the beast might spook and run.

"Get out the hand sail," he whispers to Gwen, who quietly reaches beneath the seats and finds the light, clear sail. She holds one side and waits for Pip to take the other, but Pip looks at her with bulging, terrified eyes.

"Go on," Ishmael urges.

Pip doesn't move; he seems frozen.

"I knew it," Gwen says bitterly.

"The sail, sailor!" Ishmael orders.

Quaking almost beyond control, Pip reaches for his side of the hand sail. It catches the breeze, and the chase boat begins to drift more quickly while Ishmael uses the rudder to steer.

The Great Terrafin is straight ahead of them. Ishmael is trying not to imagine what will happen if they can actually put a stick into the enormous creature. Meanwhile, a few hundred yards off the bow, in the direction the terrafin is heading, a thin spit of land juts out from the beach. Soon the beast will be forced either to reverse course or turn to the right. Ishmael decides to gamble and steer the boat toward the spot where he thinks the Great Terrafin will be in a few minutes.

Just then comes the distant hum of a drone. Ishmael grabs the two-way and hisses, "Call it off! We're close."

The drone veers off and hangs motionless in the sky, observing from a safe distance.

"You've got a visual?" Starbuck's excitement is evident even over the scratchy two-way.

"Yes, sir." Despite the polarized glasses he wears, the glittery surface makes it impossible to see where the creature is. Ishmael can only hope it's still somewhere off the port side, soon to encounter the spit of land and turn right.

"Careful," Starbuck cautions, as if Ishmael needs to be told.

The chase boat continues to glide silently, but Pip's eyes dart like small, frightened creatures. "They can't really expect us to fire a harpoon at it," he whispers. "It's madness!"

Ishmael presses a finger to his lips. Yes, it's madness, but part of him can't help feeling excited as well. Adrenaline rushes through his veins. They are pursuing what must be the largest, most dangerous creature on this planet.

The breeze continues to push the chase boat slowly toward the spot where Ishmael hopes to intersect with the beast. "Put down the sail," he whispers to Gwen and Pip.

Without the aid of the breeze they drift more slowly. There is still no sign of the Great Terrafin. Ishmael wonders if it encountered the spit of land and doubled back. Or did he miscalculate where they would meet it?

Then he hears a gasp. Gwen points off the port side. Coming toward them beneath the water's surface is not one but *two* creatures — the first is black and far smaller than the second.

Could the first one be a male? Ishmael wonders, since it doesn't appear to be fleeing. Is . . . is the Great Terrafin courting? If so, there's a chance the beast will be distracted enough that it won't notice the chase boat until Queequeg gets to fire. Ishmael's blood vibrates with excitement.

But Pip extends a trembling hand. "Give me the headset. I want to speak to Starbuck."

"Shut up," Gwen snarls under her breath.

"You don't understand," Pip protests. "I don't have to be here. I . . ."

In the bow, Queequeg quietly swings the harpoon gun around and aims. Ishmael's heart is thumping so hard it feels like it wants to climb into his throat.

For a few seconds, the bay is eerily calm.

Then, suddenly, the enormous creature speeds toward the surface, and the Great Terrafin breaches! It blocks out the sun when it leaps, torrents of seawater streaming off its white wings and three — yes, *three* — long tails!

Queequeg swings the harpoon gun upward.

Bang!

The gigantic beast crashes back into the water with a deafening *flop!* and barrels away. Huge waves rush out in every direction, and the chase boat is rocked so violently that it nearly capsizes. Line whistles off the starboard side, and Ishmael quickly starts the chase boat's engine and throws it into gear.

Pfufft . . .

The RTG cuts out and stalls. Silently cursing Perth, Ishmael tries again. Line continues to whip out in a blur. Gwen pushes the orange float over the side and shouts at Pip, "Make sure the line's clear!"

But Pip is transfixed.

Gwen points at the tub and screams, "Look out!"

The knot in the line appears so quickly that no one has time to react.

55

Whomp! The boat is yanked sideways with such force that Gwen is tossed out. Somehow Pip, Queequeg, and Ishmael hang on while the chase boat is dragged, skipping and skittering like a skimmed stone. The knotted line has caught on something in the bow, but Ishmael is being buffeted so hard he can't focus. There's no point in shouting at Pip or Queequeg to try to clear the line, because the instant either of them lets go he'll be thrown overboard, too. All they can do is hold tight.

It may be only Ishmael's imagination, but he senses that the Great Terrafin is headed for the mouth of the bay. He cranes his neck high enough to catch a glimpse of three speeding chase boats eager to put more sticks in the beast. Strangely, he counts a fourth, this one coming from behind, and catches a hint of black hull before Chase Boat Four slams into a wake broadside and goes airborne. Time momentarily slows while the boat flips over in midair and spills out the remaining crew. Ishmael feels himself flying and flailing as the bay's surface rushes toward him.

Smack! He plunges in face-first.

Seconds later, he is bobbing woozily, coughing and spitting up hot seawater. The upside-down chase boat floats nearby. Did the line snap when the boat flipped? A cacophony of confusing sounds reaches his ears — gunfire, boat engines, drones whining, distant shouts — and he spots Queequeg floating and coughing up seawater a dozen feet away.

There's no sign of their new lineman.

"Pip!" Ishmael shouts, fearing the worst. He twists around to see if Pip is behind him and instead finds the black hull of a pirate ship gliding close. Something heavy plummets down on him. A net! The pirates are gathering him and Queequeg in like scurry.

They both struggle futilely while the net rises out of the water and dumps them, drenched and dazed, on the deck. Hands reach through the netting and yank their knives out of their sheaths.

Bang! Bang! Zing! Ping! Bullets ricochet and whiz past. Ishmael and Queequeg stay curled in their PFDs on the deck under the soaking-wet netting, in no hurry to crawl out. Near them two pirates kneel against the ship's bulwark, shouting and pointing. "He's gettin' away!"

A third pirate climbs up on a capstan with a net and flings it. A minute later, a soaked, panting Pip is hauled on board and dumped next to his soggy crewmates.

"That was some righteous swimmin', boy." A pirate sneers down at Pip, displaying blackened nubs of teeth. "Too bad it didn't do ya no good."

The gunfire ceases. From the distance comes the receding hum of chase-boat engines, the slap of boat hulls, and the whine of drones. Ishmael imagines that the rest of the *Pequod*'s small armada is following the Great Terrafin out through the mouth of the bay and into the ocean. When he tries to lift his head to see, though, a heavy boot comes down painfully on his neck.

Meanwhile, pirates throw grappling hooks over the ship's rail, and soon Ishmael can see the stern of Chase Boat Four lifted out of the water so that the engine compartment can be kept from being swamped. He's surprised that the bright-red harpoon line is still attached to the bow. When a pirate pulls the line in until the harpoon appears, Ishmael realizes what happened: Queequeg didn't stick the terrafin after all. The line had simply gotten tangled in the creature's multiple tails.

The pirates gather around the captives, pointing and gloating. Apart from variations in height and bulk, they look eerily alike: eyes bloodred, hair uniformly black, faces crudely tattooed. When they blink, tattooed crossbones can be seen on their eyelids.

In a tremulous voice, Pip addresses a pirate with spiky hair and a face covered with scars. "Are you the captain? I want to speak to the captain."

"Do ya now?" the pirate replies, amused.

"Yes," says Pip through the netting. "And he'll want to speak to me once he finds out who I am."

"Really?" says the pirate. "Well, I'll be sure to mention that when I next sees him."

The nets are yanked off and the prisoners' hands and ankles are bound. While the pirates push and shove one another to get at the chase-boat crew's shoes, Queequeg whispers to Ishmael, "Where's Gwen?"

"She got thrown out of the chase boat," he whispers back.

"Maybe she was lucky," Queequeg whispers.

"Maybe." But Ishmael fears the worst. The last he saw, the chase boats were all headed out of the bay, leaving no one to rescue her.

Stripped of their shoes, the prisoners are left lying barefoot on the deck while the pirate ship motors out of the bay, gaining speed and rising up on hydrofoils.

* * *

It's difficult to judge how fast or far they travel, but it's growing dark when the pirate ship finally slows, dropping off the hydrofoils and back into the waves. Craning his neck in the dim evening light, Ishmael sees a beach strewn with debris and the rusted hulls of boats. The skeletons of other wrecks lie partly submerged in the shallows. It looks like an underwater junkyard.

The pirate ship anchors, and the prisoners are dragged through the hot shallows, across the beach littered with boat parts and garbage, and along a footpath worn into the jungle. It's not long before they come to a clearing barnacled with metal shipping containers, decrepit-looking tree houses, and other dwellings cobbled together out of wood and corrugated tin. These dwellings form a circle around a large, blackened fire pit.

Ishmael, Queequeg, and Pip are thrown into a shipping container. Even though it's past dusk, the dark container is filled with the day's residual heat and feels as hot as an oven. The door has been chained so that a gap of maybe six inches allows in some air. Sweat trickling down their faces, the chase-boat crew huddle near the gap, trying to see out.

From the distance comes the shrill squeal of an RTG being pushed to its limits while men whoop and cheer. It's almost certainly Chase Boat Four, and Ishmael wonders how much abuse the engine can take before it burns itself out.

"Wh-what are they going to do with us?" Pip stammers, wiping perspiration from his brow.

Neither Ishmael nor Queequeg answers.

"Guys?" Pip's voice rises in panic.

"Calm down," Ishmael says. "They took us hostage for a reason. And whatever it is, it probably means they want to keep us alive."

Pip considers this and relaxes.

Ishmael just hopes it's true.

56

With nightfall, the pirates wander around, pausing to drink from animal-skin sacks, after which their movements become clumsier.

"Remember him?" Pip points, and Ishmael recognizes the tall, thin, toothless pirate who chased Pip around the mess during the attack on the *Pequod* several months before. The pirate dumps an armful of sticks and branches in the fire pit.

Next, a small, scrawny pirate limps past the shipping container, dragging a limb from a tree. The fingers on his right hand are bunched together and slightly hooked.

"You there!" Pip calls. "We're thirsty. We need water."

The pirate pauses and looks in at them with dull pink eyes that aren't nearly as red as the others'.

Pip squeezes his face into the opening. "I'd like to know who's in charge here. There must be someone in a position of authority. I need to talk to that person. But first, some water."

The corners of the man's mouth curl scornfully. "Position of authority? Like the president? Or maybe you wanna speak to the king?"

Chuckling to himself, the scrawny pirate once again starts dragging the limb toward the fire pit.

"Wait! What about our water?" Pip cries.

But the pirate doesn't look back.

Soon a large blaze is burning in the fire pit. Startlingly, the pirates' tattoos have begun to glow faintly green in the dark. Dinner appears to be every man for himself. Some roast scurry on sticks over the open flames, others brown chunks of meat in handheld grills. But all who cook are warily watching other pirates who, having no food of their own, linger nearby in groups, whispering.

The scrawny pirate limps toward the fire pit with a plump white flyer tucked under his arm, but before he can roast it, a big bruiser of a man sneaks up from behind. The bigger man has a sloping forehead, deep-set eyes, and a grotesque nose that looks both crushed and bent. He tries to grab the flyer, and a tug-of-war ensues until they literally pull the creature apart, leaving the smaller man with only a wing.

The bruiser lifts the raw, bleeding carcass to his mouth and takes a bite.

In the shipping container Pip shudders. "How barbaric!"

The heinous behavior continues. Three pirates rush a fourth, who's cooking close to the flames, and two of them begin to brutally beat the man while the third grabs his food and runs off. Moments later, the two pirates give chase to the third, who's decided not to share. Now the beaten pirate joins another group that hovers near the fire, looking for someone else to steal food from.

"Complete savages," Pip murmurs.

Later, when dinner has ended and the fire has slowly begun to burn itself out, the horde gathers, sitting on tree stumps, crates, and whatever else is available. Now and then a pirate will pull a vial from his clothes and use a dropper to place a tear of glowing greenish liquid in each eye.

Terrafin serum, Ishmael thinks. *Of course.* That explains the red eyes — and the immunity to pain.

The bruiser who stole the flyer from the scrawny pirate steps into a cleared area beside the fire pit. He's bare-chested now, his skin grotesquely disfigured, covered with scars and glowing green tattoos. He folds his muscular arms across his chest and waits while the other pirates argue and gesticulate. From the shouts and laughter, Ishmael gathers that the big pirate is called Winchester and that he's waiting for someone to challenge him.

"I think they're making bets," Queequeg whispers.

Finally, another pirate pulls off his shirt and joins Winchester beside the fire pit. The audience starts to cheer while the two bare-chested men, circling each other with fists up, exchange jabs. Soon the jabs become outright punches. Even in the container, Ishmael can hear the nauseating smack and crack of knuckles against jaws and cheekbones.

The battle turns bloody and furious, the audience howling with delight while the two men stand toe-to-toe, trading ferocious blows.

But the goal of the fighters isn't merely to pummel each other. As they slug and grapple, it appears that each is trying to throw the other onto the glowing red coals in the fire pit. This, Ishmael realizes, probably accounts for the horrible scars that mark Winchester's torso.

Sure enough, the fight ends in an explosion of sparks when Winchester wraps his arms around his opponent and hurls him, screaming, into the pit. In a flash his opponent launches himself out of the fire and frantically rolls on the ground, trying to dislodge the sizzling red-hot coals stuck to his skin. Winchester raises his fist triumphantly, and pirates cheer and chant his name again and again.

When the sickening scent of scorched flesh reaches the storage container, Pip whimpers, “I have to get out of here!”

Ishmael and Queequeg share a grim look. It’s hard to foresee how that will happen.

57

In the almost-complete dark, Ishmael sits by the shipping container's chained door. Near him, Pip and Queequeg are curled on the filthy floor, asleep. Several sticks the length of men's arms lie close by. Each is bare of tree bark and blunted at the ends, apparently smoothed by years of use. Ishmael wonders what they are for. Meanwhile, the camp never becomes completely quiet. A constant, hypnotic humming—reminiscent of small RTGs—makes his eyelids grow heavy. . . .

"Ah!" Pip's cry pierces the night.

Ishmael's eyes burst open. Pip is shimmying backward toward the door while pointing at a large, shadowy creature on the floor. It's big—about the size and shape of a man's leg—and Ishmael can hear the tapping and scraping of hundreds of tiny legs as it wriggles toward them.

Now he knows what the blunted sticks are for. He grabs one and pokes at the crawling thing until it retreats into the dark depths at the back of the container.

"Wh-what was that?" Pip stammers.

"Not a clue," Ishmael answers, keeping the club close in case he needs it again.

"What's going to stop it from returning?" Pip whispers fearfully.

Ishmael suppresses a weary sigh. "I'll stay up and watch for it."

At the first gray hint of dawn, Ishmael listens to the hoots and howls of jungle creatures, the grating snores of pirates, and that constant humming sound. A light film of dew covers the rusty lock and chain that secure the container door, and he can smell the tart scent of damp coals from last night's fire. Ghostly wisps of smoke rise from the dying gray ash while small brown four-legged animals with white-striped tails sniff around the edges of the fire pit, searching for leftover bits of food.

As the world outside gradually brightens and angled light seeps in through the gap in the doorway, Ishmael sees that the back half of the shipping container is filled with gauzy webs on which rest nasty-looking, furry red-and-gray creatures the size of treestones, each with eight spindly legs. On the floor below them crawl long, thick invertebrates with hard, segmented bodies and hundreds of short legs. One of these, Ishmael thinks, is what he poked with the stick last night.

Lovely company to share a cell with.

The sun starts to rise above the trees, and the container grows hot and steamy. Thin shafts of light come through rusty holes in the ceiling, and insects fly in and out.

"Anyone thirsty?" Queequeg croaks hoarsely.

Ishmael's mouth is dust-dry, and he feels parched. If they don't get something to drink soon, will they end up a meal for the creatures in the back of the container?

A motley, haggard, and bleary-eyed group of pirates approach the container. In their midst is one Ishmael didn't notice the night before. Like the others', his black clothes are tattered and patched, and a pistol and knife hang from his belt. His face is gaunt and his hair spiked, but unlike the others', his hair is pure white. By the deferential way the men treat him, Ishmael assumes that he is their leader.

With fiery-red eyes he stares in at the captives. "What quantity of juice has he acquired thus far on this voyage?"

"Juice?" Ishmael repeats.

"Neurotoxin. From terrafins."

"Ahab?" Ishmael guesses.

"No, King Neptune. Of course I'm referring to Ahab, you dithering dimwit."

Pip squeezes beside Ishmael and presses his face into the gap. "Excuse me. My name is Pippin Xing Al-Jahani Lopez-Makarova." He waits, apparently believing this should mean something to the pirate. "Do you understand?"

But the white-haired pirate keeps his reddened eyes on Ishmael. "If you're unable to estimate the extent of his cache, perhaps you'll enlighten me as to the number of terrafins he's corralled in the past six months?"

"Please, sir, I can tell from your diction that you're an enlightened man," Pip says anxiously. "I'm of the Gilded. Surely you know what that means. If you send out word that I'm here, I promise you'll be amply rewarded."

This time, the white-haired pirate takes notice of him.

The container feels like a furnace. Ishmael knows that they won't last much longer without water, but it appears that the pirates couldn't care less. The oppressive heat and thirst make even the good-natured

Queequeg edgy. "You really think the Gilded's authority extends all the way to this planet and these pirates?" he asks Pip. "Like that white-haired pirate's on some kind of two-way right now checking out your story?"

"You have no comprehension of how powerful the Gilded are," Pip replies crossly.

Queequeg scratches the sparse beard along his jaw. "If they had any influence here on Cretacea, why haven't they gotten rid of these pirates?"

"And exactly how would you suggest they accomplish that?" Pip asks with a condescending tone. "Transport a force of specially trained mercenaries all the way here just to eliminate a minor nuisance? A complete waste of resources."

"It's got to cost them money each time these pirates attack one of their ships," Ishmael points out.

For a moment Pip gives him an odd look. He parts his lips. "You should . . ." he begins, then changes his mind. "A pittance. Easily factored into the cost of doing business."

"Right," Queequeg agrees emphatically. "That's how it always is with you people. It's all about business."

Rather than take offense, Pip seems amused. "Ah, the Lector expounds. Don't you ever tire of this absurd dream of destabilizing the world order?"

"Not *the* world order," Queequeg counters. "*Your* world order, which works really well for the Gilded and really badly for everyone else."

"If it weren't for the Gilded, there'd be no order, period," Pip snaps.

Queequeg smirks disdainfully. "At least, that's what you'd like everyone to believe."

Pip rolls his eyes. "Who constructed the Zirconia Electrolysis stations to provide the planet with oxygen? And the Natrient factories? Who pays for these missions that bring resources back to Earth?"

"Don't the Gilded have to breathe and eat as well?" Queequeg asks scornfully.

"Like we'd *ever* eat Natrient," Pip scoffs, then catches himself. His face turns red.

Queequeg chuckles bitterly. "Oh, right, I forgot. That's only for us menial laborers."

By midday, Ishmael's throat is so parched he can barely swallow. Queequeg's and Pip's faces and arms are smeared with dirt, and he's sure he doesn't look any better. They would definitely be sweating were there any moisture left in their bodies to sweat.

"Can I ask you a question, friend?" Queequeg starts in again with Pip.

"I'd rather you didn't."

"What are you doing here? In all seriousness. If you're of the Gilded, you sure don't need the money. So why are you on this planet?"

"*This planet,*" Pip repeats in a snarky tone, then shrugs like he knows it's stupid to be antagonistic. "You truly want to know? I was bored."

Ishmael cocks his head curiously. Of all the answers he might have predicted Pip giving, that wasn't one of them.

"You have no idea how dull that life is," Pip goes on. "The same people doing and saying the same things all the time. Wearing the same clothes and acting in the same ways. I was going crazy. It got to the point where I said I would run away. Not that I had the faintest idea where I'd go. It was an empty threat, but it worked, and it just so happened that there was something useful I could do here."

"Be a drone op?" Queequeg frowns.

"Cartography, if you must know. Gathering imagery to map Cretacea."

Ishmael eyes Pip curiously. "When the pirates caught you, they complimented you on your swimming. Where did you learn to swim?"

Pip looks away without answering. But in a way, that is the answer.

"Shocking, isn't it?" Queequeg says bitterly. "While the rest of us didn't have enough water to wash in, he and his type were swimming in pools of it. So Pip, bet you're sorry you're not in your nice comfortable boring world now."

Pip snorts. "You Lectors think you're so smart, so smugly righteous and morally superior." He pauses and looks at Ishmael, then appears to make up his mind about something. "Suppose I told you that your close friend here is of the Gilded, too?"

Queequeg laughs. "That's a good one."

"Tell him," Pip says to Ishmael.

Queequeg's grin fades, and he gives Ishmael an uncertain look.

"How could I be of the Gilded?" Ishmael asks. "I'm from Black Range, the armpit of the coal region. My foster parents work at a Zirconia Electrolysis station, like everyone else in Black Range who is lucky enough to have a job."

"Hold out your registry," Pip says knowingly.

Ishmael hesitates, then tells Queequeg, "Something strange is going to happen. I don't understand why, but—"

"Just do it," Pip cajoles, then says to Queequeg, "Watch closely." He crosses his left wrist over Ishmael's. In the dim light of the shipping container, there's the faintest blue spark, and once again Ishmael feels a shock.

Queequeg gives him an astonished look. Ishmael rubs his wrist and thinks back to his last night on Earth, when Old Ben's registry greeted his the same way. Old Ben was the last person Ishmael would have imagined being of the Gilded, but there were certain things about him that now make Ishmael wonder. How could such an old, broken-down, benzo-swilling husk of a man be the *manager* of the Zirconia Electrolysis station? And back at the foundling home, the way he spoke to the haughty Ms. Hussey and she listened without argument . . .

In a voice rife with misgivings, Queequeg asks, "What . . . what was that spark?"

But before the discussion can continue, the tall, toothless pirate and the scrawny one appear at the container door.

"Now whish of you gentlefellers ish Lopesh-Makaroba?" lisps the toothless one.

Pip gets to his feet. The tall, thin pirate smiles — a grisly sight. "Well, if it ain't ol' Pudgy himshelf!" He takes out his gun and aims it at Queequeg and Ishmael while he unlocks the shipping container door. "Come wish us."

Pip pauses and gives Ishmael an apologetic look.

"See if they'll give us water," Ishmael reminds him, then watches as the Gilded boy goes.

58

"Think they'll let us die?" Queequeg rasps. Hours have passed since Pip was taken away. During that time, Ishmael explained that he has no idea how he could be of the Gilded, since he'd never even heard of them until he arrived on the *Pequod.* Queequeg believes him, saying it wouldn't matter now, anyway; he knows what Ishmael is made of, Gilded or not.

Ishmael cannot recall ever being so thirsty. He can't bear the idea that he might perish here in this shipping container, not knowing what happened to his foster parents or having found Archie. *Is there truly no justice in the universe?*

"Hey." The scrawny pirate with the hooked fingers looks in at them. His left cheek and eye are red and puffy, like he's recently been on the losing end of a fight. From under his shirt he pulls an animal-skin bag that sloshes. The sound is enough to drive Ishmael mad. He's stunned when the pirate offers the bag through the gap to Queequeg and him.

They pass the animal skin back and forth, drinking quickly. At the same time, the scrawny pirate appears to be keeping an eye out for anyone coming. Suddenly he reaches in, snatches the empty bag, and slides it back under his shirt. Then, with feigned gruffness, he loudly demands, "Come on, you gotta know how many terrafins they've landed in the past six months."

A moment later he's joined by the toothless pirate. "They confirm you of anyshing, Blank?"

"I think they were just gonna, Glock."

The pirate named Glock looks in at Ishmael and Queequeg.

"Where did you take our friend?" Ishmael asks.

"Well, now, I wouldn't be conshentrated about him," Glock answers. "He's valued hish proportions in joy juice. He'll be finalized jush fine. Come on, Blank."

The scrawny pirate hesitates. "Shouldn't we try to trade them for juice, too?"

"Naw, Kalashnikov says theesh two aren't worsh a day of time," Glock says.

It takes a moment to unravel the pirate's meaning. Queequeg points at Ishmael. "They'd trade for him. He's of the Gilded, too."

"Him?" Glock scowls. "That accurshed?"

"Don't I wish," Ishmael says. "I'm afraid my friend's delirious from thirst."

Glock sneers at Queequeg. "Nicesh try, head meat."

The two pirates depart. In the container, Queequeg gives Ishmael a frustrated look. "You should have told him, Ish. You could have gotten out of here."

Ishmael settles back down on the dirty container floor. "Not without you, Queek."

* * *

That night Ishmael and Queequeg take turns batting away crawling creatures in the dark. By the morning, they're drained, and as thirsty as ever. When Glock and Blank return, the scrawny pirate cups a rifle with his bad hand. He waits for Glock to unlock the container door, then motions with the muzzle of the rifle. "Let's go."

Outside, Blank points to a couple of shovels. "Grab 'em."

Queequeg and Ishmael do what they're told, and Blank marches them barefoot through the camp. It's still early, and while a few pirates are out and about, the doors to most of the crude dwellings are locked shut. As they pass the fire pit, Ishmael feels the hard nubs and ragged edges of bones underfoot. Many appear to have come from scurry or flyers, and here and there are larger bones that might have come from some medium-size animal. A few of the bones are larger still . . . almost, Ishmael realizes with alarm, of hominid proportions.

"Any chance we could get something to drink?" Queequeg croaks.

Blank answers by poking him hard in the back with the rifle barrel. "Shut up and walk." He forces them along a thin trail through the undergrowth, past tall, limbless trees, to an open area with a hut. Buckets, metal drums, and wire screens lie about.

"Up there." Blank points at a narrow path leading up to a cave in the side of a hill.

Ishmael and Queequeg start to climb, but they stop when a sharp, unpleasant odor hits their nostrils. It's coming from the cave opening, which is barely wide enough for someone to crouch down and squeeze into. After tying a bandanna over his nose and mouth, Blank lights a torch and gestures with his weapon. "Go in."

Ishmael and Queequeg inch into the cramped, dark cave. The stench is stronger here, and Ishmael's eyes begin to sting and water. His lungs burn. Blank's torch lighting the way, they find themselves in a vast, open cavern. In its middle is a large, dark mound, which is the source of the caustic odor. Buckets lie on the ground.

"What is this?" Queequeg wheezes, wiping tears from his eyes.

"Ya new jobs." Blank jams the torch into a crack in the cavern wall. "Start diggin'. Fill those buckets."

While Queequeg tentatively jabs his shovel into the side of the mound, something catches Ishmael's eye, and he looks up at the ceiling of the cavern. At first he isn't sure what he's seeing. Then, with a start, he realizes that hanging upside down above them are thousands of horrible-looking, white-fanged, gray-and-brown creatures.

"Don't worry, they sleep durin' the day." Blank wipes his brow. "Fill ten of them buckets and bring 'em out." With that, he turns and goes back outside, where the air is fresher and it's possible to draw a full breath without gagging.

The digging is dreadfully hot, unpleasant work. Each time Ishmael or Queequeg thrusts a shovel into the mound, a new burst of sharp, acrid odor fills their noses and burns their eyes. Both have to stop several times to retch, and it's not long before the front and back of their dirty uniforms are dark with sweat.

Having filled ten buckets with the foul-smelling stuff, they eagerly lug them out of the cave and into the fresh air. Next Blank orders them to scrape the contents of the buckets through wire mesh, then mix it with charcoal from the fire pit and a white-yellow substance with a rotten odor all its own. The resulting powder is black and malodorous.

"Some water, friend, *please*?" Queequeg begs while they work under the broiling sun.

The scrawny pirate holds up his animal skin and jiggles it. This time no sloshing sounds come from within.

"Can't you get us some?" Ishmael implores.

Blank looks at them like they're crazy. "If Glock or one of the others came by and found I'd left ya alone, I'd be shot. Enough talk. Back to work."

Ishmael and Queequeg have no choice but to make more of the

black powder. Do the pirates plan to work them until they drop dead of thirst?

Not far from them, lounging in the shade of a nearby tree, Blank takes his knife from its sheath and starts whittling a small stick. Because of his bad hand, he must clench the stick in his teeth. He's concentrating deeply and not paying attention to them.

Ishmael catches Queequeg's eye. Should one of them sneak up behind the scrawny pirate and hit him over the head with his shovel? They could grab the rifle and run — but that's where the plan gets dicey. To get to the chase boat, they'd have to go back toward the pirate camp. With one gun between the two of them, what chance would they have against all those armed brigands?

Still, Ishmael isn't certain how much longer they'll last without water. And the longer they wait, the worse shape they'll be in.

He glances again at Blank, absorbed in whittling. After motioning to Queequeg to keep scraping the black stuff through the wire mesh, he picks up his shovel and starts quietly toward the tree, trying to stay out of the pirate's line of sight. Soon he's close enough. Having never hit anyone on the head with a shovel before, he isn't sure how hard to swing. Ishmael doesn't want to hurt him any more than is absolutely necessary. Blank may be a pirate, but he did sneak them water yesterday, and he doesn't seem nearly as ruthless as the others.

But at this point, it's him or them.

He raises the shovel.

Crack!

59

"Ahh!"

Caught by surprise, Blank yelps and jumps up and spins around, coming face-to-face with Ishmael. "What's goin' on? What was that noise? Why ain't you over there workin'?"

"I . . . was coming over here to tell you we're almost finished," Ishmael lies, pretending to lean casually on his shovel. He points at the source of the noise — a treestone lying beside a large rock. "A treestone fell."

But Blank's face has gone ashen and he's trembling.

"You okay, friend?" Queequeg asks hoarsely, coming toward them. "You look kind of shook up."

"I'm fine. Just don't like loud noises," Blank snaps peevishly. He knits his brow. "You ain't slowin' down, are ya? Get back to work."

But instead, Queequeg starts toward the hut.

"What're ya doin'? Stop!" Blank picks up the rifle.

Queequeg keeps going. A rusty ax is propped next to the hut, and Ishmael wonders if that's what his friend is headed for.

"Hey! I said stop!" Blank aims the rifle.

"Queek?" Ishmael says apprehensively, worried his friend may be so addled by thirst that he'll try something stupid.

Click! Blank unlocks the rifle's safety. "I swear I'll shoot!"

"Go ahead," Queequeg says. "If you won't let us drink, we're going to die anyway."

Blank's finger quivers on the trigger. Ishmael's stomach cramps anxiously. "Don't shoot him! He's delirious. From thirst." He turns to Queequeg. "Stop, Queek. Don't do this."

But Queequeg picks up the ax.

Finger slowly tightening on the rifle's trigger, Blank warns, "This is ya last chance!"

The pirate's attention is completely on Queequeg. Ishmael slowly starts to lift his shovel.

"I swear, I'll shoot!" Blank declares again, but to Ishmael the warnings have begun to sound hollow. If the pirate were going to shoot, he would have already. Queequeg comes closer with the ax. . . . And stops at the fallen treestone, which he starts to hack open.

Feeling a wave of relief, Ishmael tells Blank, "It's okay. He's just getting us something to drink."

The pirate lowers the rifle. "He's crazy. All he's gonna find inside that thing is a hard, round nut."

"I don't believe it!" Blank exclaims gleefully through a bulging cheekful of treestone meat a few minutes later. "These things're all over the place and we ignore 'em."

"You can tell the other guys and be a hero," Queequeg says, hacking open another.

Blank's face darkens. "Not a chance. Now I ain't gonna have to go anywhere near that stupid fire pit and have my scurry and flyers stolen before I can eat 'em. The rest of 'em can starve for all I care."

Queequeg gulps down the water inside another nut and wipes sweat from his forehead with the back of his hand. "Let me ask you a question, friend. If you hate the others so much, why be a pirate? Why not quit and join the crew of a scurry boat or something?"

"Not with these." Blank closes his eyes, displaying the crossbones tattoos on his eyelids. "I'm branded. No captain'll ever let me on his boat."

Having finished his treestone meat, Blank starts to whittle again. When Queequeg asks what he's doing, he explains that he's making wooden darts, then sweeps away some fronds behind a shrub and proudly shows off the crossbow he's fashioned out of wood, metal, and animal sinew. He demonstrates, firing at the trunk of a nearby tree. The dart buries itself in the bark.

"See? As lethal as a gun," the pirate says with pride. "And without all the noise, which makes it even better."

"You built this all by yourself?" Queequeg runs his fingers over the crossbow.

Blank beams.

"Shown it to the other guys?"

"Naw, they wouldn't understand. The notion of stealth is lost on 'em. They ain't big on subtlety." He glances over at the wire mesh and black powder, and Ishmael wonders if he's about to order them back to work.

"What're we making, anyway?" Ishmael asks, hoping to delay their return to the putrid-smelling cave.

"Gunpowder."

"Serious?" Queequeg gestures at the buckets of gunk they dug in the cavern. "From that stuff?"

"Don't believe me? Watch." Blank opens the door to the hut. Inside are piles of cloth bags filled with black powder, as well as several long coils of what looks like black string. He takes a scoop of the black powder and lays a short trail on the ground, then lights one end with a match he's taken from a box in the hut. Sizzling sparks and flames spurt beneath a small cloud of white smoke from one end of the black powder trail to the other.

Queequeg stares, dumbfounded. "If I didn't see that with my own eyes, I wouldn't believe it."

When it rains that night, water drips through the small, rusty holes in the roof of the shipping container. Queequeg and Ishmael lie on their backs with their mouths open, trying to catch whatever moisture they can. The water tastes metallic, and from time to time they have to pick tiny flecks of rust off their tongues, but after a day spent digging in the hot cave, they can't get enough. Then while one tries to get a few hours of fitful sleep, the other bats away the creatures that crawl out of the maze of webs at the back of their cell.

Early the next morning, Glock opens the container door. Bleary-eyed, Ishmael and Queequeg prop themselves up on their elbows. A group of men, including the white-haired pirate, has clustered outside the container. With them is Pip.

"Speak your piece, mollusk," the white-haired pirate orders Pip, who squats down to be eye level with his crewmates. With a dismayed expression, he stares at their filthy uniforms, which stink from sweat and digging in the cave.

"I'm leaving, but I didn't want to go without saying good-bye," he says, then leans close and whispers, "Tell them you're of the Gilded, Ishmael. They'll work you to death if you don't. Believe me, before I came to Cretacea, I heard stories."

Ishmael shakes his head. Suddenly Pip turns to the white-haired pirate. "Suppose I told you how to get all the joy juice you'll ever need?"

The pirate leader eyes him suspiciously. "What manner of poppycock is this?"

Pip points at Ishmael and Queequeg. "They have the means to acquire an unlimited supply of terrafin serum."

"Don't accredit him, Kalashnikov," Glock warns the white-haired pirate, and points at Pip. "He'sh imbued wish shyllogism."

Kalashnikov zeros in on Pip. "All the juice we'll ever need? Under no circumstances could that be possible."

"It is, I swear," Pip insists. "On Gilded honor."

"Explain," Kalashnikov demands, narrowing his red eyes.

Pip looks at Ishmael. "Tell them what Gwen said that foggy night on the *Pequod.*"

With dawning horror, Ishmael realizes that Pip knows about the islanders' terrafins. The night he spoke with Gwen on the ship's deck, Pip must have been on the other side of the crane mast, listening the whole time!

Inside the container, Ishmael rises to his feet. "I don't know what he's talking about."

But Pip says to Kalashnikov, "You're familiar with the islanders?"

"Those rock-hurling tree dwellers?" Kalashnikov says. "What've they to do with this?"

"Pip, don't," Ishmael warns.

Pip ignores him. "They cultivate terrafins. It provides them with an endless supply of juice."

Ishmael's insides knot. As much as he doesn't want to die, he can't bear the thought of what these barbarians will do to the peaceful islanders now that they've learned about the terrafins.

"How do I know you haven't concocted this confabulation merely to deter me from exterminating these two?" Kalashnikov indicates Queequeg and Ishmael with his gun.

"They lived with the islanders for more than a month. Long enough to learn everything about them."

"Is that true?" Kalashnikov asks Ishmael.

"No, sir," Ishmael replies. "Like you said, he's making that up to save our lives."

"For Earth's sake!" Pip spouts with aggravation and points to the tiny skivers in Ishmael's and Queequeg's ears. "Where do you think they got those? They're from baby terrafins. They came back from the island with them."

With his gun aimed carefully at Ishmael's face, Kalashnikov steps close and inspects the skivers. Glock does the same to Queequeg and says, "Well, now, I'll be atoned."

The pirate leader presses the cold metal barrel of the gun under Ishmael's chin. "Unfortunately, those miniature skivers don't necessarily alter your circumstances. At best, they merely illuminate the fact that someone here is misrepresenting the truth. If this terrafin story is indeed a figment of someone's imagination, I promise you'll be sorely regretting the day you left Earth."

Glock aims his gun at Queequeg and starts to squeeze the trigger. "Well, now, I shay why incubate, Kalashnikov? Let's shnaffle them now. They're not conforming, anyway."

"No!" Pip cries.

Before Glock can fire, Kalashnikov elbows him in the stomach. The tall, toothless pirate grunts and doubles over.

"I'll decide who lives and dies around here," the pirate leader growls, flicking the tiny skiver in Ishmael's earlobe. "We'll keep these two alive for now. It's conceivable that they'll be valuable should we need to convince the tree dwellers to drop their guard." He presses his face close to Ishmael's. "You had better pray that your Gilded colleague speaks the truth, poppet. Otherwise, I'll relish executing you *and* every one of your tree-dwelling acquaintances."

60

"I don't know how many more times I can stand having a gun shoved in my face," Queequeg grumbles later when Blank walks him and Ishmael back up the trail to the cave for another day of digging.

"Consider yaselves lucky," the scrawny pirate says. "Most of the time these idiots don't think twice about pullin' a trigger."

This isn't the first time Blank's made it plain that he's not happy being a pirate, and with the islanders' lives now at stake, Ishmael feels he must take a chance. "Help us get back to the *Pequod,* Blank. We'll tell them how you aided in our escape. They won't care about the tattoos on your eyelids. Most of the crew's covered in tattoos."

Blank's eyes dart around fearfully before he whispers, "D'ya know what would happen if Kalashnikov caught me? I'd be skinned alive and tossed into the flames. I ain't kiddin'. I seen it happen."

It's a gruesome image, and Ishmael hasn't forgotten the hominid-like bones he stepped on around the fire pit.

"He won't catch you," Ishmael says. "We'll wait until the middle of the night. You let us out of the container, then we'll grab a boat and be gone before they know it."

Blank scuffs the ground with his boot. "Couldn't happen even if I wanted it to. I ain't got the key."

"Who does?" Ishmael asks.

"Kalashnikov and Glock."

"Can you get it from one of them?" Queequeg asks.

Blank chuckles bitterly. "Oh, sure. I'll just stroll up an' ask for it."

That evening, while the pirates are distracted by the fighting beside the fire pit, Queequeg squats and Ishmael climbs onto his shoulders. Grimacing, Queequeg rises to his feet.

"You okay?" Ishmael whispers, feeling Queequeg struggle for balance beneath him.

"For now," his friend whispers.

Ishmael runs his fingertip around the edge of one of the holes in the container's ceiling. Just as he'd hoped, the rusty metal is so thin in some spots that it flakes off under his touch. He pushes one of the blunt sticks through the hole and starts to widen it. But in other places the ceiling is thicker, and he is forced to work the metal back and forth until it snaps.

The work is slow, and he must frequently climb down to give Queequeg a chance to rest his shoulders. All through the evening, he bends, twists, and breaks off as much metal as he can. By the time the pirate camp starts to grow quiet for the night, the hole is broad enough that he and Queequeg can stand on the container floor and look up through it at the dark, starlit sky. The great orb is round and bright tonight.

"Think we'll fit?" Ishmael whispers.

"You first," Queequeg whispers back.

With his friend buttressing from below, Ishmael grabs the rim of the hole and pulls himself up. It's a tight shimmy and the rough metal edges scrape his skin, but he manages to squirm through and into the night above. The sky is the deepest purple imaginable and the jungle is alive with screeches and howls. He pauses a moment to drink in the fresh air, then reaches back down. "Your turn."

They grasp each other's wrists, and Ishmael strains to pull Queequeg up to the rim. Queequeg grabs the metal edges, but even with Ishmael's help, he can't squeeze his broad shoulders through. He twists and wriggles until he's too tired to hold on anymore.

"Let's rest and try again," Ishmael whispers down. All he can see in the dark container are Queequeg's eyes.

"You're gonna have to go without me, Ish. Better one gets away than none."

Ishmael won't hear of it. "Not happening."

"If you don't go, sooner or later we're both dead meat," Queequeg insists. "You're our only chance. Besides, you heard what Kalashnikov said. He'll keep me alive to get to the islanders."

Maybe, Ishmael thinks. Or maybe the pirate leader will kill Queequeg in anger, then attack the islanders anyway. There's only one thing to do. "I'm gonna find that key," he whispers.

"You're crazy," Queequeg whispers back. "Just go. You've got a brother you need to find."

"What about you?" Ishmael asks.

"All I ever had was my father, and they took him away." Now, when Ishmael looks down into the container, all he can see is darkness.

"I'll be back," he promises, then crawls to the edge of the container roof and lowers himself to the ground. He tiptoes barefoot toward the burned-out fire pit in the middle of the camp, where coals still glow a faint red. In the orblight, he can see the dark dwellings. *Is there a way to determine which is Glock's or Kalashnikov's?*

The door of one hut is slightly ajar. He doesn't know whose hut it is, but maybe he'll be lucky, or at least find a weapon. A second later he peeks through the open doorway at what looks like an empty, unmade cot. The dark hut reeks of body odor. He slips in and presses a palm against the bedding. It's still warm. Bad news. Whoever left might return at any moment. He glances about quickly, searching for a gun or even a heavy stick — anything.

The door creaks behind him. Ishmael whirls around — and comes face-to-face with the hulking, horribly scarred pirate named Winchester. The big man fills the entire doorway, his tattoos glowing eerily green in the dark.

Ishmael lowers his head and charges, crashing into the man with more than enough force to send him flying backward out of the hut — but Winchester barely moves. His thick arms close around Ishmael and lift him off the ground.

Ishmael punches the side of Winchester's head as hard as he can. The pirate doesn't even flinch, while Ishmael's fist throbs painfully. He tries kicking, but he might as well be a small, wriggling rodent in Winchester's massive hands. The big pirate slams him to the floor.

"What're ya doin' in here?" he growls. "How'd ya get out of that container?"

Woozy from being slammed so hard, Ishmael has trouble coming up with an answer. Winchester reaches down and with one hand lifts him off the ground until they're face-to-face again. "Where's yer friend?"

Being this close to Winchester's stinking breath snaps Ishmael out of his daze. "Back in the container. He couldn't get out."

The pirate studies him with those eerie red eyes. *He's trying to decide which of a thousand ways to kill me,* Ishmael thinks, his heart beating in his throat.

Instead, Winchester tosses him into the corner like a rag. "It's gonna take me a few minutes to get my stuff together. Don't do nothin' stupid. I'd hate to have to crush yer face."

Ishmael sits up and rubs his head, sure he's misheard. "What?"

"Yer my ticket outta this garbage pit." Winchester shoves things into a sack. "We're gonna take yer boat and go out into the ocean and find a ship, and you're gonna tell 'em how I saved yer life and helped ya escape and yer convinced I don't wanna be a pirate no more. If they don't want me, they can send me back to Earth."

From under his cot Winchester slides a metal lockbox that Ishmael immediately recognizes as similar to the ones he saw in Starbuck's and Ahab's cabins. The pirate presses his huge thumb against the scanner and the top opens, releasing a small cloud of chilled vapor. Winchester removes a vial of chartreuse serum, which he carefully packs into a portable vacuum flask.

"What about food and water?" Ishmael asks. "Might take a long time to find a ship."

"Think I'm stupid?" Winchester snarls, shoving him outside. He points at two large cans of water next to the hut and gestures for Ishmael to carry them.

"What about food?" Ishmael whispers.

"Don't worry about it."

A jarring thought comes to Ishmael. He's seen this beast of a man eat a raw flyer. What if *he's* the only meal Winchester plans on bringing along?

Followed by the pirate and weighed down by the heavy cans, Ishmael trudges along the jungle path toward the beach, his mind searching for a way out of this.

Suddenly, two loud *thunks!* and a *thud!* catch him by surprise. Dropping the water cans, he spins to find Winchester sprawled facedown on the ground. Behind him stands Blank, breathing hard and holding a club in his good hand.

"Been waitin' a long time to do that." The scrawny pirate grins.

Before Ishmael can ask him why he did it, sounds of approaching voices and rustling branches come through the dark.

"Run!" Blank urges him, then disappears into the black jungle.

There's no time to go back for Queequeg. At this point, Ishmael's best hope for saving his friend is to get help. He hustles down the dark trail to the beach. In the orblight he spots Chase Boat Four anchored half a dozen yards offshore and splashes through the shallows toward it.

"Get him!" a voice shouts from behind. Looking back, Ishmael sees the silhouettes of half a dozen pirates on the beach — some kneeling and taking aim with their weapons.

Ishmael climbs into the chase boat and presses start. *Pfft*. . . . The RTG cranks and quits.

Bang! Plang! A bullet ricochets off the engine. Ishmael ducks and tries again.

This time the RTG catches, and Chase Boat Four lurches forward.

Bang! Zing!

Bullets whistle past his ears while the boat gains speed and heads for the open ocean.

With the chase boat racing over the sea, the wind in his face, and no pirates in sight, Ishmael feels the elation of escape and the wrenching agony of leaving Queequeg behind. The sky on the starboard side slowly brightens, red clouds appearing to the east. A crosswind is starting to blow, and soon the ocean swells begin building. Ishmael is forced to steer the chase boat up wave faces and down their backs, scaling liquid hills. Under thick gathering clouds, he keeps the boat going as fast as it can, hoping to outrun not only any pirates who might be pursuing him but the ominous weather as well.

The winds grow stronger, and soon the churning gray seas have foamy white peaks. The boat bounces and slaps, jarring Ishmael's tired muscles and jangled nerves.

And still the swells increase in size.

The wind is beginning to howl, and stinging salt spray hampers his vision. The chase boat is struggling up the face of a large swell when Ishmael feels the RTG hesitate, then sputter. The boat barely makes it over the crest. But halfway up the next wave, the RTG quits completely, and the chase boat slides back down into the trough.

Ishmael tries to start it, but the engine doesn't respond. Bracing himself in the turbulent seas, he lifts the top off the engine compartment. The RTG's ribbed outer shell assembly is discolored and some of the fins look wavy — evidence that they've been heated beyond their tolerance. He remembers the pirates fooling around with the chase boat just after he and Queequeg were captured.

He's surrounded by whitecaps, the whistling wind blowing foam off the crests, making streaks across the gray waves. The sea comes heaving up, and the chase boat rocks violently. Ishmael has to grab the gunwale to keep from tumbling out. Each time a wave threatens to tip the boat, he must scramble to the high side to stabilize it.

This goes on for hours, until Ishmael, exhausted and weak, gradually gives in to oblivion.

61

For an instant, Ishmael thinks he's back home under the Shroud—until he feels the boat rocking beneath him and remembers that even on Cretacea, there are nights made extra dark by thick cloud cover. Driving rain and sea spray pelt him. Soaked and shivering, he tries to get up, only to be held down by a rope lashed around his waist. He remembers that the last thing he did before he passed out was tie himself to a seat to keep from being tossed out by the riotous waves.

The rain is welcome, and Ishmael catches what he can in his hands, funneling the fresh water into his mouth. But the shower passes before he's had enough to quench his thirst. All that remains from the rain is dirty water covered with a patina of oil, sloshing around in the bottom of the chase boat. Ishmael knows what he has to do if he wants to survive. As sickening as the thought is, he lowers his face and drinks.

The sun is hot and glaring; the ocean as smooth as a mirror. Ishmael lies with his head under a seat to shield his face from the scalding rays. Thirst, he's learned, is a much harsher companion than hunger. Thirst demands; hunger merely bides its time. In the scant shadow, with his head against the floor, he listens to the never-ending slosh of sea against hull and wonders if he'll ever be found.

He has lost count of how long it's been since he escaped the pirate camp, days and nights blurring together, but there have been many. Kept barely alive by the filthy water that collects from time to time in the bottom of the boat, he does not know how much longer he can survive without food. Everything feels illusory: He can no longer distinguish between wakefulness and dreaming.

Something thumps the bottom of the chase boat. Dazed and nauseated, Ishmael drags himself to the gunwale and looks over. The sea beneath him has gone white, as though the boat is bobbing on an alabaster ocean. An enormous black eye rises out of the water a few feet away.

In it Ishmael can see his thin, haggard reflection, but he realizes this must be a dream, for staring deeper into the black sphere, he also sees lush green jungles alive with brightly colored flyers, furry tree-dwelling quadrupeds, and all manner of slithering, crawling ground creatures. He sees oceans filled with glimmering schools of scurry, and larger predatory beasts. In this black globe is an entire world, untouched and unspoiled by human hand.

As if the beast knows that she has shown him enough, she slowly slides back into the sea. Ishmael lowers himself to the floor and feels the chase boat rock when the colossal creature glides away.

* * *

"Friend or foe?" a voice calls. On the floor of the chase boat, drifting in and out of consciousness, Ishmael assumes he's dreaming again.

"Friend or foe?" the call repeats. The voice sounds like a woman's.

Another voice joins in: a boy's. "I see him! He's just lying there."

"Careful," the woman cautions. "Could be a trick. Put out the bumpers."

The chase boat shudders, and suddenly Ishmael suspects it might not be a dream after all. This time when the woman shouts "Friend or foe?" she sounds closer. A strong smell of scurry is in the air.

Ishmael gathers what little strength he still possesses and props himself up a few inches. His skull feels like it weighs a hundred pounds, and his arms and shoulders tremble with the strain. A trawler has come alongside, and two blurred figures stare down at him from the railing. The larger of the two — Ishmael thinks it's the woman — is holding something long and dark that might be a shotgun.

"Friend or foe?"

Ishmael tries to swallow. His throat is so dry and sore he isn't sure that words can crawl out, but somehow he manages to croak, "Even if . . . I were . . . a foe . . . I'd have to be . . . crazy . . . to say so."

His head drops back to the chase-boat floor. The effort to hold it up has exhausted him.

62

Sunlight pours in through a porthole. Ishmael is lying in a cushioned bunk, covered by a thin blanket. It takes several moments before he figures out that he's on the trawler, which is moving slowly, rocking this way and that. He vaguely remembers being pulled from the chase boat, and someone coming in now and then to give him water and food.

When he tries to rise, he feels woozy and dazed, but he waits for his mind to clear and slowly stands. Feeling his way along the wall to steady himself, he makes it to the head.

The face in the small mirror over the sink is gaunt and sunburned, with hollowed cheeks and protruding cheekbones. Though not thick, his mustache has grown in, as has the patch beneath his lower lip, but the hair on his chin is sparse and scraggly. Sliding his hands down his sides, Ishmael can feel his ribs and hip bones. How long was he stranded at sea? Even if he finds his way back to the *Pequod,* is he already too late to save Queequeg and prevent the pirates from attacking the islanders?

When he exits the head, he's aware of a fracas coming from above. He finds a tunic and pants, which are too large and must be cinched with rope, then climbs the steps to the deck barefoot. From the moisture in the air and the position of the sun, he can tell that it's midmorning.

The trawler is at the center of a cloud of flapping, wheeling white flyers making a tremendous ruckus. The woman and boy are in the stern, retrieving wet line through a pulley hanging from a boom overhead. They are wearing boots and bright-yellow overalls made of some slick waterproof material. The boy is young — maybe eleven or twelve. The woman has a stocky build and short gray hair; something about her is familiar. Clamped between her teeth is a stem with a small bowl at the end. Now Ishmael remembers: This is the trawler that traded pinkies for supplies with the *Pequod* months ago.

"Well, well, look who finally woke up." The woman chuckles. "Sure two days of sleep was enough for you?"

"Yes, ma'am. And thanks for saving me."

"See you found the clothes. Had to pitch your uniform overboard. Never smelled anything so awful."

"I understand, ma'am."

"Ever clean scurry?"

"Sorry, ma'am?"

The woman holds up a medium-size silver scurry. Its belly has been slit open and the innards removed, revealing pink meat.

"No, ma'am."

"Well, you're about to learn. Go back down and get yourself a bib, some boots, and gloves."

Ishmael does what he's told. While below, he sees through a porthole that Chase Boat Four has been secured to the starboard side of the trawler. If he ever gets back to the *Pequod,* Starbuck and Stubb will surely be pleased that he's brought the boat back with him.

When Ishmael returns to the deck a short time later, the woman and boy are winding in netting and the flyers are in a frenzy, diving and trying to steal whatever morsels they can. The net begins to rise out of the water, bringing with it the huge, squirming ball of sea life. Ishmael expects to see wriggling pinkies, but instead the net is filled with a squirming silver-and-blue mass of scurry.

When the net is entirely out of the water, the woman and the boy swing it over the deck, spilling out a writhing blanket of scurry in all sizes. The intense screeching of the flyers is matched by an unexpected roar of applause — the desperate clapping of hundreds of scurry flopping on the deck.

"Round 'em up before they slip through the scuppers!" the woman yells, grabbing scurry by their tails and tossing them into buckets. Ishmael and the boy join in. The deck is glazed with scurry slime, and several times Ishmael slips and almost loses his balance until finally both feet shoot out from under him and he goes down hard on his butt.

The boy offers him a hand.

As Ishmael reaches for it, their wrists graze.

The shock catches them both by surprise. The boy freezes and stares at Ishmael in confusion. Once again, Ishmael has serious doubts about Pip's claim that greeting registries are a sign of the Gilded. How could this boy be one of them? Why would any member of such an illustrious group want to crew on a smelly trawler on this harsh, backward planet?

The boy doesn't ask what the shock meant, and Ishmael doesn't offer to explain. Instead, the boy tightens his grip on Ishmael's hand and helps him up.

"Show him what to do," the woman shouts over the din of

screeching flyers while she sorts through the buckets of twitching scurry on the deck, picking out the biggest and dropping them through a hatch.

"Come with me!" The boy leads Ishmael to a narrow table covered with gouges and small iridescent scurry scales. Laying a scurry on its side, he demonstrates how to slit its belly open, and uses his gloved fingers to scoop out the entrails. The "cleaned" scurry go into pails beside the table.

Ishmael gets to work, but he is much slower than the boy, who can deftly clean a scurry in seconds. Ishmael struggles to pin the flailing, slippery creatures on the slimy table and feels uncomfortable jabbing the knife into a living thing. And even though he's wearing gloves, his hands and fingers are stuck repeatedly by the spiny fins. But he slowly catches on.

By the time they've finished with the scurry, Ishmael's hands are sore and bloody. But the day's work is still not done. He and the boy must hose down and scrub the cleaning table and deck until every bit of slime, entrail, and scurry scale has been washed through the scuppers and into the sea.

All the while, enticing smells of cooking seep out of the wheelhouse. Finally, the woman calls them to lunch in the small saloon belowdecks. The meal is fresh-cooked scurry, biscuits, and some sort of steamed green. A fold-out table is set with a tablecloth, cloth napkins, plates, and silverware.

While Ishmael eats ravenously, the boy and the woman take their time, handling their silverware with ease and refinement.

"This is delicious, ma'am." Ishmael dabs his lips with his napkin. "I really appreciate it."

"Please, call me Grace," the woman says.

Grace . . .

Ishmael stops in mid-chew. He hasn't forgotten what Old Ben said that last night back on Earth: "*All I knew were Grace and the ocean. . . . The captain of our pinkboat.*"

When Ishmael takes a moment too long to reply, Grace says, "And you are?"

"Call me Ishmael."

"Nice to have you aboard, Ishmael." Grace tilts her head toward the boy. "And this is my son, Benjamin."

Feeling light-headed, Ishmael stares at the boy. The distinguishing facial characteristics are there — the broad forehead, the thick hair, the widow's peak. Is he actually Old Ben? The thought is completely unsettling. It's not possible — is it? The old man's prophecies about Cretacea, the *Pequod,* Grace, and the pinkboat have already come true. But how in the universe could this boy end up an old wreck of a man in Black Range? How could he have lived there for more than thirty years *before* Ishmael even left for Cretacea? And yet, that last night in Black Range, hadn't Old Ben also said, "*I wasn't on a mission. Cretacea's where I grew up.*"

"Ahem." Grace clears her throat.

"Sorry." Ishmael realizes he's been staring. Grace knits her brow. "Are you okay?"

Ishmael takes a deep breath to stop his head from spinning. "Yes, ma'am."

"May I ask how you came to be floating in the middle of the ocean?" Grace asks. "In a stick boat from the *Pequod,* if I'm not mistaken."

Ishmael swallows, then tells them the story.

"You were captured by pirates?" Benjamin asks with wide-eyed wonder.

Ishmael nods.

"Well, you're in luck," Grace says. "In a few days we'll rendezvous with your ship to drop Benjamin off. He's going back to Earth."

"I said, I'm not going!" The boy crosses his arms defiantly.

"You must get an education, Benjamin," Grace says patiently, in a way that makes Ishmael think she's said this many times before.

"No, I mustn't," Benjamin protests. "I want to stay here with you."

Meanwhile, Ishmael feels his insides churn while he recalls Old Ben's warning: "Do not rendezvous with the Pequod. *When Grace tells you that's what she's going to do, you have to stop her. . . . Lives are at stake.*"

It may have once seemed impossible, but there's no longer any doubt in Ishmael's mind: This boy sitting in this trawler on this vast ocean on sun-blessed Cretacea will somehow grow into Old Ben on bleak, sooty, Shroud-covered Earth.

Unless Ishmael can stop them from meeting the *Pequod.*

63

"That story about you escaping from pirates really true?" Grace asks while she lights the bowl she has clamped in her teeth. Wisps of pungent smoke drift into the air. She and Ishmael sit on a narrow bench outside the wheelhouse and watch the sunset of pinks and purples over the vast blue ocean. They've finished dinner, and Benjamin is below in VR.

Ishmael cocks his head. "Why would you doubt it?"

"Been sailing these oceans a long time. Heard a lot of stories about pirates taking prisoners, but never heard of anyone getting away. Guess it was a good thing we found you when we did. You looked like you might not have lasted another day."

"Not sure how long I'd have lasted if I hadn't escaped in the first place," Ishmael says, once again feeling an ache about leaving Queequeg behind. "Do you ever have trouble with them?"

"The pirates? No. They're shore huggers, afraid of the open ocean. Don't have a clue about navigation. As long as we stay out at sea, we don't have to worry." She points at the tiny terrafin skivers in his ears. "What about these?"

He tells her about his time with the islanders, but not about the terrafin pens.

Grace gives him an uncertain look. "Islanders? Never heard of them."

"You're serious?" Ishmael's surprised.

"Well, like I said, we stay in deep waters because that's where the scurry and pinkies are plentiful." She relights her bowl. "Still, seems like you've covered an awful lot of ocean for someone who says he's been here only a short time."

Ishmael hears loud and clear what's gone unsaid: She'd like to believe him, but isn't convinced she should. But he's curious about her, too. "How long have you been on Cretacea?"

"More than half my life at this point." Grace lets out a puff of smoke. "I left Earth the day I found out there was a place like this, with real daylight and all sorts of living creatures and endless, beautiful ocean. Guess I was born with the sea in my blood. Why anyone would want to remain on that filthy, dark world is beyond me."

"Then why send Benjamin there?"

"All he's ever known is the ocean, but that doesn't mean it's in his blood, too. I made a choice about what kind of life I wanted to live. He deserves to have the choice as well."

"But what makes you think he'd ever choose Earth? Like you said, it's so ugly there."

"Not everywhere."

Ishmael absorbs this. It still seems incredible to him that there are places on Earth that aren't as bad as Black Range. But he knows there must be. Like High Desert, where Billy's family lives. And Pip, of course, comes from a place that must be much different, where there's enough water to fill swimming pools, and people don't depend on Natrient to survive.

But no matter where Grace thinks she's sending Benjamin, Ishmael knows that eventually the boy will end up a broken-down benzo fiend living alone in Black Range. His insides are in turmoil. He promised Old Ben that he'd do whatever he could to stop Grace from rendezvousing with the *Pequod,* but that was before he knew that Queequeg's life might depend on him getting back to the ship to organize a rescue. *And* before he knew the lives of the islanders might depend on him as well. Finally, it was before he knew that Archie was somewhere on Cretacea.

He knows he should tell Grace the truth, try to persuade her that Benjamin is better off on her pinkboat than he ever will be on Earth. That they shouldn't interact with the *Pequod* . . .

But something else has begun to niggle at him:

It was Ben who discovered him and Archie in the foundling home, and who brought Petra and Joachim to see them.

It was Ben who persuaded Ms. Hussey to let Joachim and Petra take both boys when it became obvious that they were inseparable.

It was Ben who always said they could have better lives than anything the Zirconia Electrolysis station could offer.

Finally, it was Ben who encouraged Ishmael to go on this mission.

Is it possible . . . that Ben planned this from the beginning? So that he wouldn't have to be sent back to Earth?

Has everything that's happened to Ishmael since the day Ben spotted him in the foundling home been leading to this one moment, when Ishmael has the power to change the course of the old man's life?

Has Old Ben simply been using him all this time?

No, Ishmael can't believe that. He *won't* believe that.

But even as he tells himself that, other suspicious thoughts worm their way in.

The Ψ9,000 he sent back . . . was it *really* for his foster parents?

You can't think this way, he tells himself. *You've got to trust.*

But what about meeting up with the *Pequod*?

Ben's is only *one* life. What about Queequeg and the islanders? Can he choose one man's life over so many?

The trawler rocks gently on the waves. The sun is below the horizon now, but the clouds are still orange, pink, and purple. Fifty feet off the bow, a large scurry leaps out of the sea and splashes back down.

"I thought this was a pinkboat," Ishmael says, watching the spreading rings of water where the scurry jumped. "I remember we traded with you a few months ago."

"It's a pinkboat when the pinkies are running. When they're not running, we have to take whatever we can get, which means scurry."

"Do you trade with ships besides the *Pequod*?"

Grace chuckles. "When all you've got are pinkies and scurry, you'll trade with any ship you can."

"Ever encounter one called the *Jeroboam*?" Ishmael asks.

Grace gazes off into the distance. "No."

64

In the morning Ishmael wakes to the scent of red berry. His body aches and his hands are sore from cleaning scurry the day before, but he rises and goes into the head, where he decides to shave his chin but keep the mustache and patch beneath his lip.

When he gets to the galley, he gladly accepts a steaming mug from Grace.

"Benjamin's up on the deck," she tells him. "It's a beautiful morning. Why don't you join him?"

Mug in hand, Ishmael heads abovedecks. Benjamin, wearing a gray jersey with shortened sleeves, is in the bow. Ishmael sits beside him. The trawler drifts on the nearly flat ocean.

"So what's it like on Earth, anyway?" the boy asks sullenly.

Ishmael takes a sip of red berry and answers carefully. "I guess it depends on where. Some places aren't so great. . . . But it sounds like

Grace wants to send you somewhere that's better than most." He feels a spasm of guilt. He hates being deceitful. But how can he tell this boy the truth as he knows it?

"What about the place you're from?"

Before Ishmael can reply, they become aware of a distant speck in the sky and a high-pitched whine that grows louder until a drone hovers before them. Grace comes out of the wheelhouse, and it occurs to Ishmael that this drone is here to inspect them. Trust is a rare commodity on the open seas. They are supposed to meet the *Pequod* soon, and someone on that ship wants to make sure everything on this trawler is as it should be.

The drone circles the trawler and then returns to inspect the crew, coming within a few feet of Ishmael and lingering a moment longer.

"Get the feeling someone's surprised to find you aboard?" Grace asks.

"Can't blame them," Ishmael answers.

Another moment passes, then the drone zips off.

Realizing what the drone's visit signified, Benjamin shoves his hands into his pockets and pouts. "I'm not going."

Grace lights her bowl. "There's a lot more to life than living on this boat."

"*You* like it," Benjamin shoots back petulantly.

"It's a choice I made after many years of seeing what else was out there," says Grace. "It's time for you to make your own choice."

"This *is* what I'd choose," Benjamin insists.

"You're too young to know that. You have to get an education, and then, if you decide you still want to work on a trawler, no one will stop you."

"I hate you!" The boy springs to his feet and goes below, slamming the hatch behind him.

Grace doesn't react, but Ishmael sees a great sadness in her eyes. As much as she seems convinced that this is the best thing for

Benjamin, the decision to send him so far away must be terribly painful.

Seeing her heartache, Ishmael can no longer resist the obligation he feels toward the old man he left back in Black Range: "I know this is none of my business, but have you been in touch with anyone back on Earth lately? I get the feeling that things aren't so good."

"I've been assured that he'll be well cared for." Grace waves at the nets and ropes and winches. "This is no way for a child of his age to live. No friends. Nothing to do but work. Where he's going he'll have access to . . . certain advantages. Once he experiences them, he may find he wants more from life than this."

Ishmael feels a prickly sensation spread over him. *Certain advantages?* Is she saying what he thinks she's saying — that Benjamin *really is* of the Gilded?

By midafternoon, the *Pequod* is in sight. From a distance it resembles a huge reddish-brown-and-black-striped creature. Crewmen line the railings. The drone returns and circles the trawler watchfully.

Grace tells Benjamin to get his things. The boy wrinkles his nose angrily but does what he's told. As soon as he disappears belowdecks, his mother rubs tears out of her eyes. Earlier in the day she'd told Ishmael that her husband, Benjamin's father, was washed overboard in a storm when Benjamin was still a toddler. That must make sending her son to Earth even more wrenching.

A chase boat is lowered from the *Pequod* and starts toward them. Among the crew Ishmael spots bright-yellow hair and a familiar hulking figure: Daggoo and Bunta, together again. Thanks to the drones, they must know by now that he's aboard the pinkboat. Is that why they volunteered to be part of the welcome party?

"Will you keep an eye on my son?" Grace asks, her voice almost breaking.

All at once, Ishmael knows he can't hold back any longer. The battle that has raged in his conscience has abruptly ended. He has to tell her the truth.

"Don't send him back," he blurts out. "It's bad back there, where Benjamin is going. You need to keep him here, with you."

Grace's eyes widen, then narrow. "I don't know what business it is of yours, but I told you, he's got people who'll look after him. He'll be all right."

"He won't!" Ishmael insists. "Listen to me! Something goes wrong when you send him back. I can't explain it, but I'm telling you the truth. He isn't going where you think — or even *when* you think. The Earth he's going to is dying, and he's going to die right along with it!"

Her expression hardens. "You can't possibly know that. He has to go."

The chase boat is a hundred yards away now — close enough for Ishmael to see that Starbuck is also on board.

He takes a breath and lets it out in a rush: "Please, Grace, just listen. I know it sounds crazy, but . . . I knew Benjamin back on Earth. In a bad place called Black Range. Only he wasn't a boy then. He was an old man who'd lived a very hard, very sad life. And before I left for Cretacea, he told me about you. He made me promise I wouldn't let you send him back. *'Don't let Grace rendezvous with the* Pequod. . . . *Lives are at stake.'* That's what he told me. And I promised him I wouldn't. So you can't do it, Grace. I beg you!"

While the chase boat draws closer and closer, Grace stares at him, uncomprehending. Finally, her demeanor softens. "I don't think I realized what an ordeal it must have been for you lost at sea," she says gently. "Enough to undo even the toughest of men. You'll feel better once the ship's surgeon takes a look at you."

Ishmael glances back at the approaching vessel, his heart beating madly. If Grace won't listen, then he's going to have to find another way to stop her.

He climbs up on the trawler's transom and jumps.

65

Ishmael swims until the chase boat is within shouting distance, then waves to make sure they see him. "Don't go near the pinkboat! It's infected!"

As soon as they hear him, Daggoo and Bunta turn to Starbuck. Ishmael sees the first mate's lips move. The chase boat slows but continues to approach, with Daggoo and Bunta kneeling at the gunwale.

Starbuck steps into the bow. "Don't know what you're talking about, boy. The bio scans are the same as always. Completely normal."

The chase boat stops, and Daggoo and Bunta grab Ishmael's hands and pull him from the ocean. "Then it must be some kind of infection the scanning isn't picking up, sir," Ishmael says, dripping. "Are you really willing to risk it?"

Starbuck tilts his head uncertainly. "What are the symptoms?" he asks.

Ishmael's had no time to prepare an answer. He twists around and looks at the trawler, where Grace stands with her hands on the transom, slowly shaking her head.

"Well?" Starbuck demands impatiently.

"You have to believe me, sir," Ishmael blathers. "I wouldn't lie to you. It's bad."

The first mate picks up a pair of binoculars and aims them at the pinkboat.

"What should I do, sir?" the chase boat's skipper asks.

Starbuck lowers the binoculars. "Proceed as planned."

"But, sir!" Ishmael begins. "Didn't you hear what I—"

"That's enough!" Starbuck silences him. "I don't know what sort of game you're playing, boy, but there's a considerable transport fee at stake, and we're in no position to refuse it. What were you doing on that trawler, anyway? We saw the drone imagery of the pirates getting you."

"It's a long story, sir."

"I hope it's better than this one," the first mate says, gesturing with his binoculars at the healthy-looking captain of the pinkboat in the distance. "And while you're telling stories, what of Pip and Queequeg?"

"The pirates still have Queequeg, sir. And Pip made some kind of deal with them. I . . . I assumed he was back on the *Pequod.*"

Starbuck shakes his head, and again looks through the binoculars at the trawler.

"Seriously, sir, you don't want to go near them."

The first mate exhales an exasperated sigh. "One more word out of you, and I'll have you gagged."

When Ishmael stares a moment too long at the light machine gun mounted in the stern, Daggoo "ahems" loudly.

Starbuck turns and immediately grasps the situation. "Aw, for the sea's sweet sake! Tie his hands and keep an eye on him."

And so Ishmael's hands are bound behind his back and he's placed beside Bunta.

A few moments later, they come alongside the trawler.

"How you feeling, sweetheart?" Starbuck asks Grace, then jerks his thumb at Ishmael. "Sailor boy here claims you've got some rare disease."

"I'm afraid he's spent too much time in the sun," Grace replies.

"So where'd you find him?" Starbuck asks, while Daggoo hops on board and unties the lines holding Chase Boat Four.

"Half dead and floating in the middle of nowhere. He's delusional. If I were you, I'd keep him bound until you get him to the ship's surgeon."

"I was thinking the same thing," Starbuck says. "Where's the passenger for transport?"

"I'll get him."

While Grace heads belowdecks, Daggoo brings the bowline of Chase Boat Four back and they secure it to a cleat. Starbuck looks at Ishmael. "That story about her finding you true?"

"Yes, sir."

"Awful big ocean to just run into someone."

Ishmael shrugs. "Guess it was meant to be, sir." He glances at the pinkboat, feeling the seconds slip away. "I know you don't want to hear this, sir, but you can't send the boy back to Earth. Something goes wrong when you do. He doesn't—"

"Mother of Terrafins!" Bunta jumps up and shouts.

Everyone in the chase boat stands to see. Out beyond the pinkboat's bow, a huge white mass has appeared on the surface.

66

The chase boat's engine roars to life as the skipper quickly prepares to depart.

"Wait!" Starbuck shouts.

On the pinkboat, Grace comes abovedecks with Benjamin, and catches the stunned expressions on the faces of the chase-boat crew. When she sees what they're staring at, her eyes go wide. "Take him! *Now!*" She grabs the startled boy, lifts him over the transom, and thrusts him into Starbuck's arms.

"Grace!" Benjamin screams and struggles, but the *Pequod*'s first mate holds him while Grace dashes into the pinkboat's wheelhouse.

"Go!" Starbuck shouts at the chase-boat skipper, who jams the craft into gear. With his hands bound behind him, Ishmael starts to tumble backward over the gunwale. At the last conceivable instant, Bunta yanks him back into the chase boat, pushing him down onto a seat.

Towing Chase Boat Four, they rocket back toward the *Pequod*, where the cargo rope is being lowered over the side.

"What's she doing?" Daggoo is staring behind them. All faces turn toward the Great Terrafin and the pinkboat chugging toward it, looking like a small plaything in comparison.

"Saving our skins," Starbuck grimly replies.

The davit hooks are already plummeting down when the chase boats draw alongside the *Pequod*'s hull. Except for Ishmael — who's still transfixed by the sight of the pinkboat heading toward the enormous terrafin — those aboard begin to scale the cargo rope as fast as they can. Bunta carries a whimpering Benjamin with one arm while hauling himself up with the other.

"Hey!" Ishmael shouts when he realizes he's been left behind. His hands are still tied.

Halfway up the rope, Daggoo hesitates, then starts to descend. "Don't say I never did anything nice for you, pinkie."

After Daggoo unties Ishmael, they both begin to climb the cargo rope. The *Pequod* increases power and starts to come about, propellers churning. Ishmael looks over his shoulder and sees that Grace has positioned the pinkboat between the Great Terrafin and the *Pequod*. She stands in the stern, and Ishmael knows she's been watching her son, making sure he gets safely on board the larger ship.

Ishmael reaches the bulwark and feels hands grab and pull him over. Two of those hands belong to Gwen, and it's a surprise and a relief to see that she's okay.

The sailors at the *Pequod*'s rail silently stare at the scene unfolding before them. On the pinkboat's deck, Grace has turned to face the giant creature. It's a strange, eerie moment. Even Benjamin is quiet. Why, Ishmael wonders, has the Great Terrafin surfaced in full view of both vessels?

The answer comes with terrible swiftness: One of the creature's enormous tails arcs over its body and smashes through the trawler's rigging, knocking Grace to the deck.

"Grace!" Benjamin screams, renewing his struggle against Bunta's grasp.

Shouts of horror rise from the *Pequod*'s deck while the Great Terrafin strikes again and again, thrashing the pinkboat with its tails. Remarkably, Grace is uninjured. She struggles to her feet and tries to get into the wheelhouse.

Crash! A white tail smashes down, and Grace is again thrown to the deck.

Crash! This time, the Great Terrafin crushes the wheelhouse.

Ishmael feels overcome with guilt and anguish. Was *this* why Old Ben wanted him to stop Grace from rendezvousing with the *Pequod*? Not to change the course of *his* life, but to save *hers*? Ishmael's stomach tightens with regret. He should have tried harder to keep the pinkboat from meeting them, he should have—

The crowd on the deck begins to part. Step, *clank*, step, *clank*... Ahab quickly limps through, headed for the big harpoon cannon in the bow.

Crash! A tail smashes down on the pinkboat's stern, tearing away part of the transom. *Crash!* Another blow rips away a large piece of rail. It appears that the huge creature is intent on bashing the trawler to bits.

"Grace!" Benjamin screams again and again, twisting and fighting so frantically that Charity and Tashtego must come to Bunta's aid in restraining him.

The crew watch in horror while the great beast pulverizes the pinkboat. Grace has vanished from sight, while from out of nowhere a frenzy of red-tipped gray fins cuts excitedly through the floating debris. Ishmael can see the dark, streamlined shapes of creatures racing below.

"Big-tooths," a sailor says soberly.

Benjamin no longer shrieks and thrashes. He has fallen heartbreakingly mute.

By now Ahab has positioned himself behind the harpoon

cannon. The *Pequod* has come about and is headed toward the scattered remains of the pinkboat, whose bow is still visible, poking up through the debris, and the enormous monster just beyond it.

Boom! The huge harpoon explodes out of the cannon with such force that Ishmael feels the percussive clap in his chest.

Thwack! It's a hit! The harpoon buries itself deep in one of the Great Terrafin's wings.

Instantly, the immense creature vanishes into the depths, and heavy red line begins whipping off the *Pequod*'s forecastle.

The sailors press against the ship's rail, watching.

Suddenly nearly all of them are thrown off their feet when the *Pequod*'s bow is yanked around.

Bang! At the loud crack, Ishmael looks for someone with a gun . . . until he realizes that the sound was from the snapping of the thick harpoon rope.

A quarter mile away, the Great Terrafin bursts out of the water, the huge harpoon jutting from its back and a long length of red line trailing behind it.

The *Pequod* floats silently. The sailors slowly get to their feet. Green-haired Marion is the first to speak. "Did you feel how it pulled the bow around? Like this ship was nothing but a tin can."

"That harpoon line was supposed to be unbreakable, but the beast snapped it with one good yank," mutters Flask.

"Maybe it's a beast that's not meant to be captured." Tashtego adjusts his belt around his belly. "Maybe that was a warning of what it'll do to us if we don't leave off."

But not all aboard agree. Already Ahab is shouting up to the bridge: "Hard to port! Hard to port!"

The *Pequod* begins to churn to the left, away from the wreckage of the pinkboat, toward the direction taken by the Great Terrafin.

Benjamin screams and starts to struggle again. "*Wait!* Grace! We can't leave her!"

Ishmael pushes through the crowd of sailors and plants himself in Ahab's path. "With all due respect, sir, what about the pinkboat captain?"

With a manic look in his eyes, Ahab hardly appears to see him. "Out of my way, sailor."

But Ishmael stands his ground. "The woman could have survived, sir. She could still be out there. You can't just—"

Smack! Ishmael stumbles to the side, the skin of his cheek burning from the sharp backhand blow.

"I said, out of my way!" Ahab bellows. "This is *my* ship, and that"—he points in the direction the beast has gone—"is *my* terrafin!"

Step, *clank*, step, *clank*. The captain starts toward the superstructure. Propelled by guilt over Grace and by the conviction that Ahab will see them all killed before he'll admit defeat, Ishmael jumps to his feet to try again, but hands grab him from behind.

When he twists around, Ishmael finds himself looking at his reflection in Starbuck's round black glasses.

"It's not worth it, boy," the first mate warns gravely. "Believe me."

"But he's—"

Starbuck clamps a hand over Ishmael's mouth. "Listen carefully, boy. Even if Grace had somehow survived that thrashing, the bigtooths got her for sure. There's nothing left to be done, understand?"

Ishmael breathes heavily against the first mate's palm. Starbuck gradually loosens his grip, not sure whether to trust him. But Ishmael doesn't move.

Starbuck drops his hand and studies him. "You okay?"

No, I'm not okay. I'm never going to be "okay" as long as I'm on this insane ship. Ishmael looks at the crowd of sailors who are slowly returning to their regular chores. "Where's the boy?"

"Charity took him down to the stasis lab."

67

By the time Ishmael gets down to the lab, Charity has already closed the pod and sealed the chamber. She and Gwen are in the control room behind the clear metallic-alloy window. Tongue sticking out of the corner of her mouth, Charity is concentrating on a screen displaying bars of different colors.

"He just watched his mother die, and you're sending him away?" Ishmael asks, incredulous.

"Got a better suggestion?" Charity says. "Keep him here on this ship while that madman chases his terrafin? At least on Earth, there are people who'll take care of him." She moves her finger over the screen. In the chamber, the pod begins to glow. Watching through the window, Ishmael feels a deep sense of helplessness. Benjamin is going to Earth to grow into a miserable, decrepit old man. And now he feels responsible for destroying not one, but two, lives — the boy's and Grace's.

"You're sure you sent him to the right place?" Ishmael asks. Maybe it's not too late to correct the mistakes of the past.

"I'm sending him to Earth, honey. Hard to get that one wrong."

"But I mean, you're sure about *where* on Earth . . ."

Charity swivels around to look at him. "What's your concern?"

"I—" He catches himself. If he tells her what he knows about the future, she'll think he's crazy. Just like Grace did.

"No worries, honey. The science might not be perfect, but I'm pretty good at hitting my targets. Anyway, too late to fret about it. The flyer's in the fryer, as they say."

The three of them stare through the window into the stasis chamber, where the pod continues to grow brighter. The control room goes quiet until Ishmael's eyes meet Gwen's.

"How did you make it here after the pirates attacked us?" he asks. "I thought Ahab never goes back for men overboard."

Gwen smirks. "He does if your name's Pippin Lopez-Makarova. They sent the tender to look for him and found me instead."

"Starbuck told me Pip never came back to the ship," Ishmael says. "Any idea what happened to him?"

"We assumed he was with you all this time." Charity slides her finger across the screen. Ishmael wonders if, now that Pip's had a taste of the perils of life on Cretacea, he's been whisked off to someplace safer.

"What about Queek?" Gwen asks.

A hum comes from the chamber where the pod shimmers and then fades into nothingness. Ishmael explains what happened with the pirates, and how he had no choice but to leave Queequeg behind. "I'm going back for him."

Charity looks up from the screen. "How?"

"In a chase boat."

Gwen shakes her head. "You'll never get permission."

"I don't plan to ask for it."

The control room goes silent. Both women give him dubious looks.

"Even if you're somehow able to steal a chase boat"—Gwen's tone implies how unlikely she thinks that is—"do you realize what you'll be giving up? If they get the Great Terrafin and you're AWOL, you won't get to share the bounty. You'll be left with nothing."

Charity gazes up at him with a strange expression that reminds him of the day he arrived on this ship and she scanned his registry. And suddenly it hits him that all along she's known something about him that until recently he never suspected . . . *that he's of the Gilded.* Is she wondering why he cares so much—and is willing to risk so much—for someone who doesn't even *have* a registry?

"No, Gwen, he'll get something, all right," Charity says. "He'll get to spend the rest of the voyage in the brig. That is, if the pirates don't kill him first."

Ishmael turns to Gwen. "Look, I know I owe you a lot of money, and once I go back for Queequeg, the chances of me paying you back will be . . . well, not exactly promising. But think about it, Gwen. With the money you gave me . . . er, *lent* me . . . you may have saved two lives. Thanks to you, my foster parents could be going somewhere safe."

"You really think I care about your foster parents?" Gwen snaps. "I don't even know them."

The control room goes so quiet, they could hear the tiniest terrafin skiver drop.

Gwen's face softens. "It's *you* I care about, stupid. If I need more money, I'll figure out how to make it. But right now my biggest problem is understanding how you think you can steal a chase boat and save Queequeg. Frankly, I don't think there's enough brains in that skull to do it alone."

When Ishmael realizes what she's implying, he shakes his head. "You're not coming with me. It may already be too late. Who knows what they did to Queek when they found out I escaped? You're right, this could be a suicide mission."

"Gee, you've made it sound so appealing, I guess I'll have to go, too, honey." Charity shuts down the screen.

"Seriously, both of you. I'm not looking for a crew."

Charity's countenance becomes grave. "Okay, you want to be serious? I've got a score to settle with those barbarians myself. Even if you don't take me with you, I'd probably find another way to get them."

"Didn't you say a minute ago that the pirates will kill me if I go back?" Ishmael argues. "What makes you think they won't kill you, too?"

"Not sure my chances are much better staying on this ship and going after that monster," Charity says. "But getting my hands on those pirates would be a *lot* more satisfying."

"She's got a point," Gwen agrees.

Ishmael studies them both, knowing that while the chances of saving Queequeg are slim, they're certainly better with Charity and Gwen coming along than if he goes alone.

He leans close and tells them his plan.

68

Charity's persuaded Starbuck to assign her temporarily as a lineman on Chase Boat Four, replacing Pip. Their new stickman is Flask, who did some harpooning in his earlier years. Ishmael has no doubt that the man with the viper tattoos on his face has been quietly ordered to keep an eye on him. The third mate's presence is an inconvenience, but it won't stop Ishmael from going ahead with his plan.

Within a few hours of being launched, Chase Boat Four is far enough from the *Pequod* to be out of two-way range. The drones are even farther off, scanning the ocean for the Great Terrafin.

Ishmael cuts the RTG, and the chase boat drifts silently. Flask, behind the harpoon gun in the bow, gives Ishmael a puzzled look.

"We're going to get Queequeg." From under the console, Ishmael pulls out a duffel he'd hidden earlier.

Flask blinks with surprise. "Are ya mad, boy? The captain'll keel-haul ya—assuming ya make it back in one piece." He shifts his sights to Charity. "And you, who barely survived yer first run-in with the pirates. Ya really think you'll be so lucky a second time?"

"I was on my own last time," Charity replies defiantly. "This time I've got backup."

Ishmael passes the duffel to Flask. Inside it is a survival suit that's been treated with big-tooth repellent. "The *Pequod* will pass by here in a couple of hours. They'll send a tender to get you."

Flask starts to pull the suit on. "I guess there's no convincing the three of ya that yer mad. But probably no madder than anyone else on that Earth-forsaken ship."

"Can I ask you a favor?" Ishmael says.

The third mate raises his eyebrows. "Funny time to ask fer a favor, but ya did save me considerable coin on the repairs fer this boat, so go on, tell me what ya want."

"When they pick you up and Starbuck asks what happened, tell him I forced Gwen and Charity to stay onboard. If we ever make it back to the *Pequod,* I don't want them punished."

Flask chuckles. "Sure. That'll be easy, since it's guaranteed none a' you'll be comin' back." He sits on the gunwale and activates the survival suit's rescue beacon. "Anyway, I appreciate the suit. Someone else might've just thrown me overboard in my undies. Been nice knowing ya."

He goes over the side with a splash.

A day and a half later, when Ishmael noses the chase boat through the gap in the island reef, he sees children playing on the beach and outriggers searching for scurry. A weight lifts from his chest: The pirates haven't yet attacked.

"So this is the island." Charity sounds awestruck.

An outrigger leaves shore and starts toward them, Gabriel in the bow. When the two boats meet, he reaches out and gives Ishmael's hand a welcoming grasp.

"Tis good t'see ye again," he says warmly but with a hint of caution. "Come." He signals the outrigger to turn around and head for shore. The chase boat follows.

On the beach, Fayaway, Thistle, and Billy wait. Billy's skin is the dark copper of the islanders', his body lean and wiry. His sun-bleached curly blond hair hangs in ringlets over his ears.

Charity's mouth falls open with disbelief. *"Billy?"*

He grins broadly. "Art ye surprised?"

"Shocked," Charity replies. "You're alive! And you look completely different."

Billy beams. Ishmael wonders if he even realizes he speaks like an islander now.

Gwen gives him an uncharacteristic hug. "It's good to see you again. And you, too," she adds to Fayaway.

Thistle joyfully wraps her arms around Gwen's waist. Fayaway steps close to Ishmael and touches his cheek. "Never thought we'd see ye again," she whispers.

"Neither did I."

With her finger, she traces his mustache and the patch beneath his lip. "Ye art handsome."

Ishmael feels blood rush to his face. He turns to Gabriel, expecting him to ask why they've come, but instead Fayaway's father says, "'Tis almost dinner. Will ye stay?"

When they start up the beach, Billy asks, "Where's Queek?"

Ishmael looks down at the sand. "The pirates have him."

"How?" Billy's face is chiseled with concern.

"There's a lot I need to tell you. All of you."

They leave the beach and walk along the path through the trees. Ishmael notices platforms high in the branches. "Are those new?"

Billy's expression grows pinched, and he explains that they're for the islanders to fire arrows and darts at an approaching enemy.

"Diana's convinced we must prepare for the worst. She can't believe that ye shall never tell another soul about our terrafins."

Ishmael cringes. In a little while, Diana will discover that she was right not to trust him. Not that it's his fault the pirates know about the terrafins, but had the islanders followed Diana's wishes that he and his crew not leave the island, they would be much safer right now. He hates to think that they were smart to build those platforms and prepare to defend themselves.

Still, he's not prepared for what awaits them just outside the village: A tall barricade made of sharp wooden spikes pointing outward. It is a formidable barrier, and a horrible eyesore in such a beautiful and harmonious setting.

While they wait outside the closed gate for someone to let them in, Ishmael notices something else: "There's no music."

Billy nods somberly. "Diana says there's no place for music when we must constantly be listening for the enemy."

There are fewer islanders at dinner than Ishmael recalls. Fayaway says it's because some are always posted now as lookouts in case of attack. The atmosphere at the evening meal is no longer festive. The islanders eat quietly and speak in whispers.

Still, to Charity it must seem blissful. She takes in the trees and night-blooming flowers and puts her arm around Billy's shoulder. "No wonder you decided to stay here. I feel like I'm in paradise."

"'Tis nothing compared with the way 'twas," Billy whispers glumly. "Fear of attack 'tis like an invisible shroud always over us."

After dinner Gabriel invites Ishmael to join him and Diana beside a fire.

"T'what we owe this visit?" Gabriel asks, a cautious edge to his voice.

Ishmael takes a steadying breath and tells them everything: how he, Queequeg, and their crewmate Pip were captured by pirates, how the pirates were going to kill Queequeg and him, but Pip saved their lives . . . by telling them about the islanders farming terrafins.

Diana bangs a fist against the ground. "I knew it!" She glares at Gabriel. "And ye were so certain he'd never tell!"

Ishmael hangs his head and accepts the blame. Ultimately it will make no difference that it's not actually his fault: that Pip found out about the islanders' terrafins by eavesdropping on a private conversation he was having with Gwen. All that matters now is that the islanders are in danger.

With sadness in his eyes, Gabriel speaks to Diana. "'Tis true t'we have been betrayed. Yet he has returned t'warn us. 'Twas not compelled to do this. 'Tis a mark of character."

Diana's response is a contemptuous guffaw. "We must redouble our efforts t'protect ourselves. 'Tis time t'train the older children in the arts of combat."

Ishmael steels himself for what he has to say next: "Wait. There's more. I have to ask you for a favor."

Diana stares at him in disbelief. "Art ye mad? After what ye've done t'us? Ye should be cast off forever!"

With a pained look, Gabriel watches the red sparks of the fire vanish into the night air. "What 'tis this favor?" he asks quietly.

"Ye can't be serious!" Diana sputters, but Gabriel holds up a hand to silence her.

"The pirates still have Queequeg," Ishmael says. "We may be too late to save him, but we must try. Except my friends and I can't do it alone. If we're going to have any chance of succeeding, we'll need your —"

"'Tis out of the question!" Diana spits. "Even if ye deserved our help, we need everyone here t'defend against those demons. 'Tis only a matter of time till they come."

Gabriel reflects for a moment, then speaks to Ishmael. "We

must think of more than one life. There art the lives of all our people t'consider."

Ishmael anticipated this reply—indeed, he knows he would react the same way were he in their position. "I understand. But what if I had a way to save Queequeg *and* stop the pirates from ever attacking you?"

"'Tis utter nonsense!" Diana contends. "A handful of ye against a whole host of demons? Impossible!"

But Gabriel asks, "How?"

Ishmael lays out his plan. When he's finished, Gabriel picks up a stick and stirs the coals in the fire while he thinks.

"Ye can't seriously be considering this," Diana warns him. "'Tis madness. A false promise t'get us t'help him save his friend. How many times must he mislead us before ye understand?"

Gabriel entwines his fingers and stares at the fire without answering.

With a hard look, Diana tells Ishmael, "We've heard ye and will discuss it among ourselves. But ye shan't hold t'hope."

69

While Fayaway remains behind to listen to the discussion, Ishmael, Gwen, Charity, and Billy go down to the beach. The great orb hangs in the night sky, casting a rippling, luminescent stripe across the black water.

Sitting on the shore, Charity lets the gentle tide lap at her feet. "I can't get over how beautiful it is here."

Once again, Ishmael must gulp back the guilt he feels, knowing he could be responsible for the violence and mayhem that may soon visit this place.

"How did ye come to be captured by the pirates?" Billy asks.

In the glow of the orblight, Ishmael catches Billy up on all that's happened since they left him. Though Charity and Gwen have heard the stories before, this time around Gwen seems confused by one detail: "You're saying that the pirates let Pip go once they found out he was of the Gilded? How could the Gilded be so powerful, not only on Earth but throughout the galaxy, without the rest of us even knowing they existed?"

Once again, Charity casts a curious look at Ishmael. Then she says, "What if I told you there's a whole industry devoted to making sure you don't know about the Gilded — or about much of anything, really."

They listen while she goes on to explain that between her job as the ship's stasis tech, things Starbuck said to her while under the influence of the serum, and what she's picked up from a bit of judicious snooping, she has a reasonably good understanding of what's really been going on back on Earth:

"Everything is controlled by the Trust. What was once 'the government' was sold off and privatized during the Resource Wars — when the east and west fought over Africa and Antarctica for their natural resources. Only it wasn't *countries* fighting those wars, as you were led to believe. It was corporations."

Ishmael thinks back to Pip saying that Queek had no comprehension of how powerful the Gilded were. "So, the Trust and the Gilded are the same thing?"

"When the war finally ended and the truce was signed, the few hundred families who owned the corporations got together and formed a trust that controlled everything," Charity continues. "Obviously it was in their interest not to let the rest of the citizenry know that the result of centuries of sacrifice, death, and destruction was the Gilded's enormous increase in personal wealth and power, so steps were taken to make sure no one found out."

Like a holographic image coming together over a holodeck, Ishmael sees a picture forming. "Queek said they banned the manufacture of electronic memory in tablets so that they could control the flow of information. And they outlawed Lectors, who were the only ones who could record and preserve the truth."

Billy, who's been listening quietly so far, speaks up: "Right. But the Gilded themselves still learn how t'decipher the symbols. Ye can't control information if ye can't make sense of it."

Ishmael is silent for a moment, thinking. "While we were being held by the pirates, we found out that Pip had learned how to swim on Earth. And he once slipped and said he'd never had Natrient in his entire life."

"What the Gilded eat 'tisn't much different from the scurry, meats, and vegetables the islanders eat," Billy says. "Except the Gilded's food starts as stem cells and 'tis grown in agar, micronutrients, and amino acids."

Gwen snorts. "Next you'll tell us that they live on a part of the Earth where there's no Shroud."

"No, they art under the Shroud like everyone else, but they live inside enormous domes built over the rare aquifiers not contaminated by fracking wastewater. They have artificial sunlight, filtered air, and almost unlimited amounts of fresh water."

"That can't be true," Gwen protests. "It's not possible. We would've known—"

"It's true," Ishmael breaks in. "My foster brother and I once climbed a smokestack and saw one. It was so far away that it was just a bluish-green convex shape. We didn't know what it was at the time, but now I think it must have been one of their domes."

Billy scoops up a handful of sand and lets it slip through his fingers. "Ye once asked what my family's company did. We disposed of the dead. 'Tis the one business the Gilded want nothing t'do with. We were the only non-Gilded allowed in the domes."

"Why don't they want anything to do with the dead?" Ishmael asks.

"T'cease terrifies them. 'Tis their greatest dread."

"But everyone has to die," Gwen says. "Even the Gilded."

Billy doesn't respond, and when Ishmael glances at Charity, she looks away. He senses there's still something they're not revealing.

But before he can press either of them to explain, Fayaway comes down to the beach. She kneels beside Ishmael and their shoulders touch. "'Twill not help you. 'Tis not in our nature t'be warlike. Even this"—she gestures at the defenses that have been built in the past few weeks—"'twas unnatural for us. So what ye ask . . . 'Tis too much."

The lagoon's tiny waves lap at the sand. Ishmael and Fayaway sit together. Billy has insisted that he join them against the pirates, saying Queequeg is his friend, too. Now he, Gwen, and Charity have gone back to the village.

Fayaway bites her lower lip. "When will ye leave?"

Ishmael looks at her, wondering if after tomorrow they will ever see each other again. "First thing in the morning."

Her fingers weave into his and squeeze. In this moment, in the gentle glow of the orblight, with the infinite sparkling night above and the vast ocean beyond, Ishmael wishes he could stay on this island for the rest of his years, in this place unscathed by everything the people of Earth once thought of as progress and now know to be annihilation.

70

Strangely, Ishmael sleeps soundly. Perhaps it's being in the hammock in the fresh air scented with night-fragrant flowers. Or maybe it's being among the islanders. Though he can't remember his dreams, he knows they were pleasant. But then he wakes, and the agreeable sensations vanish.

The islanders have prepared a breakfast of purple and yellow plant foods and treestone meat, but Ishmael is too wound up to eat. There will be four of them, armed only with blowguns — alas, that only Billy has learned to use — against dozens of heavily armed and benumbed pirates. What chance can they possibly have? Ishmael is haunted by the thought that he is leading this small band toward certain death. Even if his plan were to somehow miraculously succeed, it isn't conceivable that they will all return unharmed.

While they eat, Gabriel tries one more time to dissuade him. "Ye don't even know 'tis Queequeg still alive."

For a moment, Ishmael contemplates abandoning the mission. He and the others could stay here and help defend the island. But no sooner does he think this than he sees the foolishness of it. Even with all of Diana's preparations, the islanders wouldn't stand a chance. Now that the pirates know about the terrafins, they will be relentless, sooner or later breaching the island defenses. Ishmael has already spent too much time imagining the terrible cataclysm that will follow.

He holds Gabriel's gaze. "I appreciate your concern. I may not live through this, but I couldn't live with myself if I didn't try."

When it's time to embark, Fayaway is not among the islanders who come to the beach to see the crew off. Ishmael suspects that she can't face him, knowing what his fate will probably be.

While the crew board Chase Boat Four, Gabriel and Diana stand at the water's edge, engaged in a low, heated debate. At one point Diana raises her voice enough for Ishmael to hear her say, "No! They may have saved Thistle, but ye don't owe them ye life in return."

Gabriel looks up and locks eyes with Ishmael. The two stare . . . and then Fayaway's father appears to make a decision. He wades into the shallows toward the chase boat while Diana watches, stone-faced.

"'Twill come with ye," he says when he reaches them. "But one of ye must stay here."

"Why?" Charity asks.

Ishmael can guess: "To make sure that if we succeed in freeing our friend, we'll come back and not just abandon you?"

"'Tis a foolish notion," Gabriel allows, "but also a way for Diana t'save face in front of the others."

"That's ridiculous," Gwen says. "Of course we'll—"

"We don't have time to argue," Ishmael tells his crew. "Gabriel could be our key to defeating the pirates. He swims well and knows how to navigate by the stars and traverse the jungle in silence.

And he's a skilled hunter. Whoever stays behind could help the islanders prepare for an attack, in case we don't succeed. . . ."

He eyes Billy, who shakes his head. "Gabriel and I art the only ones who know the blowguns. Ye shall need us."

Next, Ishmael tries Charity, who shakes her head firmly. "Don't even think about it, honey."

That leaves Gwen. She looks ready to argue, but then exhales an exasperated breath. "So it has to be me. All right, as long as you promise to give those pirates what they deserve, okay?"

The others promise they will. Gwen climbs out.

And Gabriel climbs in.

The night sky is cloudy and, without benefit of orblight, very dark. The chase boat floats a dozen yards from shore. In addition to the nightly cacophony of jungle creatures, the sound of a raucous fight and the flicker of firelight come through the trees from the pirate camp. It has taken the chase boat several days to get here. The air is thick with nervous energy.

Gabriel's head pops out of the inky sea and he swims quietly to the boat. Grabbing a gunwale, he whispers up to Ishmael, "Art two guards in the jungle."

Ishmael doesn't remember there being guards before. Does this mean the pirates believe that a rescue party will come for Queequeg?—in which case, he might still be alive!

A few moments later, Ishmael noses the chase boat onto the beach. They walk quietly along the thin ribbon of sand until they're only a few hundred yards from the howls of violence, and then head into the jungle and station themselves behind trees. Gabriel, Charity, and Ishmael pick up fallen treestones while Billy moves farther away into the dark.

During a lull in the bedlam, Billy makes loud, unintelligible mumbling sounds, hoping to draw the pirate guards toward him. Sure enough, it's not long before Ishmael hears footsteps and the rustle of underbrush.

Heart bumping in his chest, he presses close to a tree. The footsteps grow louder when the guards tramp through the dark jungle. Ishmael catches a glimpse of movement between nearby tree trunks, but there are no telltale glow-in-the-dark tattoos. *How can that be?*

Deeper in the woods, Billy again starts mumbling. But rather than going toward the noise, the footsteps stop.

For a moment the only sounds are the nightly jungle chorus and the distant voices of cavorting pirates.

Thunk! . . . *Thunk!* . . . *Thump!* . . . Sudden loud thuds and the rattle of brush close by make Ishmael jump. But no sounds follow. Was it treestones falling?

He remains still, pulse hammering. The pirate guards must be there among the trees and vines somewhere; he would have heard their footsteps had they departed. *Why haven't they moved? What are they waiting for?*

There's the slightest crackle to his right. Turning his head slowly, he surveys the dark trees. For a brief moment, orblight breaks through the clouds, and Ishmael catches a glimpse of a hulking figure. A pirate!

Ishmael realizes what's happened: When the guards heard Billy's mumbling, they foresaw a trap. They came noisily through the jungle at first to make it seem like they were falling for the ambush. But once they got close, they stopped to blacken the glowing tattoos on their faces and arms. Now they are proceeding much more quietly, undoubtedly spreading out and hoping to surprise the ambushers. Instead of being the hunters, Ishmael and his companions have become the prey.

He needs to warn the others. But surely if he takes a step, the pirate to his right will spot him. Staying perfectly still, the rough bark of the tree pressing against his cheek, he tries to figure out what to do. Right now, the loudest sound in his ears is the beating of his heart.

Then he hears a faint *puff* followed by a *slap!*

Thud! The figure near Ishmael crumples into the underbrush.

Gabriel must have gotten the man with a dart. Ishmael senses movement as another figure slips through the dark trees toward the fallen pirate. He thinks it must be Gabriel, and needs to warn him that the other pirate might be nearby. But before he can, Gabriel reaches the spot where the pirate fell.

Suddenly from out of the dark come the grunts and thrashing of a struggle. Ishmael can't see what's going on. He starts toward the altercation, then stops. If another pirate is close, he and Gabriel might both be captured. It takes every ounce of willpower that Ishmael has to remain hidden in the shadows, listening until the struggle ceases and is replaced by heaving breaths.

Two figures rise in the darkness, one appearing to hold the other in a headlock.

"All right, listen up, the rest a' yous!" a voice calls, and Ishmael instantly realizes that the pirate has overpowered Gabriel. But how? He was hit by a dart, Ishmael's sure of it.

The pirate continues: "I got a knife to this tree dweller's throat. If ya don't show yerselves this instant, I'll have his blood on my blade."

71

Deep in the jungle shadows, Ishmael, Charity, and Billy don't move.

"I'm warning ya," the pirate snarls. "Show yerselves now."

There's a rustling sound, and Billy's silhouette appears between the trees, his hands raised.

"I know there's more of ya," the pirate says. "This is yer last chance. Come out with yer hands up."

"All right, I'm coming out. Don't hurt him!" Ishmael calls, and steps out of the darkness. When he gets closer to the pirate holding Gabriel, he can see the glitter of a thin track of blood running down the islander's neck. "I'm the last one." Ishmael raises his hands. "You can lower your knife."

"Just three of ya come to take us all on?" the pirate asks suspiciously.

"We weren't planning on taking anyone on," Ishmael says. "We wanted to sneak in and save our friend. He's still here, right?"

"Yeah, he's around," the pirate replies. "Though he sure wishes he wasn't. Hey, Wesson, mate!" he calls into the dark. "Come out. I got 'em all."

The pirate's partner, Wesson, starts to tromp toward them through the trees.

"That was easy, huh, Wes?" the first pirate gloats, still holding his knife to Gabriel's neck.

Wesson grunts.

"I bet we'll be gettin' some extra joy juice for bringin' them in, ya know?"

Wesson grunts again.

The pirate with the knife scowls. "What's with ya, Wes? Got a bug in your throat?"

In one swift movement, Wesson pulls a branch from behind his back and swings hard, catching the other pirate on the side of the head. *Crack!* The branch breaks against the man's skull, the knife flies into the dark, and the pirate goes down to his knees. But not for long. An instant later he's starting to rise when Wesson pounces on him, quickly lashing his wrists together with rope and jamming a rag into his mouth.

If that was unexpected, Ishmael is even more surprised by what happens next: Wesson furiously begins to strip off his clothes.

"Get these filthy, disgusting things off me!" Charity says, struggling out of the pirate's tunic and pants.

Suddenly Ishmael remembers: "Those thumps we heard before. That was you?"

"He passed right in front of me," Charity says, kicking the pirate's pants off her ankles. "When I realized they were sneaking up on us, I clocked him with my treestone. It took two conks before he went down. They must both be full of neurotoxin."

Billy kneels beside the fallen pirate. "'Twasn't he hit with a dart? Why didn't it work?"

Gabriel presses his fingers against the cut on his neck. "Don't know. But what if it shan't work on the others? 'Twill we do for weapons?"

"We'll have to improvise." Ishmael points at the fallen pirate. "In the meantime, we'll tie this one's legs and secure the gag, then find the one Charity conked on the head and do the same."

Not long after that, a familiar, sickeningly tart odor greets them as they tiptoe out of the jungle beside the hut near the cave. Behind them through the dark overgrowth come the loud shouts and cheers of yet another brawl.

Charity wrinkles her nose. "What's that smell?"

"The stuff I told you about." Ishmael opens the door to the hut. "Help me move these bags up the trail."

They lug a dozen bags of gunpowder from the hut up to the entrance to the cave. Then, while Billy, Charity, and Gabriel run a long fuse back down the trail, Ishmael lays a second fuse from the hut itself, where dozens more bags are still stored.

"Everything here is set." Ishmael hands Charity the box of matches from the hut. "You guys know what to do?"

"Why do Billy and I *both* have to wait here to light the fuses?" Charity asks in frustration. "You two can't possibly take on all those pirates by yourselves. Let me come with you."

"No, I need to be absolutely certain this gets done," Ishmael tells her. "It's the most important part of the plan. You want revenge? Blowing up this cave is the worst thing you can do. Without gunpowder, the pirates'll be helpless. That means no attacking the islanders — and no more kidnapping either."

Charity makes a face, but she doesn't object.

"Remember," Ishmael continues, "wait half an hour, light the fuses, and get back to the boat as fast as you can. If Gabriel and I aren't there, leave without us."

"But—" Billy begins to argue.

"I mean it," Ishmael insists. "There's no reason for all of us to risk our lives. And once the cave is sealed, someone has to go back to the islanders to let them know they're safe."

Ishmael and Gabriel creep through the dark jungle. Firelight glimmers through the trees, and raucous shouts and cheers greet their ears. With jumpy adrenaline coursing through his veins, Ishmael is surprised to see that Gabriel is empty-handed.

"You left the blowgun?" he whispers.

"'Tis useless against these men," Gabriel whispers back.

Ishmael thinks of the ferocious fights he witnessed among the pirates, and of how unstoppable they were when they raided the *Pequod.*

"Why don't the islanders take the nectar to make them impervious to pain, too?" he asks.

"To be numb to pain 'tis to be numb to pleasure. 'Tisn't living, what the pirates do. 'Tis merely running from what 'tis natural."

"From ceasing, you mean?"

"'Tisn't a thing t'run from. 'Tis a thing t'respect and, when the time comes, accept." By now they've crept to the side of the shipping container. Crouched in the shadows, Ishmael peers through the gap in the chained door, where he can barely make out a figure sitting, head tilted forward as if asleep.

Relief floods through him: The pirate guard back in the jungle was telling the truth. Queequeg is still alive!

"Queek," he whispers.

The figure in the container doesn't move.

Ishmael inches closer to the chained door and whispers again. "Queek!"

When his friend still doesn't rouse, Ishmael reaches through the gap to touch his shoulder, then recoils in horror. Beneath the cloth of Queequeg's uniform is nothing but bones!

It's . . . a skeleton!

A light suddenly bursts on, blinding Ishmael and Gabriel.

A voice growls, "Put yer hands up!"

72

"Well, well, conshider who jush couldn't reshist returnment," Glock lisps, and starts to pat Ishmael and Gabriel down.

"You let him starve to death?" Ishmael lashes out in rage. Several large pirates struggle to hold him while Glock ties his wrists with rope. "Savages!" Ishmael tries to fight free of his captors. "I'll kill you for this!"

The white-haired Kalashnikov jabs him hard in the ribs with the muzzle of his rifle, and Ishmael doubles over in pain. "Enough of your useless bluster, poppet."

Turning next to Gabriel, Kalashnikov blinks with surprise. "A tree dweller? Well, isn't this an unexpected gift! I imagine your people will pay handsomely for your return. You should be worth every drop of juice they possess."

Ishmael's shoes are taken, Gabriel's hands are tied, and the two are marched through the camp. The fighting has stopped, and around the fire pit figures with glowing green tattoos stare at the captives. Ishmael feels the bumpy hardness of bones under his bare feet.

He and Gabriel are forced along a narrow trail lined with thorny brush. Thick loops of vine hang from branches overhead, and the ground turns spongy and wet as they near the edge of a dark, shadowy swamp.

Above, the clouds have started to thin, and in the faint orblight, Ishmael sees something that makes him draw a sharp breath: On the swampy shore are the same large, scaly beasts that attacked them in the river when they rescued Thistle. When the pirates approach, the creatures slither into the water and lurk submerged except for their bulging eyes and bumpy backs.

Kalashnikov points at a thick tree limb extending out over the swamp. From it hang several large baskets made from sticks and vines. Slumped in one of the baskets is a thin figure. Ishmael's eyes go wide. It's Queequeg!

Kalashnikov chuckles. "Your friend remains among the living—at least the last time anyone inquired."

"Queek!" Ishmael calls, but Queequeg doesn't respond or even lift his head to see who's said his name.

"Save your breath, poppet," Kalashnikov growls, then tells Glock to cut the rope around Gabriel's wrists. The pirate leader motions toward the tree with his rifle. "Ascend, tree dweller. You should feel right at home." Next he turns his gun on Ishmael. "As for you, I'd be sure to keep a firm grip on the branches. You wouldn't want to join our slimy green comrades below."

The rope around Ishmael's wrists is cut, and he clambers up the tree, anxious to get a closer look at Queequeg. But when he starts for his friend's cage, Kalashnikov aims his rifle.

"Tut-tut, poppet. You're not up there to play nursemaid."

Reluctantly, Ishmael lowers himself into the basket next to Queequeg's. Glock is sent up to clamp each basket shut, then settles himself on a platform hammered into the juncture of the tree limb and trunk. The night watch, Ishmael assumes.

Poked and scratched by the sticks that make up his new accommodations, Ishmael squats and peers worriedly at the shadowy shape in the next basket. Pale and ghostly in the dark, Queequeg looks frighteningly gaunt.

"Queek?"

His friend stirs. Ishmael feels a great wave of relief. He's alive! Just barely, perhaps, but alive all the same.

Ishmael considers his options. There are only two paths for escape: get past Glock somehow, or drop into the beast-filled swamp and face certain death. And that's assuming he can figure out how to get out of the basket. For several minutes Ishmael quietly feels around the latch overhead, but it won't open. The basket itself is lashed together tightly, making it impossible to spread the sticks enough to squeeze through. Ishmael shifts uncomfortably, his thoughts casting fitfully about for a solution. *Can it be that this time there really is no escape?* He lets his head lean back. Maybe all he can do now is wait for the explosions that will seal the cave and destroy the pirates' supply of gunpowder. At least the islanders will be safe.

The minutes pass, and jungle noises fill his ears. Below, a wobbly, long-legged animal with white-spotted brown fur slinks out of the dark and makes its way to the swamp's edge. No sooner has the creature lowered its snout to drink than one of the gnarled beasts bursts from under the surface, clamps its toothy jaws around the animal's throat, and drags it into the swamp. The water roils briefly while spindly legs thrash . . . then vanish into the murk.

The swamp becomes quiet again. There's nothing for Ishmael to do except wait for the explosions and try not to imagine what these vengeful pirates will do once they realize what those blasts mean.

So it's a complete surprise when he hears snoring from the platform where Glock is supposed to be watching them. Once again, Ishmael pokes his fingers up through the sticks that form the roof of his basket, trying in vain to reach the latch.

In the basket next to him, Gabriel is also feverishly exploring the gaps between the sticks overhead. If they can get out before Charity and Billy blow up the hut and the cave entrance, they just might be able to escape!

But despite their desperate attempts, the latches prove impossible to breach. With every passing second, Ishmael grows more distressed. The explosions should have come by now, and he's beginning to worry that something's gone wrong. If Charity and Billy have been discovered, not only will they all be doomed, but the islanders as well.

Just then, in the shadows of the dark trees that circle the swamp, movement catches his eye. It's Charity and Billy, tiptoeing through the underbrush.

Ishmael's gut twists with consternation. Why didn't they blow up the cave and gunpowder hut? They probably think they're being heroes by coming to save him, Gabriel, and Queequeg, but they're risking everything!

Billy reaches the base of the tree and begins to climb.

Snap! A twig breaks.

On his platform higher up, the dozing Glock snorts and shifts position. Ishmael cranes his neck to see if Gabriel is aware of what's going on. He is, watching with gritted teeth and fearful eyes. Billy remains motionless until the pirate's snoring becomes steady again. Then he reaches up for another branch.

Snap! The second twig is even louder when it breaks. Glock jerks his head up and blinks. Ishmael can hardly breathe. If the pirate glances down, he'll be looking directly at Billy.

It feels like forever until Glock starts to doze again, and Billy continues climbing. Nerves on jagged edge, Ishmael can't see how Billy expects to get them out of the baskets and past Glock without waking him.

But Billy doesn't stop at their branch. He keeps climbing. *What does he think he's doing?*

73

A minute later Ishmael is startled by sudden loud crashing that comes from above. It sounds like something is tearing through the foliage.

On the platform, Glock's eyes burst open and he jerks his head up.

Too late.

Wham! Swinging through the branches on a vine, Billy knocks the pirate off the platform.

"*Ahhhh!*" Screaming, Glock plunges into the swamp with a loud *splash!*

The scaly beasts are on him instantly, tails thrashing and jaws snapping. With a strangled gurgle, the pirate disappears into the dark, turbulent water.

Billy swings back to the limb from which the baskets are suspended. Scampering agilely along the thick branch, he pries open the latch of Ishmael's basket, then reaches down to him. "Time t'go, my friend."

"What about blowing up the cave and hut?" Ishmael asks.

"No worries." Billy gives him a hand.

"But the pirates must have heard Glock scream." Ishmael climbs out of his basket. "They're probably on their way here, and we don't have time to —"

Ka-Boom!

The explosion is so enormous that it shakes the trees, sending small rocks and twigs showering down and splashing into the swamp — and almost knocking Ishmael off the branch.

Billy grabs him. "Steady!"

"Think that was the cave or the hut?" Charity calls from the base of the tree.

Ka-Boom!

More debris rains down around them.

"Both." Billy rakes dirt and bits of leaves out of his hair.

Ishmael shakes his head in wonder, then helps Billy to free the others. Queequeg is so weak that Gabriel and Ishmael must carry him down together.

On the ground, Charity greets them with hugs, but the celebration is short-lived. Angry shouts echo through the jungle from the pirate camp.

"This way!" Billy leads them into the dense greenery. But it's slow going as they fight their way through the trees and brush in the dark, getting tangled in vines and tripping on rocks and stumps. Carrying Queequeg on his back, Gabriel frequently stumbles, and the others must help steady him.

When they finally emerge from the thick vegetation and run onto the beach, the soft sand slows their pace even more.

From the jungle comes the furious crashing of pirates storming through the underbrush. It sounds like they've split into two groups: one headed for the beach, the other charging ahead, hoping to cut the fleeing group off.

"Come on!" Billy urges. "Faster!"

Gabriel falters, and Ishmael drops back to help him. They each take one of Queequeg's arms, leaving his feet to drag through the sand.

Bang! A shot rings out, and they all cower but keep going.

Bang! A bullet whistles past Ishmael's ear. He risks a glance back. Some of the pirates have reached the beach behind them.

"Hurry!" Charity urges, but the only way to go any faster would be to leave Queequeg behind.

Bang! Bang! More bullets whiz past, and Ishmael can hear the second group of pirates bounding through the jungle, closing in. But the chase boat isn't far now, less than fifty yards away.

If they can just reach it . . .

Twenty yards ahead, two pirates burst out of the trees, breathing hard and holding guns. A moment later, several more join them.

Ishmael and the others stop on the beach and fight for breath. There are pirates in front of them and behind them. To their left is the ocean; to their right, the jungle.

They're trapped.

With weapons raised, the pirates approach them from both sides. From the group ahead, a single beam bursts on, blinding Ishmael with its glare. As his eyes begin to adjust, he sees that it's Kalashnikov holding the light.

The white-haired pirate leader stops half a dozen feet away and regards them coldly. "Did you really think that destroying our cache of gunpowder would protect your tree-dwelling friends?"

"No," Ishmael admits. "That's why we also made sure to seal the cave forever."

A moment of shocked silence follows, and then Kalashnikov's eyes bug out in rage. "Kill them!"

Gabriel and Ishmael lower Queequeg to the sand and clench their fists. Charity grabs a piece of driftwood from the beach. Billy picks up a round piece of coral.

Better to go down fighting . . .

"Unh!" a pirate cries and falls face-first onto the sand, his hand reaching for the side of his neck. The others look down at him, trying to figure out what happened.

"Ach!" another pirate howls, then staggers a few feet and falls.

The pirates begin to look around, the light sweeping across the tree trunks lining the beach. "What's going—?" a third pirate starts to ask, then grabs his side and doubles over. The others begin to back away in fear.

"Aah!" When a fourth pirate goes down, the rest start to scatter, running in panic into the jungle.

"Return at once, you wriggling invertebrates!" Kalashnikov shouts. But his men don't listen. Left alone, the pirate leader spins around and aims his gun at Ishmael. "I was so hoping not to have to sully my hands. Alas, you first, poppet."

Ishmael's heart is pounding so hard he can feel it in his temples. He can't believe that this is how it ends—never finding Archie or seeing Petra and Joachim again. . . .

Suddenly the gun falls from Kalashnikov's hand. In the light, Ishmael can see a projectile sticking out from Kalashnikov's forearm. It's bigger than a blow dart, but beyond that, Ishmael can't make sense of it. The pirate leader stares at it, then starts to bend down for his gun.

"Argh!" His hand goes to his shoulder, where a second projectile now juts.

But he yanks it out and picks up his gun.

Again he aims at Ishmael. "Sweet dreams, poppet."

The next projectile hits him in the hand, knocking the gun away again.

The next strikes him in the knee.

With a roar of frustration, Kalashnikov turns and disappears into the jungle.

Ishmael and the others are alone on the beach. Small waves fold onto the shore, and up in the night sky more stars are beginning to peek out from behind the clouds. In the distance they can still hear the pirates thrashing in retreat through the trees toward their camp.

"What happened?" Charity asks.

Ishmael shakes his head.

Then a scrawny figure emerges from the dark jungle.

It's Blank . . . and his crossbow.

The pirate gestures down the beach at the chase boat. "Got room for one more?"

74

The *Pequod*'s brig is sweltering. Close by, the ship's nuclear reactor is running full ahead. According to Starbuck, they've been in pursuit of the Great Terrafin for the past month — and Ahab was none too pleased to have to slow down to let a few deserters back on board three days ago.

Ishmael lies shirtless, his face and chest slick with sweat. With sleep impossible, there is nothing to do but reflect on what's happened since they saved Queequeg.

Ishmael was thrown in the brig the moment he returned. Stripped of his rank of skipper, disqualified from whatever share of the pot might have been his, he has been relegated to the position of prisoner, no longer even a member of the crew. He surmises that the only reason he hasn't been sent back to Earth is that there's no one aboard who knows how to operate the stasis chamber.

After they'd spent a week on the island, waiting for Queequeg to regain some strength, Charity and Blank decided to stay. They and the islanders had wanted Gwen, Queequeg, and Ishmael to remain, too. Even Diana had tried to change their minds; not only was she grateful for what Ishmael had done to disarm the pirates, but she had finally learned from Gwen how, exactly, the pirates had found out about the terrafin pens in the first place.

"Art sorry to have doubted ye," Diana had told Ishmael. "Ye've been a good friend. We shall be honored t'welcome ye to our island."

But despite the temptation, Ishmael couldn't accept. Not as long as Archie, Joachim, and Petra were somewhere out there, no doubt as worried about him as he was about them.

And while Gwen and Queequeg had insisted that they needed to return to the ship in order to earn more money, Ishmael suspected that they were really going out of loyalty to him. He'd only hoped neither of them would be punished.

When the time came to leave, they'd stocked Chase Boat Four with water and food and set out. After several weeks on the vast ocean, they'd gotten lucky, coming across a trawler whose captain had had two-way contact with the *Pequod* only a few days before. Having gotten a sense of the ship's course from him, the chase-boat crew found the *Pequod* a week later.

"Blast, it's hot down here," a voice murmurs in the dark.

Ishmael sits up, surprised to hear footsteps. In the dimness he makes out the silhouettes of an unlikely trio: Fleece, Stubb, and Marion. He can't imagine what they're doing down here.

The bulky cook wipes sweat off his glistening forehead. "Melville's mercy, a few more days in this and you'll be slow-roasted and juicy."

Marion passes a canteen through the bars.

"Thanks." Ishmael drinks. "From the pace of the reactor, I figure Ahab must have the Great Terrafin on drone imagery."

"That he does," Fleece says. "They think the beast has been slowed by that big harpoon in its wing. But a creature that's wounded is all the more dangerous. Seems like madness to pursue the terrafin after that business with the pinkboat, don't it?"

"A suicide mission," Marion adds.

This isn't news. Everyone on the ship knows it. "So what brings you down here?" Ishmael asks.

Marion drops her voice. "Some of us has been askin' ourselves what all the money Ahab's offerin' is worth if we ain't gonna be alive to spend it."

Fleece smooths his fan of a beard. "To be blunt, urchin, I never dreamed that such a day would arrive. I've been a salty dog my entire life and cherished most every moment. But this marks my last voyage, and unlike these other miscreants, I've amassed a nice little cache of coin. All I aspire to now is surviving to enjoy it."

Of the three, Stubb is the one Ishmael is most curious about. Why is he here? The fussy second mate is usually the enforcer, not breaker, of rules.

Stubb removes his glasses and wipes them with a fine cloth. "Mr. Bildad and the other senior directors have concluded that the actions of Captain Ahab are no longer in the best interests of the Trust. He is considered a rogue captain and will face charges of dereliction of duties. As a result, I have been authorized to take whatever action is necessary to protect the ship and its crew, and to terminate the voyage as soon as possible."

"What's this got to do with me?" Ishmael asks.

Marion's upper lip is dotted with perspiration. "Ever since you went AWOL and risked your life to save your friend, you've become somethin' of a hero to the crew. They talk about how you stood up to Starbuck and even to Captain Ahab himself. If we can tell the others we have your support . . ."

"To do what, exactly?" Ishmael asks.

"To strike," she explains. "If we can get the majority behind us, we can stop Ahab from going after that monster. He can't do it without a crew."

"You mean mutiny?"

"With the approval of the Trust," Stubb quickly stresses. "So no one will be punished."

Fleece presses his bearded visage close to the bars. "Can we count on your support?"

Ishmael can see the desperation in their eyes. Even though he gave his word to Ahab, he has no desire to risk his life, either. But what about the rest of the crew? Are they equally as reluctant to pursue the beast, or are they still blinded by the promise of enormous riches? Ishmael feels like he needs to stall until he knows more. "I need twenty-four hours to think about it. In the meantime, I promise I won't say anything to anyone."

The trio glance at one another.

"All right. Twenty-four hours," Marion says. "One of us will be back tomorrow night for your answer."

Fleece squeezes a fleshy arm through the bars and claps Ishmael on the shoulder. "Consider the crew, urchin. Lives hang in the balance."

75

Managing only a few hours of fitful sleep, Ishmael is awake in time to watch through the small porthole as the sun rises. At some point he dozes off again, because he next opens his eyes to a clinking sound: Starbuck unlocking the cell door.

"Captain wants to see you."

Ishmael sits up, immediately apprehensive. Does the captain know that Fleece, Marion, and Stubb paid him a visit last night?

The first mate holds the cell door open. "Well, you coming?"

Ishmael slides off the metal slab and starts to follow.

"That story about Charity and Billy staying with those tree dwellers true?" Starbuck asks as they start climbing the ladderways.

"Queequeg and Gwen told you, sir?"

"That's right. Guess I shouldn't blame her." Starbuck sounds wistful. At the top of the ladderway, he stops. "You may not believe this, boy, but I've always tried to do the right thing. For the men, for the ship, for the Trust."

"What about for yourself, sir?" Ishmael asks.

"For myself?" Starbuck repeats, surprised. "I had dreams, boy."

There's something fatalistic in his tone. While his eyes remain hidden behind those dark glasses, Ishmael imagines they're filled with regret.

"Know what the problem with dreams is?" the first mate goes on. "Sometimes you don't know when to stop dreaming. One leads to the next, and it seems like there's always something bigger and better just over the next wave. But in the meantime, life passes. Your wife gets tired of waiting. Your kids grow up, have families of their own and don't know who you are. One day you realize that for every dream you've achieved, you've lost something or someone equally important. Only by then it's too late."

Ishmael recalls the holograph in the first mate's cabin of the attractive blond woman and three children. Are they the kids who are now grown with families of their own? Not for the first time he wonders how long Starbuck's been away from Earth. "If you really believe that, sir, why not stop now?"

The first mate lifts one of his gnarled hands and studies the scarred knuckles. "I've come too far and given up too much to quit now. But I promise you, boy: This is the end. When it's over, I'm done."

Ishmael recalls Tarnmoor saying something similar about Ahab.

There'll be no turning back . . .

They start up another set of steps. The *Pequod* seems quiet today; presumably the chase boats are all out stalking the Great Terrafin. At the top of the next ladderway, Starbuck unexpectedly leads Ishmael outside.

After three days in the brig, Ishmael squints in the bright sunlight, but even with his eyes nearly closed, he is aware that something is different. The deck is unusually hushed—absent voices, the cries of flyers, and the clamor of sailors at work. As soon as his eyes adjust, he sees why: Two figures hang from cranes overhead, slowly turning in the warm breeze.

He draws a sharp, involuntary breath. Marion and Stubb are suspended by hooks snagging the backs of their PFDs. Their hands are bound, and gags are stuffed in their mouths. The good news is they're alive.

So much for the mutiny, he thinks. He searches around for Fleece but doesn't see him.

"Looking for someone?" Starbuck asks pointedly. "If it's the cook, he's been confined to his cabin." The first mate leans close and lowers his voice. "If I find out you were involved in that scheme, so help me, boy, you won't swing from one of those cranes for a day like those two. You'll be up there for the rest of the voyage."

They climb the remaining ladderways to the bridge, where Ahab is holding a pair of binoculars to his eyes, his long black hair lifted gently by the breeze. Starbuck leaves Ishmael there and departs.

After several moments of silence, the captain speaks: "You puzzle me, sailor. You persist in risking your own hide to help others when it will mean no material gain for yourself. What do you think is to be earned by this? Everlasting glory? Entrance into Valhalla? Sainthood?"

Though uncertain what the words mean, Ishmael senses that no answer is required.

"We're born alone, sailor," the captain continues, "and should the day come when we die, we'll depart in the same condition. After that, nothing matters."

Not far off the bow, a decent-size basher leaps into the air and splashes back down, but Ahab takes no notice.

"Can't recall when last we had a sailor who'd spent quite as much time in the brig as you," the captain remarks. "Like it down there?"

"Not particularly, sir."

Ahab lowers the binoculars. "Then how would you like to be pardoned . . . again?"

"For the rest of the voyage, sir, or just until the Great Terrafin is captured?"

A wry smirk creases Ahab's thin lips. "I'd heard there were brains to go along with your bravery. A good combination, and one that could make you extraordinarily rich. For the rest of the voyage, sailor. Your share of the pot reinstated. Would you like that?"

"You want me to go out after the Great Terrafin, sir?" Ishmael asks.

Ahab turns toward the sea and lifts the binoculars back to his eyes. "The beast is wounded. She won't be able to run much longer. When the time comes, we'll need every available man to bring her in." Out in the distance the basher leaps again. "Just tell me one thing, sailor. How do I know you won't run off a second time?"

"I didn't run off, sir. I went to get Queequeg. And if I had to, I'd do it again. But I don't, because he's here."

Ahab continues to scan the ocean. "All right. I'll let you go back out, but this time you'll have a drone watching you. And mark my words: one wrong move and next time it won't be the brig. Next time I'll feed you to the big-tooths myself."

The blue VRgog light is flashing when Ishmael gets down to the men's berth. It's been many weeks since he's heard anything, and he eagerly slips them on. It's an audio clip from Joachim!

"mael . . . condit . . . very bad. . . . Ben said you sent . . . enough to get us out . . . can't thank you enough. . . . But . . . terrible news . . . *Jeroboam* lost . . . in a storm . . . all . . . presumed dead. . . . We are leaving . . . Earth . . . heartbroken. . . . So very sorry . . . communications shutting . . . this . . . last time. . . . We love you."

76

Beneath Ishmael's feet the deck of the *Pequod* shivers. The drones are locked on the Great Terrafin, and the crew have been assembled. Around him sailors radiate nervous anticipation — adjusting PFDs, sharpening knives. The fidgeting of preparations.

But for Ishmael, a nearly unbearable sadness has bullied out any sense of fear or anticipation. The *Jeroboam* has been lost in a storm, and all aboard are presumed dead. The news feels like a harpoon through his heart. The relief and joy he should be feeling about his foster parents getting off Earth is crushed beneath the weight of his grief.

Gwen slides an arm around his waist and Queequeg squeezes his shoulder. They say nothing, but then, there's nothing they can say.

Ahab and Starbuck are up on the bridge, looking down at the crew. The captain's hands are tight on the bridge rail. "This is it, men!" he yells with maniacal elation. "I can feel it in my bones! The

Great Terrafin is wounded and vulnerable. But mind you, we ain't the only ones after her. There's big-tooths on her tails. So our task is to get the beast before those scavengers do!"

"We're gonna be rich!" Bunta shouts from down in the crowd. The sailors on the deck cheer until the captain hushes them.

"Don't be lulled into thinking this will be easy!" Ahab warns. "Injured or not, no more ferocious creature exists anywhere in the universe, and none that will fight harder for its freedom. You're in for the battle of your lives, men. . . . But once we succeed — and we *will* succeed! — you'll have wealth beyond anything you've ever dreamed of. Keep that in mind, sailors. Today's the day we've been waiting for!"

More wild, raucous cheers fill the air.

Ahab retreats from the bridge, and Starbuck takes over, explaining the strategy the chase boats will use, sticking as many harpoons as possible into the creature to create a web of lines — special green lines that have been reinforced with steel filament — from which the beast will be unable to extricate itself. Once the web is in place, the lines will be blended into two giant strands, one for each of the two enormous winches at the stern of the *Pequod.*

"At that point your jobs will change," Starbuck tells the chase-boat crews. "You can be certain that once the big-tooths sense the trapped creature in their midst, they'll be on her. Your job'll be to fire on those big-tooths — kill 'em, herd 'em away, do whatever you can to keep 'em off the terrafin."

He goes on to say that because the creature is far too large to get up the slipway whole, they'll need to winch the beast as close to the stern as they can and get its head out of the water, at which point they'll kill it. Once it's dead, they can begin cleaving and dragging the parts up the slipway for processing.

"As for how you attack it," Starbuck continues from the bridge, "you'll come at it in pairs, one boat on each side of the beast, and fire your harpoons at the same time. That should confuse it and, hopefully, keep it from going after one boat or the other. After you fire, you'll circle about a quarter mile out to give the next boats room to move in. Got it?"

The crews reply in the affirmative.

Starbuck consults a tablet. "Chase Boats Two and Four will be on the beast's port side, with Boats One and Three on its starboard. One and Four will go in first, followed by Two and Three. Go in, fire, and get out fast. No dawdling. Everyone got that? Now prepare to launch."

Three of the four chase-boat teams hurry off, but the crew of Chase Boat Four remain in place, Ishmael's gloom over Archie so great that he is almost unable to process the activity around him.

For several long moments, Gwen and Queequeg stand near him, waiting to see what he'll do.

Finally, Gwen breaks the shroud of sorrow. "Listen, I don't mean to be insensitive, but if we don't get to our boat, Starbuck'll probably throw all three of us in the brig."

Queequeg snorts scornfully. He's shaved off the scraggly beard but kept his hair long and now ties it back. "Considering what Ahab wants us to do, it's likely the safest place to be."

"What makes you think there's room?" Ishmael asks bitterly. "Aren't Fleece, Marion, and Stubb already down there?"

Starbuck comes out of a hatch and approaches them. "You're short a lineman. You need to choose someone now." He goes off.

"What do you want to do?" Gwen asks Ishmael.

"We're with you, friend, whatever you decide," Queequeg adds. Ishmael takes a steadying breath. Standing before him are two of the most loyal allies a person could hope for. He shouldn't care about the Great Terrafin, but he feels like the three of them have come so far . . . like it's their destiny to see this to the end. And with Archie gone, does anything really matter anyway?

"Who's left that we can —" Ishmael begins, then sees something unexpected: Tarnmoor is up on deck in the bright sun, feeling his way uncertainly toward them along the bulwark, unnoticed in the commotion.

Ishmael takes a few steps and places a hand on the old man's arm. "What are you doing up here?"

"Ah, Ishmael, the one I beens searchin' for," the old blind swabbie replies. "I heared yer shorts a lineman. Takes me with ya, lad. I promises I won't get in yer way."

Ishmael doesn't know what to say. "You can't—"

"Takes me along, lad!" Tarnmoor begs. "For land's sake, I've followed this beast for more'n a lifetime, I haved. The sames as Ahab and Starbuck. Just 'cause I can't sees no more don't means I don't burn with revenge as strong as thems two."

"Whipped acrost the eyes, I were. Left floatin' on a piece a' deckin' whiles all around me mens screamed and cried as the big-tooths moved in and mades a feast a' them."

Ishmael stares at the bent old swabbie. "All right, Tarnmoor, welcome aboard."

Gwen blanches. "Are you crazy?"

Probably, Ishmael thinks. "We don't need a second lineman. The plan is to stick the terrafin, then throw the line and float overboard. The three of us can do that ourselves."

Gwen and Queequeg exchange a long look, then Queequeg says, "If that's what you want, Ish."

Ishmael guides the old man across the deck. Surprisingly, when Starbuck sees them, he doesn't interfere. *He knows that the old man needs to be out there,* Ishmael concludes.

They're almost to the chase boat when Ishmael sees Fedallah sitting in the shade of one of the huge winches, carefully sharpening the point of the same long, spearlike harpoon he'd given Ishmael to use the time he saved Daggoo—the stick that must be jabbed by hand into the vulnerable spot behind the terrafin's head. Amid the frantic preparations, the white-haired harpooner calmly concentrates on this single chore.

Ishmael hands Tarnmoor off to Queequeg and stops a few feet from Fedallah. "You're serious?"

"The smallest insect can kill a man many times its size." Fedallah holds the spear up, the tip gleaming in the sun. "It is ready."

Ishmael squats. "Why, Fedallah?"

The man runs a finger along the stick's slim metal shaft. "To give meaning and purpose to that which lacks both. For some, it is a choice. For others, it is as deep in the genes as the will to survive itself. It is not important which you are. What is important is that, whichever you are, you are true to yourself."

77

Chase Boat Four bobs beside the hull of the *Pequod.* Tarnmoor is sitting on the bench seat, white-knuckling the gunwales, but with a grin as big as the crescent orb.

"Bless ya, my friends." He takes a deep sniff. "Feels good to be close to the sea again."

Gwen and Queequeg share a wary look. Ishmael knows what they're thinking: Old Tarnmoor may feel good now, but how will it be once they encounter the Great Terrafin?

At the console, Ishmael brushes his hair out of his eyes and hits the starter . . . the RTG sputters and cuts out. He tries again. This time the engine starts — though Ishmael can't shake a deep sense of foreboding. It will be treacherous enough to pursue the beast with a functioning chase boat. What chance will they have with an engine that isn't reliable?

But they are committed to this thing now. With a drone following overhead, Ishmael's and Fedallah's boats set out side by side from the *Pequod.* Daggoo's and Tashtego's boats follow a quarter mile behind. A slight breeze ripples the ocean's surface. The sky is a patchwork of blue and gray, shafts of the sun's rays breaking through the clouds. The chase boats pass in and out of sunlight and shadow. Tarnmoor clings to the gunwale and faces forward, the rushing air and sea spray on his pasty, wrinkled face.

Ahead Ishmael can make out three specks circling low in the sky, converging like airborne scavengers over wounded prey. Not flyers — drones. Queequeg points at the ocean below the drones, where the red-tipped fins of big-tooths cut back and forth in agitation.

Beyond the big-tooths a splash on the surface reveals what looks like the tip of one of the Great Terrafin's white wings. The enormous creature is surfacing, and soon its vast back is visible, looking from a distance like an island of white sand. Ancient, rusted harpoons jut from its torso, mere splinters to a creature its size. Ishmael's blood tingles with equal amounts of excitement and fear.

As the first two chase boats close in on the target, they spread out. Ishmael keeps expecting the Great Terrafin to sense their approach and dive, but it remains floating on the surface, making him wonder if it is unable to muster the energy to escape.

Ishmael and Fedallah are running two hundred yards apart, and in a few moments the creature will be between them. Drones whir and dart overhead.

Starbuck's voice comes over the two-way: "Boats One and Four, prepare to fire your bow guns on my count. Three . . . two . . . one!"

"Now!" Ishmael shouts.

BOOM! Queequeg fires.

Boom! From across the way comes the blast of Fedallah's gun.

Both harpoons strike the great beast in the back, where they stick out like pins. And yet the huge creature remains unmoving on the surface. Is it sick? Exhausted? Has it lost the will to live?

Gwen heaves the green steel-reinforced line and the big orange float over the side, and both chase boats peel away to make room for the next two.

Chase Boats Two and Three race in. *Boom! Boom!* The thunder of harpoon guns rings in the air. Lines and floats are thrown overboard and the boats speed away. Still, the giant terrafin doesn't react.

Over the two-way comes the first mate's voice again: "Boats One and Four, ready your shoulder launchers."

Ishmael signals Queequeg, who knows what to do. The chase boat cants while they circle back around on their second approach. "Boats One and Four, prepare to fire again on my count," Starbuck orders. "Three . . . two . . . one!"

BANG! Bang! The harpooners fire their shoulder-mounted sticks, and then the chase boats veer off. Ishmael steers away, watching over his shoulder as Gwen throws out another line and float. Finally, the great beast appears to rouse at the onslaught of harpoons, but only by slowly raising its vast left wing out of the water, then letting it drop with a huge splash.

"Cease fire!" Starbuck shouts over the two-way. "Boats Two and Three, stand clear!"

Tashtego's skipper obeys the command and turns away, but Daggoo's chase boat, on the left side of the terrafin, continues toward the target.

"Stand clear, Boat Two!" the first mate repeats. "Do not fire! Do you copy? Stand clear!"

But Chase Boat Two continues to close in, Daggoo standing in the bow with the shoulder launcher while the Great Terrafin again raises its left wing.

"What's happening?" Tarnmoor asks, his blind eyes turned toward the beast.

"Chase Boat Two's going in," Queequeg says. "Looks like Daggoo wants a shot at the underside of the wing."

"Daggoo!" Starbuck shouts over the two-way. "Back off!"

But now Daggoo is close enough to fire the shoulder stick.

Bang! With a puff of white smoke, the stick bursts from the shoulder launcher.

"The fool!" Tarnmoor cries.

The Great Terrafin's wing plunges down.

Crash!

Chase Boat Two disappears.

78

A strange quiet fills the air. The three remaining boats rock in the waves spreading away from the beast. Using binoculars, Ishmael scans the surface near the terrafin, looking for a sign that someone from Daggoo's boat has survived. Debris floats near the creature's left wing, and the crumpled remnants of Chase Boat Two's hull drift upside down. The red-tipped fins of big-tooths slice frantic, jagged paths through the water.

"That Daggoo were always a brash one," Tarnmoor laments. "Long on nerves but short on sense."

Over the two-way, Starbuck curses and orders the chase boats to give the terrafin wide berth. Ishmael tries to start his engine, but once again it sputters and stalls. He holds his breath and tries again. This time the engine starts, and he motors a safe distance away to await his next orders.

Were things going according to plan, the next step would be to collect the ends of the harpoon lines and bring them back to the *Pequod.* But after what happened to Daggoo and his crew, Ishmael is in no hurry to go anywhere near the beast.

"Here's what I don't get," Gwen says. "If the terrafin has the strength to raise its wing and crush a chase boat, why's it sitting there? Why doesn't it swim away? Or dive? It could easily drag the floats down with it."

"Maybe that was its last bit of strength," Queequeg speculates. "They've been chasing it for weeks, never giving it time to rest or feed."

Ishmael studies Tarnmoor's face. Is it a trick of the light, or does he detect tension in the set of the old man's jaw? What does this blind sailor see that the others don't?

Gwen points behind them. The *Pequod* has appeared on the horizon. At the same time, the Great Terrafin starts to swim slowly, towing the green lines and orange floats behind it like long tendrils.

Starbuck orders the chase boats to follow, but at a distance. While the floats and lines extend far enough from the terrafin to be collected out of harm's way, should the beast suddenly turn and attack, there would be little the crews in the chase boats could do to defend themselves. Reason enough for Starbuck to have them keep far behind.

When they pass the spot where Daggoo's boat was destroyed, Gwen gasps. Amid the debris, the mauled remains of a body float facedown on the surface, the bright-yellow hair unmistakable. Ishmael radios in the discovery.

"Follow the beast," Starbuck replies. "We'll pick up the body later."

"Fat chance," Gwen utters.

The creature continues slowly, relying more on its right wing, in a way that makes Ishmael wonder if its left is losing strength. The big-tooths and chase boats have no trouble keeping up with it, but the *Pequod* remains farther behind, almost out of sight.

After several hours, the Great Terrafin again stops on the surface. Ishmael and Tashtego bring their chase boats to a halt, but Fedallah's boat slowly glides forward until it is only a few hundred feet from the beast.

"What in the cosmos is he doing?" Queequeg whispers, while in Chase Boat One Fedallah strips off his uniform. Picking up the long, narrow spear, he climbs over the side of the boat and slips into the water.

"He can't be serious," Gwen says. "Going after the Great Terrafin with that little stick? He has to be out of his mind."

"And what about the big-tooths?" Queequeg adds.

Ishmael eyes Tarnmoor, who has remained curiously quiet.

They watch as Fedallah begins to swim with his arms extended forward, holding the spear straight out in front of him like the long snout of a basher, and kicking with both legs together like a tail. The result is not the typical splashing of arms and feet, but the graceful undulations of a creature native to the sea. It is precisely the way he swam that day many months ago when Daggoo almost rammed Ishmael's chase boat.

"Ever see anyone swim like that?" Queequeg asks in wonder.

"Likes a beast, is he?" Tarnmoor guesses. "Likes something the Great Terrafin and big-tooths be used to? Yes? Yes?"

"Yes," Ishmael answers. This is what Fedallah has lived for. To some, like the islanders, just being alive, just being able to take a breath of air and watch a beautiful sunset, is enough. But for others, a life without purpose is no life at all. They need a higher goal to strive for, and they are willing to risk everything to reach it.

"Uh-oh." Queequeg points. "The big-tooths have noticed him."

Red-tipped fins have begun to circle the harpooner. Fedallah continues his serpentine swim, passing right through the spiraling pod.

"How can he keep going with all those nasty things around him?" Gwen asks, amazed.

"No choice," Tarnmoor replies. "If he breaks stride now, them'll be on him like flyers on scurry."

Still, it's hard to imagine the steel nerves necessary to swim through such vicious beasts, and toward such an enormously dangerous creature.

When he is perhaps forty feet from the Great Terrafin, Fedallah stops swimming. The harpooner lifts his free hand and softly pats the water, much the way Ishmael once watched the islander woman do. The huge white beast stirs, and then slips below the surface, moving slowly toward Fedallah.

"If I wasn't seeing this with my own eyes, I wouldn't believe it," Queequeg whispers as the creature swims closer and closer to the spot where the harpooner floats.

"What sees ya? What? What?" Tarnmoor asks eagerly. "Tell me!"

Before Queequeg can answer, the great beast glides beneath Fedallah.

The harpooner takes a breath and dives.

"What's happening?" Tarnmoor begs.

No one answers. Both the terrafin and Fedallah disappear beneath the glistening surface. The ocean grows still. The sun's rays glint between the clouds. The chase boats bob gently, the sailors aboard them quiet, waiting. The seconds drift past. Ishmael realizes he's holding his breath.

"What? What? Tell me!" Tarnmoor beseeches.

"The monster swam under Fedallah, and he dove after it." Gwen sounds awestruck. "Now we can't see either of them."

"How vain and foolish, for mans to try to comprehends this

wondrous beast, by merely poring over his dead attenuated skeleton," Tarnmoor mutters mysteriously.

At any moment, Ishmael expects the Great Terrafin to burst through the surface, wings flapping, trailing streams of sparkling seawater as it soars into the air and then lands with a tremendous crashing *flop*, sending choppy waves and white spray hundreds of feet in every direction.

But this doesn't happen. The ocean's surface remains flat and still, and the chase boats continue to float quietly. Even the bigtooths disperse, their red-tipped fins spreading away and gradually disappearing.

"That's it?" Queequeg asks, mystified.

Ishmael trains his binoculars on Fedallah's chase boat, and then on Tashtego's. Their crews are staring down into the water. Suddenly Tashtego twists around and his mouth falls open. Ishmael turns to look. Several hundred yards away, a liquid mountain is bearing down on them.

79

The Great Terrafin smashes into Chase Boat One hard enough to launch it into the air and throw Fedallah's crew overboard. Almost instantly, the big-tooths reappear, turning their huge, sharp incisors on the floundering sailors.

Ishmael guns the chase boat toward the survivors, his crew shouting and banging on the sides of the boat — doing anything they can think of to scare the big-tooths off. But the seagoing scavengers are monomaniacal in their pursuit, and before Chase Boat Four can reach the sailors, their screams die out and the churning water grows red. The carnage over, the big-tooths vanish once again.

Ishmael cuts the engine and drifts through the debris. Here floats a shoe, and there a first-aid kit. Worst of all are the empty PFDs.

Queequeg reaches over the side of the boat and lifts up strands of long white hair.

They're all that remain of Fedallah.

Starbuck reports that the Great Terrafin has resurfaced a few miles to the south. As Ishmael steers Chase Boat Four to the location, the mood on board is somber and grim. Even wounded and weakened, the huge creature is clearly capable of bursts of enormous strength and murderous aggression.

"Why does it keep stopping?" Gwen asks again. "If it has enough strength left to fight, why doesn't it swim away?"

Tarnmoor scoffs. "The mightiest beast in the oceans don't runs away. She stays and fights to the death."

"What makes you such an expert?" Gwen asks. She doesn't say, "You can't even see," but the words hang in the air all the same.

The normally garrulous Tarnmoor remains quiet.

"It was like this with the *Essex,* wasn't it?" Ishmael guesses. "The beast pretending to be weaker than she really was?"

The old man twists around to face Ishmael with his unseeing eyes. "Aye, it were like this. We was on her tails for weeks, never givin' her times to feed or rest — barely givin' ourselves times either. She gots slower and slower, and — we thoughts — weaker and weaker. But it were all an act. Once we let our defenses down, that's when she struck."

"You . . . you've fought the Great Terrafin before?" Gwen asks, astounded.

"Aye." Tarnmoor nods. "Me an' Ahab an' Starbuck."

"Starbuck was on the *Essex*?" Ishmael asks. "You didn't tell me that." The old man had hinted that Starbuck had been on another ship before the *Pequod,* but not that it was the *Essex.*

"There's much I ain'ts yet said, lad. It's a complicated hand whats must be dealt slowly."

But before more can be told, the crew spots the vast white back of the great beast ahead, where it once again floats idly on the ocean's surface, looking for all the world like an exhausted, defeated creature. The two remaining chase boats slip warily closer.

"Anyone feel like it's setting a trap?" Queequeg asks nervously.

Just then, Starbuck issues new orders over the two-way. "Chase Boats Three and Four: Gather the ends of the lines and return to the ship."

"Does he really think the terrafin's going to sit there and let us do that?" Gwen says doubtfully.

"What do you think, Tarnmoor?" Ishmael asks.

The old man stares blankly out to sea. "If the beast wants us dead, ya can bets it'll have its way — whether we gets our hands on them lines or not."

Ishmael steers Chase Boat Four slowly toward the orange floats. Queequeg stands in the bow with a boat hook at the ready. The crew watch apprehensively while he snares the first float, then the next and the next. Tashtego's crew pick up the other three floats and lines. Relieved, Ishmael starts to steer away from the enormous creature.

Perhaps the Great Terrafin has been distracted by the big-tooths that close in, emboldened by the great beast's apparent malaise. When one of the scavengers charges and clamps its teeth onto the edge of a wing, the huge beast flings the big-tooth away. Another big-tooth attacks, and another, each one grabbing hold briefly before being tossed off.

"Whoa!" Queequeg says.

"What? What?" Tarnmoor squawks.

"Looks like the big-tooths are on the attack."

The drones have picked up the activity, and the two-way crackles to life. Starbuck orders the harpooners to man their machine guns.

"Unload on any big-tooth that comes within range. We can't let those wastrels get her!"

It's not long before an unsuspecting creature ventures nearby.

RAT-A-TAT-TAT-TAT! Queequeg fires, and the big-tooth goes into spasms. Its comrades instantly attack it in a mayhem of churning pink froth.

Meanwhile, the *Pequod* is growing larger as it nears, no doubt running full ahead to reach the scene before the big-tooths resume their attack on the Great Terrafin.

Queequeg and Tashtego intermittently fire on the big-tooths, wounding enough of them to distract their fellow predators from their ultimate goal. Finally the *Pequod* arrives, and sailors collect the green ropes from the chase boats. Faces line the ship's rusty rails, watching the proceedings with jumpy fascination.

The *Pequod*'s winches start to turn.

"Well? Well?" Tarnmoor demands.

"They're winching in the lines," Ishmael reports.

The old man cups his hands behind his ears and frowns. "Without a splash nor struggle?"

"Looks that way."

Tarnmoor lowers his hands to his lap. "Never thought I'd sees the day — not that I'm seein' it, minds ya. The mad cap'n must be beside hisself with joy."

Ishmael looks up at the sailors pressed against the rails of the *Pequod,* expecting to see the craggy face of the captain among them, but he can't find him.

Gwen points at the winch control tower. "If you're looking for Ahab . . ." The captain stands just outside the control booth, no doubt eager to make sure nothing goes wrong.

The green lines grow taut, and still the huge beast floats, nearly dormant.

"Don't know why we're bothering with big-tooths," Queequeg says after spraying yet another scavenger with bullets. "Look at the size of that thing. Even if all the big-tooths in the ocean attacked it, they'd hardly make a dent."

But Ishmael knows that Ahab is too greedy for that. After a life-time of waiting, he wants all of the Great Terrafin. Every last bit.

"So? So?" Tarnmoor asks eagerly.

"Looks like everything's proceeding according to plan," Ishmael answers, though it's hard to believe.

"So Ahab's gots 'er at last!" Tarnmoor cackles. "Never did I thinked this day would come. *Never!* This'll change things, mind ya. Change 'em in big, big ways. The riches we'll see! Anythin' ya can dreams up you'll be havin' multiplied! Anythin'!"

But Ishmael can't share in the old man's glee. No amount of wealth will bring Archie back. Nor the crews of Chase Boats One and Two.

Rat-a-tat! . . . *Rat-a-tat!* Not far away, Tashtego fires again on big-tooths that have gotten too close to the Great Terrafin. At the same time, the crew of Chase Boat Four watch seawater begin to seep out between the ever-tightening strands of green line, signaling that the rope is being stretched to the extreme. At any moment, Ishmael expects to see the Great Terrafin being drawn nearer to the ship. But the giant beast remains immobile.

Instead, the sea behind the *Pequod* begins to churn.

"What's happenin'? What's happenin'?" Tarnmoor cups his hands behind his ears again.

"It's . . . I think it's pulling back," Gwen answers, confounded.

80

Indeed, the colossal creature has started to resist. The terrafin's huge wings have slowly begun to rise and fall, and the beast is angling down toward the deep. The green lines squeak and cry under the strain, and the sea behind the *Pequod* is frothy with the propellers' efforts to keep the Great Terrafin from sounding.

Suddenly the huge creature flaps its white wings so hard that the ocean erupts.

Queequeg's jaw drops. "The stern's going down!"

As the huge winches turn, the *Pequod*'s stern gradually dips lower and lower. Ishmael can imagine an impossibly huge anchor causing that to happen, but not a living creature.

"Stern's going down, ya says? Down!" Tarnmoor grips the sides of the chase boat and presses his face forward.

It seems unimaginable, but the *Pequod*'s aft continues to dip, seawater inching up the slipway, while the ocean behind the ship is a swirling cauldron.

Aboard the ship, sailors press against the bulwarks, alarm creasing their faces while they witness the tug-of-war between beast and vessel.

"This can't be happening," marvels Queequeg.

"You'd think the lines would snap," says Gwen.

"Not them lines," Tarnmoor tells her. "Not when there's six a' them all reinforced with steel an' the strength a' hawsers."

Suddenly, the huge winches halt, and the sea behind the ship stops roiling. The sailors lining the deck seem to give a collective sigh of relief.

But the reprieve is short-lived. A furious-looking Ahab yanks open the control booth door and hauls the winch operator out by the collar, throwing him off the tower. The captain enters the booth, and the winches resume their toil.

The stern of the *Pequod* dips deeper.

Sailors have begun fleeing forward, clutching rails as they struggle upward toward the bow. The two remaining chase-boat crews watch in stunned silence. Ishmael thinks back to how weak the terrafin appeared just a short time ago, how even the skittish bigtooths sensed the moment had come to pounce.

Was it only putting on an act? Pretending to be weak in order to be towed close to the *Pequod*'s stern, where it knew it could do the most damage?

No. It can't know what it means to pretend. It's a wild beast, an animal. . . .

And yet . . .

Ishmael turns to Tarnmoor. "How did the Great Terrafin destroy the *Essex*?"

A cloud passes over the old man's features. "We followed hers into a vast, broad bay, but it were a lot shallower than it looked. The next thing we knowed, the tide goed out and the *Essex* were aground, keel stuck on the bottom, unable to budge. And that's when she went to works."

Ishmael shivers. "What do you mean, 'went to work'?"

"Attacked, lad. Battered the *Essex* with her wings and tails till there were nothin' left but some broken masts and a crumpled hull."

"When it could have just as easily escaped?" Queequeg asks.

"Aye."

"You said that happened in a vast, shallow bay?" Gwen looks rattled. "Like the one we were in when we first saw the terrafin."

"Ahab kept the *Pequod* outside," Queequeg adds. "By the bay's entrance."

"The wreck we saw!" Gwen gasps. "The one that was covered with orange and red coral? Was that the *Essex*?"

Ishmael starts to shake his head. "It couldn't be. Queek, you said that wreck must've been down there for hundreds of years to have so much coral on . . ." But as he says this, he realizes that this is *exactly* what happened. Gabriel said the undiluted neurotoxin could change men in "unnatural" ways. It's kept Tarnmoor, Ahab, and Starbuck alive far beyond their "natural" life spans.

He looks again to Tarnmoor. "Do you think . . . is it possible the Great Terrafin *led* the *Essex* into that bay, knowing the ship would run aground and become an easy target?"

For a few moments the old man is quiet. "Never thinked a' it that way. Just figured she suddenly found herself cornered, and likes any trapped wild animal, she turned on her pursuer. Buts it *were* an awful big bay," he adds, almost to himself. "Ya gots to wonder, how trapped were she really?"

"Look!" Queequeg points into the sky over the *Pequod*'s stern, where white-and-gray flyers have begun to wheel and dart. Above them, larger black fork-tail flyers circle. . . . And even higher overhead glide half a dozen huge winged beasts like the one that snatched Thistle.

Hundreds of red-tipped dorsal fins cut through the water around the ship. By now the *Pequod*'s tilting aft section is nearly deserted. Almost all the sailors have fled to the bow and many have begun to don PFDs.

The huge winches keep turning, and it seems impossible that the Great Terrafin can put up such a tremendous fight for much longer. They may have underestimated the beast's reserves of strength, but it *is* just an animal. It has to grow tired eventually.

As the level of the sea slowly continues to rise up the slipway, a single figure works his way aft, hand over hand, along the ship's railing, heading for the tower where Ahab controls the winches.

Ishmael focuses the binoculars.

It's Starbuck.

81

“What’s happening? What? What?” Tarnmoor pleads.

Chase Boat Four is quiet while the crew watch Starbuck brace himself with one hand and bang on the control booth door with the other.

“Starbuck’s trying to get into the control tower,” Queequeg says.

“What? To stops our supreme lord and dictator?” Tarnmoor laughs maniacally. “Ahab’ll never give in. Never!”

Through the binoculars, Ishmael can see Starbuck’s jaw working while he hammers at the door with his fist and shouts.

The turbulence at the stern of the ship continues to excite the flocks of flyers. The small gray-and-white ones skim along the surface, snatching scurry that’ve been tossed up in the mayhem. The medium-size black ones plunge into the waves, scooping up larger scurry thrust to the surface by the beating of the Great Terrafin’s wings. Only the huge green flyers continue to glide high above the rest, ominously waiting for still larger prey.

In the stern of the *Pequod,* Starbuck backs away from the control booth door and looks around. Ishmael narrates for Tarnmoor as the first mate makes his way aft, searching, then starts back.

"What's he gots with him?" Tarnmoor asks.

"Nothing. He—" Ishmael catches himself. Through the binoculars he sees that Starbuck *does* have something with him. "Looks like the handle of a hand winch. . . ."

"For tryin' to breaks down the door," Tarnmoor says.

By now the *Pequod*'s stern is nearly submerged, the bow of the ship poking into the air like the high end of a seesaw. On the steeply slanting deck, a group of sailors struggle to lower a tender. Others grasp the ship's rail, staring in horror at the red-tipped fins of the bigtooths slicing through the sea close to the *Pequod*'s hull.

Just as Tarnmoor predicted, Starbuck swings the winch handle at the window in the door of the control tower, the crack of breaking glass inaudible against the screeching of flyers and the churning of the ocean. The first mate starts to reach through the opening—then suddenly staggers backward like someone struck by a blow, losing his balance and slamming into a large, mushroom-shaped metal chock.

"Ouch!" Queequeg winces sympathetically. "That must've hurt."

"Starbuck or Ahab?" Tarnmoor asks.

"Starbuck," answers Ishmael.

"Aye, there'll be no stoppin' the madman now."

The winches still turn, the *Pequod*'s aft section dipping even farther into the ocean while its bow climbs higher in the air. The tender has been lowered not quite to the sea, but already sailors have begun scampering over the rail and down the cargo rope.

Within minutes the tender is filled with sailors, yet more keep climbing down. Those already in the boat swing oars and kick at those still attempting to board. A sailor loses his balance and falls into the water, having barely enough time to scream before the big-tooths are on him.

And still Ahab will not stop the winches.

More screams and shouts fill the air. Up in the bow, a sailor loses his grip and tumbles toward the stern before smashing into the base of a crane. And now, under the weight of so many fleeing sailors, the cargo rope has started to tear away from the *Pequod*'s railing. Half a dozen sailors lose their grip and plummet into the overcrowded tender below, while others fall straight into the sea and are immediately set upon by big-tooths.

The tender is now a writhing mass of arms, legs, and bodies, riding so low in the water that every wave crests over the gunwales.

"They're going to capsize!" Gwen shouts.

Feeling like he's suddenly been shaken from a dream, Ishmael tries to start the chase boat's RTG, but it stalls. He curses and tries again.

But the engine still won't start. Picking up the two-way, he calls over to Tashtego. "I'm dead in the water. Can you help them?"

"Someone must be watchin' out for you, son," comes the harpooner's pensive reply. "They'll take us down with 'em if we go anywhere near."

In frustration Ishmael tosses the two-way aside. Moments later, when the tender swamps and tips over, he and the others are forced to watch in helpless horror as all aboard fall into the hungry jaws of the frenzied big-tooths.

The sea around the capsized tender has turned red. Tarnmoor has once again gone quiet; the desperate cries of dying men tell him all he needs to know.

The winches continue to turn. The ocean now laps at the *Pequod*'s stern bulwark. If the ship dips only a few feet more, the sea will flood over the aft deck, which is riddled with rust and soft spots.

A handful of sailors are still clustered in the ship's bow, literally holding on for dear life.

"Look!" Gwen gasps. In the *Pequod*'s stern, Starbuck's head comes into view as he grips the gunwale and pulls himself up. Ishmael doesn't need the binoculars to see the blood running from the bright-red gash on the first mate's forehead. Once again, Starbuck struggles toward the tower, the walkway now so steep that he must climb along the railing, clutching each baluster like a rung on a ladder.

But the water has breached the stern bulwark and starts to flood the aft deck. The *Pequod*'s bow rises even higher, the ship now angled more than forty-five degrees.

Starbuck, on his belly now, crawls to the open booth door and reaches in. An instant later, Ahab comes tumbling out, caught unawares by the hand that grasped his false leg. Both men fall down the walkway, but Starbuck grabs a baluster and stops his descent, while Ahab crashes gruesomely off the bulwark and disappears from sight.

Blood pouring down his face, the first mate once again begins to drag himself along the walkway, desperately trying to reach the winch booth before it's too late.

"What's happenin', lad? What? What?" Tarnmoor pleads.

His eyes pressed to the binoculars, Ishmael tells the old man everything he sees. "There's still a chance. If Starbuck can stop the winches before too much water goes over the *Pequod*'s stern . . ."

"He'll do it or die tryin'," Tarnmoor says. "He always dids have heart, that one. Damaged heart, true, buts heart just the same."

The *Pequod* juts up unnaturally from the seething sea, portholes along the hull blowing open as trapped air forces its way out. Flyers shriek, but the screams of the sailors have ceased. The tender floats upside down, the only sign of life in the bloody sea around it the red-tipped dorsal fins still slicing hungrily to and fro.

Through the binoculars Ishmael can see the agonized grimace on

Starbuck's bloody face as he hauls himself hand over hand toward the control booth.

He's . . . almost . . . there . . .

"He made it!" Ishmael exhales with relief as the first mate heaves himself into the control booth. A moment later, the huge winches stop, then begin to spin freely in reverse as the Great Terrafin escapes, stripping the green lines off the massive drums in a blur.

An instant later, the lines pull free of the winches and disappear into the deep.

82

Stillness again descends. Flyers circle but have ceased to cry. The bigtooths glide smoothly through the water, calmer now that their feast is over.

The forward section of the *Pequod* stands almost perpendicular to the ocean.

"How's that possible?" Queequeg asks.

"What now? What?" Tarnmoor begs.

Ishmael tells him, and the old man blinks his unseeing eyes. "Aye, she's been breached, then." He speaks glumly. "Taked in too much a' the sea. She's in the ocean's unmerciful grip. It's hell *and* high water fer all."

Even as Tarnmoor speaks, more portholes burst, trapped air hissing out, and the upright ship begins to sink slowly almost straight down. Foot by foot, the hull disappears beneath the surface—reluctantly at first, but then gradually accelerating as seawater pours in through every rusty hole, burst porthole, and unsecured hatch. As the ship fills with water, the air swells with the clangs and groans of rending metal.

The few remaining sailors in the bow leap desperately into the ocean, thrashing frantically to get as far away from the ship as possible. But they don't stand a chance: Big-tooths slash through the water, and once again the chase-boat crews watch in helpless horror as men and women flail and scream and are pulled under. Flyers cry and reel above, and through them now plunges a great green winged beast, claws outstretched until it plucks a sailor from the sea and carries him off, wailing, into the sky.

With a deafening hiss of steam escaping the flooded nuclear reactor, the *Pequod* drops deeper and deeper into the sea, until finally only the forecastle with its mighty harpoon cannon protrudes above the waves.

It pauses there for an instant, as if gasping for one last breath.

And then it's gone.

Where the *Pequod* was, there now is a gruesome calm. Nothing remains except torn, empty PFDs, floating debris, and pink-tinted bubbles bursting at the surface. The big-tooths have disappeared. The cries of the flyers diminish as they cease circling and begin to settle down.

In the chase boat, Tarnmoor breaks the silence. "She gone?"

"Yes."

"Ahab with her?"

"I think so."

"Starbuck?"

"Him, too."

"Big-tooths got the rest?"

"Looks like it."

The old blind man turns his face away. "However mans may brag a' his science and skill, and however much, in a flattering future, that science and skill may augment; yet forever and forever, to the crack a' doom, the sea will insult and murder him, and pulverize the stateliest, stiffest frigate he can makes."

Ishmael is still staring at the spot where the *Pequod* was only moments before, finding it difficult to believe that the ship truly is no more.

Suddenly a box pops back up to the surface.

Then a barrel.

Then, two gasping sailors in PFDs!

Ishmael reaches for Chase Boat Four's controls, but the RTG sputters and stalls. He curses and tries again. Meanwhile, Tashtego's chase boat has started toward the floating men, hoping to get to them before the big-tooths do.

Ishmael is still trying to start the engine when the white-and-gray flyers dotting the surface abruptly begin flapping their wings. They take off all at once, squawking loudly.

"What is it?" Tarnmoor asks urgently. "What's spooked 'em?"

"Probably Tashtego's boat," answers Queequeg. "He's going for two sailors in the water."

Just then Chase Boat Four's RTG catches and starts.

"No! Don't!" Tarnmoor cries. "Don't go near 'em! Don't!"

"If we don't get them, the big-tooths—" Ishmael doesn't have time to finish the sentence. Two hundred yards away, the ocean erupts as the Great Terrafin bursts out of the sea, water streaming off its huge wings, still trailing half a dozen green harpoon lines from its back.

For an instant Tashtego's chase boat and the two sailors in the water are covered by an ominous shadow as the enormous beast blocks out the sun.

CRASH!

The Great Terrafin smashes back down.

Waves roll away from the huge creature. On the only craft left afloat, Ishmael, Queequeg, Gwen, and Tarnmoor—all aware that escape is impossible—wait to see if it will turn on them next.

The monster floats, motionless. Perhaps it's Ishmael's imagination, but he could swear that the Great Terrafin is looking at them with one of its huge, fathomless black eyes.

"What's it doing?" Gwen asks softly.

It's Tarnmoor who has the answer: "Deciding."

83

Ishmael's vision is blurry and his mind foggy, but he knows he's not aboard a ship because the floor beneath him does not rock. He's lying on a cot in some kind of tent. From behind him, clear liquid runs down a thin tube and through the infuser attached to his arm. A band around his left wrist holds a sensor to his registry, no doubt feeding a constant stream of medical information to a monitor somewhere.

Fragments of memories emerge from the mist in his mind:

Drifting for days on a calm sea under the blistering hot sun. Parched, starving, dying of thirst. Lying with the others on the bottom of the chase boat, their heads under seats to keep their faces from being severely burned.

Then a strange, pulsing storm from above. Wind and spray whipping around them while some roaring airborne thing hovered overhead. One by one they were lifted into the belly of the mechanical flying beast.

Next a shadow over his face amid the roar, and a gentle hand behind his neck, tilting his head forward. Something hard and cool pressed against his lips. The fantastic sensation of fresh water in his mouth and against his tongue.

"Try to drink," a voice had said. "You're badly dehydrated."

Strangely, the voice had sounded like Pip's.

Ishmael opens his eyes.

"He's awake," someone says.

Two unfamiliar people come into view and look down at him. One is a lanky man wearing a dark suit. His face is grave and lined, and his sandy gray hair falls onto his forehead. The other is a woman with a polished, egg-shaped head who is wearing a silver-gray suit. A man in the pale-blue jumpsuit of a medic removes the sensor from Ishmael's left arm and scans his registry, purple light illuminating the elaborate gold filigree.

"He's stable," the medic says, then leaves.

The man in the dark suit and the bald woman gaze at each other.

"It's undoubtedly him," the man says in a stern and authoritative manner. "The filigree, the lineage, the STR core loci. . . . It all corresponds perfectly."

"But look at him." The bald woman sounds repulsed. "It's not possible."

"You doubt the registry? The testing?"

"Well . . . what do you imagine Mr. Bildad will do when he learns of this?"

Ishmael listens with half an ear. He's worried about Tarnmoor, Queequeg, and Gwen. Where are they? He props himself up and sees that his is the only bed in the tent, and there are two uniformed guards at the entrance. To his surprise, the effort to sit up leaves him breathless.

"Easy, now." The man gently presses him back onto the cot.

"Where am I?" Ishmael asks.

"In a medical tent," the woman answers.

"Yes, but where?" Overhead, daylight filters in and the sun is a glowing yellow spot against the gauzy tent material.

"Please relax," the man tells him, then looks at the woman. "To answer your question, I'm not sure that what Mr. Bildad thinks is our concern."

"I'd love to hear you tell *him* that," the woman says abrasively.

The medic in the pale-blue jumpsuit returns and holds a straw to Ishmael's lips. He takes a sip. The liquid is sweet, thick, and chalky. . . . It's Natrient!

"Yuck." Ishmael turns his head away.

"You have to drink it," the medic says in a soothing tone. "You're severely malnourished, and you've been further weakened by a parasitic infection. This is easy to digest. It'll help you get your strength back."

Ishmael reluctantly takes the straw between his lips. The thick glop makes him shiver with memories of life back on Earth. Archie. Petra and Joachim. Old Ben. The dark dustiness of Black Range. Not even a year since he left, and yet it feels like a lifetime ago.

"If you're finished, you may go, Nazik." The woman flicks her hand as if shooing away an annoying insect. "Please inform the guards that they are not to let anyone else in."

She looks back down at Ishmael. There is something odd about her eyes, but he can't figure out what it is. "I am Chief Compliance Officer Valente, and this gentleman is Bartleby. There's much we need to know about what happened to the *Pequod*. Especially pertaining to the matter of—"

Ishmael cuts her short. "There were three others with me. Are they okay? Do you know where they are?"

The bald woman appears annoyed that he's interrupted her.

"Why don't you give him the HMD?" Bartleby suggests.

"I thought I could ask some questions first," she protests.

Bartleby remains firm. "The HMD."

She sighs and hands Ishmael a head-mounted display. "From a friend of yours."

Ishmael puts on the HMD. It's a private Z-pack, which must be activated by his registry. The next thing he knows, he's in a large room dominated by a long, polished oval table. The walls are paneled with dark wood, and the heavy maroon curtains that frame the windows are held by thick gold ropes. The air feels cool and smells slightly of fresh paint.

"Greetings!" Ishmael finds himself facing Pip, dressed in an ornate gold-embroidered tunic. He's smiling. "I'm so absolutely delighted that you've survived. After the initial reports, we thought that everyone on board the *Pequod* had perished. I know you must be worried about Gwen and Queequeg, but be assured that they're being treated well and are not far from you.

"You'll probably learn a lot in the coming days that will be surprising. I had hoped to be the one to brief you on the situation, but I'm afraid things are rather chaotic at the moment and I've had to entrust the task to others. For now, please answer all of CCO Valente's questions about the destruction of the *Pequod.* Your cooperation will be greatly appreciated."

The scene morphs, the room fading away, leaving Pip's head and shoulders against a shimmering silver background. "I always knew you were someone special, my friend. I'm glad to be proved right about that."

The Z-pack ends and Ishmael takes off the HMD, feeling even more confused. What was Pip talking about? And where is Pip, anyway? He can't have gone back to Earth. Is he still here on Cretacea? Or has he gone to one of the other feeder planets?

The good news is that Gwen and Queequeg are alive. But Pip said nothing about Tarnmoor. "There was an old blind man with us," Ishmael says. "Tarnmoor, the *Pequod*'s swabbie."

Valente and Bartleby cast questioning looks across the cot. Then Bartleby says, "There were only three of you in the chase boat."

Ishmael's memory may be foggy, but he thinks he'd remember if something had happened to Tarnmoor. "Could you please check?"

Valente frowns. "There's a great deal of more pertinent information I have to gather. This really isn't the time —"

Bartleby breaks in. "Considering this young man's acts of heroism, I suggest you look into it."

Ishmael isn't sure what acts of heroism Bartleby is referring to, but he's not about to argue.

The bald woman sighs. "What was the name again?"

Ishmael tells her, and she speaks to her tablet: "Find Tarnmoor, swabbie on the *Pequod*."

While they wait for the results, Bartleby has the faraway look of someone listening to something through an earbud. Valente's impatient scowl grows deeper with each passing moment. Finally, the tablet reports back: "Tarnmoor, rank of first mate, perished in the *Essex* disaster."

Bartleby clears his throat. "Approximately a hundred and seventy-five years ago, if I'm not mistaken."

"No, he survived the *Essex* disaster," Ishmael insists. "He was a swabbie on the *Pequod* and was with us in the chase boat when the *Pequod* was pulled under."

Valente's carefully manicured eyebrows jump. "'Pulled under'? Don't tell me you're also going to claim the ship was destroyed by a mythical enormous white three-tailed terrafin?"

Ishmael is shocked by the accusation. "There's nothing mythical about it," he says. "It's as real as you and me. Ask anyone who was on —" He was going to say "on the *Pequod*" but remembers that Pip said everyone else had perished.

"The only ones left are you and your two friends," Valente replies. "And the three of you were found in a state of delirium. If it's any consolation, you're not the first sailors to experience collective delusions under extreme duress. The brain is a remarkable and often confounding organ."

"But there must be drone imagery," Ishmael argues.

Bartleby shakes his head. "If there was, it was lost with the *Pequod.*"

Ishmael fights the urge to laugh at the absurdity of what Valente's saying. "We didn't just *see* the terrafin. We fought it. We saw it kill people. It nearly killed *us.*"

Bartleby leans close, his voice gentle. "I understand that you sincerely believe everything you've said, Ishmael. But the myth of the giant white terrafin has been around for as long as men and women have been coming to Cretacea. We've repeatedly consulted the experts: scientists, historians, archaeologists. They all agree that if such a mammoth creature ever existed, there would be evidence in the fossil record."

Ishmael can't fathom this. "Fossil record? But the Great Terrafin isn't a fossil. It's alive. It's out there now, at this very moment!"

Valente sighs impatiently. "There is not now, nor was there ever, any sort of 'giant terrafin' here on Earth. What you and your friends saw — what you *think* you saw — was a figment of your overexcited imaginations. Hallucinations brought on by trauma and severe malnourishment."

But Ishmael hasn't heard anything after "here on Earth." *What is Valente talking about?* he wonders, staring at the yellow disc of sun still glowing through the gauzy material overhead. "Aren't we still on Cretacea?"

Valente shoots Bartleby an exasperated look.

The stern-faced man fixes Ishmael with his gray-blue eyes. "What I'm about to tell you may come as a shock: There is no difference. Earth *is* Cretacea, and Cretacea *is* Earth."

84

Over the next hour, Bartleby explains. As Pip predicted in his Z-pack, Ishmael has a hard time believing at first. It sounds unreal: A millennium ago, while working on something called the Large Hadron Collider, scientists discovered how to create wormholes — tunnels between different points in space-time.

"Cretacea, Triassica, and Permia aren't other planets," Bartleby tells him. "They're the names we've given to the missions taking place in different periods of Earth's history."

Ishmael's head is spinning. "Why?"

"To harvest the past for the resources we need in the future. We chose times prior to extinction events in the hope that whatever, er, *alterations* we caused wouldn't carry over. Of course, all of that is now moot, as the time you and I came from — the Anthropocene Epoch — has ended." Bartleby pauses and shakes his head regretfully. "The sixth and most profound extinction event of them all. Almost one hundred percent of life on Earth, including man, is gone."

As Ishmael absorbs this, a sudden realization appears like a light in a swirling fog. This explains how Benjamin could have been the same Old Ben whom Ishmael knew when he was growing up. When Benjamin's pod shimmered and vanished from the *Pequod*'s stasis chamber, it wasn't traveling through *space* to Earth, but through *time* . . . to the future, roughly thirty years before Ishmael was born!

"My foster parents," Ishmael says. "They . . . I . . . someone I know supposedly got them out of the Anthropocene. Is it possible they're here?"

The lanky man looks down at Ishmael and shakes his head. "We'd know if they were in this settlement."

"Then is there a way to find out where they are?" Ishmael asks.

"Things are very disorganized right now," Valente says impatiently. "As the Anthropocene Extinction Event nears completion, there's been a significant diaspora of humans, and none of the available databases are proving to be as reliable as we'd hoped. It's nearly impossible to track down even those of us who are . . ."

She doesn't finish the sentence, but she doesn't need to. If they can't keep track of their *own* kind, what chance is there that they've bothered with anyone who's not of the Gilded?

Trying to cover up her blunder, Valente continues: "If your foster parents were able to get out, then they're quite lucky, no matter where they wound up. You're fortunate to be here yourself, Ishmael. Our scientists have determined that the Cretaceous period offers some of history's richest resources, as well as many relatively stable millennia without any recorded major cataclysmic events."

"We estimate that the next extinction event here, the Cretaceous-Tertiary, won't occur for at least twenty million years," adds Bartleby.

But Archie came here to Cretacea, and now he's dead, Ishmael thinks. Cataclysmic events aren't the only threats to life.

His ire and the pain of losing his foster brother return. He can't help thinking that if the Gilded hadn't been so rapacious, there might not have been the need for so many missions — or to take volunteers so ill-suited for the task. If Archie had remained behind, maybe Old Ben could have smuggled him out, too. And then he'd still be alive.

"So"— Valente manufactures a pleasant expression —"perhaps *now* we can discuss the circumstances surrounding the destruction of the *Pequod*?"

If there's one thing Ishmael's ascertained about the Gilded, it's that they're not interested in others unless they have something they want. And he has no qualms about using that very trait against them. "I'll be glad to discuss the *Pequod* . . . just as soon as you give me a definitive answer about my foster parents."

"But . . . that's not possible," Valente says, flustered. "You're being completely unreasonable."

"Ishmael, thousands of pods had to depart the Anthropocene very quickly," Bartleby tries to explain. "Right now there's a moratorium on destasis until we've built adequate accommodations. As a result, there are long queues of them up and down the time line, waiting in stasis. It's going to take centuries."

"I need to know about my foster parents." Ishmael remains firm.

Valente's neck reddens and her eyes narrow. "Well, if I wasn't convinced before, I certainly am now: You are undoubtedly your mother's son. But I'd like to remind you, Ishmael, that regardless of what's happened in your life up to the present, you are still one of us, and it would serve you well to be more cooperative." She spins on her heel and departs.

Ishmael is left alone with Bartleby. The tall man's face is inscrutable. "I feel I must warn you that there are those among us who were, quite frankly, shocked to learn of your existence. Not everyone is happy about your uncanny knack for survival. The situation here is quite unsettled. You must be careful whom you choose to trust."

Ishmael glances toward the entrance to the tent. "Is that why those guards are here? To protect me?"

The question appears to amuse Bartleby. "Who said they're here to keep people out?"

The realization catches Ishmael by surprise: They're here . . . to keep him in? Make sure he doesn't escape again?

"Why?" he asks. "Who am I?"

85

Ishmael's earliest memories are vague, vaporous, the least to be trusted: nestling in the silky softness of a blouse, a perfumed fragrance enveloping him, his ear pressed close to a warm, soft bosom, the peaceful beating of a heart beneath. Then loud crashes and shouts from somewhere in a house. A violent struggle close by. Panicked scurrying. Frightened voices as he was bundled into scratchy, unfamiliar clothes and passed tearfully into a stranger's hands.

Were the memories credible? Or just the confabulations of a lonely young boy who'd never known who his real parents were?

The medic, whose name is Nazik, helps Ishmael to his feet.

"You've been summoned by the executive board." He gives Ishmael a cane. "This will help while you regain your strength."

Several days have passed since Ishmael first awoke in this tent. Since then he has learned much about Earth, about "Cretacea," about himself. He is the son of Eliza, after whom Eliza's Law was named. Bartleby had known his mother when she inherited her chair on the Trust's executive board from her parents. He spoke of her with fondness, but also with great sadness. Eliza had devoted her life to protecting children and the disadvantaged, something that had earned her both admiration and many powerful enemies. Then, one night seventeen years ago, Eliza and Ishmael's father were killed in a fire that was rumored to have had suspicious origins. Ishmael himself was presumed dead, though his remains were never recovered.

Tarnmoor's words come back to him: *"Where's the foundling's father hidden? Our souls is like those a' orphans. The secret a' our paternity lies in their grave."*

It's been a lot to take in, and as Ishmael follows Nazik out of the tent, he is still reeling from it all.

The day is gray and humid, and a light rain falls. The medic offers to cover Ishmael with a shawl, but he refuses it; he prefers the sensation of rain on his face.

They start down a narrow wooden walkway, part of an elevated camp with platforms for tents and huts. The camp smells of freshly cut wood, and the thatching on the roofs is green. But unlike the islanders' elevated village, the construction here is crude and clumsy. The walkway creaks and dips unsteadily, and instead of having finely carved joints, the woodwork is amateurishly lashed together with strips of rope and vine.

Still weak and needing to pause and catch his breath, Ishmael watches while a handful of men and women on the ground attempt to raise a newly built hut onto an elevated platform. It's plain to see that they're not used to manual labor. Their polished shoes sink into the mud, and the men's tight trousers and rain-soaked tunics hinder their movements. There is fevered shouting as some of them tug on ropes attached to pulleys, hoisting the small dwelling into the air, while others attempt to guide it over the platform.

Snap! Crash! A hoist rope breaks. Workers cry out and dive for safety as the hut smashes to the ground and splinters apart.

"Third one this week," Nazik mutters, helping Ishmael along. "Yet still they act surprised."

Ahead on the walkway, an irate woman with two children is complaining loudly to a harried-looking man holding a tablet. The woman and children are dressed in gold-trimmed finery and have the same ashen-skinned and plump look Pip had when he first arrived on the *Pequod.* The woman lugs a heavy bag in one hand while using a purse to shield her head with the other. The children cling to armloads of electronic toys.

The woman gestures at a thatch-roofed hut. "*This* is where you want us to live?"

"It's the best we can offer right now, madam," the man apologizes.

The woman peers inside. "It's so tiny and dark."

"We hope to have lighting soon."

"And the washroom?"

The man blushes and points down a walkway at two small structures. The nicer one—with a metal roof and small skylight—has a human figure painted in gold on the door. The other is made of rough-hewn wood and has a thatched roof. Instead of a door, there hangs a sheet with a crude outline of a worker with a shovel.

"You . . . expect us to *share* a toilet?" the woman asks, aghast.

"It is only temporary, madam," the man replies. "We are working to remedy the situation as soon as possible."

"Excuse us," Nazik says as he and Ishmael go past.

Ishmael can feel the woman and children gawking at his darkly tanned skin, terrafin skiver–pierced ears, and rain-matted hair.

They come across more bewildered refugees from the future. Though he knows it's only wishful thinking, Ishmael can't help looking for his foster parents in the crush.

At last Nazik and Ishmael arrive at a large thatched structure that is sturdier and better built than any of the others they've seen. A long line of well-dressed, disgruntled-looking people wait outside, trying to keep the rain off their heads with palm leaves or pieces of clothing. As the two pass, they overhear irate grumblings about the oppressive heat, overcrowding, lack of furniture, and shared bathroom facilities.

Two guards stand at the building's entrance while a third scans visitors' wrists before allowing them in. Nazik leads Ishmael past those waiting in line.

"We are here at the behest of the executive vice president," Nazik tells a guard, who regards Ishmael with suspicion. The guard reaches out and touches the tiny skivers in his ears. Does he really think they could be some kind of weapon? As soon as Ishmael's registry is scanned, the guard's demeanor changes. The two visitors are politely ushered inside.

The building, which appears to be some sort of headquarters, is still under construction, with half a dozen workers hammering, sawing, and plastering. Nazik guides Ishmael to the end of a long hallway and knocks on a heavy wooden door. A voice inside bids them enter.

Ishmael steps into the room, sees the table and heavy maroon curtains, and knows he's been here before . . . in VR with Pip.

86

The air is cool and dry, and the floor is thickly carpeted. A group of elegantly dressed men and women sit around the large oval table. Ishmael recognizes Bartleby and the shiny-headed Valente.

At one end of the table sits a distinguished-looking, dark-haired man in a sharply pressed dark-blue suit with gold buttons and a gold pocket square. A pointed beard grows on his chin, his fingers are adorned with heavy gold rings, and he's wearing earbuds so as to receive outside information while attending this meeting.

At the other end of the table sits a silver-haired woman wearing gold-rimmed glasses. To Ishmael's befuddlement, Pip is rising from the chair next to hers. Like the others, he is dressed in finery and appears to be quite at home in these surroundings.

Pip tells Nazik he can go, then comes over and squeezes Ishmael's hand. "It's so good to see you."

Ishmael allows himself to be led to a seat at the table. The men and women stare at him with expressions ranging from guarded to amazed.

The silver-haired woman smiles benignly at Ishmael. "We of the executive board are surprised, but of course delighted, that you are here. Those of us who knew your mother admired her enormously. It was a great tragedy when she and your father died."

Some around the table nod in agreement, though Valente and a few others remain stone-faced. The man in the dark-blue suit shoots his cuffs, displaying a heavy gold wrist tablet. He leans forward and addresses the silver-haired woman with carefully calibrated words. "You must forgive me for injecting a note of skepticism, but I imagine I'm not the only one here who feels that it is extremely *convenient* that Eliza's son and heir not only is still alive but has shown up in the very time and place where the Trust has chosen to establish this epoch's headquarters, Executive Vice President Lopez-Makarova."

Lopez-Makarova? Ishmael gawks at Pip, who tosses off a self-conscious shrug.

The silver-haired woman appraises the distinguished-looking man with practiced impartiality. "Thank you, Mr. Bildad. Convenient though it may seem, there can be no doubt in the matter. The registry data is conclusive. In addition, you are welcome to speak to my nephew about Ishmael's service aboard the *Pequod.* He has proved himself to be invested with the best of both his parents."

Mr. Bildad leans back, presses his fingertips together, and gives an obsequious reply: "As you are the most senior corporate officer on Cretacea and this epoch is under your jurisdiction, Executive Vice President Lopez-Makarova, who am I to argue?"

"Thank you, Mr. Bildad. I certainly appreciate your heartfelt vote of confidence," Pip's aunt replies smoothly. The tension between these two is as thick as the pirate Winchester's skull. The executive vice president turns her attention to Ishmael. "One of the reasons we've asked you here today is that we hope you can assist us. As I'm sure you've seen, we are trying to cope with many of the challenges people face when suddenly thrust into a new and unfamiliar environment. My nephew informs us that you've spent time with the group of people he calls the islanders, who apparently have been quite successful in adapting to the conditions of this epoch. We would like to reach out to these people, to ask their assistance in how to best adapt to this place and time."

Ishmael tries to imagine the overdressed Gilded wearing the meager clothes of the islanders, climbing limbless trees to shake down treestones, and sleeping on floor mats in windowless huts.

"What you're really saying is you want me to get them to help you build your settlement," he says.

"We can easily persuade them to do that," Mr. Bildad says with unsettling calm.

Pip's aunt shoots Bildad a dismayed look, then turns back to Ishmael, her appearance once again serene. "I'm sure you've seen our poor attempts at building with the materials we have at hand. We've concluded that the only way to complete this settlement in a timely fashion — and to the standards to which our colleagues are accustomed — is to employ the services of more skillful laborers. We will, of course, compensate them for their time. In addition, we are hoping that you might have suggestions as to what other incentives we can offer them."

"We've been led to understand that they live very . . . primitively," Valente adds. "Perhaps they could benefit from our advanced knowledge of medicine?"

"From what I can tell, they don't need any assistance in that area," Ishmael replies, choosing his words carefully.

"Then perhaps something in the area of education, or entertainment, or . . . fashion," suggests a woman dressed in a lavish green gown with polished gold buttons and sharp lapels, over which is draped a long gold-and-black sash.

"That's a very generous offer," Ishmael says. "But the islanders take pleasure in things that nature, not humans, provides. I honestly can't think of anything you could offer that would interest them."

The faces around the table grow frustrated — except for Mr. Bildad's. He appears preoccupied with the feeds from his earbuds. In the lull in conversation, Ishmael studies this rarefied group his birth parents once belonged to — that *he* supposedly *still* belongs to. Without doubt, they are the healthiest, best-groomed people he has ever seen, and yet there is something unsettling about their appearance. They're *too* perfect-looking, all with teeth that are uniformly straight and unnaturally white, and hair that has an artificial luster. Ishmael peeks at the hands of the man next to him. The skin is almost translucent, allowing the blue veins to show through. He looks at the eyes of the people across from him and realizes that the whites are *too* white. There's no sign of any redness, not even tiny capillaries.

And that's when it hits him: They're *all* using the terrafin neurotoxin. Hadn't Billy and Charity been trying to tell him as much? The one thing the Gilded fear more than anything is death — and the way to avoid death is to use the green serum. No wonder Ahab was so confident these people would pay whatever he demanded for it.

But unlike the pirates and the highest-ranking officers of the *Pequod*, the Gilded have had their teeth fixed and their eyes whitened so that the effects of their addiction won't show. And there will soon be *thousands* of the Gilded here, all demanding neurotoxin to stay alive long beyond their natural life spans.

Ishmael stares at the golden ropes holding back the long maroon drapes. *Once they find out the islanders farm terrafins . . .*

The executive vice president leans forward, interrupting his thoughts. "Ishmael, this is extremely important. Are you saying that there's *nothing* they want?"

"I think the islanders are perfectly content with their lives just as they are," he answers. "But they're a very generous people. I'm sure they'd be happy to share their building skills with you without demanding payment."

Amid the flabbergasted expressions that ring the table, Mr. Bildad slowly removes his earbuds. "It's not only skills we need, it's manpower." He places his hands flat on the tabletop. "I believe we've heard enough. I see no other option than to proceed with the approach I originally proposed — before this young man made his . . . unexpected appearance. Any objections, Madam Executive Vice President?"

Barely able to mask her irritation with Bildad, Pip's aunt looks away without replying. Ishmael glances at Pip, hoping for an explanation, but his friend won't meet his eye.

When the meeting ends, protocol demands that people leave the room by official rank. Mr. Bildad and Pip's aunt exit at the same time, though through different doors. Pip and Ishmael are the last to depart.

"When you said your father was acquainted with some people . . ." Ishmael begins, using the cane for support as they walk back down the long hallway.

"She's his sister," Pip says.

"You knew all along that Cretacea was Earth?"

"Yes."

"So that story about collecting drone data for cartography was just another lie?"

Pip grimaces at the reminder that he's told so many untruths. "No, that was true. The coastlines in this period are quite different from those a hundred million years in the future." He stops and gives Ishmael a bemused look. "I always thought one of you would figure out that this was Earth. Didn't you think it was strange that the days here are the same length as the days on the Earth you left? Every planet rotates at its own unique speed, so if this really were another planet, the days would be a different length."

Ishmael shakes his head. It's just one more piece of information he never knew. "What about Gwen and Queek? In the Z-pack you sent me—"

Pip stops and presses a finger to his lips. He looks up and down the hallway and then shoos Ishmael through a door and into a sitting room . . . where Gwen and Queequeg are waiting.

87

His friends are dressed in threadbare coveralls, their hair is shorn, the skivers no longer in their ears. They look as thin as they did the day they first arrived on Cretacea. And Queequeg is limping.

After hugging him joyously, Ishmael asks what happened.

"Work accident," Queequeg responds matter-of-factly. "Log fell on it."

"What did the doctor say?"

"Doctor?" Gwen snorts bitterly. "Not for us mere peons." She shoots Pip an angry look.

"I told you before," Pip says in a hushed voice. "Even if I have favorites, I can't be seen showing it."

Gwen turns to Ishmael and smirks. "How do you like that? We're Pip's favorite slaves."

"Easy, Gwen," Queequeg cautions.

Pip looks at Gwen. "Did it ever occur to you to wonder how that rotorcraft found you in the middle of the ocean? When the *Pequod* vanished, there were no reports of survivors. I spent days and nights scanning the ocean with a high-altitude drone I wasn't even authorized to use."

"Oh, you're *such* a hero," Gwen says contemptuously. "That's why the only people who've been transported here have been your precious Gilded." Her voice rising, she adds, "What about the millions of non-Gilded who got left behind on Earth — or in the future or whenever? The people who weren't considered *worth* saving?"

Pip hangs his head. "There was a limited number of pods, and yes, most of those spots went to the Gilded, since they were the ones who could pay. . . ." He stares at his feet. "I don't know what more you want from me, Gwen. I can't apologize for who I am, but you know me well enough —"

The door swings open and a guard looks in. When he sees Pip and the others, his mouth falls open. Pip instantly changes his tone. "How did you two get in here? Guard, take them outside and hold them until I can deal with them myself."

As the guard hustles Queequeg and Gwen out, she replies scornfully, "Know you? You're so wrong. We don't know you at all!"

When they're gone, Pip slumps onto a divan, shoulders sagging, hands pressed between his knees. "That wasn't fair. I mean, what she said. I didn't create this system, I was born into it . . . like you." Pip looks up searchingly, and Ishmael knows he wants him to agree that they have a common bond. But Ishmael can't help wondering if he and Pip have anything in common at all.

"What's Bildad planning to do?" he asks.

Speaking a hair above a whisper, Pip says, "Invade the island and enslave everyone they capture."

"What if the islanders resist?"

Instead of answering, Pip looks away. "We should be going. The guards will get suspicious."

Pip leads him out of the building, past the long line of unhappy Gilded still waiting to voice their grievances. Water drips from the eaves, but the rain has stopped and the sun is gradually breaking through the clouds.

The guard is waiting on the walkway with Gwen and Queequeg. "I'll take them from here," Pip tells him. "Return to your duties."

As soon as the guard departs, Pip drops the officious act. "Take a few moments to catch up, but don't be too long or you'll attract suspicion. You and Queek are supposed to be down in the workers' camp."

"How could we ever forget?" Gwen snaps sarcastically.

Pip shakes his head sadly, then turns to go.

"He's not that bad," Ishmael says in a low voice when Pip's out of earshot.

"You can't be serious," Gwen spits. "Do you have any idea what his kind have been doing to the rest of us for the past five hundred years?"

"Yeah, but think about it," Queequeg says. "You can't blame Pip for everything the Gilded do." He raises his hand when Gwen begins to protest. "Wait. I'm not saying he's a saint, but he did try to save me and Ish when the pirates had us. And we wouldn't be alive if he hadn't found us with that drone."

Gwen's forehead wrinkles, but she doesn't argue.

"Ish, before we go back to the camp, there's something we think you should see," says Queequeg.

They lead him down a creaky walkway that extends over lush jungle. In the distance Ishmael hears a steady *clang! clang! clang!* that grows louder the farther they go. Eventually the walkway ends, and they look out over the jungle at a broad green valley and a sparkling blue-green bay. Flyers of different sizes and shapes glide on air currents, and unseen animals clamor in the trees. Ishmael still finds it mind-boggling to see how much vegetation there is here compared with the barren gray Earth of the future. An Earth that can no longer support life.

Another settlement is being built on a nearby hill, and hundreds of yards below it, where the jungle ends at the water's edge, construction has begun on what appears to be a dock, flanked by the framework of several large, low buildings. The clanging sound is coming from a tall machine on a barge that is driving pilings into the shallows offshore.

Gwen points farther up the hill, where a camp of white tents is nestled among the trees. "That's where we live. There are about a hundred of us, including engineers and construction managers. It's not nearly enough people to do all the work."

Queequeg gazes down at the new construction. "My father used to say that in the entire history of the planet Earth, no other creature — not the dinosaurs, nor the apes, nor any other living thing — ever saw fit to radically change the environment to accommodate its whims. When you think about it, humans have been the most successful invasive species of all time. In the space of three thousand years — a mere blink on the cosmic time line — we destroyed a world that was four and a half *billion* years in the making. It's what the Lectors have always said. This is the human legacy: the sixth and final mass extinction event. Complete ecocide."

Now, in addition to the *clang! clang! clang!* of the pile driver comes a distant crashing from somewhere in the valley.

Queequeg points to a spot where three large machines are slowly plowing through the jungle, knocking down and scraping away all the trees and vegetation before them, leaving a ribbon of brown road behind. "It's going to be the same thing all over again. These people will always live under a shroud, if not of darkness and pollution then of greed and selfishness. They'll take everything they can to make themselves rich and comfortable while they ruin the world around them. How long will it take them to destroy Earth in this epoch? Two thousand years? A thousand? And you know what they'll do then?"

The question is rhetorical, but Gwen answers anyway: "Go back even farther into the past and do it all over again."

88

That night, Ishmael is kept awake not only by the booming thunder and flashing lightning of a storm, but by his mounting concern over Bildad's plans. He may barely be able to remember his mother, but he's certain she would have stood up to the executive board and fought for the rights of *all* people — islanders, the non-Gilded, and Gilded alike. But what can he do with only Gwen, Queequeg, and, maybe, Pip on his side?

He's barely slept when he feels a hand gently shake him. In the dim predawn light, he finds Pip crouched beside his cot. "Get up, we have to go."

"Where?" Ishmael yawns.

"Just come. I'll explain later." Pip holds up a robe to show there's no time for Ishmael to dress. Ishmael grabs his cane, and they leave the tent. The gray air is heavy with warm mist.

"What happened to the guards?" Ishmael asks.

"Don't worry about that," Pip whispers. "Hurry."

Leaning heavily on the cane, Ishmael hobbles down the walkway, still slick from last night's rains. "What's going on?"

"You'll see in a moment."

But suddenly feeling apprehensive, Ishmael stops on the wet walkway. "Where are you taking me, Pip?"

Pip stops and looks back at him. "Don't you realize what's at stake? The future of the planet could hinge on what happens *here*, right now, between us."

Despite all he's been through in the past twenty-four hours, Ishmael can't help eyeing Pip with wary amusement. "Sounds kind of grandiose, don't you think? I mean, we're just two people who—"

"Suppose I tell Bildad that you're plotting to warn the islanders of his attack?" Pip challenges him. "Don't bother denying it; there's no way you'd sit idly by while the island is invaded and its people are taken into slavery."

Ishmael tenses and grips the head of his cane, his thoughts galloping. Has Gwen been right about Pip all along? Is he just like the other Gilded—concerned only about those with privilege?

"And why shouldn't I tell Bildad?" Pip goes on. "I mean, look how Gwen acts even after everything I went through to save the three of you? Maybe my fellow Gilded are right when they say you people don't appreciate anything we do for you."

Ishmael looks over the walkway. It's a long way down. If it comes to a choice, can he do what has to be done to stop Pip from telling Bildad?

A crooked smile inches across Pip's lips. "Always worrying about other people, aren't you."

Ishmael isn't sure how to respond. But it doesn't seem to matter. Pip says, "That's why I'm not going to tell Bildad anything. Because I admire you, Ishmael."

Ishmael feels his forehead wrinkle.

"And I'm going to help you protect the islanders," Pip adds.

"How?"

Pip's smile turns impish. "You can't attack something if you don't know where it is."

Ishmael blinks with astonishment. "The maps you were charting . . ."

"I might have missed an island." Pip winks.

"But won't that make it incredibly difficult for the Gilded to survive here?" Ishmael asks. "I mean, no offense, but those people have no concept of what work is."

"I told you I came to Cretacea because I found that life boring," Pip says. "Maybe if we can learn to be self-sufficient here, we won't become what we used to be — an arrogant class of self-indulgent sycophants with nothing to do except entertain and play."

Now Ishmael understands that Pip might not have been exaggerating: The future *could* hinge on this moment. If the Gilded are forced to relearn basic life skills of survival instead of simply bending the wills of the weaker and less fortunate to do their bidding . . . If the islanders are allowed to continue their way of life undisturbed . . . Perhaps some new kind of society could eventually evolve. One *not* based on greed and the old animal instincts of survival of the fittest but on shared industry, compassion, kindness, and respect for nature. A world that values the worth of all individuals equally and respects the great circle of life and death. If such thinking is spawned now and inherited by subsequent generations, then maybe the future history of Earth *could* be rewritten — perhaps the Anthropocene Extinction Event might never have to happen.

If Pip is really to be believed about wanting to help him . . .

Wisps of mist drift across the elevated walkway. From somewhere below comes the sound of a creature scuttling through the underbrush.

"Come on, there isn't much time," Pip urges.

But Ishmael doesn't move. Is this a trick? He already knows that some of the Gilded don't want him around because of how much like his mother he appears to be. Or because his allegiance is so obviously with the islanders. Or because, despite his birthright, he is so obviously *not* of the Gilded.

Pip frowns, then shakes his head. "You *still* don't trust me?" he ask. "All right, suppose I show you something that'll convince you once and for all?"

Gwen and Queequeg are waiting in Chase Boat Four, which is anchored in the bay just off the beach. The clouds have thickened, and it's begun to rain again. Pip helps Ishmael wade out to the boat.

"There's food, water, and this." Knee-deep in the water, Pip takes a small, thick tablet from inside his tunic. "You know what this is?"

"A tablet with memory?" Queequeg guesses.

Pip nods. "It's got the only copy of the true map. Once you reach the island, I suggest you destroy it."

"You could come with us," Gwen says.

"If Ishmael and I both disappear, they'll think he kidnapped me. They'll never stop looking for me. You never know, they might accidentally stumble upon the island. I'm better off staying here and helping my aunt get this place up and running." He pauses, then chuckles as if he's had another thought. "Besides, could you really see me strolling around in those things the islanders wear?"

The rain's begun to fall harder, matting down their hair and pocking the water all around them. A small green-and-yellow flyer with a bright-red head alights on the chase boat's breasthook and shakes itself out.

"One more thing, Ishmael," Pip says. "Your foster parents made it off Earth. They're coming here."

Ishmael feels his mouth fall open.

"They're in the queue and probably won't be up for destasis for another three hundred years. But they'll make it."

Ishmael sags with relief. He will never get to see them, but at least they'll be able to live out their lives in a place with sunlight and fresh air. His gaze falls on the water, on the multitude of ever-widening rings caused by the rain. He has Old Ben to thank for what's happened. That night in the storm back in Black Range, the old man had tried to save all of them — himself, Grace, and Ishmael's family. He almost succeeded.

Gwen leans over the gunwale and hugs Pip. "I never thought I'd ever hear myself say this, but thank you."

Queequeg rubs Pip on the head. "We're grateful to you, friend."

"You won't tell them about the islanders farming terrafins?" Ishmael asks.

Pip shakes his head.

"Or the Great Terrafin?" asks Queequeg.

"Not unless I want them to think I'm as crazy as you three," Pip replies with a wink.

Ishmael clasps Pip's hand thankfully. "You're a good person, Pippin Xing Al-Jahani Lopez-Makarova."

"If that's true, it's only because of what I learned from all of you." Pip pats the chase boat's RTG. Ishmael presses the starter. The engine engages immediately — and hums smoothly.

"Almost forgot to tell you." Pip grins. "That's a brand-new RTG. No more stalling. Guess money and power do have some perks after all, huh? Now you'd better get out of here before anyone notices you're gone."

The crew wave and steer for the open ocean, raindrops stinging their faces as the chase boat picks up speed. Behind them the settlement grows small, then finally vanishes in the misty air.

89

The islanders — and Charity, Blank, and Billy — greeted the arrival of Chase Boat Four with jubilation and an hours-long celebration, despite the mixed news that Ishmael and the others bore: that no matter what Pip promised, the possibility remained that someday the Gilded might stumble upon them.

Gabriel said, "Should these Gilded ever find us, and should they mean us harm, we shall defend ourselves. 'Twill be okay, Ishmael. 'Twill be strong. 'Twill survive."

"'Twill never, *ever* be a slave t'anyone," Diana added.

"But . . ." Gabriel gave her a serious look. "We shall dismantle the barricade and have music again."

Diana hesitated, then agreed. "For now."

It's very dark, and the fires are little more than glowing red embers. Almost everyone has climbed into a hammock or crawled into a hut, and Ishmael longs to do the same, but Fayaway is pulling him down a walkway.

"'Tis a thing ye must see," she says.

At the edge of the village, she picks up a torch and leads him through the jungle and up the hill to the cave where the islanders' ancestors first found shelter after being shipwrecked many generations ago. The great orb is full, and the night sky is awash with twinkling pinpricks, but the entrance to the cave is ominously dark. Torch in hand, Fayaway leads him inside. The air is stale, but thankfully not rancid like in the pirates' cave. In the flickering orange light she shows him crude wall paintings.

"They tell a story." She guides the torch along the wall.

It takes Ishmael's eyes a moment to adjust — not only to the dim light but to the crude drawings. Gradually, he starts to make sense of what he's seeing.

The first illustration is of a ship lying on its side while people wearing PFDs struggle and lifeboats row away through tall waves.

The next drawing is of an entrance to a cave like this, with small figures playing outside and larger ones carrying bows and game.

Next, people in waist-high water, using nets to catch scurry.

Next —

Ishmael's heart jumps into his throat when Fayaway points out a figure with long dark hair, leaning on crutches, his thin legs dragging behind him, surrounded by children.

Can it possibly be?

He follows her torchlight to a larger drawing of the man on the crutches again. Rising above the figure like a halo is Archie's favorite design — the circle with the tree inside, the tattoo that all the islanders have on their necks.

Ishmael's heart drums, and despite the cool cave air, sweat breaks out on his forehead. He points deeper into the cave, still in the dark. "What's back there?"

"Old things," Fayaway says.

"Of the survivors?"

When she nods, he starts toward the back of the cave. Fayaway follows, the glimmering torch illuminating old crudely made pottery, broken bows, shreds of old fishnets, a shoe, some rope, and—

Ishmael drops to his knees. With tears welling in his eyes, he picks up a rusted leg brace with torn, decaying Syncro straps.

"This"—he chokes, tears running down his cheeks—"belonged to my foster brother. To Archie."

Fayaway kneels beside him. "Then 'tis Archie in the paintings. 'Twas here hundreds of years ago. 'Twas one of the survivors of the wreck."

"The *Jeroboam,*" Ishmael croaks.

"He has not left," Fayaway whispers. "'Tis still here in all of us. In the air and the ground. In the wood of our walkways and the thatch on our huts. And in our hearts and minds. Ye have found him, Ishmael, and so long as ye art here, ye shall always be with him."

Fayaway leans forward so that her forehead presses against Ishmael's. He smiles through his tears. *I feel you, Archie,* he thinks. *In these gentle people. In their strength and kindness. In this beautiful place. You and me together. Always.*

He rises to his feet and takes Fayaway's hand. They leave the dark cave and step out into the orblight beneath a sky of shimmering stars and galaxies. He pauses to take a deep breath of the night air. He's reached the final harbor, whence he will unmoor no more.

He's back home, with Archie. Finally.

END NOTE

The Cretaceous period lasted from the end of the Jurassic (roughly 145 million years ago) until the beginning of the Paleogene (roughly 66 million years ago). During that time, the climate on Earth was considerably warmer than it is today. Tropical sea surface temperatures may have gotten as warm as 107°F (think: really hot shower). This is roughly 30°F warmer than the warmest oceans are at the present.

Scientists believe the increased temperatures were caused by widespread volcanic activity, which produced heightened levels of carbon dioxide. The production of large amounts of magma, or molten rock, possibly caused by the movement of the Earth's crust (also called plate tectonics), also pushed ocean levels up, so that vast areas of the continental crust were covered with shallow seas.

As a result, more than 80 percent of the Earth was covered with water, compared with roughly 70 percent today.

In addition, the position of Earth's landmasses changed considerably during the Cretaceous period. At the beginning of the period there existed two supercontinents, Gondwana in the south, and Laurasia in the north. By the end of the Cretaceous, the positions of the various continents were nearly the same as those shown on maps today.

GLOSSARY

Aft situated toward or at the stern

Amidships of, pertaining to, or located in the middle part of a ship

Anthropecene a geologic chronological term for the epoch that began when human activities had a significant global impact on the Earth's ecosystems

AWOL absent without leave. Away from duties without permission

Baclum bacterial luminescence. Luminescent bacteria emit light as the result of a chemical reaction during which chemical energy is converted to light energy

Bait special reward

Berth sleeping accommodation on boats and ships

Bow the forward end of a vessel

Breasthook a V-shaped timber or plate connecting ship timbers or stringers of opposite sides where they run into the bow

Bridge the forward part of a ship's superstructure from which the ship is navigated

Bulwark the side of a ship above the upper deck

Bumper a device for absorbing shock or preventing damage (as in collision)

Capstan a vertical-axled rotating machine developed for use on ships to apply force to ropes, cables, and hawsers

Chock a heavy metal casting with two short horn-shaped arms curving inward between which ropes or hawsers may pass for mooring or towing

Cleat a fitting on ships to which ropes are tied

Cleaving deck a deck on which large creatures are flensed and cleaved

Cutting in *See* **Flense**

Davit a system that is used to lower or raise a smaller craft from or onto a larger one

Davit hooks hooks used to hold a smaller boat

Derma-jet infuser a type of medical injecting syringe that uses a high-pressure narrow jet of the injection liquid instead of a hypodermic needle to penetrate the epidermis

Fathom a unit of length equal to six feet (1.8 meters)

Flank speed a ship's true maximum speed

Flense (v.) to remove the blubber or skin of large beasts

Fluke the part of the anchor that catches in the ground, especially the flat triangular piece at the end of each arm

Forecastle the forward upper deck, or part, of a ship

Full ahead flank speed

Gunwale the top edge of the side of a boat

Grappling hook a device with multiple flukes attached to a rope

HMD head-mounted display. Worn while in virtual reality

Hawser a thick cable or rope used in mooring or towing a ship

Head a ship's toilet

Hold the cargo space belowdecks in a ship

Keelhaul a form of punishment meted out to sailors at sea. The sailor was tied to a line that looped beneath the vessel, thrown overboard on one side of the ship, and dragged under the ship's keel

Lee side the sheltered side; the side away from the wind

PFD personal flotation device, life jacket

Port left

Pot the accumulated funds from which individual bonuses are paid

RTG radioisotope thermoelectric generator. An electrical generator that uses heat released by the decay of radioactive materials to create power

Scupper a hole in a ship's side to carry water overboard from the deck

Sick bay a room on a ship set aside for the treatment or accommodation of the sick

Slipway a ramp at the stern of a ship to assist in hauling harpooned creatures onto the flensing deck

Sound (v.) to dive swiftly downward. Used of a marine mammal or a fish

Starboard right

Stern the back part of a boat or ship

Stick a harpoon

Superstructure the parts of a ship built above its hull and main deck

Swabbie a member of the crew, typically of low rank

Swell a rolling ocean wave; not cresting

Tender a boat for communication or transportation between larger ships or shore

Thwart a structural crosspiece forming a seat in a boat

Transom the planking forming the stern of a square-ended boat

Turnbuckle a device for adjusting the tension or length of ropes or cables

Virtual reality (VR) a computer-simulated environment that creates physical presence in the real world or imagined worlds. Virtual reality replicates all sensory experiences, including taste, sight, smell, sound, and touch

Wheelhouse also called a pilothouse, a glass-enclosed room from which a ship is controlled by the ship's pilot

Windlass a machine used to let out and heave up equipment such as an anchor

Z-pack a zettabyte packet. A unit of information used in virtual reality

Zirconia electrolysis a process, based on oxygen-ion-conducting zirconia electrolytes, that electrochemically reduces carbon dioxide to oxygen and carbon monoxide

ACKNOWLEDGMENTS

With oceans of paternal pride, I gratefully acknowledge my daughter, Lia, who created the cover illustration for this book, and my son, Geoff, who read a nearly five-hundred-page version of the manuscript and made many insightful and useful editorial suggestions. It's not only more than enough to make the old man proud; it brings a tear to his eye as well. I love you both, and thank you both. I am also indebted to my wonderful and benevolent editor, Kaylan Adair, who devoted many extra hours to this endeavor. With patience and aplomb, she handled the editing with one hand and her newborn son with the other. Thanks also to all the other supportive and dedicated folks at Candlewick who helped make this novel happen. Finally, to Barb — my anchor, my muse, my PFD — with love.